Jadesola James loves summ
Barbara Cartland novels, lo
buttered toast and copious amounts of cake and tea. She writes glamorous escapist tales designed to sweep you away. When she isn't writing, she's a university reference librarian. Her hobbies include collecting vintage romance paperbacks and fantasy shopping online for summer cottages in the north of England. Jadesola currently lives in the UAE. Check out what she's up to at: www.facebook.com/jadesolajameswriter!

Canadian **Dani Collins** knew in high school that she wanted to write romance for a living. Twenty-five years later, after marrying her high school sweetheart, having two kids with him, working at several generic office jobs and submitting countless manuscripts, she got The Call. Her first Mills & Boon novel won the eviewers' Choice Award for Best First in Series *RT Book Reviews*. She now works in her ce, writing romance.

Also by Jadesola James

Redeemed by His New York Cinderella

Jet-Set Billionaires collection

The Royal Baby He Must Claim

Passionately Ever After… collection

The Princess He Must Marry

Also by Dani Collins

Marrying the Enemy
Husband for the Holidays
His Highness's Hidden Heir

Diamonds of the Rich and Famous collection

Her Billion-Dollar Bump

CONVENIENTLY HIS

JADESOLA JAMES

DANI COLLINS

MILLS & BOON

First published in Great Britain 2025
by Mills & Boon, an imprint of HarperCollins*Publishers* Ltd,
1 London Bridge Street, London, SE1 9GF

www.harpercollins.co.uk

HarperCollins*Publishers*, Macken House, 39/40 Mayor Street Upper,
Dublin 1, D01 C9W8, Ireland

ISBN: 978-0-263-34457-8

03/25

This book contains FSC™ certified paper
and other controlled sources to ensure responsible forest management.

For more information visit www.harpercollins.co.uk/green.

Printed and Bound in the UK using 100% Renewable Electricity
at CPI Group (UK) Ltd, Croydon, CR0 4YY

BILLION-DOLLAR RING RUSE

JADESOLA JAMES

MILLS & BOON

To my fellow romance authors,
both at Mills & Boon Modern and beyond.

Thanks for all the advice, support
and encouragement along the way.

CHAPTER ONE

WITH HIS BACK to his guests and his eyes closed tight, Desmond Tesfay was counting backward from ten. No, twenty. Ten seconds was nowhere near sufficient to clear the clouds of irritation now hovering like a mist over his senses.

The origin of these clouds was teenage heiress Hind Al-Bahri, who was chattering away behind his back. She'd been shadowing him in his office since nine o'clock that morning at the behest of her father, who was the new president of aviation for the oil-rich nation of Bahr Al-Dahab and the biggest potential client Desmond had welcomed that year.

Hell, the biggest potential client he'd *ever* welcomed. There was money, and there was *money*. It also meant a way into a market with unlimited possibilities. He'd have tap-danced naked in front of Buckingham Palace in order to get this man's attention, so letting a spoiled teenager trail him for a day in order to get a "feel for business" was easy in comparison.

And, if all went well, he would land a deal that would not only make Tesfay International a giant in the aviation industry, but would also ensure its reputation as an innovator. A *pioneer.*

Ten long years of hard work would finally pay off.

Desmond shifted a bit and ran a finger under the collar

of his snow-white shirt. It felt as if it were choking him beneath his midnight blue, slim-cut suit. His whole body was sparking with nervous, devastated energy.

Father. His heart cried out the word, though his lips were still.

It had been nearly ten years since his father, Abram Tesfay, had lost his life in the smoking remains of EssentialAire Flight 0718. Ten years since his father's business, as broken as Desmond's heart, had been passed to him, a graduate with barely a year of work experience.

Ten years since his whole world had shattered.

Ten years since his vow to rebuild his father's legacy, whatever the cost.

He'd spent years clawing upward toward the sun. And he'd finally—finally!—broken through to light.

Desmond closed his eyes and tried to picture his father's face. The most frightening thing was how poorly he was able to recall his father's features outside of photographs.

Those pictures were hidden in his office now, buried by the PR teams that had come and gone after the tragedy in a bid to ensure potential clients forgot what had happened.

But they hadn't forgotten, had they?

No major international airline wanted to be seen doing business with the firm, but all that was about to change.

Desmond finished counting, rearranged his features, and mentally snapped back into the persona he donned every morning like the custom suits he favored. He wrapped himself in it so tightly that nothing could escape.

Laconic. Wry. Charming. *Light.*

Not a hint of the grief he carried could show in anything he said or did. Though the memorial of his father's death was a mere twenty-four hours away, his dark mood was buried deep down inside where no one could see it.

He took a breath, turned around and blanched. With her slim gold-plated mobile, Hind was zooming in on one of the many model airplane interiors he had displayed on the boardroom table, thinking that something visual might be of interest to the teenager. She was mouthing the lyrics to a song he vaguely recognized and flashing the peace sign at her imaginary audience.

Was she streaming *live*?

"Hind!" he snapped.

She peered up at him through several layers of mascara, lips tilted in a glossy pout.

"Those are *confidential*." Even he could hear how stuffy he sounded. He hadn't shown her any of the really confidential work of his firm—he wasn't a fool—but he didn't want any unfinished work leaked on the internet, no matter how good it was. "As I mentioned earlier, it's work for a client who wouldn't appreciate it being leaked to the competition before launch day."

Hind blinked, bringing to mind a confused puppy, albeit a very expensively dressed one. She pushed a lock of glossy dark hair behind one ear, Cartier dangling from both her earlobes and her wrist. "But you said, *yanni*, they were toys?"

"Models, Hind." A vein was beginning to throb at his temple, and he glanced discreetly down at his watch. Four forty-five. "Anyway, kindly delete that footage and let's take a walk down to advertising, where you'll see some of the specifics of our latest campaign, and then, *finally*, we can head out for an early dinner…"

Hind sighed loudly.

"You'll feel better once you get some food into you," Desmond said dryly. "Come on, Sheikha." He waited for Hind to gather herself together with much dramatic effect, restraining the impulse to roll his eyes until her back was to him. He pressed the button for the automatic doors, and followed her out.

It must be nice, he thought, to have a life so uncomplicated that one could afford to squander opportunities.

Val Montgomery had been forgotten. Again. On her birthday, no less.

A bare two days after Valentine's Day, which she'd also spent alone.

Another person might have decided to wallow in self-pity. Val shrugged it off in the darkened conference room and stood, slipping her feet into the sensible pumps she'd been wearing since morning.

She was used to being invisible, and she was used to being alone. It didn't bother her; on the contrary, she supposed it meant she was doing her job well. Being a personal assistant to one of the wealthiest heiresses in the Gulf did require a certain degree of discretion, and the most successful domestic servants knew how to be both invisible and indispensable at the same time. As to the birthday bit, well… She hadn't celebrated one since that disastrous milestone nearly ten years ago when her husband had shown her his true colors.

She'd been *happy* to be alone since then, and reminded herself of that at every opportunity. There was no solitude that was worse than being mistreated.

Val scooped up Hind's custom lipstick-red couture handbag, hoisting her own high-street leather satchel onto her shoulder, and hurried for the door.

Just ahead of her, Hind and Desmond's voices were bouncing off the walls of the corridor. This part of the office was designed to look like a high-tech but extremely luxurious hangar bay, with vivid lighting, sleek furniture in icy chrome that looked uncomfortable but somehow hugged the body in the most ergonomic way, and mock-ups of aircraft that hung from high ceilings on thin chains.

Tesfay International had clearly been designed to impress everyone who stepped foot inside, and although Val had spent nearly a decade in some of the finest architectural structures the Gulf had to offer, she still found herself gawking at the interior.

She'd barely managed, thank goodness, to keep from gawking at the sight of its owner. Not that it would have mattered, she thought with an internal sigh, quickening her pace. For all the notice Desmond Tesfay took of her that morning she might as well have been one of the leather chairs that circled the marble-topped boardroom table.

Val had seen him before, of course. He'd been courting Sheikh Rashid for months, and no one who saw the Englishman could forget him. He'd left his stamp all over Europe, transforming budget airlines into everyday luxuries, and now he was expanding into the Middle East.

It was a wise decision. The oil-rich oasis of the Gulf had been Val's home for more than a decade and the wealth she saw on a daily basis still amazed her, even now. Bahr Al-Dahab, while the smallest country by far out of the many that clustered round the balmy turquoise-blue waters of the Gulf, was the richest. It had been a small cluster of Bedouin settlements a couple of generations ago, and then oil had been discovered in the region. Now it surpassed its bigger cousins in riches, and investors were pouring into the region, making men like Hind's father into billionaires practically overnight.

"But I'll need my *bag* for that," Val heard Hind whine,

and she snapped back to attention, hurrying forward to hand over the handbag.

"Thank you so much, Val," the girl said sweetly, although she didn't look up because she was scrolling through her mobile. "We're to go to dinner with Desmond this evening, he tells me, and I'll need to change."

Val looked up from placing the bag on Hind's arm and then arranging her sleeve to meet Desmond's eyes, and her skin heated.

She thought she'd been dead to the effects of men for years, and for very good reason. But Desmond had been having this effect on her all day, much to her confusion. It was because he was basically a celebrity, she told herself. A celebrity with warm bronzed skin, brandy-dark eyes framed by heavy lashes, and his mouth—

What was *wrong* with her? She closed her eyes briefly, willing the apparition to disappear. Unfortunately, doing so merely heightened her other senses, and she was overwhelmed by the clean, crisp scent of him. Something woodsy, spicy and soft all at once…

When she opened her eyes he was peering down at her curiously, and she took a step back, casting her eyes down to the floor. She was thirty-nine, she reminded herself sternly. One year left until forty. Much too old to be fluttering round *any* man in this manner. He'd just taken her by surprise, was all…

"Will you be joining us?" he asked.

Hind answered for her, huffing through her nose. "She has to," she groused. "Daddy won't let me go anywhere in London without a companion. Like it's 1890 or something…"

"He wants to keep you safe," Desmond said, soothingly.

Hind snorted. "You *would* take his side. I'm going to

freshen up," she announced, and clattered off for the toilets before either of them could answer. Val was left with Desmond, her stomach curling into an impossible knot. The corners of his mouth tipped upward, although he wasn't actually smiling. His face screamed irritation.

"Are you her…nursemaid, or something?" he asked. She could hear the tints of London in the rich baritone of his voice, and something else, something reminiscent of the Gulf. She ignored the sarcasm and replied in the dulcet tones she always adopted at work with the standard answer.

"I am Sheikha Al-Bahri's companion and personal assistant. I…travel with her."

"Because she's not married."

So Desmond Tesfay was familiar with the country's upper-class culture, then. Valentina compressed her lips, tasting the waxy lipstick she'd worn that morning. It served as a distraction only for a moment.

"Do you have a name?"

A flush rose under her skin. "Of course I do." *Why* had her voice risen three octaves?

He waited patiently.

"Val Montgomery," she said through clenched teeth.

"Miss Montgomery," he said softly, as if committing it to memory. Her stomach roiled with the unexpected intimacy of it. She took a breath, craning her neck to peer up at the air-conditioning vent—was the thing even working? "Did you come from an agency, or are you on a free visa?"

That was unexpected. Val was able to look him directly in the face for the first time. She registered his utter handsomeness, of course, but then the small details you couldn't get from a distance began to seep through. It was a kind face, and its businesslike sternness contrasted with eyes that looked almost…amused. It was the face of someone who'd never been bothered with the sort of burdens she carried. And he was…young.

Too young for her skin to be as hot as it was now, and much too inappropriate.

Pull yourself together!

Val lifted her chin. Her hands immediately went to smooth the creases in her tailored wool dress. The shapewear she wore beneath—and which felt like a steel cage—was specifically designed to banish even the *suggestion* of unsightly lumps and bumps. She straightened her spine until it no longer pinched, and she felt in control again.

She was human, after all—occasionally her body reminded her that desire existed—but her brain and sensibility would always prevail. She would make sure of that.

"I'm afraid I cannot divulge the specifics of my employment with His Highness—"

His heavy black brows jumped upward. "You're American," he stated. "Or Canadian?"

"American, but—"

"How on earth did you end up in Bahr Al-Dahab, of all places, and babysitting *her*?"

"I'm not babysitting." Though some days it felt like she was. Irritation yanked her chin up another fraction of an inch. "I suggest," she added haughtily, "that we limit our conversation to business matters."

"Fine." The insufferable man leaned back with a glint in his eye that made him even more absurdly good-looking. Really, he was almost a caricature of a book billionaire at this point. There was an ease to his manner, too, that for some reason she didn't believe. He smiled, but the lightness wasn't quite convincing; his eyes were darting around as if she were *boring* him. "Tell me how I can get on well with Sheikh Rashid, then. I want his business."

"How you can *get on well* with—" Val was at a loss for words.

"I want his business," he repeated.

"And you're asking me?"

"Why not?" Desmond flashed her a smile, one that transformed his face from being ridiculously attractive to being devastatingly handsome. It was no closer to changing that odd detachment in his eyes, however. "Let's not dissemble, Miss Montgomery. You're as much an outsider to Bahr Al-Dahab as I am, and you know as well as I do that connections and personal relations are more important than profit."

So he knew that much, at least. Val's estimation of him rose a bit; she'd seen many expats with their heads far enough up their own asses that they didn't even realize when they'd blown it with her volatile boss. "I—"

"I take any advantage where I find it." He tilted his dark head. "You understand."

"What makes you think I have an advantage?" Val countered. "I just *babysit* his daughter, as you said."

"Fair enough." Desmond laughed, but it was a hollow sound. "But I'm going to count the fact that he sent her to me today as a good sign."

Val restrained a snort with some difficulty. While her primary function was "babysitting," as Desmond had pointed out, she'd worked for the sheikh for over eight years now and had witnessed enough family meals and functions to know that there was little about this man that had made a lasting impression with her boss. Hind's father was notoriously straitlaced and conservative, and Desmond Tesfay's flashy persona wouldn't impress the man at all.

She rearranged her features back into the cool blankness she'd cultivated over the years, but it was too late. Desmond's eyes narrowed. "What?"

"Nothing," she mumbled, taking a step backward.

"No, no, no, no, no." Desmond was stepping closer as she stepped back, that gleam in those brandy-dark eyes darkening them all the more. "You were going to say something. Or you were *thinking* something, at the very least. Spit it out."

"I wasn't—"

"Spit it out, Miss Montgomery."

What *was* it about the way the man's voice wrapped around the vowels of her surname that turned her lower belly to melting honey? Val lifted her hands to pat her cheeks. She took a breath and pictured herself encased in ice, a trick she'd learned from one of her meditation apps and which she put to use on Hind's particularly bratty days. Snow, mountain peaks glittering white, a pool of still, turquoise-blue water. "I'm sure I don't know what you're talking about, Mr. Tesfay."

"Yes, you do."

Was he going to wrangle with her like a three-year-old? "Mr. Tesfay—"

He had the gall to lift his finger as if to wag it at her, but the reappearance of Hind thankfully interrupted his interrogation.

"I'm ready!"

Flustered, Val turned to her, clearing her throat. Hind thrust her handbag in Val's direction without a word and set off down the hallway, chattering into her mobile as she went.

Val's face burned with embarrassment, and Desmond had seen it all. She knew because her skin was tingling where his eyes grazed her.

"She's normally not…" Val's voice trailed off. What was the point?

"Miss Montgomery…" he began.

"Dinner!" she said, clapping her hands to break the tension as she skittered forward. She jumped when Desmond slipped up behind her, and a large warm hand hovered over hers, but stopped short of touching her.

"Allow me," he said, and she nodded. She sincerely hoped her light-headed breathlessness was the result of not drinking enough water today, and not as a result of her proximity to Desmond. His hand closed over the handle of Hind's behemoth handbag, and his fingers rested on her elbow a fraction of a second before he stepped away.

"My man will take it at the door. Come on, let's go." He began striding toward the door, and Val gave herself a good shake, reprimanding herself severely.

Years ago, she'd had an intense physical reaction to a man just as young and just as handsome, if not quite as successful. All she'd gotten from that was a heart that was smashed to bits and a colossal mess she was still cleaning up.

Well, she told herself, this was different; she had about as much chance of starting anything with Desmond Tesfay as she did of flying to the moon. And, frankly, she was grateful for it.

She was content just to look, and comforted to know that no one would ever know how silly she had been.

CHAPTER TWO

HAD TEENAGE GIRLS, Desmond wondered, been this tedious when he was a teen himself? He couldn't remember that far back. All he knew was that the evening was nearing an end, and he was grateful. He wanted badly to be back home, alone.

He supposed Hind felt the same; she had stopped pretending to be interested in anything he was saying over an hour ago.

"Couldn't you have got us in at the Soho Club?" she queried, pushing aside her plate.

"You're under*age*."

Hind sighed and rose to her feet, seemingly overcome by the unfairness of it all. "Fine." She reached for the massive red handbag she'd kept close to her side since they'd entered. "I'm going to the loo," she said. "And I don't need you, Val. Be right back!"

She left in a cloud of perfume and that now-familiar clatter of high heels. Desmond was finally able to take a breath. He was going to hear that damned *tap-tap* noise in his sleep.

Her minder, or whoever Miss Montgomery was, was sipping from a little brass-handled pot of Turkish coffee. She hadn't said a word throughout their meal, aside from gentle reprimands to Hind whenever the latter had been rude, which was more than once. He couldn't have said a word about the meal if his life depended on it.

But now Hind was gone, and his eyes flicked over to the woman sitting across from him.

She was petite, with soft small hands that busied themselves quietly and unobtrusively with knife and fork. Her feet were tucked neatly beneath her chair. Her dark hair was combed back into a sleek ponytail and thick lashes framed her downcast eyes. A beauty spot sat just below a generous lower lip. He found himself lingering on that small black mark despite himself. It called attention to the lush fullness of her mouth—

She cleared her throat and he blinked, then wanted to laugh out loud. That annoying teenager had wound him up so much that he'd been ogling her *nanny* as a way to escape the situation.

He wanted to return to the question of how she could help him win Hind's father as a client. That was the only reason he was anxious to hear her speak again.

Because of the deal, of course.

Before he could open his mouth, though, she said, "I can't help you, Mr. Tesfay."

Is she psychic?

"I'm not sure you—"

"You've been assessing me since Hind left." She picked up a napkin and began to dab at her mouth.

"I'm sure I don't–"

"Don't you?" she looked up at him then, and he found himself taking a breath despite himself. The horn-rims she was wearing had slipped down her nose and she regarded him over the top of them.

It was giving a "sexy librarian" vibe and he was very much into it. He would have laughed at himself again, but she was explaining why she couldn't—or wouldn't—help him. Her voice was soft and modulated, with a drawl that was reminiscent of the magnolia trees and fragrant honeysuckle he'd seen on trips to the American South. That voice took the sting out of what might have been a very sarcastic line of conversation.

When she smiled, when the soft brown glow of her cheek dented into a single, perfect dimple, he'd decided that this Miss Montgomery was very, very attractive indeed.

"And that's why I can't help you," she finished, and he realized he'd checked out for a moment. She picked up her napkin and shook it out with a flourish. Desmond half rose from his chair, but she shook her head. "No, please don't trouble yourself. I'm going to check on Hind," she said, and was gone, with Desmond determinedly *not* watching her walk away. Oh, who was he kidding? He watched, and he enjoyed every single second. Her small waist sloped dramatically into hips that topped a full, heart-shaped bottom that swayed seductively as she walked—

He shook his head and forced himself to look away.

It was probably the most clichéd thing about the poor-little-rich-boy that he was, but he did appreciate a beautiful woman. There had been many since his father's death. He didn't use them as a means to forget—nothing could ever do that—but things like good food, good wine, pleasure found between soft willing thighs—

It was the only time he could shut off, just a little. And God knew he was tired.

Desmond had slowed down a little since turning thirty approached—not with the business, but in his playboy affairs—yet this was neither the time, the place, nor the woman.

He had a deal to close. The Sheikh seemed no closer to

committing than when Desmond had started courting him as a client, and he had a feeling that this attempt to ingratiate himself had been a waste of time. He pressed his lips together in irritation and glanced down again at the vintage gold watch on his wrist; he'd put it on the day he'd learned of his father's death, and it had barely left his arm since then.

If he could get out of here in the next hour, perhaps he could salvage the evening at least…

But he was interrupted by the sudden appearance of Miss Montgomery, whose poise was very different from the controlled haughtiness she'd wielded like a blade on her way out. Now she was breathing hard, and she looked panicked. He stood, but she didn't seem to notice. Her eyes were wild.

"Hind's gone!" she cried.

"Hind's *gone*?"

Val ignored Desmond, dialing Hind's mobile for the fifth time in seven minutes. By her calculations it was nearly twenty-five minutes since her charge had disappeared. Twenty-five minutes in which anything could have happened. Her mind, as it was prone to do, leaped to the worst-case scenarios, and then some. Hind, kidnapped by her father's enemies. Hind, robbed and left for dead behind the restaurant—

"She probably just went home."

The phone was ringing. Val pursed her lips and pressed it closer to her ear. Three rings. Four. Five—

"She wasn't exactly overcome with joy at our company," he added, dryly.

"Hind wouldn't do that," Val said through clenched teeth, although she wasn't sure why she was so confident. "And anyway, I'll find her in a jiffy," she said, more to herself than to Desmond. "Her watch has a tracker in it."

"You mean *this* watch?" Desmond said, and held up the slim Cartier timepiece, which lay beneath the rim of Hind's plate. A sound of distress escaped Val's lips before she could suppress it, and she closed her eyes tightly.

"I'm pretty sure tracking her is illegal—unethical at least." Desmond's voice broke through the smudge of darkness behind her closed lids. Did he sound…*amused*? "When I was her age, I'd have probably done the same. I remember slipping out of an Eid celebration when I was a kid, and I met up with friends at Glastonbury—"

Why was he *still* talking? She had to think. She reached out, placed her hand on his arm, and pulled out the commanding tone she usually reserved for the rambunctious boys she'd nannied for before Hind. "For a moment, Mr. Tesfay, please *stop talking*."

He stopped, lifting those perfectly groomed brows to their limit, then looked cross at the fact that he'd instinctively obeyed.

"I have to think," she said apologetically—but not really—and drew back. In the moment after speaking she'd become suddenly very aware of the muscles flexing beneath the fine soft wool of his dinner jacket.

He looked slightly less put out. "Has she ever done this before?"

"Only in the mall, and I'm not worried about her there."

Oh, why would Hind try this, and here?

"Does she have any friends in London?" Before she could answer, Desmond Tesfay continued speaking with that butter-rich baritone that was making her insides soften, despite herself. She wanted to scream. "And Hind is—What is she, seventeen?"

"Not till August," Val gritted out.

"Ah, a Leo. Come on," Desmond added, when that observance didn't elicit a smile. "She's got her mobile, it's on, she'll call you when she's ready. It's London. She's not a baby, and she knows who to call if she gets into trouble."

"I pity you if you can't see what a disaster this is," Val spat out.

"You're right," he drawled. "I mean, it might be bad for you, Nanny McPhee, but—"

Nanny McPhee? Oh, he was going to get it. Val drew herself up to her full height, feeling her shapewear stretch as she did so.

"Just so you know, you're never going to land this deal. You're too shortsighted and ignorant to close it."

That got his attention. A spark of what could be anger darkened his eyes to near-black. Finally, a real emotion had broken through all the bland, ice-cool charm. The change sent a thrill through her. She forced it down, and resisted the urge to take a step back.

"Shortsighted and ignorant?" he echoed softly, and took a step forward. She fancied she could feel the heat radiating from his body. This close, she could certainly smell him, the layers unfolding with each second—cloves, cinnamon, a hint of orange. There was also something heavier, like brandy, or a touch of fine-honed leather. He tilted his head and surveyed her face. She felt heat rising inside her, and her body began to vibrate with the intensity of his presence, overcoming the panic she'd felt at Hind's disappearance.

But she had bigger things to worry about this evening, including a job she couldn't afford to lose. But none of that changed the fact that this man was the sexiest person she'd spoken to in a very, very long time.

All amusement had left his voice, as well as his face. The practiced charmer was gone, replaced by someone much less amused, and—if it were possible—much more attractive.

"I realize that you're likely terrified for your position," he said in a voice so cold she felt it running up her spine in an involuntary shiver. "But I fail to see how that affects my business prospects, so if you would be so kind as to enlighten me as to why…?"

Oh, she'd enlighten him, all right. She swallowed hard, summoning every bit of self-control she'd learned in her years in the Gulf.

"First of all," she said, relieved that her voice came out clipped and measured, "you have no idea how much of an honor it is for Sheikh Rashid to have left you, a single man, with his precious daughter all day. He entrusted you with his favorite—scratch that, *only*—daughter, and what did you do? You took her out to dinner, and you *lost* her. Yes, she acted independently, and yes, I am her chaperone, but *you're* her host, and *you're* the one who wants this deal. Why would he trust you with his business if he cannot trust you with his child?"

She took a shaky breath, while Desmond sat in stony silence.

"We'll find her." His voice was full of controlled fury. "Come, Miss Montgomery, collect your things. Let's go."

CHAPTER THREE

DESMOND CALLED FOR a car after telling himself that it was the business deal and *not* the fact that he'd just gone through one hell of a telling-off by a very sexy librarian-slash-nanny that made him do so.

It was, arguably, not a solution, but at least it would give them a semi-private place to brainstorm, and it made him feel as if he was doing something to find that insufferable teenager. Val hadn't met his eyes since that moment between them in the restaurant; the spitfire was completely gone, replaced by the slightly distant coolness she'd maintained till dinner.

He wished she would look at him, he was surprised to realize. He couldn't remember the last time a woman had told him off or avoided his gaze. They usually sought it, if anything. But Val Montgomery had barely looked at him all day.

It bothered him more than it should.

He cleared his throat in a bid to displace the thought and focus on the task at hand. Strangely, the absurdity of the situation had eaten entirely through the clouds of gloom that had threatened to engulf him all evening.

"Has she got a location app on her mobile?"

"If you were running away from someone, would you leave it on?" she said tartly.

Desmond recoiled. “Listen, I’m just trying to help—”

“I know. I know.” While her voice wasn’t nearly as contrite as it could have been, she did look at him then, lifting soft fingertips to massage her temples. “I apologize—it’s been a very long day.”

Slightly mollified, Desmond continued. “Does she have any friends or relatives in London she might have met up with? A boyfriend?”

“I hope not,” Val muttered, but her eyes widened all the same. “Friends in London—I can’t believe I didn’t think of it before.”

“What?”

“I was so busy sniping at you I didn’t think.”

Well, at least she realized she’d been sniping. He took a moment to enjoy the self-righteousness as she dug through the enormous handbag at her side, produced her mobile phone, and opened an app. He leaned in, peering over her shoulder, and was immediately taken in by a soft, powdery fragrance cut with something sharper, more vivid. She shifted and the movement caused her softness to be pressed against his side for a moment; he enjoyed it much more than he should have before she moved away.

“She’s got a dummy account,” Val said by way of explanation, sliding her horn-rims up her nose in order to see better. “I’ve been following her for years. No new posts, but—Oh, dear. Oh, *dear*.”

She sank back as if overcome, and Desmond took the opportunity to look at her phone, then laughed out loud. It was a real laugh that bubbled from deep inside his chest. The sound so startled him that he paused for a moment.

“What’s so funny?” she demanded crossly.

“#FleeFromNannyMcPhee?” He was *cackling*. “Great minds think alike.”

“I’m not her nanny,” Val said hotly. “I’m her—”

“Personal assistant,” Desmond said soothingly. “We know. Don’t take it personally. This is probably what she calls you to her friends.”

Val huffed, and the movement made her rather ample chest expand in a way that was *very* distracting. He brought his mind back to the matter at hand. “You can stop worrying. At least you know where she is.” He passed the phone back. “Her grammar, though, is appalling. Either that or she typed in a hurry.”

“She’s a perfect speller!” Val sputtered, but she was looking more horrified at each line.

Jailbrk! I ditched Nany McFee! Ready 4 my #1niteinLondon <3

Heddin 2 the #roylоperahouse 2 c the <3 of my llife.

Pic comin up, wait 4 it!

#fleefromNannyMcPhee

“Love of her *life*?” Val fairly shrieked.

Desmond was trying very hard not to laugh again, despite himself. “I don’t think she’s talking about a boy, if it makes you feel better.” A thirty-second search produced ticket sales for a popular K-pop band that performed their concerts opera-style. Val took one look and buried her face in her hands.

“Is she a fan?” he queried, politely.

“Of *course* she’s a fan of that moronic group. She begged for tickets, but her father said no.” Val drew in breath as if it were all too much. “Finding her in that crowd will be—”

"Virtually impossible." Desmond tapped his wrist in memory of the watch left behind. "It's a ninety-minute show, according to this. When does her father expect her back?"

"He doesn't. He's in Manchester till tomorrow morning." Val sagged back onto the rich leather seat, placing her hands on her head as if it ached. The hem of her dress hitched up with the movement, and Desmond saw just a hint of lace and the soft dimpled skin of her thighs before the hem dropped again. Was she wearing lace-top stockings? The thought made something tighten in his middle.

If he were being honest, he had no shortage of access to women keen to spend time with him, each more beautiful than the last. None of them stayed, although some certainly did try. Some wanted his money, and those were the easiest to flush out. Some wanted his network of contacts and business partners. Some—and these repulsed him the most—were soft and starry-eyed, looking at him as a devoted prince who would ride in and save them.

Val Montgomery was none of these things; she looked more like she wanted to push him out of the car while it was in motion, but she certainly had caught his attention. And though he had no idea where this evening was taking them, he knew one thing: he wanted more of her. In what capacity, he still wasn't sure, but he did know that solving her problem with Hind would help.

"This is what we'll do," he said, cool reassurance taking over his voice. "We'll go to the Royal Opera House—it's about twenty minutes from here. We'll keep an eye on Hind's feed. If we're lucky we'll spot her in the crowd coming out. If we don't, at least we know where she's going next on her jailbreak night."

"Not funny."

"Sorry."

There was a moment of silence punctuated only by traffic sounds outside the steel-wrapped oasis of their car. Val took a breath and turned to look at him.

"I was a little short before," she said, in that soft, cultured voice with a hint of— It was bugging him. What was that accent? The American South? He'd had a classmate from Atlanta while attending school in London that spoke a little like her. "I appreciate your help. And I hope this won't affect your opinion of Hind, or the family. She really is a good girl, just a little…bored."

"Do you like working for the family?"

"I do." Val sat up straight, and he saw, again, a distracting flash of lace and brown skin before it disappeared. "It's not the most exciting line of work. But it pays well, and I need the money." She said the last line almost too quietly to hear, in a way that was more reflective than anything else. She lifted a hand to fiddle with one of the small pearls earring she wore.

"Student loans?" he ventured after a moment. America was notorious for that, he'd heard.

She smiled a little. "No. Not many college degrees in how to be a nanny," she said with a self-deprecating laugh.

"What did you go to school for?"

"My mother was a dressmaker. She had a small business, back home." She was still twisting the earring, almost nervously now. Long lashes swept down over her cheeks then lifted, and she fixed her enormous brown eyes back on him. "I went to trade school for a couple of years, intending that when I graduated I'd help her. I still design—kind of. Hind has a business selling hand-sewn abayas to her friends and other girls. I help her with the technical work. It keeps Hind out of trouble and brings something extra for me."

"You seem very close."

"I've been working with the family since she was nine," Valentina said softly.

"How did you get to know them?"

Something in her eyes closed off subtly; there was a tightening around her mouth, and her lashes fluttered down.

"I got to know Sheikh Rashid through an old…acquaintance," she said, after a long pause. "He is the best and kindest of men."

A ringing endorsement of her boss was to be expected, but the very slight quaver he heard in Val's voice, the first of its kind he'd seen in her all evening, was not. He felt his eyebrows lift; exactly what was the older man to her? "That's a very telling statement. His reputation is that he's a bit of a—"

"His reputation comes from people who don't know him at all," she said sharply. "I *do*, and I know what he's done for people. Myself included."

Very interesting. "You know him well, then?"

"Well enough." She cleared her throat, the moment gone. "Well enough to know that we need to find this girl and get her home where she belongs. And thank goodness, there it is." She nodded, indicating the Royal Opera House a little way in front. She stopped speaking, leaving Desmond to his thoughts. Finally, some spark of emotion from Hind's no-nonsense companion, and it'd been Sheikh Rashid who'd pulled it out of her. Her fearsome, older boss, of all people?

Could she and Hind's father be—?

As soon as the thought flitted across his mind he banished it with an internal laugh. That was a fairly major leap of imagination, and not worthy of either of them. Val frowned at him. "What is it?"

"Nothing." Aside from it being completely inappropriate, Desmond strongly suspected Val Montgomery would not enjoy hearing that his first thought was that she was engaged in a liaison with her boss. "Let's go and find our girl, shall we?"

"She's hardly *ours*," Val grumbled. The driver deftly pulled the car close to the curb.

"Don't bother with the door—traffic's a mess," Desmond called up to his driver, reaching for the door handle. Val began scooting over, then yelped as the car jerked forward, pushing her hard against Desmond's body.

"Henry!"

"Apologies, sir, there's a van behind us letting down a wheelchair. I should have said," the driver called back.

"For Christ's sake. We'd have been flat on the curb if the door was open." He opened the door quickly, freeing himself from the pleasant warmth of Val, who'd shifted back almost immediately. "Sorry," he said, and held out a hand.

She was rattled enough to take it, and hauled herself out of the car with no further incidence.

"Are you all right?" he asked.

"Just fine!" She was shaking out her coat, looking disproportionately flustered. "I— Can we just go, please?"

"Fine," he said, and they set off.

What a little hypocrite you are, Val Montgomery.

She'd reprimanded Desmond Tesfay in a very public place barely half an hour ago. She was currently trying to hunt down her charge, in a chase that might very well result in the loss of a job she needed very badly. And now, after the minutest bit of close contact with him, she was so flustered she hadn't been able to say a word for the past five minutes.

She hadn't felt desire in so long that its arrival this evening had startled her with its intensity. But their closeness in the car had sparked it, and she was still unsettled by the strength of its pull. She'd thought those feelings had been squashed long ago, banished by the exhaustion of poverty, of abandonment, of heartbreak. But here it was, burning as brightly inside her as kindling stirred to flame.

She was helpless against it. But she knew better. *She knew better.*

She wouldn't slip up again.

Outside, they could see a crowd forming that was clearly there for the same show as Hind, streaming into the Royal Opera House, its soft yellowed light penetrating the dusk of early evening. It looked beautiful in this light, tall and imposing, a fitting background for the fading blue sky behind it. Young fans were dressed in their best in velvet miniskirts or backless, barely-there dresses, light catching the sparkles of youthful enthusiasm. Val suddenly felt very silly, and more than a little old.

Thirty-nine years old today, to be precise. Quite honestly, she'd forgotten, in all the excitement. And she was much too old to allow herself to be lost to fantasy, even for a moment. Desmond's rich brown eyes and full, curving mouth were the stuff of fantasy, no matter how solid he seemed by her side.

He was a man. A rich and ambitious man. Nothing but trouble in a pretty suit. She'd spent the last eight years working her fingers to the bone so she could be free of men like him for good; so she could finally be completely independent.

"We'll never find her in this crush," Val murmured.

"We might not need to. Has she updated anything?"

Val scrolled. Hind was ensconced in one of the opera house's plush red velvet seats, winking cheekily and flashing her fingers in salute. A background of crimson and gold illuminated her lovely face. At least she'd had the sense to cover the lower half of her face with a rhinestone-studded mask. If her notoriously private father *ever* saw these posts, he wouldn't be able to identify her.

Hopefully.

"She's inside."

"Great." Desmond's hand was at her back now, hovering close enough for her to feel the heat of him without actually touching her, steering her deftly through the crowds. "We'll go to the bar, have a drink, and scoop the little stinker up on her way out. Watch your step!"

Everybody in the crowd seemed to be young, female and beautiful, and a few were shooting Desmond appreciative looks. He was oblivious, concentrating on his job of steering Val forward without incident. His jaw was rigid; those limpid, bedroom-sleepy eyes lowered.

"I have a private box here," he said, so close to her ear that she nearly jumped. A shiver went down her spine as his breath caressed her ear lobe.

"How convenient for you," she managed, gripping the straps of her handbag for dear life. At the bar, Desmond procured two seats out of thin air. She nodded her thanks, blurted out something inane about needing to powder her nose, and made a run for the ladies'.

Miraculously, the place was empty except for a couple of women chatting in hushed tones while washing their hands. Val ducked into a stall, made use of the facilities and then stood with her dress unzipped for a long moment, willing the air-conditioning to cool her skin.

Her whole body felt primed for touch.

She carefully rolled down her stockings and took off her tight shapewear, then fanned air on her bare skin. She splashed cold water on her wrists and touched them to her face, then patted the skin dry and reapplied a few drops of perfume on her wrists and neck. It smelled far too sweet to match whatever pheromones her body was absolutely vibrating with at the moment. She gave herself a mental shake, then dressed herself, reapplied her lipstick, and prepared to face him again.

She headed back out to the Champagne Bar, determined not to be so silly. She was met by Desmond, who was looking devastatingly handsome and holding aloft two empty glasses.

He wasn't going to make this easy, was he? He already had that devil-may-care look on his face—the look of a man who couldn't relate to even a third of what she had to deal with on a daily basis. And he was sporting that charming smile that said everything and nothing. She knew that smile; she'd fallen for a similar one before and look where that had got her.

"You made it clear how serious this is," he said, handing her a glass, "with the force of an angry monsoon. But you have to admit that this is a little funny—chasing a sixteen-year-old across London, I mean."

Val felt her mouth creeping up at the side. "It is," she allowed. "But water for me, please."

Desmond made a sound of displeasure deep in his throat. "I was going to let you choose the bottle."

"I'm working," she said a bit primly. "And so are you, for that matter."

"Do you not drink?"

"That isn't the point—"

"I'll admit to having an ulterior motive," he said, and stepped aside, offering a hand to assist her onto the barstool. "Can I help you?"

"I'm not sure I should take either the help or the drink if you've got an ulterior motive."

He laughed. "My *motive* is to ply you with champagne and good conversation over the course of the next hour, until you're willing to give me some tips—good, *discreet* tips—to help me win the Sheikh's business. And," he added, cutting her off, "I'll have the added advantage of time with a beautiful and intelligent companion—"

"Don't ruin your chances before you begin," Val said archly. Her cheeks were flaming hot, but her insides felt pleasantly warm. How long had it been since a man had flirted with her, in any capacity? It felt…nice. And there was an odd edge of kindness shaping Desmond's countenance that she couldn't identify; she only knew it was there, and she could feel it, drawing her to him despite herself.

Val took a step closer, offered him her hand, and his lips tipped up.

"Need a boost?"

"Please."

In one breathless moment his hand was on the small of her back, burning through her clothes again, and she was up on the barstool. Had he lifted her? Had she floated? She had no idea. He was still standing, his head hovering well above hers.

She pressed her knees together, tugging to make sure the lace at the top of her stockings remained hidden; he caught the gesture and she saw something in his eyes kindle.

He was closer to her now, or was that her imagination? Val took a breath, giving herself a minute to look around at their opulent surroundings, trying to focus on anything but his face. There had been a time, years ago, when beauty had moved her. Her husband had been an expert when it came to scenes like this one: glamorous surroundings, a handsome face, a solicitous hand on her lower back. But it had all been a front, a smoke screen to nothingness.

She didn't know what was behind the curtain with Desmond Tesfay. All she knew was that she had no intention of lifting it.

"Tell me how I'm really doing," he murmured.

He's closer!

She pushed the thought away with some effort and cleared her throat. "With the Sheikh?" her voice sounded unnaturally high.

"Yes." He reached behind her and produced a tall glass of water, which he handed to her. She took a grateful sip. "I need something that will help me seal the deal."

"I can't divulge anything about my clients—"

"Yes, you can." His dark eyes were glittering. "Or you can tell me what I must absolutely avoid. Come on, Miss Montgomery. You've seen my office, my setup, and heard a summary of my pitch."

Yes, she had. And it was good—very good. What she'd seen of his campaign revealed the painstaking detail of his research into the region as well as the Sheikh. It had made her admire him more, really. The way his eyes had lit up—he had a vision for the region that was more than sparkly gadgets and flashy flight attendants.

"It was good," she said with sincerity. Desmond straightened a little when she said that, and she was touched, despite herself. Her feedback mattered to him, and that showed a humility that was sorely lacking in the men she'd been interacting with over the past ten years. "You're very young to have achieved so much," she added.

He laughed out loud. "How old do you think I am? You're talking as if you should be nannying *me*."

"Heaven forbid."

Desmond was leaning in closer now, with a different sort of intensity than the flirtation he'd started with, but this version made her pulse race just as quickly. "I just meant…the scope of Tesfay International is impressive."

Desmond leaned back, focusing his eyes on some glittering object some distance away from them. "I suppose."

"Have you been in the Gulf long?"

He shook his dark head. "This is a bit of an expansion move." His expression was suddenly wary and she wasn't sure what had prompted that. "We've mostly been in the European market up until now."

"*We*'ve?"

"My father. It's his company, really. *Was* his company." Desmond's voice was growing crisper by the moment. "Hence the youth of which you so charmingly spoke—I'm a nepo baby."

"And he sent you here?"

"He's dead, sweetheart," Desmond said, his voice drawing out the words to something long and almost lazy. He'd tilted his head back so that his face was momentarily in shadow, and she was unable to see his expression as clearly as she had before.

Val felt mortification wash over her at her own tactlessness. "I'm sorry—I shouldn't have pried." Val paused to tuck a lock of hair behind her ear, then stilled the nervous movement; there was no hair there, of course. The amount of gel and edge control she used on a daily basis would have defeated even the most errant curl.

"No need to apologize. You weren't to know." His words were carefully enunciated, as if he'd rehearsed the lines many times but was still uncertain as to how to deliver them.

"I'm sorry for your loss." And there she was, apologizing again. He lifted the corners of his mouth but it wasn't a true smile.

"You're very kind."

They sat in silence for a moment, lost in their own thoughts as soft conversations and the strains of Chopin hung faintly in the air.

"It's not something I talk about in public," Desmond said, after a while. His eyes still seemed to be focused on something far away. "He died in an accident some years back. Plane crash."

The words were said so baldly that Val's breath caught in her throat. "That must have been devastating."

"It was." His face hadn't changed expression but his voice had quieted; she had to lean in to hear him above the chatter and clinking glassware. "I am privileged enough to ensure with my business—our business…that his legacy didn't die with him."

"That's very…noble." Val hoped her words sounded sincere; she meant them, but there was something about Desmond in this moment that meant she didn't trust her voice.

He looked at her; his eyes were dark and liquid and she involuntarily lifted a hand to her neck. His gaze was making her pulse thrum like a hummingbird in her throat. "He would be so proud."

The storm in those eyes had increased till the color was nearly obliterated; all she could see was black. "Kind words," he said after a moment, and bitterness entered his voice. "Empty, but kind."

What?

"I did not intend—"

"My father might hate what I've done with this company. How would you know? *I* barely know what he would think."

She had no idea what to say to that.

"Are your parents proud of you, Miss Montgomery?" he asked coldly.

Well, *that* was certainly a shift in conversation. A lump rose hard and fast to the same place where her pulse beat. "My, um—"

"I'm just curious."

"Well, I—"

Desmond's eyes fell on her lap where she knotted her hands, and he raised his brows.

"Am I making you nervous, Miss Montgomery?"

"A little." She might as well be frank. "This conversation…"

"Has become a little heavy?"

"Well…"

He smiled, and in a flash the introspection was gone, replaced by the familiar smirk. "My apologies. Consider us back in shallow waters."

"No, I didn't mean…" Val fumbled. Oh, how had she managed to bungle this up so badly? And why did she mind so much that he'd withdrawn from her, despite her relief that his question had ended up being rhetorical? He'd clearly launched that question out at her like a grenade to throw her off balance, and it had worked. "Mr. Tesfay—"

"No, no, no need to explain."

"Well…all right."

"I need something. Anything at all," Desmond continued, taking up his former line of conversation with ease. "You know as well as I do that these things often come down to some arbitrary thing. A shared interest, membership of the same club, a brand of whiskey…? Although I know he doesn't drink," he added.

Shallow waters. It was much easier to breathe now that he

had changed the subject, that was for sure. She found herself licking her lips, gathering her wits and answering in kind.

"Ignoring the fact that revealing information like this would be very indiscreet of me, that would be giving you quite the unfair advantage, wouldn't it?"

"It absolutely would."

He said it so confidently that Val had to cover her mouth with a hand, stifling the laugh that burbled forth. When he smiled, it was like the sun coming out after a storm. She knew it was real and involuntary because it made fine lines fan out of the corners of his eyes, as if he were a man who laughed often.

"Well?"

Why shouldn't she? Why shouldn't she give him some harmless nugget of information that would help him—and more importantly, prolong the conversation?

She did want to prolong the conversation, didn't she, despite that horribly awkward exchange a few moments ago? He was still very close to her, and looking at her keenly, as if he were trying to find the key to a puzzle. It was an oddly penetrating look that made her grope awkwardly for the champagne flute.

"We're drinking now?" Desmond asked, rather triumphantly.

"One glass," she allowed.

"What's your choice?"

"I don't care." She eased the death grip on her handbag and took a deep breath. She was having a drink at the Royal Opera House in the Champagne Bar with a man as rich as Croesus while her sixteen-year-old charge was presumably dancing to K-pop inside. She must be in a fever dream.

"ID, please!"

The bartender's voice startled her. She fumbled in her

bag, identified the slim rectangle, and pushed it forward. The pigtailed woman squinted at it, then at her, then returned it with a straight face.

"Happy birthday, Valentina!" she said chirpily, and poured, then disappeared. She felt heat shoot up to her cheeks. Desmond was staring at her, as if seeing her for the first time.

"Valentina?" he said, and that was all it took. His low voice curved around the syllables of her name. If calling her *Ms. Montgomery* gave her butterflies, then using her full name made a quiver go up from her tummy to her throat.

She jerked as if she'd been burned. "Don't call me that!"

"*She* called you that."

"It's on my ID, that's why." Damn the bartender and her presumption. Val took a large sip from her glass to bolster herself. She registered icy cold first, then bubbles burst on her tongue with a delightful apple-like crispness. She closed her eyes for a second and wished Desmond gone. When she opened her eyes he was looking at her curiously.

"It's a beautiful name," he said with that odd gentleness that occasionally characterized his speech. She pressed her knees together so hard it hurt.

"It's ridiculously sentimental," she said tightly. "My father named me that because I was due on—"

"Valentine's Day! Of course!" Now he sounded a bit amused. "And it's the sixteenth. You missed it by a hair."

"I suppose I did."

"Do you really hate the name that much?"

"I don't *hate* it, I just…" She used to *love* it, actually. She used to think it was elegant and old-fashioned and a little romantic, just like her. She'd liked the association with what had once been her favorite holiday. But *now*…

Well. Life had been diligent about showing her how dangerous sentiment and romance could be, hadn't it? And the name she'd once loved mocked her whenever she heard it.

"Val is easier to pronounce than Valentina where I live," she said. It wasn't quite the truth, but it was close enough. "It's Val now."

"*I* think your full name suits you much better," he declared.

"*I* think what *you* think matters little in this case," she said acidly.

Irritatingly, the man wasn't put off. Instead, he topped off her glass and offered a half smile. "And it's your birthday. Valentina," he said, as if testing out the name.

There it was, again, that liquid fissure beginning to creep between her thighs. "Don't call me that," she said automatically, burying her nose in her glass, although her voice was perhaps not as sharp as she'd intended.

When she resurfaced, he was gazing at her thoughtfully. "I'm sorry. This is a dreadful way to celebrate, isn't it?"

She shrugged. "It's not as if I had any other plans."

"Oh, that's too–"

"No, it isn't bad. It isn't bad at all," she said crisply. Despite whatever…attraction she felt, at the end of the day her rules remained the same. "It's lovely, actually. No stress, no obligations, no parties, no *men*," she said pointedly. "Just another day, exactly as I want it."

To her surprise he laughed. "I can relate. I haven't celebrated a birthday for years."

"Why not?"

A shadow crossed his face. "No time," he said, briskly. "Work. And my…family lives quite a distance away."

There was something he wasn't telling her, and she was surprised to find herself wanting to know what it was.

"But enough about me," he said quickly. "How old—?"

"Older than you. And no, I'm not telling you." She was old enough to think back on the girl she'd been, and how she'd screwed up badly enough to put her in this position on her thirty-ninth birthday. Images raced through her mind of the shy, neglected girl she'd been: a whirlwind courtship with a man she'd met by chance at Mardi Gras in her native New Orleans; a marriage—a short, terrible marriage; and finally—

Val abruptly stood. She didn't want to go down this road tonight, even though she knew it was inevitable. At the very least she could wait until she was in the privacy of her own room. "I should find Hind," she said firmly. "Thank you for the drink."

"Where is she now?"

"I'm going to try and scoop her up on the way out."

"And if you're unsuccessful? Listen—" And there it was again. Tha*t look*. Flickering down the length of her body, almost too quick to note. He seemed…

When was the last time anyone had looked at her like that? And since when had she cared that they did? Desmond Tesfay was eroding every single vow she had made and that had kept her safe for the past decade. Champagne. Closeness. Flirting. Him saying her *name*. And she was terrified at how much she liked it.

His voice, rich and low, broke into her thoughts, quieting them. "I've got as much at stake as you do, don't I? Let me help you."

When she tilted her head, he raised both hands in surrender. "No funny business. And consider your full name forgotten."

She gritted her teeth. "Will you keep haranguing me for information about the Sheikh?"

"Not if you don't want me to."

There it was again, that easy smile. Those unreadable, yet oddly intense dark eyes.

Shallow waters.

She paused for a long moment to regain her composure.

“Fine,” she finally forced out, and he nodded.

“It’ll be a birthday to remember, if nothing else,” he said lightly, and offered his arm. Val took it.

A birthday to remember.

Really, the man had no idea.

CHAPTER FOUR

THEY DID NOT manage to "scoop" Hind up in front of the Royal Opera House, much to Val's dismay and Desmond's amusement, despite himself. The little minx was proving more slippery than an ice cube on a marble floor, and her rapid-fire posts seemed more a mockery of their incompetence than anything else. When he told Val so, she glared at him. Any relaxation she'd managed to achieve in the Champagne Bar seemed to have evaporated with the realization that once again Hind was loose on the streets of London, and the time was nearing ten o'clock. She was looking crosser and crosser by the minute.

"Are you really finding this amusing?" she asked. "Running off to some basement jazz club, off all places," Val sputtered. "Ronnie Scott's—can you imagine? She just *came* from a concert."

Desmond stifled a smirk with some difficulty. Calling Ronnie Scott's "some basement jazz club" definitely wouldn't go over well in Soho, but they were already back in his car with his driver patiently navigating his way through late-night traffic. "It's not the actual Ronnie Scott's—it's a club *close* to it. A dupe, I believe she said. She's catching the tail end of a friend's set," he said in the soberest voice he could manage.

"She's not meant to have any friends!"

Desmond laughed out loud; it was a real laugh as well, and he wondered how many of them this woman had pulled from him this evening. Val was staring hard out of the car window, as if she could conjure Hind by sheer will. Desmond reached out and tapped the leather seat just next to her thigh, and she jumped.

"We're almost there," he said. She nodded with a smile that didn't quite reach her eyes. She looked worried, and tired and more than a little defeated, and he wasn't sure it was entirely related to Hind's misbehavior. Something bloomed in his chest, something warm and fierce—a desire to lift some of that heaviness from her in some way. Which was mad in and of itself. He didn't even know her! Digging beneath the surface of a person, shifting those sands, only led to more complications. Since his tumultuous early years, he'd managed to live a life free of complications in the personal relationship department.

He was man enough to admit that he was a little afraid of taking off the mask; the results would likely be catastrophic. And Val had already made him say too much. His father's death was public information, but the real reason he worked himself half to death and was determined to break into the Gulf market was *not*.

And with one question and one little flutter of her lashes, *Valentina* Montgomery had made him say more than he ever had to anyone else.

It was increasingly difficult not to slip up and call her by her full name.

The car stopped a little distance from Chez Dodo and Val immediately leaped out of the car and began speed-walking toward the club without a backward glance. Desmond's long legs ate up the distance quickly, but she still managed to enter before he did. When he ducked through the door, navigating the throng of people, he was surprised to see her standing with her arms crossed, just to the right of the stage.

"There she is," she said in a subdued voice, and nodded, pointing with her chin. It took Desmond a full minute to recognize Hind; the teenager was sitting in the midst of a group of girls who more or less looked like her, chattering nonstop.

"She looks so happy," Val said, and there was a wobble in her voice that made Desmond draw a little closer to her, despite himself. "I could go over there now, and get her, but..."

"We could give her a bit of time?" Desmond suggested. He steered Val to a benched area with a partial view of the stage. It was clearly designed for intimacy because the moment they sat, it was as if they became ensconced in their own little world, a wood-and leather-sealed sanctuary that smelled of gin and dust and sweat and perfume. Desmond was suddenly very aware of the softness of her thigh, pressed close to his, of that powdery sweetness that lingered on the soft skin of her neck, of the curve of her breasts beneath her tight black dress, of her small waist and full lips.

This was a setting made for closeness, for pressing a warm body against yours and kissing them, deliberate and sweet, until they sighed and softened and melted into you. Normally, Desmond would do exactly this, but not with a woman like Valentina Montgomery.

He reminded himself of that, and sternly.

She was chewing that deliciously full lower lip and when she released it, it was plump and cherry red. Desmond completely gave up any denial of the lust he was feeling. Apparently, he could add sexy librarian to his list of kinks. He cleared his throat. "Are you going to get her?"

Her eyes were still fixed on her charge, and she sighed. "No."

"No?"

"She…she looks so happy, and she rarely gets to have fun like this. Bahr Al-Dahab isn't like let's say, Dubai or Qatar. Beautiful architecture, amazing food and a great educational system, but not much in the way of teenage fun. She can't get in trouble now because I'm watching her." She sounded as if she were convincing herself rather than him. She cleared her throat and released her death grip on her handbag. "You've been so kind, and you're so busy. Since I can actually see her now, I can take it from here. I'll take her home in a cab after the set."

Desmond raised his brows to their limit. "Surely this isn't the same woman who reamed me out only a couple of hours ago?"

"I know, I *know*." Val pressed her hands to her cheeks. "I was…distraught. I apologize. You've been very nice about this mess of an evening."

It *had* been an evening, hadn't it? And one that he otherwise would have spent in his apartment, brooding. Or pacing. Or working feverishly. An evening like this, when they'd been thrust together so unconventionally, could be good two ways, couldn't it?

An in with Sheikh Rashid, and more time with a beautiful woman, who had his body humming with an anticipation to which it had no right.

"I'll stay with you, if it's all right," he said. "Let me buy you dinner, at least."

"It's after ten!"

"A second dinner," he amended, and laughed. "When was the last time you were out on the town, Miss Montgomery?"

"A very, very long time ago," she admitted with a rueful smile.

Warmth blossomed in his chest.

"I am a bit hungry," she admitted.

"Say no more." Desmond stood and waved the waiter over.

Perhaps it was seeing the youthful, happy glow on Hind's beautiful face that did it, or perhaps it was the handsome man at her side, dark eyes boring into her as if he'd discovered something surprisingly precious, but Val found she wasn't ready to go home. Not at all. And those rules she held so tight to, well her heart was eroding them away piece by piece, with every second of enjoyment.

That strange dark moment in the Champagne Bar was behind them, and she *wanted* to be pressed improperly close to Desmond Tesfay as the silky strains of Gershwin hung in the air. She *wanted* to cut into the perfectly cooked steak in front of her, fragrant with rosemary and glistening with butter and pan juices. She *wanted* to feel the smoky burn of fine whiskey on her tongue.

She wanted to laugh, as she hadn't in months. Years, really. And most of all, she wanted to revel in the fact that Desmond Tesfay's eyes were devouring her.

When he wasn't being obnoxious, Desmond Tesfay was as skilled a conversationalist as he was handsome and he drew her out with easy, innocuous questions. How long had she been in the Gulf? Which countries had she worked in? Did she enjoy it? Nothing personal at all, nothing about—thank goodness—dead fathers, or birth names, and nothing she wouldn't share in any casual conversation.

She felt herself relaxing. Yes, she'd worked in Abu Dhabi, Bahrain, Qatar and now for Sheikh Rashid. She couldn't name her clients of course, but she'd worked for an ambassador for the UAE, a brother of the Omani sultan, a famous Emirati influencer, a Qatari princess. She understood Gulf Arabic perfectly, but her accent was dreadful, and she spoke fluent French. Her favorite food in the region had to be chicken *mandi*…

She found herself chattering away in a manner that probably would have appalled her had she been in her right mind. Any protests about the fine wine, the food, any of it were met with a laconic "It's your birthday, after all," and one of the slow vulpine smiles that made her stomach flop to her feet. And then he'd *look* at her.

He wasn't even trying to hide it, she thought with an internal shiver. Every time his eyes flickered over her face or body, she pressed her thighs together against the heat kindling there. She was no untried virgin and nor was she frigid; the fact that she found it so easy to be swept away was why she'd kept her defenses so rigidly in place all these years. Being with a man she'd wanted wildly had ended in nothing but disaster and a feeling of emptiness that had lingered through till this very night.

And yet…

She cleared her throat in a bid to clear her head. It didn't work, but she forged on anyway. "I've talked so much that I think I need to resort to clichés at this point." He smiled noncommittally and she felt a stab of nervousness. "Do you come here often? Is it quite fashionable? I'd heard of Ronnie Scott's but not this place."

"I come here once in a while, when a client who fancies himself a music aficionado wants a must-see spot." Desmond was toying with the remains of his own dinner, eyes fixed lazily on her face. "Do you like it?"

"At the risk of sounding pretentious, it's extraordinary."

"Good." Were his eyes drifting down her body now? And if she was not mistaken, that was desire in his eyes… She was disturbed to find herself tilting toward him, her body arching under his gaze. "I intend for you to enjoy *everything* we do this evening."

Val choked, then placed her whiskey glass down, chasing the mouthful with ice water. In an effort to calm herself, she closed her eyes.

"Do you like the music?"

"It's amazing." At this point, keeping her eyes closed seemed safer. Now that Desmond was shut out, the music became more than a backdrop; she could make out melody, cadence, rhythm. While Val wasn't a music aficionado by any means, jazz had always been a part of her life. She licked her lips, lowered her shoulders and bid tension in her body to leave through exhaled breath. And to her surprise, it did.

She eased back into the seat, but it was no longer buttery soft leather; Desmond's arm was there. It was rigid and soft all at once, and it pulsed with warmth. He'd clearly taken the opportunity to move even closer. She was…well, she was practically in his arms. And it made her fizz inside.

"My father played as part of a jazz combo when I was a child," she said. The smell of him was dizzying.

"Where was that, again?" His voice was low and rich and she could feel it tightening at the tender points of her body; her breasts, the soft secret place between her thighs.

"New Orleans," she said after a moment. "He passed away when I was a child. That's why I was so embarrassed about…before. I shouldn't make such tactless comments."

Desmond made a noise of acknowledgement deep in his throat, and Val felt the sound resonate down to her toes, leaving a very pleasant tingle. Those beautiful eyes were masked, completely and she didn't know whether to be disappointed or to be relieved.

"I'm sorry for your loss," he said after a beat, and his voice was gentle.

"Oh, you don't have to be. I was young. My mum married again, and my stepfather was just fine—" And now she was babbling like a nervous teenager. She stopped and took a deep, steadying breath, then closed her eyes. Desmond's body was a warm mass at her side, pulsing with something she dared not name.

"He played an upright bass, my father," she continued. "In a restaurant. It was an unapologetic tourist trap that served nothing but frozen hurricanes—"

"Hurricanes?"

"It's a drink that'll have you on your back in a half hour. And they had the best lobster and shrimp pot pies. I can taste them even now…"

"Val," he said with an amused tone. "Your eyes are still shut."

She bit her lower lip hard and nodded.

"Are you afraid to look at me?"

Yes, she was. Because he was too attractive, and because this was inappropriate—and most of all because the fire raging inside her at this very moment was much too reminiscent of the young woman she'd been, a woman too easily swept away by passion into dangerous currents. She'd almost been lost—no, she *had* been lost, for a very long time. And now she was here, in the arms of possibly the most attractive man in all of England, while technically working. And he was telling her to *open her eyes*.

"I am," she said, and she wondered how the hell her voice had gone so soft and smoky. She hadn't sounded like that, not since—

The sound he made in response lived halfway between a laugh and a sigh. "Well, at least I know you feel it, too."

Val's eyes flicked open, and she knew right away it'd been a mistake. Desmond had shifted his body and was peering intently into her face, with those dark eyes and their honey-tinged irises glowing in the dimness of the lounge, like a cat's. Want sliced razor-sharp through her, and he thumbed her chin, his touch whisper-soft. She swallowed. And the words that came out of her mouth next shocked the hell out of her.

"You might as well just do it," she said a little acidly, sounding like herself for the first time since they'd sat down, and his lips twitched.

"Am I that obvious?"

"Weren't you trying to be?"

"Don't be so eager to rush a beautiful thing, Miss Montgomery."

"Val," she corrected, her heart thumping like a rabbit's. If this was happening, she couldn't let it happen with him calling her *Miss Montgomery* or, worse yet, Valentina. Not with his liquid, rich voice simply dripping with all the dirty things she presumed he could do to her—it was bringing to the surface something she wasn't ready to explore. Not with him.

And yet, her thoughts were going in directions she couldn't control, while she sat in the booth, heart thudding, mentally grasping at them as they floated beyond her fingertips into places that sent back heated, urgent images that took her breath away with their sensuality. His mouth on her neck, his lips on hers, the softness of his breath on her ear. His hands on her breasts, hips, bottom, thighs. Stroking. Exploring.

Gripping.

Her face bloomed with heat, and it left her body in the softest of exhales before he *finally* kissed her. It was soft and heated and spicy with whiskey and honey sweet, all at once. His lips knew exactly where to go. First he explored her mouth with the tenderness of one who'd been a long-time lover, then to that pulsing hollow in her throat that had always left her a quivering mess and finally to her collarbone, dangerously close to the dip in her neckline—

"Desmond!" she gasped.

"I shouldn't," he said quietly against her skin. "I don't think you're the type to—"

"How would you know what type I am at all?" she said a little haughtily.

He made an amused sound without looking up. "Okay, you've convinced me."

He didn't want any more interruptions to this, and when his mouth skittered up and to her lips again, she didn't protest. She just sighed a little, tipped her head back, and lifted her arms to encircle his neck. He was kissing her more urgently now, muttering things she couldn't quite understand, and then his mouth was at her ear again—

"You smell so damned good," he rasped. She realized vaguely that he had stood up and was facing her now, hands resting on her thighs. She wanted to pull up her dress so she could draw him between her thighs—

"It's all right," she almost said. After all, he was shielding her, and the booth they were in was private and dark, but that would be ridiculous. As ridiculous as the fact that his fingers were tracing slow, lazy circles over that tender bit of skin between her stocking tops and her underwear, and she was incredibly close to letting out a whimper that she might not recover from. And there was still—

Hind!

She must have uttered the name out loud as she thought it, because Desmond pulled back abruptly. She noticed dimly that his breathing was ragged—*she'd* done that to him, she thought, astonished. And from a few simple kisses. And despite their very public location, despite Hind, she didn't want to move. To emerge from this little cocoon of lust they'd created would mean a forcible ejection back into the real world, one that might never allow the throbbing want she felt to bubble back up to the surface again.

How long had it been since she'd felt this near wild longing to be touched, kissed?

At least ten years. And it was happening now, and with a man who was significantly younger than her.

That was sobering enough. Val cleared her throat and stood, taking a very large step sideways in order to move herself from Desmond's immediate area of contact. He stood as well. His head was tilted and he was looking down at her, an odd half smile in place.

"Don't spoil it by talking about how sorry you are for being so impulsive. Or say it was the champagne. Or tell me you never do this."

She blinked. He'd taken the words right out of her mouth. He reached out with his long, slim fingers and touched her chin.

"Don't be sad."

She felt tears prick beneath her lids. She wasn't sad. She was *lonely.* She was angry because the actions of one man had turned her life into this—a woman who was trying very hard not to romanticize kissing a stranger at least a decade younger than her in the basement of a club. And the fact that he'd recognized it so easily made her feel even worse.

"I'm not sad," she whispered. "And you're right. I never do this. And for very good reason, too."

"Which is?"

Val lifted a hand to cradle the side of his face; he tilted

his head so that it perfectly fit into the hollow of her palm. "Because kisses are bad for me," she said, matter-of-factly. "I always end up paying for them, Desmond. I don't want to do that with you."

"Why? Are you afraid of getting attached?" His eyes were glittering in the dark.

"I used to be. Not anymore."

"What happened?"

"I met a man as handsome as you are." His hands tightened at her waist. "Unfortunately, he turned out to be… not very nice."

She felt his arm loosen and grow rigid. "Did he—?"

"No! Not that." There was that prickling behind her lids again. "I just… I lost myself in him, Desmond. I got in so deep that I didn't recognize who I was after a while. And I told myself that would never happen again. Not to me. And here I am, with you…"

He released her then, and she felt so bereft she actually ached. She wanted to cry out, to press herself against him again, to feel that delicious hardness and warmth. But she couldn't.

Could she?

A tinny clash of cymbals signaled the end of the set, followed by enthusiastic applause, and the two of them scooted even further apart.

She cleared her throat in an attempt to come back to herself.

Now was the time to scoop up Hind, to get home, to shower off the taste, smell and essence of the man in front of her, and to go to sleep like a responsible human being. She swallowed hard past the lump in her throat. The chattering from the audience filtered in little by little, breaking the stillness. The evening escapade was over. Desmond fumbled about for his mobile while Val pressed her hands to her burning cheeks.

It didn't help.

Desmond scrolled, then smiled a little. "It looks like our girl's headed back to The Ritz."

"Really?" Val peered over his shoulder. Indeed, Hind's new story announced:

Tired and HAPPY af!!!! Headed home. <3 you London

"Oh, thank goodness," Val exhaled. But then her breath was gone again because Desmond was very close, peering down into her face, and his eyes were so dark that she took a full step back.

"If I pressured you at *all*, Val, I truly am sorry."

She was shaking her head hard before he even finished. "You didn't."

Relief lightened his features ever so slightly, and at that she was oddly touched. "All right."

She could feel him withdrawing both physically and emotionally, and her body throbbed with the loss. Her resolve was gone. It'd dissolved like salt in boiling water. There was no point in getting it back, really.

You could enjoy the night, a little voice inside her whispered, fanned by the heat lapping in her lower tummy. *Just this once. You know you want him. He's not going to stick around—he'll probably be relieved that you don't want him to. You can go right back to your rules.*

She'd made the rules for herself to avoid entanglements. She'd make sure this wouldn't turn into one. She wasn't the naive, vapid, impressionable girl her who had been seduced and abandoned.

She was *Val*.

And Desmond was…young. A little full of himself, yes. But he had stopped when she'd asked him and he'd *listened.*

And if she were truly honest with herself, she wanted him rather badly.

"Desmond?"

He turned and her mouth went dry. She stepped forward and, on her tiptoes, she pressed her mouth to his. Before she could even register the skin on skin, he'd wrapped one long, muscled arm round her waist and was drawing her close with a surety that was becoming all too familiar. He stopped only when her breasts were flush against his chest and the inches between them evaporated like mist over the Gulf on humid August mornings.

"Make sure she gets home," he said, his lips a whisper away from her own. Her body was surging to life—again. Oh, she was in *trouble.* "All right, Valentina? If this is what I think it is—"

"It is," she said hoarsely against his mouth.

"Come home with me, then."

"Desmond—"

"I *want* you," he warned, his eyes glittering. "And if that's ever not okay, I'll stop and send you home. But I want you, Valentina Montgomery. And I'm not going to apologize for that."

Oh, wow.

Desmond was cupping her face now, looking hard into her eyes. "I'm not him, whoever he was," he said simply and firmly, and she closed her eyes, as much to shut him out as anything else.

"I know," she whispered.

CHAPTER FIVE

SHE DIDN'T GO home with him. She took him home with *her*.

She said, in between those soft gasps that came on the tail end of every breath while he was kissing her, that she had to be close to Hind in case anyone called her during the night. But she didn't use that as an excuse to stop this madness, like a sensible, responsible woman would. No. She was as swept away as he.

She took *him* home, instead—or what served as home on this particular trip to London. Her own room at The Ritz was some distance from the presidential suite where Hind was staying with her father. Once she'd made sure that Hind was tucked safely in her bed and the security team was notified that she was in for the night, she returned to her room where Desmond was waiting.

He barely registered a small, impeccably clean hotel room much humbler than the suites he was accustomed to—if one could call any room at The Ritz humble—before his eyes fell on the large bed in the center of the room. She squeaked when his hands descended to the fullness of that magnificent bottom of hers and squeezed. Val distanced herself from his arms and reached over his shoulder for the light.

Desmond shook his head. "Leave it on," he said, and the words came out hoarse with desire. He wanted to see every single inch of her, and wanted it vivid in his memory. He'd wanted many women in his past, and had won them, but never with this type of urgency. This *impulsiveness*. He leaned forward and kissed the melting sweetness of her mouth again; the texture of it was addictive.

He forced himself to keep it soft. Slow. He wanted her squirming for him to go faster, to demand it before he did. What was it she'd said? *Kisses are bad for me.*

He barely knew her, but he was determined that his would never be.

"You're a very good kisser," he rasped, and she smiled in a way that made him wonder if she were thinking of other things. She reached up and threaded her fingers through his hair.

"I'm being kissed at The Ritz by a billionaire," she said, almost to herself.

Desmond laughed. "On your birthday."

"On my—" Those lovely eyes widened. "I'd forgotten about that."

"I'll sing the song for you later."

After he kissed her some more. And got her naked—or maybe he'd leave the stockings on? Whatever made her feel sexy.

"It's been a while…" She sighed, but her face was taut with desire—desire that was overcoming reticence, prudence, common sense and professionalism. He'd had many beautiful women in his day but he'd never seen one with such naked passion vibrating through her body.

Her pupils were large, dilated. Her makeup was smudged in a way that spoke of smoky desire. Something both wild and sensual had taken her, and his own body throbbed in response.

"Please."

It was the soft entreaty through those full, wet lips that did it. It drove him wild when women asked for it so nakedly and unashamedly. Lust clouded his brain as he pulled her toward him by the wrists and kissed her—hard, this time, and she grunted approval. This, at least he knew how to do, and do well. Tenderness, though, was new. And he wasn't going to risk thinking about that right now.

Val's mouth had the sweetness of honey and the softness of velvet all at once; it was decadent, like the world's richest dessert. Her body yielded to him and she punctuated the kisses with soft little exhales of pleasure that sparked a familiar ache low between his thighs. He shifted, gripping her hips. He didn't want to hide what she was doing to him, and from the way she was squirming she didn't mind at all.

His fingers found the zipper on the back of her dress; it came down easily, and his hands tightened even more on her, holding her steady as she stepped out of it, kicking it away. Beneath the dress, the rounded swell of her breasts was invitingly full, and moving rapidly with every breath, and he noted how the lacy stockings hugged the butter-soft skin of her thighs. The scent of her was suddenly there too, a sweet feminine musk that was perfume and soap and hairspray and *her*. If he was hard before, it was nearly unbearable now.

"Desmond…" she whispered.

"Off," he said, with a voice he was finding increasingly hard to control. For goodness' sake, why was the woman wearing so many layers? He knew it was to hide the lushness of her body in the context of her work for the conservative sheikh, but he was very much enjoying having her gradually bared to his gaze now. His fingers raced down to the small of her back to reveal skin so soft and fragrant that the experience didn't quite seem real.

He bit back a groan. Her breasts were absolutely beautiful—full and heavy and lush—and her rapid breaths made them move in a way that made him harder still. Her nipples were large and swollen, and he couldn't resist cupping her breasts.

"I had no idea, Miss Montgomery."

"Don't call me that!"

"Under this tight little dress… All these layers… They've been rubbing against your nipples all evening, haven't they?" He used the pads of his thumbs to circle the unbelievably soft skin, bending to kiss the hollow between her breasts. "You smell so unbelievably good."

"Desmond," she said, and the second set of syllables of his name broke. "*Please…*"

"What?"

"Please…"

His mouth was watering, but he was going to draw this out as long as he could. He passed his thumb dangerously close to the pouting nub, and she buckled against him, then managed to draw herself up with that proud tilt of her head that he was growing to find so damned attractive. The movement exposed the gentle pulse in her throat and he shifted his mouth to that spot and spoke against it. "Tell me."

Her tongue darted out and she licked her lips, making them glossy under the soft light of the room.

"They ache…"

"Do they?" Desmond began rubbing them gently with his thumbs, enjoying her gasps. And then he bent and drew one copper-hued, pouting nipple into his mouth.

She cried out then, and he felt his own body surge almost violently in response. She tasted as delicious as she looked, and her nipple swelled and pouted all the more, plump and tender in his mouth. Val moaned softly when he bit down gently, adding just enough pain to balance out the pleasure, rasping his tongue to soothe the skin, while the fingers of his other hand tugged and pinched, matching the rhythm of his mouth. Her thighs were parting; her fingers were an iron grip on his upper arms. She was thrusting her breasts up to meet his mouth, and he intensified the pressure, sucking harder. He was so hungry for her.

It suddenly seemed too hot in the small room, and she was trembling more with every second, almost as if—

Desmond was plenty vain, but he wasn't vain enough to assume he could make a woman climax just by touching her breasts. But here they were, Val quaking with pleasure, her body stiffening, lids fluttering shut, back arching, head tipping backward. For that one intense moment, it seemed as if he were the only thing holding her up.

Then, she cried out.

Val didn't know what she'd die of first, mortification or pleasure.

The latter was still pulsing through her body, each wave a little less intense than the last. In the circle of Desmond's arms she was ensconced in a cocoon of cloves, oranges and clean sweat. He was breathing as hard as she was; it was almost as if they'd become one.

"You all right?" he asked after a moment.

She nodded, squeezing her eyes shut. When he stepped back she felt cool air waft over painfully tight nipples and she automatically lifted her hands to cover them.

"Don't you dare."

Long, sensitive fingers were caressing her body and then they were stumbling toward the bed and he was there with her, lips skittering over her breasts, her belly and her hips. His breath tickled her skin and the laughter that came turned to something else entirely when he found that hot secret place between her thighs, first with his fingers, then his mouth. And when he finally dragged his head up to kiss her, she was quivering so much he asked her if she was all right again.

"Yes," she managed. *Barely.* They lay in silence for a moment, her ragged breath the only sound in the room.

"Well. Happy birthday, I suppose."

It took a moment for her addled brain to register *that*, as well as the smirk on his face. She sat up in mock outrage, trying to bite back the laugh that threatened to bubble up. "You—"

"Yes. Me," he confirmed, and then he was lunging forward, and his lips were on hers again, but gentle this time. She could taste the odd sharpness that was her, and the spiced, smooth sweetness that was all Desmond. Finally, it was her turn to explore his body.

She did so almost greedily. As a single woman in her position, alone in the Gulf, it had been years since she'd had so much as a warm hug, let alone meaningful physical contact with a man.

Not that this was meaningful, she told herself, sternly. And that was the last cohesive thought she had.

Examining Desmond's body, unbuttoning the tailored sky blue shirt he wore, was a thing of delight. His skin was a warm and gold-hued brown, and lean muscle rippled below the surface, moving and tensing with every touch. His breaths were measured and deep, and his eyes were heavy-lidded with sooty lashes. In a way, she was grateful that he mostly kept them lowered because true intimacy wasn't an option. Not tonight, not ever.

Desmond shifted his hips forward when her exploring

hands finally dropped to his abdomen, and the sound that escaped her when she found *him*, hard and curved and rising against her hand, sounded alarmingly like a purr.

Was this really her?

"There you are, love," he said huskily, and she had to grip her thighs together hard at the sharpening ache between them.

"Desmond..." The tip of her tongue escaped her mouth, skittering over her lips.

"Touch me."

The command was rasped low and deep into her ear and she shivered. He drew her so close it was as if they were fused into one. As her fingers closed round the warm, silken girth of him, the hiss he let out reverberated through her body. His head tilted and his mouth sought out the tender skin of her peaked nipples. The silence in the room was pierced by a cry—not his, hers.

"Just like that," he said in a near growl as her hands found their rhythm, stroking, thumb passing over the swollen tip of him, circling, slicking the moisture she found there. He tore his mouth from her breasts, his face tight with both pleasure and urgency. She'd forgotten what it was like to move with someone, to find their rhythm and they yours, to have your bodies fit together tightly, skin on skin.

She'd forgotten how addictive being swept away by passion could be. Desmond had ripped wide open something she'd held tight for years.

She drew back, and his mouth released her nipple with a soft pop. She looked at him steadily. His eyes were nearly black with an open hunger that made her insides twist. His lean, powerful, elegant body was, at this moment in time, hers. He was still swelling against the pressure of her hand and she wondered if it was painful for him. She trailed her fingertips down the length of him, tracing softly to where the tip of him pulsed and flushed.

He clenched his jaw and clenched the sheets in his fists. Val lowered her head, and opened her mouth, taking all of him inside.

"Oh, my—" he began, but got no further.

CHAPTER SIX

THE AFTERMATH WAS sweat soaked and punctuated with heavy breathing. Desmond and Val lay together, entangled in the bed sheets. His head was resting on her lower belly, and her fingers were threading through his hair absent-mindedly. Too absent-mindedly. As much as he wanted to stay there and revel in the softness of her, he knew it would be a mistake.

She looked the most beautiful she'd been all night. Her hair had escaped its slick ponytail and now haloed her face and her lips were swollen.

Desmond considered for a moment, then reached across her body to where the room phone sat on the ornate night-stand. When he did, his arm brushed across her breasts, skimming nipples that were still full and pouting; he felt heat surge down— *Again?* Surely not. He ignored it and dialed.

Val sat bolt upright. "What are you doing?"

"I'm hungry," he said patiently. "You've kept us rather busy for the past couple of hours."

"*I've* kept us—!" She was speechless. He waggled his brows at her and half turned as the concierge answered, holding back his laughter with some effort. This was precisely what he wanted—something to tip power back into his hands after she'd undone every bit of the control he'd thought he had. His body was still humming from the aftermath.

More than that, she'd made him *care*.

"Can I ask you to hold for a moment, sir?"

"Of course."

"Are you crazy? You can't order room service to my—"

"Why not? Don't you eat?" He cleared his throat as the concierge came back on. "Hello, thanks. I feel like slumming it tonight. I'll have the Wagyu burger, medium rare, and the black truffle *frites*. And for the lady…?" He nodded in her direction.

"The *lady* isn't having anything! You can't… I can't… I…"

"You wanted me to leave? Is that it?"

There was a quick flash of guilt in her eyes. "It isn't unreasonable, Desmond. *Technically* I'm still at work."

"If the sheikh is knocking at your door at—" he peered at his watch "—three a.m., I'd be a little curious about the nature of the work you do! No, sir, we still haven't made a decision," he said to the concierge. "Perhaps we could look at the menu and call you ba—"

Val made a noise of frustration that sounded so like a growl it stopped him dead, and he dropped the phone, surprising himself by bursting into laughter as he did so. Val, who'd tried lunging for it again, was half on top of him now, her small, soft fingers anchoring his wrists to the bed with sudden strength. And now he was officially getting hard again. This woman was full of surprises!

"I. Am. Not. Feeding. You," she gritted out. He saw her eyes drift down to where he was stiffening then dart back to his face as if she were correcting herself.

"Do you want me to leave?" he asked softly.

She released his wrists without answering, sucking in

her breath as she did so, and, heaven help him, there were her breasts again, heavy and round, perfectly in his line of vision, jiggling softly with every breath she took. Even before his eyes, her plump copper-brown nipples were growing painfully full and tight.

He reached up and palmed her breasts. Her breathing quickened.

"You know I will if you say the word," he said mildly, and he punctuated his statement with a twist of one of the hardening buds; he'd observed enough during their union to know she liked that, a *lot*. She gasped softly.

"Don't move," he said, then raised his head high enough to draw that nipple's twin into his mouth. As he sucked, his fingers inched down her tummy to where she was slick and swollen; she jerked upward when he touched her and he shook his head, releasing her breasts.

"No. Don't go back. Forward, sweetheart. Let me taste you."

"Desmond—"

"*Do* it."

She inched forward, crying out softly when he parted her, her thighs spread open inches above him, all glistening skin and the sharp, delicious scent of arousal. He reached up and dug his fingers into the glorious softness of her hips, then pulled her down till he was able to taste her. She trembled and shook and cried out, all reticence completely gone. She tried to pull away, but he held her fast. And when she finally fell forward, spent and gasping, he rolled over and drew her into his arms, his face fierce.

"Desmond," she gasped out. He thought there was dampness on her cheeks.

"It's all right," he said, kissing the shell of her ear and biting down gently.

He didn't know when she shattered in his arms; he was too far gone, himself. Her heart was drumming so fast it echoed the flow of blood in his ears and her breathing was as ragged as his.

It was the hottest thing he'd ever experienced, knowing that he'd done this to her. No—that *they'd* created this moment. Together. They both knew this had no future, but for just this moment—this heat-filled, sticky, sweat-drenched moment punctuated by gasps of air and tangled limbs—they were together.

Impulsively he reached out and cradled her face in his hands.

"I want to stay," he said simply, surprised at the honesty in his words. He wished that navigating life wasn't such a strain for him and that the aftermath of his father's death—and his role in it—hadn't consumed him so much. "May I?"

Even as the words hovered in the air, he couldn't believe he'd said them. He'd once been the type of man to say such things, but that version of Desmond Tesfay had been buried in the smoking wreckage of Flight 0718, ten years ago. He should be planning a smooth exit; ego aside, he should be thrilled that she wanted him out of the room. It was rare that a woman made it so easy for him. But there was something beyond her stern facade, something that made him want to stay.

"This was nice," he finished, lamely.

"It was," she agreed. "It's been a long time. Thank you, Desmond." She sat up, drawing her knees together almost primly; the ladylike employee of the sheikh was back. "I'm going to..." She gestured to the washroom.

"Go ahead," he said.

Then she was up and moving swiftly toward the bathroom, leaving only rumpled sheets and a faint hint of perfume and sex behind. Desmond was left at the foot of the bed, feeling curiously bereft. He missed her already, and that was strange. Unsettling.

"Room service?" he called out to the closed door, forcing lightness into his voice. The last thing he wanted to do was appear *needy.*

An aggravated huff came out in response, drifting over the sound of running water. "*Fine.* But after food, you go."

A buzz from her mobile woke Val in the morning.

Automatically, her fingers groped for the slim rectangle and she held it blearily to her face, still overcome by the fog of sleep. Her lids were stuck together and she rubbed her eyes to release them, then froze as the events of the night before—well, only a few hours before, if she were being honest—filtered through her mind.

There was Champagne. Steak. Slow, slow kissing. Not so slow kissing. Laughter. Conversation. And then…and then…

Passion. Unhinged, unrestrained passion, here on this very bed. And afterward, when they'd both been too worn out to move, they'd finally had those damned Wagyu burgers, at nearly five in the morning. They'd eaten them in languid respite, at first lazily and then rapidly, as their hunger overtook them, shoving piping-hot truffle fries soaked in ketchup down as if they were uni students trying to soak up their beers at a pub after a late night.

They hadn't slept. And he hadn't left. He'd asked to stay with her, and she knew the memory of the look in his eyes at that moment wouldn't leave her for a long time.

Then they'd *talked.*

In the pale light of dawn, Desmond seemed to have shed the layers of flippancy he'd wrapped himself in all evening.

And Val realized how much she missed both the intimacy of sex and of conversation.

They'd chatted about inane things at first, tried to watch a replay of *Coronation Street* that neither could follow, and drowned their gluttony in ice-cold Cokes from the minibar.

Then he'd asked about her father, and she'd been loose enough with serotonin and food and a pleasant tiredness to answer. His body was lean and chiseled, standing out against rumpled snow-white sheets. The playfulness had gone; his eyes were curious and kind.

"What do you want to know?"

He lifted his slim shoulders, an odd little smile playing round his mouth. "I don't know," he said slowly. "It's something we have in common and I feel oddly close to you right now."

The words hung between them for a long moment. Val cleared her throat and pursed her lips. "Do you always say exactly what you mean?"

"You don't have to answer, you know," he pointed out.

She knew. She reached up to smooth her hair and knew she was going to have one hell of a time detangling it in the morning. When last had she forgotten to put on a silk scarf before climbing into bed?

"You mentioned a stepfather."

"Yeah. Russell," she said, and even as she uttered his name, his face came to memory. Prematurely wrinkling skin the color of coffee with cream. A little too eager to please with a tendency to lecture, but altogether a decent man, most of the time. "He was…kind. At least, in the early years he was. I was happy when he came because my mother wasn't crying anymore."

Desmond nodded, his face unreadable.

"She'd been so unhappy, up until then. And it was okay—

it was really okay. He didn't treat me like his daughter, but he treated me fairly. And then he and my mum had my siblings—Joy, Michaela and Sam. He wanted kids right from the beginning."

"Are you close?"

"Not really." A familiar lump was rising in her throat. "It was good for a while, but as I got older, I felt really out of step with the rest of them. I was the one reminder of my mum's life before. I feel like it was sad for both of them in that way…" Her voice trailed off.

Desmond's fingers rested loosely on her hip, and it was pleasantly distracting. "But?"

"I don't know. I don't really look like them." Her little brother and sisters, with their cinnamon-colored curls and wide gray eyes were sweet in their own way, but spoiled. And her parents had doted on them. "I was…quieter. Russell is very hearty, and a little loud. I always felt like I was spoiling their fun, their *look*, and my mum was anxious to make sure I wasn't being left out, and that just made me feel awkward."

"And then?"

"I heard them talking one night. I was probably about sixteen at the time, maybe Hind's age. I'd been looking at colleges and Russell was talking to my mum about cost. He was saying that I was an okay student but not a brilliant one, and he was worried about financial aid, and maybe it would be better for me to go to a technical school for a bit or get a job first—find my sea legs, he said. And he said, 'Remember, we have a family to take care of, and we can't compromise that.' Excluding me, basically."

"He didn't think of you as his."

"Exactly. It wasn't the advice that he was giving that hurt so much—it was good advice. It was just hearing him talking about me as if I were a problem to get rid of so they could carry on with their *real* family. I was determined to get out of New Orleans and prove I was worth more than what he thought I deserved. I ended up here." She lifted her shoulders, ignoring the knot forming deep in her tummy. She hadn't told Desmond even half of the story, but that was all she wanted to share right now.

"It's easy not to visit much when the distance is so great. And they don't seem to miss me, honestly, so..."

She wished the words back the second they came out of her mouth; she sounded so self-pitying. Desmond didn't seem to mind, though. She scuttled closer to him and rested her cheek on his shoulder. He kissed her softly, gently, caringly.

She hadn't wanted to sleep because sleeping meant waking up and it being the next day when she would have to return to her real life. But fatigue had taken over and they'd both finally slept.

And now it was 9:00 a.m. and she'd missed breakfast with Hind *and Desmond was still there.*

The watery light of the early morning so particular to London illuminated his golden-brown skin; he was sprawled face down beside her, gently snoring into his pillow, and she felt grateful she could not see his face. She bit her lip hard and turned her attention back to her phone.

There was a text from Hind canceling breakfast on account of being exhausted. *Thank goodness.* Of course Hind was exhausted after yesterday's shenanigans.

The second and third messages were the same ones she received every month, from the Bahr Al-Dahab National Bank. And if there had been even a little fairy dust left from the night before, she was dropped squarely back to earth by the texts. The first:

Your salary has been credited to your account.

And then, almost immediately after:

Your loan installment of 18,483 riyals has been successfully paid.

Just about half her salary, the amount legally allowed for the bank to take. With trembling fingers, Val logged into her banking app and sent another five thousand into her loan account, leaving just enough to get through the rest of the month.

This dissolved the afterglow rather rapidly. Val bent over and shook Desmond's shoulder, then again but harder. For the first time since yesterday, looking at him gave her no fluttery feelings because she was consumed by the cold, hard chains of reality. "Desmond!"

He muttered something and yanked a pillow over his head.

"You have to go," she said briskly, and when he didn't respond she clapped her hands. "Desmond!"

He groaned and pitched the pillow at her playfully. "What, no breakfast in bed?"

"Desmond!"

He yawned, and rolled over, wrapping the coverlet tightly round him.

Val let out an outraged squawk, then yanked the coverlet with all her strength. She slid out of bed, wrapping the coverlet round her as she went. Desmond dived for her and secured the end. The two engaged in a rather undignified struggle before Val emerged panting and victorious. His eyebrows climbed.

"Oh, no, you don't. Time to go," she ordered, although

she couldn't hold back the smile creeping across her face, despite the way her morning had begun. "You're impossible."

"And you," he said simply, "are absolutely enchanting, Valentina Montgomery."

That seemed to undo something in her. For a moment worry was shoved aside and she kissed him, her body fitting as perfectly against his as it had last night. He didn't push for anything else, just kissed her back. Val felt relief—of course she did.

This was goodbye.

She pulled back and looked pointedly at the door. It was time to get back to reality.

He got the message.

"I'll go," he said. "This was fun."

CHAPTER SEVEN

THIS WAS FUN.

In the shower, Val dropped her sponge three times before she gave up and let hot water cascade down on her back and shoulders. She was tired—every bone in her body ached, it seemed—but she'd also never felt so alive. Her body thrummed with a lot of things, but none of it was regret.

Yes, she'd been impulsive, immature, unprofessional even, but it had been nearly a decade since she'd done something for herself in this way. Since she'd given in to what she wanted without considering the consequences. Had it been worth it?

The tingle between her legs suggested that it had been very much worth it. Val began to scrub herself vigorously in small circles on her smooth brown skin. It was startling to feel so different and yet look exactly the same. But she *was* the same, she told herself sternly. She would emerge from the bathroom. She would put on one of her plain work outfits and do her job. Desmond would do his and there would likely never be any reason for them to interact again.

She'd be *safe*. And if she had been as prudent with her husband as she was being today, she'd have saved herself a whole lifetime of hurt.

Val watched grimly as the bubbles slid toward the drain, then stepped out of the shower. She dried herself, hung the towel up and went through her usual routine—a generous slathering of baby oil, a generous spritz of apple-vanilla perfume, and as if to make up for her behavior the night before, she dragged on the most forbidding of her wool work dresses, one with long tight sleeves and a stiff linen collar. A glance at the clock told her she'd barely taken fifteen minutes to get ready. She wouldn't even be late to see Hind this morning. She shouldered her bag, making a point of *not* looking at the disheveled bed behind her, and opened the door. What she saw turned her blood to ice.

There was Desmond, talking animatedly and Hind, with a silver tray in her hands.

And Sheikh Rashid, looking angrier than she'd ever seen him.

No, not angry. The man's face was florid with rage. She registered dimly that Desmond was trying to placate the older man, but she was too shocked to pick up more than a word or two. The few she did register landed like lead weights in her brain.

Appalling. Unprofessional. Disgrace.

What did he think happened? Well, that much was clear. He'd likely seen a very disheveled-looking Desmond Tesfay emerge from her room this morning, and his daughter—who in his eyes was young and impressionable and innocent—had spent the day with him.

Val didn't have a single word with which to defend herself.

"Val," Hind was saying, and the girl tugged her hand. Val meekly allowed herself to be steered back into her room, and Hind shut the door on the two men. The sheikh's voice faded away, and Hind, her eyes as round and glistening as the enormous diamond solitaires she wore, thrust the tray in her direction.

"Baba marched me down here to apologize for ditching you last night," she said. "Apparently someone saw me coming in and snitched, but we saw Desmond coming out of your room. What…?"

At the confirmation of her worst fears, Val covered her burning face. She would *not* give in to the final humiliation of crying in front of her charge, however desperately she wanted to.

"You and Desmond *Tesfay*?" Hind's voice was high with incredulity. "But you're so—"

Proper? Boring? Old? They were all possibilities, and each one was worse than the last, as well as being completely true. "That's enough, Hind," Val said sharply, somehow summoning her professional tone even though her body was hot with embarrassment. "You did plenty yourself last night."

"And it's all forgotten now, thanks to you!" the girl said almost gleefully. "Baba's going to *kill* you. But Desmond Tesfay, Val. I mean, *really*."

Val closed her eyes, willing Hind out of the room. The girl had no idea.

"I wonder what they're saying," Hind said. Val opened her eyes in time to see Hind pressing an ear on the door. A hard knock nearly made her tumble to the ground, and she scrambled backward as the sheikh and Desmond entered the room. The man's face was as hard and cold as granite.

Val bit the inside of her cheek in an effort to show no emotion. He would fire her and cancel her visa. Her years of careful client cultivation in the Gulf would be lost with this death blow to her reputation. And her debt… What about her debt?

"I am extremely disappointed in you, Val," said Sheikh Rashid.

Of course he was. "Sir—"

The sheikh held up one hand to silence her, his expression darkening. "You not only carried on a relationship behind my back, but you went as far as to marry—"

A marriage? *What?*

"—without my knowledge!"

Her eyes darted to Desmond; he was looking at her steadily.

Don't say anything, his expression seemed to command.

"At the very least I would have expected you to tell me that your circumstances were likely to change. I consider you a part of my household, Val. And you not only carried on with this relationship behind my back, but you didn't allow me to celebrate you as I should have!"

Val was dimly aware of Desmond coming to her side, his hand seeking hers. "I told her not to, Your Excellency. I felt it would be a conflict of interest, given I was actively seeking your business."

Sheikh Rashid's eyes were darting back and forth between their faces. "How did you even *meet*?"

"You and I have been in talks for over a year, Sheikh Rashid," Desmond said blandly. "In the early days I spent quite a bit of time in your magnificent waiting rooms. She came in with Hind one day and was kind enough to direct me through the labyrinth of rooms, and by the time I emerged I was so enchanted that I invented a cousin in need of her tutoring services. By the time she'd figured out my ruse..."

Val closed her eyes. She was going to be struck dead at any second, she was sure, because this story was growing more outrageous by the moment. She would even welcome it, at this point; at least it would make him stop talking!

"...and that's it. We got married in the courts about a

month ago. We'd planned the white wedding for sometime next year, or even later, and we were going to announce it officially, then. Val is so dedicated to her duties and she didn't want to abandon Hind until she was ready to leave for university."

"I had no idea. She gives nothing away, I swear."

"Can I be a bridal attendant?"

"I flew to New Orleans to meet her parents, and if you think it's hot in the *Gulf*..."

The conversations were melding into one. Val was having an out-of-body experience and watched herself accept hearty congratulations from Sheikh Rashid and soft but effusive kisses from Hind. She saw herself give her arm to Desmond and allowed herself to be steered away from Hind and her father, who was smiling now. Desmond ushered her further back into her room and whispered rapidly in her ear.

"Sorry to spring that on you," he said, his English accent growing crisper with every word. "But you know how particular they are in Bahr Al-Dahab about contact between unmarried men and women, and too much was at risk. Your job, my deal..."

"And *this* was the best way to handle with it?" Val countered. She groped behind her until she found the single guest chair in the room, and sank into it. "I'm— But— What— You did it so *easily*! That outrageous story!"

"Yes," said Desmond. Something hardened in his face, something that took away the youthfulness completely, something that made ice creep up Val's spine. Ambition. She'd seen that look before and knew what it meant to have her life—her happiness—be dependent upon it.

There was nothing more ruthless than an ambitious man. You'd always come second to it.

That was what had got her into the biggest trouble of her life in the first place, and here she was again, swept away by passion, then trapped in a web of her own impulsive foolishness.

"I'm not going to apologize for lying," Desmond said. He lifted his broad shoulders and shoved his hands deep into his pockets. That beautiful, lush mouth of his had tightened into a line. "Not when it could lose me everything I've been working to achieve. I've been trying to break into the Middle East market for years. This has more far-reaching effects than you could possibly imagine, Val. And this way you get to keep your job and your reputation."

His patronizing words were more than she could take. She stood abruptly and crossed to the wide windows overlooking Mayfair, pressing her forehead against the glass. The Sheikh and Hind were still talking rapidly together by the door to the hotel room and the tiny room was suddenly stifling in its opulence.

"It doesn't have to be for long, Val," he said quietly as he came over and joined her. "A few parties, a few dinners, a handful of social events. Once the contract is signed, we'll go our separate ways. Discreetly."

Yes, everything had an easy answer when you were young and handsome and had nothing to think about but your deals. She felt her shoulders drooping, forfeiting the posture she usually fought so hard to maintain.

Desmond drew close and placed a hand on her lower back. "You look tired."

"Well, I didn't sleep much, and I have to admit to my employer that this whole fairy tale you concocted is a scam and I will lose my job and my visa—."

"What? No, Val. I thought we talked about this!"

"No. *You* talked about it, and decided that *you'd* fixed

everything," Val responded hotly. Desmond looked up at her harsh tone, so her next words were softer, though no less forceful in their intent. "Well, you don't know anything. And even if I wanted to go along with this madness, Desmond, I couldn't."

"Because you're so *moral*," Desmond said, rolling his eyes.

"No, Desmond." Val's mouth curved, ironically, even as her stomach twisted so much it hurt. "Because I'm already married !"

"I can't imagine what you have to tell me that would justify making me a co-adulterer without my consent!" Desmond hissed.

Val was sitting across from him in a ludicrously powder-pink chair, and the two of them were speaking in hushed, rather vicious whispers across the round marble table, where an opulent spread for afternoon tea in a private room at Claridge's sat untouched between them. It was the first moment they'd had alone since she'd dropped her bomb earlier in the day. Right after she'd said it, Hind had come in and dragged Val off to work, and Desmond realized belatedly that he didn't even have the woman's *number*.

His next opportunity to speak to Val came that afternoon. Hind, who'd arranged this happy little gathering to toast the couple, was on a video call in the lobby that certainly wouldn't last forever. They were utilizing this opportunity to row very well, though. In the time he'd known her—which, granted, had been less than twenty-four hours—he'd never seen her so enraged.

"You never said a word!" Desmond continued. "Not one word!"

" It just—never seemed like the right time! I was in the moment," she defended herself.

"You certainly were," he muttered, then gritted his teeth. The conversation was growing more ridiculous by the moment, and he just couldn't reconcile the soft, yielding woman who'd kissed him and looked at him with such wonder the night before with the type of person that would sleep with him, knowing she was *married.*

"If you'd get off your moral high horse for just a moment, I could explain." Val's voice had grown frayed.

Moral high horse? Ha!

"I haven't seen him in over eight years. And no, I don't know where he is. We were living in Dubai at the time, and he…left me."

"Left you," Desmond repeated, looking keenly into her face. It was tight and very carefully controlled and there was a pinched line between her eyes that hadn't been there before.

"He left me," she repeated. "Technically I could file for divorce on the grounds of desertion. No, I haven't talked to him since then, and yes, he's still alive. His family confirmed that much, although they won't say a word about where he is. And frankly, I don't want to find him. Not at this point."

The words hung between them for a long moment then Desmond sank back into his chair, his fury spent. "Huh."

Val pressed her knees together and leaned forward, decanting steaming amber tea into both their cups. Her hand was shaking. "Lemon? Milk?"

"Neither." He winced when she picked up her cup and took a long sip; she didn't seem to notice the heat that probably would have burned off the tip of his tongue. "Val."

She said nothing and didn't look up. Her lashes cast shadows over her soft brown cheeks; he forced himself not to notice. "I didn't know."

"How could you have known?" she said. Desmond was struck with a sudden urge to hold her; to comfort her. There was some element in her that roused his protectiveness—maybe he'd sensed the sadness in her.

"Would you do me the honor of letting me sympathize with you, at least?" he said after a moment. He picked up his own tea and took a less aggressive sip.

"First of all, you're about eight years too late. And second of all, no sympathy's needed. It was a long time ago," she said. "And it's irrelevant, anyway. What's relevant is that you've put me in the most appalling position, Desmond Tesfay. I can't make this much money anywhere else in the world, and I… I need it."

Her voice broke a little over that last hesitation. Desmond wanted to find out why, but she continued before he could open his mouth.

"I have…debts to pay. Lots of them. Financially I'll be where I need to be in about three years, if I keep working for the sheikh. He's got cash to burn. But if I lose my job… Everyone knows everyone in these circles, Desmond, and if I mess up with one employer then I've lost them all."

The despair in her voice pricked at a soft place inside that he thought impenetrable by any entreaty; he'd been so hyperfocused on his own troubles for such a long time that he'd long since pushed aside close relationships. How could he share in another's burdens, when his own were crushing him?

"I cannot lose Sheikh Rashid's good opinion," she said. "He's done so much for me already."

There it was again, that regard for the older man that niggled at him in ways he had no right to feel. Desmond took a long, calming breath, one that allowed him to regain full control over his faculties, then leaned forward, picked up a pair of silver tongs, and began loading a fine china plate with some of the more mouth-watering titbits on the table. "I bet you haven't eaten since this morning."

"I'm not hungry."

"Eat," he said, his voice firm. "I'm here to listen. I know you have no reason to trust me, but I'd like to help. If I can."

There. He'd said it.

It was the first time in ten years he'd offered to help anyone when there was nothing in it for him. First, he'd asked the woman to let him stay with her, and now this?

What the hell was Valentina Montgomery doing to him?

He dropped his eyes to the plate he was arranging and discovered he'd piled enough sandwiches on it to feed a small horse. Hurriedly he decanted half back onto the serving tray and handed her the plate.

"You don't have to explain if you don't want to."

She shook her head quickly to cut him off. "No. It's fine. I want to."

CHAPTER EIGHT

SHE SHOULDN'T TALK. She shouldn't want to talk. But whatever fairy dust Desmond had sprinkled in the room the night before must be in effect again, because she began telling him her story.

"I met him one night when he dropped his wallet," she said. "It was Mardi Gras, when I was still young and excited enough to go. He was visiting New Orleans, trying to get a buyer for some new energy drink he claimed would keep people partying all night long. I was with my friends, and I'm really not the party type, so when I returned his wallet and he gratefully asked me to dinner as a reward, I agreed."

It was surreal, how narrating the events of that evening so many years ago was bringing back smells, colors, and sounds: music from a brass band several meters away; an acrobat dressed in neon yellow, contorting himself into shapes just to her right; the smell of barbecue and burnt sugar. And Malik's dark, handsome face, peering into hers as if surprised and pleased at what he'd stumbled across.

"His life sounded so exciting. His business ventures. He'd opened a chalet in Aspen, had food trucks in Oklahoma, traded crypto currency. He'd been to so many places, and… well, I was feeling a little trapped then, so meeting him felt like some kind of release. We started dating right away, and

I followed him out to Dubai, where he was wrapped up in something there—horse racing, I think?"

"It's pretty lucrative in the Gulf."

"Not the way he did it." There was acid in her voice, but she didn't care. "I got a job as a teacher and I sponsored him while he worked on his business ventures. There were loans he took out, things he had me sign..." She realized then that she was sounding increasingly disjointed, but she couldn't have explained it better.

"I was a fool."

"Hey, now," Desmond said, quietly.

"No, no, I *was*," she said resolutely. "I don't mind admitting it."

"You were *married*."

"I was a fool," she said crisply. "And he was dismissive and mean. I thought it was because he didn't have money, because he was waiting for that one big thing to pay off. Right before everything fell apart, he looked me right in the eye, like he actually saw me for the first time. He told me that he was glad he'd married me, because not many women would have put up with him."

"Was he that bad?"

"That's not the point." Val gave a quick shake of the head. "The point is that—I don't know how to articulate it—but I felt like such a *pushover*. Like he'd stayed with me simply because I wouldn't call him out on his shadiness, and all those years I thought he'd want to change for me, but I was fooling myself."

"Why didn't you leave?" Desmond looked faintly impatient.

A lump was rapidly rising in her throat. "Because I'm pathetic."

The words hung in the air between them. Desmond sighed, all traces of impatience gone from his face.

"You're not pathetic," he said simply. "I can think of *many* pathetic things, and you being taken advantage of isn't one of them."

She nodded. She had no idea why he was being so sympathetic, but he was looking intently at her, as if willing her to absorb every word she was saying.

"Val, do you hear me?" He leaned forward and took her hands. "Don't give him power by blaming yourself. Especially when it wasn't your fault!"

Tears stung Val's eyes. The validating words were unexpected, brief, and yet touched something in a place she'd kept protected for years. "All I've wanted since then is to be free of him. To be free of men, really. And then—"

Comprehension dawned in his eyes. "I've mucked things up for you nicely, haven't I?"

"Something like that."

"How much do you owe him?"

She swallowed. "I don't see how that's—"

"How much, Valentina?"

"I am nearly a million riyals in debt." She looked at him to gauge his reaction. He kept his face carefully blank.

"That's a lot of money."

She felt her insides twist. "Not to *you*, I would imagine."

"You seem very close with Sheikh Rashid…"

Her lips twitched. "You have no idea."

"Is he aware of your situation? Have you ever asked him for help?"

Laughter broke from her although the situation was far from funny. "Aware? He was a business partner of my husband's. He was also the one who bailed me out of jail when I was locked up for debt."

"What?"

"Yes." Bile rose to her throat at the memory—the humiliation, the small, hot women's dormitory at the debtor's prison, the hopelessness she felt. The invasive questions she'd been asked, the courtroom. "I'd been helping Hind with her reading—I used to tutor, just to keep myself busy—and she was quite attached to me. I don't know why Sheikh Rashid believed me, but he did."

Desmond crossed his arms and leaned back in his chair. "Probably because your husband ran off with some of his money as well."

"We made an agreement that I'd work for him and in exchange he'd become the guarantor for my loan." She paused, swallowed hard. "I haven't exactly been up front with him, either. I'm fairly sure he assumes I'm divorced by now, which is why he believed your story."

Desmond was looking at her steadily and her heart quickened. What was he thinking?

"I have a proposition for you. You've got your goals, Val, and I've got mine. And right now, they intersect."

"That's a little presumptuous to say."

"Help me do this," he challenged. "If I get the deal with Sheikh Rashid, I'll pay off your debts. All of them."

What?

"Desmond—"

"Trust me, I can afford it." The words sounded arrogant, even to him, but he pressed on. "This is about elevating my business, Val, not necessarily just about the money. We're in a position to help each other."

Help each other? Valentina stared at him, her insides in turmoil. She was feeling so many things at once that she didn't know which to address first. There was a residual warmth from the memory of his hands on her body just hours ago, coaxing pleasure from her.

She forced the thought away as quickly as it'd come. Desmond Tesfay was not an option for any type of lingering thoughts. Wasn't that why she'd chosen to spend the night with him in the first place?

"If you're trying to kill that napkin, there must be better ways than slow strangulation," Desmond said dryly.

She looked down to see the mangled white linen in her lap.

"I—"

"There are no downsides to this, Valentina."

There it was, her full name again, his voice warm and honeyed around the syllables. Would it be hypocritical of her to insist he not use it again, since it sparked such warmth in her? She closed her eyes and tried to steady herself.

Emotions are weaknesses to be exploited.

Never put the power to hurt you into anybody's hands.

She repeated the mantras in an attempt to control her thumping heart, willing that new softness inside her to a place where it could not affect what she said to the man looking at her now.

"It's *Val*, as I told you before," she said haughtily. "And let's be frank, Desmond. I've been *trapped* in a position to help you." Part of her wanted to cringe at her own frankness. She could hear the note of bitterness in her voice. "I don't want to owe you anything."

"It'd be an equal and fair exchange!"

"You don't understand. It's never that simple." She swore softly and laughed at the shock on his face. "Think of the consequences!"

"Only if you choose to see it that way, Val."

"Yes, everything's about the *spin* in your line of business, isn't it," she said a little archly. "Are you this dismissive of everything?"

"Only of things that shouldn't matter." Desmond sighed. "I'm sorry for what happened to you. You shouldn't have to pay for his mistakes."

"Pretty words."

"I mean it." His eyes were intense. "Why won't you let me help you? It's a *bargain*, Val, not a way to trap you. I have no desire to trap you."

She swallowed and focused on the fine china on the table in front of her. Ultimately, she had no choice, because the lie had already been sold to the sheikh, and the thought made her want to cry from frustration.

When she spoke, her voice cracked the way she feared it would.

"Fine."

She didn't like it, and Desmond didn't like the fact that he felt so uncomfortable about the situation. It tainted their night with an ugliness that reeked of coercion—something he recoiled from with all of his sensibilities.

And so, to his surprise, he found himself saying, "Forget it."

Her dark head jerked up, those enormous eyes fixed on him in surprise.

"I mean, I still want you to *help* me, don't get me wrong," he said crossly. "But I don't like how this feels."

He wanted that horrible cornered look to be gone from her face.

He wanted her to look at him the way she had the night before.

He reached down and picked up his leather laptop bag that held the assortment of devices that never left his side.

He placed an electronic tablet in front of her and handed her the stylus.

"Give me the details of your loan account," he said.

One of her hands flew up to her throat. *"What?"*

"No strings. Consider it compensation for a very painful lie," he continued, somewhat dryly. "You don't have to influence Sheikh Rashid on my behalf, either. My work can, and should, stand on its own. Just allow me to maintain this…fiction, for both our sakes, until I hear either way."

He didn't know what he was doing, but he had no idea how else to lift that burden from her shoulders, and have her accept it. Even if she left his life completely, after this, he had plenty of his own sins to atone for.

Shock had drained her rich brown skin of its glow and she looked wrung out. He wanted to tell her his real motivations—that he knew exactly what it was like to be trapped by circumstance, and that something as banal as money would not be a barrier to freedom in a just world—but he said nothing.

She was shaking her head. "No. It's very generous, but I can't accept that." Her mind was racing; he could tell by the way her full mouth was pinching in the middle. "I—I won't deny that this will get me out of a terrible situation that has crushed me for years, Desmond. I won't deny it. But I have to…earn this. I'll help you with Sheikh Rashid."

"Valentina—"

She stuck out her hand, still not looking at his face.

He took it, and in an instant, it was there, that absurd desire, overcoming all propriety, all common sense. Familiar heat was coiling low and slow in his abdomen. Last night was coming back to him in sounds and images that were brief but intense. Sighs. Gasps. Moans. Those nails on his skin.

Desmond, please...

He could still taste her on his tongue if he tried hard enough, that honeyed sweetness born of arousal she hadn't even known how to hide.

"Your husband," he said softly, "must have been out of his mind." He wanted desperately to lift a hand and stroke her cheek with his fingers the way he had last night.

She closed her eyes briefly as if gathering strength, then looked at him steadily.

"This can't be part of…whatever this is, Desmond," she said after a beat. "You know it would be a terrible idea. We have to keep our minds clear if this is going to work. It's got to be—"

"Strictly business," Desmond finished for her.

"Yes." He saw her throat contract as she swallowed. "When we go back to the real world, *my* real world, I need to be able to separate what's real and what's not. This was… lovely. It was the loveliest night I've had in a very long time. Magical, really—"

Desmond held up a hand. He felt as if he were being rejected, although he completely agreed with every word she was saying. Not to mention her husband, for goodness' sake, and his own…complications.

"We mustn't be greedy, must we?" she said, but it seemed more like she was telling herself rather than him.

"And we can be friends, can't we?" she added with a bit of a wobbly smile.

Of course they could. They had their dead fathers in common, after all.

Dead fathers.

Oh, damn it. *Damn it. Damn it!*

Val, of course, noticed the change in his expression immediately. "Is everything okay?"

"Yes, yes, it is." Except it wasn't. He glanced down at his watch—his father's watch—and looked at the time, groaning inwardly. Croydon was at least an hour and a half away in current traffic, an hour if he was lucky, and he'd forgotten. He'd never forgotten, not once in nearly ten years.

"What's happened? You look worried."

He let out a short, barking laugh. She didn't know the half of it. To his surprise, he found himself answering honestly. "Memorial service. For my dad and the other people… in the accident he was in. I go every year. This is the first time I've forgotten. I can't believe it."

He was fully aware that he must sound unhinged. He clenched his hands for a moment, then stood. "I don't even have time to change…"

Val's brown eyes were wide and soft. "I'm so sorry. I kept you…"

"No. No, it wasn't you at all." Except, of course, it was. He sometimes, especially in the early years, would go on a bender around this time. Val certainly wasn't the first woman who'd ended up in his bed a couple of nights before. But today he'd *forgotten.* He raked his fingers through his hair and swallowed back that choking feeling threatening to tighten round his chest. "I'm so sorry but I've got to go."

"Do you…do you want some company?"

Those words stopped him in his tracks.

He took a deep breath to tell her no, and found himself saying, instead, "Sure. Fine. Let's go. But—Hind?"

Val gave him a wobbly smile. "I haven't asked for an afternoon off in years. This is more important."

CHAPTER NINE

WITH ITS GRAY sheets of rain and a persistent dampness that crept into the innermost regions of even the most waterproof jackets, London had risen to the occasion for the Flight 0718 memorial with weather that matched Desmond's mood perfectly.

He'd attended this memorial service without fail every single year since the accident. It was always held here in the little gray church in Croydon.

This was the first time he'd ever come with someone, he realized. The first time in all that time he hadn't wanted to be alone. It was strange to have to give context, to explain what all the other attendees already knew.

"One of the passengers was the vicar here," he whispered to Val. "He would have been serving here twenty-two years, had he lived."

Val made a soft sound in response, and reached out and placed one of her hands on his arm. He resisted, with some effort, the urge to shake her off as they entered the church's dim interior. She began following an usher who smiled and offered her a hothouse orchid—the favorite flower of another victim of the crash, who'd been a florist in Kent—but Desmond shook his head.

"Back here," he mouthed, and gestured to the corner of the last row but one on the left-hand side. They sat and Val blew on her hands to warm them; wordlessly, he dragged off his gloves and handed them to her.

The vicar's eldest son, a tall, broad, tow-headed twelve-year-old, read out the same passage from the Psalms that was read every year. He'd been a mere toddler in his mother's arms at that first, horrible service. Val fixed her eyes on the boy and did not look at Desmond, for which he was grateful. He worried the program until the cover page sliced into his thumb; Val gently took it from him.

He watched the blood trickle down his finger with an odd sense of detachment. He was glad for the sting; it would keep him centered. He barely reacted when Val produced a pristine handkerchief from her handbag, pressed it into his hand.

Candlelight flickered on the walls, which were worn soft and gray from years of worship. Desmond knew already that after the service the families of the victims would hug each other, chat, perhaps even laugh; nearly ten years of shared grief lent an intimacy to the occasion. Some of them were friends now and met outside of this yearly memorial. Some brought new partners to the service, more and more each year. Babies had been born; children had finished school, or gotten married.

For Desmond, though, each service might as well have been the first one. And he regretted with every minute that passed giving in to Val's offer in his moment of weakness.

He clenched his teeth so hard that his jaw ached. Candles were lit for every lost victim, while the congregation breathed the damp, frigid air in the silence of remembrance.

Every year since the accident he'd mourned alone, but tonight Val tugged off her borrowed glove, then slipped her hand into his. And, desperate for something to anchor him down, he held on and closed his eyes.

Afterward it was a little easier, but not by much. He stood a little way from the throng, close to the door, Val's hand still folded in his. He didn't speak to anyone, other than cursory nods or greetings when he was approached.

No one ever came to Desmond for more than a few seconds; his presence at the memorial was acknowledged, but there was no warm welcome for him as there was for the others. A couple of people eyed Val with curiosity, but he had no relationships here that would lead to any introductions. And Val, bless her, was quiet and unobtrusive. She'd somehow managed to read the situation, even though he hadn't had the words to explain.

He'd lost his father, yes; his only parent, the man who'd raised him alone. But his father was also responsible for the loss of the many who lay dead.

And that, they could not ignore, even though it was not Desmond's fault. Desmond had a right to grieve as much as they. But his presence here today, and every other time, was…complicated.

No one ever invited Desmond home for a cup of tea, or to the pub where they had a customary drink afterward, or to the weddings and christenings of the relatives of the deceased. No, Desmond would usually wind his scarf around his neck, set his shoulders, and move silently into the rain alone, the first one out of the church; breathing hard through his mouth and blinking the rain out of his eyes; swallowing hard over and over again, harder and harder, and counting his breaths until the thing that threatened to break past his stoicism settled back deep inside him, where it belonged.

But this year was different. Val's small figure was beside him, resolute, gripping his hand as if their lives depended on it. Eventually the last guest had filtered out onto the stoop, exclaiming over the rain and arranging a rideshare in a loud hearty voice, and they were alone. It was only then that she finally looked at him. And from her expression he could tell that he hadn't been very good at hiding his emotions after all.

"Oh, Desmond," she whispered, and then she was on her toes, cradling his face and kissing him on the cheek. He couldn't respond. His body, his mind, his lips—they were all frozen.

"We should go," Val whispered, tugging at his hand. Her eyes had kindled with something that hadn't been there before, something frightening in its intensity.

He nodded and followed her out into the rain.

He should have pulled away from her, made some dry comment about the folly of kissing in a church, or something—anything to bring them back to normal. But he was just so numb, and so cold, and so absolutely burned out. It'd been exhausting, keeping up this facade for so long.

But he'd be back at it tomorrow; he didn't know any other way to be.

He shouldn't accept her pity; he shouldn't accept her comfort. He didn't deserve either. He hadn't asked for it from the other people in the church. It would have been an unbearable cruelty to seek that from them.

After all, his father wasn't the only one responsible, and Desmond had been hiding behind the protection of a dead man all this time.

The Notting Hill address that Desmond gave to the taxi driver through chattering teeth meant nothing to Val, who only knew of the area from movies. The trip was ruinously expensive and Val saw their driver peering at the bedraggled pair in his rearview mirror, as if wondering who they were. Desmond certainly hadn't given him a hint. After handing over the address, he didn't say a word, just leaned back on the seat with a sigh and closed his eyes.

"I'll send you back to the hotel, once we get there and get you dried off." And that was all he said, the whole hour-plus drive back through the heart of London. When they pulled up to the enormous detached house, Val barely registered red brick, darkened by the sky, electronic parking with two sleek, covered cars atop an elevated platform or the dark shapes that seemed to indicate a garden. Most of the details were obscured by rain. Desmond punched in a key code and there was a tinny sort of beep, and then he shouldered his way through the heavy black door.

Val found herself blinking rapidly in the soft light of an entryway flanked by floor-to-ceiling stained-glass windows that would look magnificent in the daylight. She slipped out of her sodden pumps, feeling awkward about dripping on the floor. Desmond fetched her a towel of such softness and absorbency that she caught her breath a little as it touched her skin. She luxuriated in it for a moment, and when she looked up Desmond was unbuttoning his shirt, his jacket and coat already on the floor.

"You need to get out of those wet things," he said.

"What, here?" she squeaked, realizing how silly she sounded. Desmond had already seen her naked from every imaginable angle.

And he didn't seem to notice her statement. He was grimly unbuttoning the dark suit trousers he wore. He stood there, shadows dancing across lean muscle, his skin gleaming with water, drops trickling down and disappearing into the waistband of his black boxers. He stared down at her, looking grimmer still, with a completely indecipherable expression on his narrow, hard face. It was completely at odds with the laconic, smooth-tongued businessman she'd spent yesterday evening with; this was a silent, hollow-eyed stranger.

Yet, Val still felt an impulse to reach for him, to *touch* him—

He turned from her and walked with his usual easy gait over tiles that were as clear and as reflective as glass. Heated, too, possibly, if the warmth circulating from the soles of her feet upward were to be believed.

"Come," was all he said,

She glanced behind her at the abandoned entryway with its sad little pile of discarded clothing; he hadn't said a word about calling that cab to take her back to The Ritz. She probably should—

"Val!"

She draped the towel around her neck and hurried after him.

"Welcome," he said, throwing out one arm to the side in a half-hearted attempt at a grand gesture. It was the first hint of his old self she'd seen in hours.

The space opened up into a long, wide hall with glowing walls the color of fresh cream on which enormous paintings hung, gallery style; she recognized Andy Warhol, Kehinde Wiley and others that looked vaguely familiar whose names she could not place.

But she could not slow down to enjoy them because her host was stalking impatiently forward. Almost in a blur, she saw glimpses of a sitting room with a large fireplace, a room with a faded Persian carpet and a massive dining table, and a sunroom that looked as if it ran round the entire western perimeter of the house. In daylight it must be stunning. The house was like Desmond, in a sense—luxurious without being ostentatious, stylish without being flashy. Understated. Elegant. Relaxed.

They reached the end of the hall, where the enormous doors of a lift were covered with slabs of the palest pink marble gleaming beneath the lights. There were no buttons, just a panel that Desmond, still half-naked, let his finger hover over.

The doors slid open smoothly and he stepped in, as if it were a portal to another kingdom. He looked over his shoulder but said nothing.

She swallowed and stepped in beside him. His presence filled the entire space; the sweet spiciness of his skin seemed to have been amplified by the rain. The air between them was so very charged, full of pent-up energy built from the tension of the evening that she had no idea what to do with.

She wanted to rest her head in the hollow between his shoulders. And it wasn't just about sex, either—it was about closeness; something she suspected he needed.

Desmond was the only person who'd tempted her for so long. And here she was, in his home. After knowing him for only two days. Wanting to comfort him.

Perhaps, she thought, knotting her hands in the towel clutched tight round her shoulders, it was the pain she'd seen weigh him down this evening. It was the pain of loss, but something more, too. He had the look of a man who knew he couldn't fix what was wrong.

That, she understood, if nothing else.

"I'm taking you to one of the guest wings," he said as the lift doors opened. *First floor.* This hallway was also lined by paintings, though she didn't recognize the artists of these. The ones downstairs were meant to impress; these were meant to add atmosphere. "You'll find everything you need there. Have a hot shower if you want, and get out of your wet things."

Despite herself, the words were finding their way under her skin, warm and sinuous.

"Will you—?"

"I'm going to do the same. Do you think you can find your way back down to the main floor?"

She nodded.

"Great. Meet me there. Half hour." And then he was gone, leaving just a faint suggestion of warmth, sweat, rainfall and cloves.

Val stood there silently for a long moment, wrapped in her towel. It was so quiet in the house.

In the bathroom, she stripped off her soaked clothing and quickly showered to warm herself up. She got out and wrapped herself in a crimson dressing gown that had been folded on the foot of the bed and which smelled faintly of mint and eucalyptus. The silk fabric was light and luxurious, the sleeves rolled back into heavy, embroidered cuffs. She wadded the hem in her hand to keep from tripping as she went to the vanity to inspect her hair. It had frizzed completely, haloing her face with soft dark fuzz.

"Get it together," she hissed to her reflection. Her eyes looked wide and questioning, and the fabric clung to her body. She barely recognized herself. Val straightened to her full height and left in search of the lift.

When she stepped out onto the main floor, Desmond was there, his hands folded behind him. His hair was wet and coiling tightly against his head, and he wore a simple black crewneck and knit trousers hanging low on his narrow hips. He was more casually dressed than she'd ever seen him.

He's beautiful.

The thought came without her permission.

"Hey," he said.

She looked up.

It was a mistake. She could feel heat suffusing her face. This was too intimate. She'd barely had meaningful human contact in years, and she'd shared so much with this man in only two days.

Silence thronged between them for one second, two, three…

"Thank you," was all he said when eventually he spoke.

She nodded, her mouth dry.

"Shall we get something to eat, then?"

CHAPTER TEN

"COME WITH ME."

She tightened her robe across her chest, feeling rather silly in it, but her clothes were hanging in the bathroom and still soaked through. She trailed her companion through the house while outside rain lashed the roof and windows, and the occasional tree branch made a tapping noise against the glass. They emerged into another part of the house, one that immediately looked more intimate.

"This is where I spend most of my time—the part you saw earlier is for entertaining. My office is there." He gestured at a closed door. "I eat in here."

The room in question was delightful, rendered in shades of muted rust and gold, and featuring a sunken floor with enormous cushions around a low table. Candles flickered on the table enhancing the soft warm light spilling from lamps around the room and the glow from a fire that sparked and crackled in the ornate fireplace. Val lowered herself onto a squashy cushion on the floor. The slippery fabric of her dressing gown was hard to manage and she pulled it round her legs and back up over her breasts just in time.

His eyes flickered over her, and she felt a familiar flush of heat when she realized he had noticed.

"Sorry about the dressing gown," he said. "My stepmother keeps them for guests, but it's not very practical, is it?"

"It's fine. It's beautiful," she said, and forced a smile.

"I could give you something of mine—"

"Oh, no. No. I'm perfectly all right." The thought of wearing his clothes, of wrapping herself in what was sure to be his scent… "This is lovely. Thank you."

"I'll have something brought over for you." He came to join her, easing himself down against the cushions of the low seat. He exhaled as if his body hurt, then bent over the table to uncover the dishes. He obviously had a discreet staff member—or three—who had set up the room and produced the food. Steam curled up from the plates and Val felt her stomach tighten with hunger. There was a small dish to her right with a steaming hot towel on it; she picked it up and wiped her hands.

"I hope you like lamb. And Ethiopian food," Desmond said.

Val nodded. "Yes, I do." She recognized it immediately. "Some of my colleagues are Ethiopian. And Eritrean," she added as an afterthought.

"Yes, I've heard there are quite a few in Bahr Al-Dahab." He lifted the woven lid of the *mesob* with a flourish, gesturing that she should take one of the springy flatbread pieces within. "Help yourself."

"Thank you." When her *injara* was safely on her plate, he offered her the bowl of stew. Her stomach growled audibly as she spooned some onto the flatbread. She waited until he'd served himself, then lifted the first bite to her lips.

It was delicious—fatty, tender lamb cooked in a spicy, flavorful stew seasoned with chili oil. She looked up to see Desmond regarding her with amusement.

"What?" she said, covering her mouth with her hand.

He laughed, and the sound added warmth to the room. “My father would have been impressed at your eating with your hands.”

“Are you Ethiopian?”

“I was born in Surrey. My father left Ethiopia in the eighties, during the hunger crisis.” He paused to tear off a bit of bread, deftly spooning stew in one quick motion.

“Your mother?”

“Oh, they got divorced early on, and she went home. She married again. I stayed with my father here.”

“Oh, I see.”

“He was the youngest of six brothers. They all worked, got themselves through school, combined resources, and started a business. All things aviation. Airplane parts. Maintenance. Consulting.” He gestured at himself. “Tesfay Aviation Solutions was what it was called. They really capitalized on the boom in affordable air travel. My father was a tagalong teenager for most of it, but he really came into his own when he convinced them to let him start a marketing and advertising leg of the business. He did well, for a really long time—he’s responsible for a lot of the advertising for smaller international airlines. *Was*,” he corrected himself.

Val nodded, encouraging him to continue.

“It was amazing,” he said quietly, looking up and meeting her eyes. “They built a fortune in one generation. That’s them, there,” he said, gesturing to a painting on the wall.

Val rose to her feet and crossed over to the painting, wanting a closer look. The men were all lean and handsome and had something of Desmond in their faces, in the sinewy build, in the beautiful skin. The traditional style of the portrait and the soft brushstrokes made it difficult to identify features too closely. She squinted, wishing she had her glasses, then stepped back, bumping directly into Desmond.

"Oh! Sorry!" She hadn't even heard him come up behind her.

"Not an issue at all." She could feel the warmth of his body radiating into her back.

"That's Abuna, Abel, Selama, Thaddaeus, my father Abram, and Markos."

"They're very handsome."

"Yeah, they would say that, too."

"Are they still in London?"

"Some of them. A couple went to the US. Uncle Abel's in Ethiopia at the moment." She sensed hesitation from him and she turned to face him. "We're not…terribly close," he said. A shadow passed over his face. "There was a bit of a break, a few years ago."

"What happened?"

"It's a long story."

"We have time." She didn't know why she was pushing, especially because his face was growing darker and darker. She was convinced he would change the subject and the moment would be over.

"The flight he was on…it was an airline that he and my brothers developed with the firm from inception to the first flight. It was in response to increased budget tourism, and my father wrote an absolutely magnificent campaign. What he designed… I've never seen anything like that before. I was so proud of him—" Desmond's voice became so frayed that Val felt a stab of physical pain herself. She inhaled to steady herself and found that the air was heavy with the sweetness of lemon candle wax, the spicy richness of chili oil and meat, and… Desmond.

"When the flight was lost, shares plunged. It was an ugly

story. My uncles were fighting among each other, throwing around accusations of blame… in the end, they sold all their shares to me, wanting to wash their hands of it. And now here I am. Carrying that legacy."

"And you— haven't seen them since then?"

Desmond shook his head. "They blamed my father, you see," he said. "That made it…impossible for me to stay with them."

There was no sound in the room other than the rain drumming on the skylights above. Desmond rubbed a hand over the top of his head, looking wearier than she'd seen him before, and so different from the cool, sardonic bachelor she'd met only yesterday.

We're all hiding something, she thought.

Some just buried it deeper than others. And in this moment, she felt his loneliness. Earlier that day, at the memorial, she'd recognized self-blame—both were emotions she herself felt on a daily basis.

Right now, she was feeling so many things: admiration for all he'd accomplished and for his ambition, sorrow at the fact that he'd been so alone in that church just a couple of hours ago and now, incredibly close to him in a way she hadn't expected.

Desmond's voice had grown hoarse; he seemed to be transfixed by the portrait of his father and uncles. His jaw was so rigid that Val wanted to reach up and caress it into relaxation.

To comfort him.

"Europe is completely shot for us as a market. People won't forget a tragedy that resulted in the loss of so many people. But the Gulf is still open, and young enough to throw money at us, and—" He stopped and cleared his throat.

"I have to do this," he finished. "For him. For my father. I can't let his legacy die, Val. I simply can't. Not when—" His eyes were dark pools that glimmered in the candlelight. Val waited breathlessly for him to finish what he was going to say, but he turned away from her with visible effort. "Come on. Our food's getting cold."

They sat down again, companionably close this time, and ate from the same dish, their fingers brushing occasionally. They didn't speak until the food was nearly gone.

"I suppose," he said, with the first hint of humor she'd heard in his voice since they'd raced to the church for the memorial, "we should get to know each other, since we are supposed to be married." He was clearly forcing levity back into the conversation, and the smirk on his face told her he was being playful. She decided, for his sake, not to push things, and instead matched his lighter tone.

"I've been trying not to think about it!"

"You should see your face," he jeered. There was laughter in his voice, and she was glad for it. "Well. What are the most important things?"

"Family, religion, allergies…?"

"You've met them—" he gestured at the wall "—Orthodox, and mushrooms. Yourself?"

"Well, you've heard my story about my family. We're Baptist, although I haven't entered a church since my wedding. No allergies except cats."

She paused, wanting desperately to segue into something less…serious. "I suppose we could talk about Sheikh Rashid again. And your deal."

"You don't have to."

"Do you have to argue about everything?" she said crossly. "I said I would. Now, listen."

He covered his mouth rather dramatically, and she rolled her eyes.

"Nostalgia," she said.

Confusion crossed Desmond's face. Val crossed her arms over her chest; her breasts were aching beneath the fabric that covered them. She forced herself to focus on Desmond.

"Bahr Al-Dahab," she continued. "It means—"

"Sea of gold."

"Yes." She nodded. "It's very glamorous, the concept of a nation built of a single material. Liquid gold, as it were. Your competitors have worn that idea out. But Sheikh Rashid, he loves history above all else. Bahr Al-Dahab is his beating heart, even more so than the king."

Desmond's eyes were darker than they'd been earlier, if that were possible. "Tell me more."

"Ask him about the history of Bahr Al-Dahab and he'll be delighted to tell you the story."

"Why don't you tell me?" Desmond countered, and his mouth curved up slightly. "You have the loveliest voice, you know."

He needed to stop saying things like that—and in *that* voice. Talking was calming her down, cooling the blood that still thrummed in her ears, her temples, and he was undoing it. "The country grew from an historic port city that thrived in the late sixteen hundreds and early seventeen hundreds. Merchants from Asia, Africa and even Europe would sail to its shores, bringing with them myriad goods and stories, and exporting baskets of the most beautiful pearls—there's a luminous, creamy color that's unique to the region."

"All right," he said, after a moment.

"There's stunning architecture that has been preserved there better than anywhere else in the Gulf—souks in their original settings and an enormous harbor. There's a pearl festival every year to celebrate the origins of the nation. You don't hear much about us internationally because we've been overshadowed by our neighbors and their skyscrapers. Dubai. Qatar. Bahrain, even."

"Yes, I know."

"That's what he cares about," she said. "The legacy. An appreciation of what their fathers sacrificed. Every single person that pitches to him tries to sell him a vision of the future, without stopping to appreciate the past. And if you can focus on that, you'll stand out."

The words hung between them for a moment in the small space; Desmond looked at her keenly.

"Legacy," he echoed.

"It's strangely fitting, isn't it?" she asked, and forced a smile, forced her trembling limbs to still. Why was he *looking* at her like that? "Consider what you're doing for your father. After all, this is all for him."

A muscle worked in the long column of his throat.

"I suppose," he said a little hoarsely, and the naked sorrow was so vivid on his face that she completely pushed aside all reservations and offered her hand. He hesitated for only a moment, then shifted closer to her and took it.

They sat in silence for a moment in the cocoon of heat and cushions, and the look on his face was twice as intense as it'd been in the shadows of the jazz club. That same hot, irresistible, dreadful impulse that had taken her over just one night ago was prickling at her senses now, overcoming decorum, good sense, propriety, good taste—all of it was quickly fading…

It was different from last night. Then, it had been lust. Indulgence. Fun.

Now she felt as if something in her was cracking open to warmth. To light.

To possibility.

And a desire to comfort a man that she'd somehow grown to care for immensely, in a very short period of time.

"Desmond," she said, as a warning, a final attempt to curtail whatever this was. But it didn't come out as sternly as she'd intended; instead, it was more like a sigh. And then Desmond's face was so close to hers, and his eyes were so very gentle, and she was tipping her lips up for the kiss he was offering.

Again.

They kissed until the moment faded into something that no longer made sense. When they were both breathless and hot, Val pulled back slowly, swollen lips parted, and sank back against the cushions of the low sofa. Yes, he knew he didn't deserve her, but she was here, and she wanted to comfort him. As long as he didn't let it spark anything else...

Right?

Desire was hot in her eyes, mixed with an uncertainty that touched him. What was she uncertain about? Him? His desire for her? Allowing a man who was grieving his father to kiss her after a night of remembrance?

"Desmond..." she started to say, and he knew he had to stop this from getting any more emotionally intimate.

"Listen," he said huskily, staring deep into her eyes so that she'd believe the lie. "I'm fine. It was a long time ago."

"I know, but—"

Desmond's response was to pull his sweater over his head, as much to hide his face as anything else. When he dropped it on the floor he saw that it'd worked. Her eyes were clouded with want and she shifted as if uncomfortable, pressing her knees together and fiddling with the belt on her robe. The movement drew his eyes to her body, where the thin material of the robe clung to her waist and hips. Her full breasts were especially prominent beneath the fabric. It brought to mind the way they hung heavy and hot when they were exposed, the way her nipples grew hard and long and almost unbearably sensitive when touched or sucked.

Had they really only had one night together? He felt like he knew her body so well already. He brushed a hand where the material gaped on her legs then ran it up the silken length of her thigh.

He remembered the intensity of the first time he'd touched her, and amid his growing arousal he felt a pinch of nostalgia. It was never going to be like this again, these two nights in London. They'd got so close, so fast. And now she was looking at him, with that heavy-lidded gaze, and if he didn't know better—

He didn't complete the thought, because Val rose to her knees on the sofa, leaned forward, and kissed him. Hesitantly at first, asking for permission, and when his hands slipped up almost automatically to grip her waist, her hips, she parted her lips and there it was again, that honeyed sweetness that he knew would nudge at the edges of his dreams for nights to come. Though it would never be better than it was in person. Her tongue slid against his and he tasted spice and mint. He pressed forward to kiss her harder but she pulled back a little and shook her head, her eyes glittering.

"No," she said, and her voice was husky with want. "Let me, Desmond. *Please.*"

Damn, her voice sent fire straight down to his groin and he was hard, so hard. Her eyes flicked down to where he swelled against his trousers and her tongue skimmed her lower lip. Her hand followed and huffed out breath. "Val. Are you sure?"

"I'm sure," she whispered against his lips, and then she gasped a little when his hands tightened on her hips. He yanked her forward and she rose to her knees and straddled his hips. "I just… I want to relax. I want *this*…"

So she'd felt it too, that lightning-bright connection. And she'd come looking for *him*. His chest sparked.

She'd come to him. She'd come to him because she wanted him badly enough to shed her natural reticence and to ask for it. "Val…"

"Please stop talking," she said softly.

She drew the crimson silk of her dressing gown from her shoulders in a seductive shimmy that had him catching his breath. She was naked beneath it, as he suspected. Her skin was warm and scented. Desmond shifted back to accommodate her, and her breath vented in a low hiss as she rubbed that slick, sensitive part of her against the roughness of his trousers. She threw her head back, eyes closed, and he was almost wild with desire. If he couldn't bury himself *deep* in her in about thirty seconds, he was going to—

"Touch me."

She took his wrist and guided it down to where he knew she was swollen and aching. She swore, and a shudder went through her that made her breasts shake. He passed his thumb against her center, and the *sound* she let out…

CHAPTER ELEVEN

VAL CRIED OUT as she shattered in his arms, harder than she ever had before. The entire day she'd been trying to slow her thudding heart, pressing her thighs together at the dampness that collected there. And now, for the first time ever, she'd gone after what she wanted and got it. She'd bared her body to him and told him she needed him.

She fumbled urgently at the hem of his shirt and at the buttons of his trousers, wanting him as naked as she was. As she'd commanded, he didn't say a word, and when he was finally bare and smooth and warm beneath her, he tipped her chin down so she was forced to watch her thighs open as he parted her slick, swollen flesh and he filled her. He throbbed and grew inside of her, grinding against her exactly where she needed him, building, pushing, tightening until they shuddered and came together.

It wasn't until the stars behind her eyes faded that she realized she hadn't even considered contraception. And neither had he. She closed her eyes again and rested her head on his shoulder, feeling him slide, slick and warm, from her. She'd get a morning-after pill tomorrow. It'd be *fine.* She didn't want to leave this blissful state, not yet. She didn't want to come back down to earth.

There was something about Desmond that made her believe it might be possible to escape the existence she'd been stuck in for so long.

Desmond's hand was on her head, smoothing down the fluffy curls as they dried in the warmth of the room. "Are you all right?"

She nodded.

"Let's go to bed."

Going to *his* bed meant waking up in his arms, and… well, things had already been messy enough tonight. But going to *her* bed meant waking up alone when the man she ached for was in the same house.

Would it really be so harmful, allowing herself one more night?

Of course it would be. She couldn't risk it.

"Not yet."

"Not yet," he agreed, and shifted to cradle her close.

When Desmond woke the morning after the memorial service, the rain had stopped completely and light was filtering across his bed from the enormous skylights in his room. It felt as if he were emerging from a spell. The soft yellow pool completely illuminated Val, who was sleeping on her side with her silk dressing gown clinging to her body. Her hair stood out from her head in soft shining puffs of black while her lashes curled low on her cheeks.

She looked so beautiful and it was with some effort that he resisted reaching out to touch the satiny smoothness of her cheek, or the bare shoulder that emerged from the pool of crimson silk. Instead, he eased himself from the sheets with practiced quiet, barely disturbing the bed, and moved soundlessly to the enormous alabaster marble bathroom.

Desmond washed his face and brushed his teeth. Then he sank down on the chair his barber normally used for shaving, trying to collect himself before he had to go out there and face her.

What the hell had happened last night?

Not only had he brought her home—something he'd never done with any woman he'd slept with casually—but he'd also taken her to his father's memorial. And spending the night and subsequent day with her had made him forget the event was even taking place—which hadn't happened in ten years.

What the hell had this woman *done* to him? Why had he opened up? The combination of beauty, maturity and kindness that radiated from her like light probably had something to do with it…

How could he have been so careless?

Maybe this is something you've needed for a long time.

The thought came to him unbidden.

He shoved it away violently.

Their night together wasn't the issue; he'd self-medicated between the soft, willing thighs of many women over the years. But this…this *intrusion* into his home, into his *heart…*

He could not risk either. Not now, and not for the foreseeable future.

Desmond began counting breaths, tapping rapidly on his leg as he did so. He had to be calm when he left this bathroom, when Val was awake and looking at him with her usual gentleness, the gentleness he clearly had responded to so intensely the night before.

Had they really only known each other for two days?

The softest of noises in the doorway made him look up; Val stood there in the dressing gown, which was now anchored securely around her curves. Though the silk clung just as suggestively to her body as it had the night before, he did not feel any lust. Instead, he felt a tug in his chest that was much more disconcerting.

In the warm, natural light of the early morning she looked lovelier than he'd ever seen her. She was carefully expressionless.

"Good morning." The huskiness in his voice surprised him.

"Good morning."

"Did you sleep well?" Why was this painfully awkward already?

"As well as you did, I think." There was a flicker of a smile on her face, enough to make him feel a bit better.

"It's all right," he said, careful to match her neutral expression with his own.

"I—I appreciate your trusting me enough to bring me to your father's memorial service. I didn't know him, but I'm sure, I'm sure he would be so touched. This deal is… it's important for both of you, and I'll help you in any way I possibly can."

He waited for a moment. She said nothing else, only folded her hands.

"Thank you," he said after a moment.

She cleared her throat and drew the crimson silk more tightly across her chest. "I should…get dressed."

"I'll walk you back to the guest wing…"

She shook her head. "I can find my way. And, Desmond…" she hesitated.

"Yes?" His heart was pounding in his ears, a dull rush of blood.

"I want to find him."

"Find…?"

Val continued, stating her words carefully and decisively. "I don't want to be married to him anymore. I want to be free. I want to put that bit of my life behind me, officially. I think the past couple of days have made me see things differently."

Desmond's heart was squeezed so tight in his chest he found it hard to breathe. "Go on."

"You're getting better at the listening bit," she remarked, crossing her arms.

"You're a good example. Go on, then."

"Every single moment married to Malik felt like work. He was so—" She cut herself off; as if she wasn't quite ready to discuss all that. "Exhausting," she said as a compromise. "His ambition was great, and it was exhausting. And then he left, and that was exhausting. And then I found out about the debts. I was arrested, and then everything became a struggle. Getting up. Taking care of myself. It was all exhausting. Even sleeping was exhausting, because my mind was constantly racing. Where the hell would I get that kind of money?"

He nodded. "I wondered why your family didn't help, but given what you've told me about them…"

She shook her head, one short sharp movement. "They think I'm out here by choice. I…couldn't. Too many of them warned me about Malik, but I married him anyway." She sighed. "You had your own break with your family, and I had mine. I couldn't… I couldn't burden them with this, not when they didn't want me there."

"Valentina—"

"Living a life where you're constantly reminding yourself how foolish you've been—" She broke off. "Pursuing a divorce would have been another thing I had to do, and I was already so tired." She paused, blinking hard, but a telltale wetness was already making its way down her cheek. "I wish I had a better excuse."

Sweetheart. The endearment came to him so naturally, though he didn't say it out loud. "You don't have to justify anything to me," Desmond said huskily.

"What happened here in London… I realized I want a different kind of…existence. I've never confronted him about what he did to me, whether directly or indirectly." Her voice lowered. "I've been pathetic."

Desmond made a hissing sound through his teeth. "Are you ever going to stop calling yourself names when it comes to that moron you were married to?"

"I don't," Val retorted. "All I meant was—"

"All you meant was that this is your fault. Again. But it's not." He paused to let that sink in, then leaned forward in his chair until their faces were very close. "He must have done a real number on you to make you think you're not as extraordinary as you are."

"Desm—" She couldn't finish the word.

And Desmond found himself peering into her face. Their noses were almost touching, and he felt dizzy suddenly. Her eyes were soft and serious all at once. He had to make her listen. He reached down, took her hands.

"I think you already believe me, somewhere deep inside," he said quietly. "Please don't absorb one unworthy man's bad opinion, Valentina. It will rob so much from you."

Val bit her lower lip. Her exhalation of breath danced whisper-soft against his skin.

And there it was.

He kissed her, just for a fraction of a second, feeling warmth seep all the way to his toes, and when she opened her eyes, she was still looking at him with that oddly tender expression on her face.

And then he felt it again.

That tug of desire for something more.

Something that transcended sex.

Something that was not possible for them, and certainly not while she still wasn't free of her first husband. Desmond wasn't sure what the future held, or if he even could be a part of it. But suddenly it felt like possibilities were within his reach, each more beautiful than the last. It gave him a warm glow inside.

It gave him hope.

"Valentina," he said quietly, and reached out to cup her face.

"Using my full name again, I see," she said lightly.

"It suits you better, I think." And maybe it did, now that the reason she'd shunned it in the first place seemed to be dissipating with each day. She laughed, a choked sound, and he thumbed away the dampness at the corners of her eyes. And for the first time in years he allowed what was on his heart to leave his lips.

"Get your divorce," he said, simply. "I'll help. Then, marry me, Valentina. For real this time. And come back to London with me, after I've solidified this deal. Let me have some part in starting your new life."

Val considered this for a minute, chewing hard on the inside of her lip, trying to breathe through the emotions currently roiling through her. He couldn't read her mind, but he would bet his fortune that what he saw reflected in the stunning clarity of those eyes was—

Hope.

It was a long time before she spoke and Desmond waited patiently.

"His name is Malik Ali," she said finally.

CHAPTER TWELVE

VAL BARELY RECOGNIZED the woman staring back at her.

Nothing physical had changed; she was wearing a silk jersey wrap dress that was constantly in her rotation during summer months. Her hair had been conditioned, detangled and smoothed back into soft puffs that adorned the back of her head. Her long-line bra and underwear were still digging into the tender flesh of her torso—a little more than usual, actually—but she was ready to leave London for Bahr Al-Dahab.

Desmond had *somehow* sweet-talked Sheikh Rashid into letting her off duty with Hind during the evenings. He'd been taking her to London's finest restaurants every single night, and her stomach seemed to be reacting to the bewildering variety of Michelin-starred meals by ensuring every single calorie went straight to her hips and bum.

Desmond. She raised her fingers up to massage her temples. Whenever she thought about her experiences over the past week and a half, her head would start to throb.

Desmond loved to eat; she'd discovered that about him. He loved to talk, often gesticulating wildly as he did so, flinging food into his mouth every now and then. She'd never met a person in her life infused with such raw energy. He attacked every hour of the day ferociously, without looking back, without any of the hesitation or overanalysis that characterized Val's days. When they ate together, he drew her into the conversation, showed her what he was working on and listened with concentration. He drank from Val's water glass and laughed when she pointed it out; he cut the choicest bits from his plate for her to try and smirked at her when she scolded him.

He wanted to marry her.

After his heart-stopping announcement, he'd explained, of course, still cradling her in his arms as if it were the most natural thing in the world.

"I like you," he'd said, simply. "And I want this to be—real, at least to the degree that we can make it. It seems all right for now, but you're not going to feel right, lying to Sheikh Rashid for however long this lasts, and—well, I won't, either. There are more reasons to marry than love, Valentina. I want you to consider it. I can promise you will never regret this."

He seemed determined—she could see it on his face when he thought she wasn't looking—that she would never have a reason to be uncomfortable in his presence, that she'd have every reason to accept his wild proposal.

And if she were honest, it was this that made her uncomfortable. It was too much.

She wasn't used to such consideration, from anyone. Her stepfather had been tolerant. Malik had been…overbearingly self-interested. And here she was, with a man who sent cars to pick her up so she wouldn't have to walk, who gave her an Amex black card in her name for "anything she needed" and who texted her every night to wish her sweet dreams.

She wished he was the shallow young man she'd assumed he was before she met him. It would have made their resolution so much easier. But he wasn't. He'd proven that much, that night in Notting Hill. And then he'd look at her, and he'd smile, a slow deliberate smile that lit something inside her and made her feel sparks down to her fingertips. It wasn't a crush or the beginnings of love or anything like that, but it was *something*. The pleasure of being *seen* perhaps, and the realization that after nearly a decade of resting in an emotionally fetal position, she now *wanted* to be seen. And it was having an effect on her that she couldn't deny. What might it look like if she were free? Truly free?

Even now, in her old clothes, she looked so different—the type of difference that radiated from within. She was *glowing*. Being desired so nakedly by Desmond Tesfay had made her see her body in a different light. Her wobbly bits had been transformed to lush softness; her lips looked tender and red, even without the benefit of gloss. She was flushed and warm with passion—unbelievable passion—both given and received. Words. Kisses. Hands and lips skimming every inch of her body. Heat and sweetness and a pleasure that overwhelmed every bit of common sense.

Yes, Desmond Tesfay was a skilled lover. And she, Ms. Pragmatic, Ms. Practical, Ms. Prudish, even, had blossomed under his touch like one of the moss roses on her balcony that she guarded so carefully from the Gulf heat.

Val liked sure things; she liked answers. Embarking on this—could she even call it an affair?—was unsettling, at best. And in the days that had followed she'd waited in vain to see another glimpse of the man who'd taken her to his home that night and told her a story that had made her heart break for him.

But despite his loving gestures, that man never appeared again.

Would that be enough for her? Another marriage to a

man who was masking his true self from her, even though he was considerably kinder than the last one?

A discreet tap at the door startled her. Goodness, she'd been deep in thought! She shoved her feet into her pumps, and when she opened the door she recognized the grizzle-haired concierge who'd been tasked with taking care of Sheikh Rashid's family for the duration of the visit.

"Mr. Tesfay's car is waiting downstairs, ma'am," the man said respectfully.

Waiting among the black taxis at the curb of the hotel was a sleek champagne-colored Tesla that glowed in the light of the early morning. A smart driver in a tailored suit opened the door for her, and Val slid in, her eyes widening in surprise as she did.

The interior of the car was a surprise after the staid gray dignity of Mayfair. It smelled faintly of rosewater and something else too, something sharper and suggestive of essential oils. While she was figuring it out, the driver flipped open a carved wooden box and lifted out a rolled white cloth with a pair of tongs. He draped the steaming cloth over her hands, pointed out the glass water bottles and snack bar built into the armrest, then shut the door.

Traffic seemed to part as if by magic for the Tesla meaning the ride to the airport was quick and smooth. When she arrived, she was handed over to an agent who escorted her to a private check-in and security desk, and yet another car was waiting to whisk her off to a plane waiting at the edge of the tarmac. The distinct light blue, white and pale gold of Bahr Al-Dahab's flag fluttered next to a strip of red carpet leading to the steps up to the aircraft. And when she caught sight of Desmond, tall and erect and impeccably dressed with his arms full of delicate, star-shaped flowers, her heart began to thud, and her throat tightened.

He smiled as she approached him. The scent of the flowers was so strong and sweet that she could smell them even from a distance. When she grew close he laid them carefully in her arms.

"You look good," he said, kissing her cheek.

She swallowed. "Desmond, I don't think—"

"Flowers a bit too much?" He peered into her face.

"Well, yes—"

"They're Arabian jasmine—the Bahr Al-Dahab variety, as I'm sure you know. The design team thought they were overkill as well, you know, with allergies in the cabin and whatnot…"

He was trotting up the boarding steps as he spoke, leaving Val with a very hot face and an armful of flowers.

Desmond frowned down at her from the top of the steps. "Are you coming?"

Val loosened her hold on the flowers and ascended with as much dignity as she could manage. He was grinning so widely when she reached the top that she narrowed her eyes in his direction. "*What?*"

"You've a lovely walk," he said, and laughed out loud when she swung her handbag at him. She was secretly grateful though, because his nonsense dissolved some of the tension.

"I agree with your design team," she said with hauteur, ignoring his statement and shouldering her handbag. "It's too much. Perhaps stick to lavish arrangements in the lounge?"

"We're having jasmine cultivated specially for the airline," he confided.

"Before you even get the deal?"

Desmond shrugged, but there was a gleam in his eye that she was beginning to recognize. "I was chasing a deal once to market private cabanas. I built an entire villa from the ground up to show the client. He ended up going with someone else, but he was so impressed he bought the thing for himself. Come on."

Despite her discomfort, Val was quite impressed by what she saw; it was impossible not to be. The inside of the jet was modeled, Desmond explained, after the first-class cabin he planned for GoldenEye.

"GoldenEye?"

"It's only a working title, don't worry," he said with a laugh. "My team will come up with something more suitable by the launch. I was hoping to get Hind involved in naming it, but she had about as much interest in the project as I have in her social media reels. Come, I'll give you a tour."

A smiling flight attendant dressed in an impeccably tailored suit dress rendered in those same shades of pale blue and gold-tinged ivory accepted the bouquet from Val with a smile. Desmond pointed out the details: real gold watch and enormous sixties-style pearl stud earrings.

"They're locally caught, and of the highest quality," he explained. "Hijabi flight attendants have a brooch they'll use to fasten their *shaylas* that are the same style. The fabric was also sourced locally from a family of textile artists from India who've been here for generations."

"It's impeccable," Val said, impressed.

"There's gold silk thread woven into the fabric so it catches the light. All the jewelry is locally made as well, and the cabin..."

The cabin was *breathtaking.* Val had flown private on occasion with Hind, of course, but the discreet taste and modernity of the cabin was a stark contrast to the Sheikh's eighties-style opulence. The hardware was all gold-tinged cream; the seats were upholstered in pale blue; the paneling was Lebanese cedar, glass-smooth, polished and sealed to a soft glow; and the floors featured handwoven carpets crafted by local artisans.

Desmond and Val sat in adjoining chairs that were so luxurious that Val felt as if every muscle in her body was relaxing one by one. When she asked Desmond what it was, he grinned.

"Just call it space-age memory foam."

A flight attendant surfaced, her finery covered completely by a filmy apron with long sleeves. She offered Val an exquisitely plated amuse-bouche: locally sourced caviar perched atop a delicate blini, perfectly crisped with saffron round the edges with a drizzle of saffron-infused crème fraîche and a dusting of gold leaf to finish off the bite.

After his initial bursts of enthusiasm, Desmond fell into a silence that felt oddly moody. Under the guise of enjoying the selections brought from the caviar and oyster bar, Val watched him carefully. He began to tap his left thumb on his armrest in a tic she had come to recognize. He answered every question she asked of him quickly and politely, but he was clearly distracted. Before takeoff he asked the flight attendant to bring him the safety checks and logs and everyone sat in silence for twenty-five minutes while he looked them over.

Val didn't mention it; it was understandable, she thought with a stab of sympathy, for someone who'd lost his father in a plane crash.

"Thinking about work?" she ventured after they'd taxied and taken off in silence, and the crew had disappeared.

"What? Oh, yes," he said briefly. It was the first time he'd been this quiet all week.

Val looked out of the window, but when she turned back to him she was surprised to find his eyes fixed on her face.

"Sorry if I'm being terrible company," he said abruptly. His voice was clipped but apologetic. "Just shifting into work mode, I think."

She nodded. Marriage to an incredibly moody person—and one with an awful temper, to boot—had schooled her well in dealing with men and their moods. Silence paired with wide-eyed attention—but not too wide-eyed—was the best course of action.

She hated that she remembered this, and she hated that Desmond's moodiness had caused her body to tense with that memory.

But Desmond *wasn't* Malik. He was nothing like Malik, and he'd proven that over and over. But this was a good reminder that even so, she still had a lot of healing to do.

And for once, it actually seemed possible.

Desmond sat up, startling her back into the present. "Damn it. I almost forgot." He hit the call button, finally looking a bit more animated. The flight attendant appeared so silently that Val jumped, then flushed. They hadn't been doing more than talk, she reminded herself, and were supposed to be a married couple besides, but she wasn't used to feeling so…good.

"The trays," he said.

"Yes, sir." The woman first performed some complicated operation that transformed the space in front of them into a proper dining table, complete with white linen with sharp corners.

"I'm not hungry yet," Val protested.

"It's not food, although we've got a lobster thermidor back there that will surely change your mind. Ah, perfect, thank you," he said, as the flight attendant appeared with two companions. Each of them placed a tray before her. One was lined with a deep emerald green, one ruby red and the third…

“Tiffany blue,” Desmond confirmed, his eyes beginning to sparkle just a bit. “Pick a ring. I’ve got one that I think will look amazing on you, but since this isn’t quite a traditional proposal, you might as well have full choice…”

“I don’t need a ring!” Val drew back in horror. There had to be millions of pounds’ worth of diamonds and gemstones sparkling in front of her, catching the very flattering lighting on the interior of the plane.

“You’re going to get one.” Desmond pointed. “Green tray is from Van Cleef, the blue from Tiffany, and the red are either antique or locally made. All responsibly sourced gems. And no protesting—you’re not going to make me look cheap. The official story is that you’ve been hiding it along with our relationship, but now that our happy union is out in the open—” here, a lilt crept into his voice “—you’re going to flaunt this absolutely beautiful, carefully designed token of our love.”

“You’re ridiculous,” she muttered, and sat on her hands.

“*You’re* being ridiculous.” His long slim fingers hovered over the Tiffany tray, and he plucked one at random—a cushion-cut yellow diamond. He twirled it once and held it up for her inspection. “This is a little…”

“Flashy? I’d never wear that,” she said without thinking, and looked up to see him grinning.

“Oh, fine!” She filled her cheeks with air, then released them with a huff. “I wouldn’t even know where to begin.”

“What kind of ring did your husband give you?”

“He didn’t,” she said automatically. “I had a gold band that I bought myself. He didn’t—” His words came back to her. “He said there were better things to spend money on.”

Desmond gave her a look that conveyed precisely what he thought of *that* sentiment, and she pursed her lips, refusing to engage any further.

"I had a librarian," Desmond said, "when I was in school. You look incredibly similar to—"

"Oh, hush!"

He smiled at her then, and her heart thumped deep in her chest because it had finally reached his eyes.

"Fine!" She bent over the trays in an effort to hide her face as much as to look closely at the rings.

"I could tell you the one that I thought looked most like you. But you pick one. I'd like to see how I did. No thinking about the cost, or anything like that, please. Choose the one you genuinely like the most."

Val examined one or two, and finally picked up a simple solitaire set in a wide band rendered in a warm, rich shade of gold. It reminded her of the jewelry she'd seen while out with Hind in the souks. The teenager dismissed them as being deplorably old-fashioned, but Val liked the simplicity.

"Ah," said Desmond softly. He took the ring from her, lifted up her left hand, and slid it onto her finger. It sparkled brilliantly. "Three carats. Simplest setting out of all of them. Beautiful, elegant and a little old-fashioned, like you."

"How very gallant of you." Oddly she could feel tears stinging at the corners of her eyes. What a tableau this was, but it was strangely touching.

"You'll see over the next few days just how gallant I can be. This is just the beginning."

Something had shifted between them.

The rest of the flight was spent companionably, with no deep, dark secrets revealed. It was as if they had some unspoken agreement to make the rest of their time as pleasant as possible and indulge in a fantasy that seemed to come from the clouds themselves. They ate their saffron-infused lobster thermidor and ate hot freshly baked bread and seasoned yellow rice, then washed their fingers in cool rosewater and applied a lotion that smelt of sun-warmed flowers. After dinner, the flight attendant came round and set up the entertainment system. Val elected to watch a Turkish drama that had been popular years ago, and they lost themselves in tales of sultans and princesses and desert intrigues until her eyes grew heavy and her head drooped down on his shoulder.

The soft, low light in the cabin made her ring sparkle. Impulsively, Desmond picked up her hand and kissed it. It felt so very natural, this little bubble of comfort, so removed from what lay ahead.

It would have been nice to linger there forever, but reality awaited them.

At that thought, Desmond's jaw tightened. He lowered her hand back to her armrest and rearranged the linen and cashmere blend cabin blanket across her lap before drifting into a dreamless sleep, himself.

When he woke, it was to chatter in the cabin. He sat up blearily, rubbing his eyes as if he were four years old. He wondered when the last time was that he'd slept so deeply, anywhere? The flight attendants were preparing the cabin for landing and he sat up straight, yawning till his jaw cracked. Val was gone.

"She's using the facilities," a voice cut through his sleepiness as if reading his mind. A flight attendant shimmered over, offering a kit with mouthwash, a toothbrush, a small jar of La Mer and a rolled-up linen towel of unbelievable softness. He buried his face in it, inhaling jasmine and amber. When he lifted his head, Val stood before him as if conjured from the longings of his own mind and his body was suffused with warmth.

"Hello," she said, smiling down at him, that dimple in her round cheek deepening. She was dressed in an abaya of shimmering blush pink that just touched the floor round her feet; the sleeves were long, bell-shaped and dramatically wide. The pale *shayla*, draped loosely round her shoulders, was a creamy color with just a hint of pink that made her skin glow. Tiny seed pearls adorned the sleeves and hem of the garment.

"National dress," she said, as if it warranted some explanation. "Hind and I designed it."

"You look beautiful," he said softly.

She did not squirm in embarrassment or self-consciousness. Instead, she looked at him steadily, as if trying to figure out the answer to some question, before moving forward. The two halves of the abaya opened to reveal wide-legged trousers and a blouse in the same shade as the *shayla*. She eased herself back into her seat, crossing her legs at the ankle. "Black is the standard in the Gulf, of course," she said, twisting her ring round her finger, "but the wife of the king is hugely popular, and she favors pastel colors. For this style of dress, all the colors of the rainbow are available, but soft, soft as if shrouded by a cloud. This fashion is called Al Farashat. Butterflies," she translated. "The fabric is so gently woven that it flutters with even the slightest touch of wind."

"Aptly named."

"Yes." She smiled and folded her hands. "Hind and Sheikh Rashid are eager to welcome you."

His answer was cut off by the returning flight attendant, who complimented Val's dress, helped her fasten her seatbelt and put their seats back into the upright position. Then they were making a slow, leisurely descent into a blazing sunset, with Val leaning over him and smelling sweetly of a floral scent.

"Do you see how the sun shimmers on the water, just like that?" Her voice was hushed, almost reverent, as if the landscape demanded it. "It looks like acres of gold, shining through the surface of the sea. A philosopher explored here in the eighteenth century and described the famous sunsets, and that's how the country got its name. And there—" she indicated a string of irregularly shaped round islands "—that's Lulu Island, on account of it looking like a woman's pearl necklace. The mainland is that big one, right in the center. The old pearling port is there, and see that dome? That's the Gold Palace, and the government buildings, and—"

"Hey," Desmond said quietly. His heart was thrumming in his chest and his eyes were fixed on the soft berry-brown of her mouth. "I did the research."

"Oh." He watched her throat constrict as she swallowed. *She's nervous.* He felt a surge of protectiveness. "I'm sorry. I just—"

"It's not a complaint." He was close enough to kiss her, if he wanted to. And he wanted to, so badly.

The thought was disconcerting, as well as felt so natural.

Bahr Al-Dahab looked even more extraordinary from the ground. The series of islands ranged from a twenty-minute to a two-hour drive from tip to tip and formed a semicircle that hugged the coast of Oman, which loomed purple gray in the distance, jagged mountains meeting desert, meeting crystal-blue water.

The airport was in the middle of one of the islands, and a troop of snow-white Land Rovers was there to meet them when they arrived.

Val glided out across the tarmac, smiling broadly and calling greetings; obviously, the drivers were well-known to her. It was fascinating to see her with this new confidence in her role as a trusted member of Sheikh Rashid's household.

The motorcade drove sedately up a long corniche with palm trees and carefully tended Gulf rose bushes on either side. They passed through downtown, with its skyscrapers in reflective blue-gray glass that seemed to kiss the sky; drove over the bumpy cobblestones that lined the streets of the old souk, where vendors peered at the cars' dark tinted windows, smiling and gesturing to their shops; snaked around the Culture Village which was dedicated to museums and sculpture and past the shining cream and marble domes of the city's first mosque.

The line of Land Rovers eventually left the city and made their way up a quiet street to a white villa in a contemporary style reminiscent of Palm Beach, perhaps. As they pulled into the reddish-brown flagstone driveway, the doors flew open and Hind stood there in a pink linen abaya, grinning broadly.

"Surprise!" she cried.

Val rushed to greet her, while Desmond looked past them into the villa. It was tastefully simple, with a pearl-white tiled floor and walls, and comfortable furnishings.

"Baba said you'll stay here while you're in town. Let me give you a tour," Hind said, setting off in a cloud of vanilla, jasmine, amber and oud. "Then you'll come to our place for dinner, and the driver will bring you both back tonight."

"This villa is for us?" Desmond murmured.

"Yes."

"And we're *both* coming back tonight?"

"Not now," Val said through her teeth. "We're *married*, remember?"

They followed Hind into the villa.

There was a bright, contemporary *majlis*; three bedrooms, including an impressive master; a large, modern open kitchen with a dining room with floor-to-ceiling windows that overlooked the sea. Val explained quietly that this was one of the many real estate investments Sheik Rashid owned in the country. This was one of the nicer, more modern neighborhoods, a place often chosen by young expat couples.

"I have an apartment on the sheikh's estate," Val added softly, falling a little behind Hind. "But with you in town…"

"Got it."

After the tour they freshened up while Hind waited impatiently downstairs, chattering into her mobile. The three of them then went to Sheikh Rashid's sprawling estate for a barbecue dinner, eaten outside in the garden, reclining on lush, embroidered cushions.

"Is this a good sign?" he asked Val under the cover of a troupe of traditional drummers, which were the evening's entertainment.

"What do *you* think?" she said a little acidly. She was a little preoccupied, he found. She smiled about a fraction of a second too late when something was said to her and looked at her phone more often than was strictly polite. She frowned down at her phone and he couldn't help mentioning it.

"Am I really that boring of a companion?" he asked dryly.

She started violently. "I—I'm sorry. This is inexcusable. I contacted Malik, through his family—texted his parents, at the last number I have for them. I wanted to see if maybe—"

Ah. Malik. The feckless husband.

He felt a flash of discomfort, one that took quite a bit of the enjoyment from the evening. In a quiet moment, he took out his mobile and sent a couple of text messages of his own.

CHAPTER THIRTEEN

DESMOND DIDN'T WANT to credit Malik Ali for his insomnia that night, but the evidence, unfortunately, was damning.

Desmond's team emailed information about Val's husband to him within two hours. It was almost laughable, how quickly they were able to locate him. The fool hadn't even been hiding well.

On paper he seemed harmless enough: Malik Ali of the Bronx, New York, married to Valentina Montgomery in Dubai, twelve summers ago. His lawyer had included a passport photo and a wedding photo. Desmond stared at the latter until his vision grew blurry.

So this was the kind of man that could get Val Montgomery to the altar.

In the picture, Val was wearing an ivory column dress in a style and cut that he recognized as being typical for her. A demure square neckline, her curves sheathed but not concealed in the least by the tight silhouette. Her chin was lifted and half her face was covered by a fascinator and net. Malik was tall, broad-shouldered, dark with an expression that gave nothing away. He didn't look like the type that would abandon his wife and skip town while nearly two million dirhams in debt.

Then again, Desmond didn't look like the type of person he was at heart, either. And when it came down to brass tacks, wasn't it about money? The fact that his motivations were somewhat noble didn't make him better than any other capitalistic grasper. And Val…

She was another man's wife, no matter how unworthy the husband.

"Run me through it," Desmond said to his agent.

The scope of the story was incredible, even though he was hearing it for the second time. She'd married him after a whirlwind courtship. There were debts in his name, with Val named as guarantor, and a period of nonpayment that had lasted a year, during which his visa had expired. He'd exited on a visa change to the United States, and hadn't returned. And when Val left months later, presumably to look for him, she was scooped up in the airport by the authorities, jailed for a month, and released when Sheikh Rashid bailed her out.

"Find out where her husband is," he said briskly. "Is there an Interpol case against him?"

"Presumably, yes. But he isn't high on their list. They have slightly bigger things to worry about."

Now Desmond eased himself from the crisp white sheets, barely disturbing them, then grabbed his laptop from its place of honor beside the bed. Out on the balcony, people were still up; he could hear chattering and laughter, could smell smoky green apple shisha and barbecue. He liked the bustle below him, liked to hear people's conversations. It distracted him from the fact that he was completely alone, alone in the midst of many. Perhaps that was why he'd felt such a strong connection to Valentina Montgomery. They had debts that had separated them from the world, although, unlike hers, he could never pay his back. Nothing could match the cost of human life, could it?

And Val was somewhere on the ground floor in her bedroom, presumably asleep. His body stirred, despite himself. He remembered the smoothness of her skin against cool sheets, the curve of her hip as she lay on her side, her long lashes resting on her cheeks.

And heaven help him, he missed her. He attempted a breathing exercise to calm himself: breathe in for four, hold for seven, exhale.

It helped a little. Not enough.

Despite the lavish dinner they'd shared only hours ago, he felt his stomach rumble. Not bothering with a shirt, he headed downstairs. He pushed open the heavy wooden door, blinking at the warm, yellow light spilling out.

Val was standing at the kitchen island, pouring a glass of suspiciously dark red liquid into a wineglass. When the door creaked she jumped, startled, liquid blooming red on her shirt.

"Oh, no. No, no, no!" She unbuttoned her white linen shirt and thrust the soft material under the faucet of the granite sink. Underneath, she was wearing a blush-colored camisole of lacy pink—no bra, he observed when she finally turned, looking flustered.

"Eyes *up*," she snapped, crossing her arms.

He was a little taken aback; then he laughed out loud, and the sound dispelled the tension in the room just a little. After all, he *had* been looking. "Sorry."

"At least you didn't deny it." For a moment, she looked as prim as possible, then she lifted her chin and slowly dropped her arms. "I couldn't sleep."

"Neither could I." He crossed over to the fridge and picked up a foil-covered tray that looked interestingly lumpy; when he lifted the corner he saw that it was indeed the lamb from earlier. "Leftovers?" He tossed the tray onto the island, pulled the first bone off and ripped into it with his teeth.

Val cleared her throat, looking much more flustered than when he'd surprised her. She self-consciously yanked up the neckline of her camisole.

He wanted to tell her not to bother. Her nipples were dark and swollen and looked as if they were trying their best to break the confines of the thin garment and, frankly, the sight was just as erotic as when he'd had her naked, spread open, touching and tasting her with lips and tongue. But he dragged his mind away from it and instead said the one thing he knew would kill the mood and kill it *completely.*

"I'm working hard on looking for your husband," he said.

She startled to attention, her eyes wide as a deer's.

"I have some updates," he added gently. She looked at him, chewing on the soft fullness of her lower lip. "Have a seat. And don't look so terrified, sweetheart."

Between bites of cold lamb, garlicky *toom*, sweet ketchup and swigs of the bittersweet fresh pomegranate juice she'd been pouring when he'd entered the kitchen, the two talked quietly, side by side at the kitchen island, elbows and fingertips brushing occasionally. It felt incredibly domestic, even if neither allowed the conversation to veer in that direction. He kept his eyes on her face and she did not attempt to criticize any use of silverware, or lack of it. But the unspoken thing between them lingered like the woodsmoke from yesterday's barbecue, and Desmond did not quite know how to make it go away.

She asked about Malik in soft dulcet tones, and Desmond told her what he knew. His new home, close to the Canadian border, in New York State. His return to the horse racing business. The fact that he'd be notified Monday morning by email of her intention to file for divorce.

"If he doesn't contest it, you could be before the judge in

a matter of months," he concluded. He couldn't read her expression; it was tight, closed. "And it would be over, finally."

He waited for her to speak for a long moment. When she didn't he continued.

"My wish—my offer still stands," he said, simply. "Come with me to England, Valentina. Back to Notting Hill." His pulse was thrumming in his ears so loud it was distorting his voice, but he ignored it. "We'll go back and forth—together. And then we can marry—" He found he had to stop to swallow. "If it is still agreeable to you, that is—"

He couldn't continue. Instead, he drew back, trying to will the blood back from his burning face. Valentina was looking at him steadily, and her face was guarded.

"Desmond," she said, so quietly that he had to lean in to hear her and again, that delicious scent that was part of her skin hovered around them both.

If he touched that smooth skin the scent would linger in his nostrils well into the next day. He would not. He *could* not.

Her eyes were soft and warm and resting on him with an intimacy that he had to face. It had been there almost since the beginning; that had been *growing*, never acknowledged.

"Don't you see?" she said, gently. She moved close to him, cupped his face in her hands. "This—marriage, Desmond. What do you anticipate it looking like? Is there a possibility that you'll ever want more than this? And if the answer is no, is that fair to both of us?"

"Valentina—"

"I'm possibly in the most—vulnerable place I've been in a very long time. I can't guarantee I won't fall in love with you. That's the problem," she said. "And if you don't want that possibility…" She hesitated.

And then he wanted to respond the only way a man who

felt the way he did about her should: he wanted to pull her into his arms and kiss her. And possibly even say the words that were already forming on his lips. He knew in that instant why he'd so impulsively asked her to marry him, to come to London with him. It had little to do with Sheikh Rashid.

It was because he was so very lonely, had been that way for almost ten years, and was half in love with her already.

Desmond's face was transformed. It became tense. Unyielding. And at the sight of his changed expression, Val felt her own stomach lurch in anticipation of something she remembered all too well.

Rejection.

She knew the words, and what they would be, even before he said them. And she listened with only half an ear because something hot and loud and painful was roaring in her head. She could see his lips moving but could barely comprehend him—not that it mattered, because she understood his meaning without having to hear the specifics. Her entire being was engaged with keeping her back perfectly erect.

She was only waiting for the excuse she knew was coming.

His voice was tired. All of a sudden he looked years older, and it occurred to Val that she might be looking at the real Desmond for the first time.

"I know what you're thinking," he said.

Did he, though?

"You're thinking I shouldn't have asked this of you," he said. And then his hands were on her face, stroking with his thumbs, a little at a time, as if he were trying to commit all of her to memory. "I'm not in a place to do that. And to be honest, you aren't either, are you?"

She shook her head. Partially because she didn't trust herself to speak, partly because he was right. A lump was threatening to push past her throat into a sob, and she couldn't do that. Not after he'd opened up to her, been vulnerable with her, and not after he'd rejected her so thoroughly in the same conversation.

"You have," he said, and his voice was rough again, "captured my attention in a way no other woman ever has. You're the first person who's ever tempted me into thinking…"

The silence stretched between them like an abyss, and when Val spoke her voice sounded small and strained, even to her.

"Into thinking what?"

He was chewing the inside of his cheek, the way he did when he was thinking hard about something, and Val felt her stomach constrict and knot up. In the brief time she'd known him, she'd gotten to know his idiosyncrasies so well; Desmond was an open book if you knew how to read him, and that was incredibly attractive. More than the money, the looks or the incredible sex. He'd made her forget every bit of professionalism she'd cultivated and to which she'd clung stubbornly over the years. He'd made her forget the age difference between them, and throw caution to the wind.

She found herself pressing her thighs together to ease the ache; felt a pull of desire so intense it actually hurt. The ghost of a smile skidded across his face.

"You see?" he said.

Though her cheeks burned, she looked at him steadily.

"You've already been tied to a man who left you to repay debts he racked up," he said gently. "You don't need to carry my baggage too, Valentina. No one does." His fingers crept down, laced through hers. It was a very long moment before he spoke, and she didn't try, either.

She didn't know what to say.

"*I* am the reason my father was on that plane," he said. "*I* killed him, as surely as if I'd done it with my own hands. The least I can do is carry on the legacy he left behind. Make sure it isn't lost the way he was."

"Desmond—"

"I have to tell it all at once, or I won't tell it at all," he warned.

His voice was clipped, though not dispassionate; he was clear he was forcing out every word. "It was a budget airline. We took them over, to manage in-house. It was my first big project, right out of uni. Baba was so proud of me, his smartass son. I led advertising for that campaign. The flight was packed that day because of a promotion *I* ran. *None* of those people would have been there if it wasn't for me."

"Oh, Desmond," she whispered, her hand creeping up to her mouth.

His mouth had compressed into a thin line. "At least I can talk about it without throwing up now. That's progress, I guess. That memorial service? I go every year. No one's made the connection between me and that flight, not yet. People pointed fingers at the owners accusing them of corporate manslaughter and they got sued into the ground. But—"

"Desmond, it was an accident. How could you possibly think—?"

"The promotion I designed was a marketing stunt." He carried on speaking as if he hadn't heard her. "I called it Flight Forward Live. I recruited a ton of people to film their experiences, documentary style, on different flights that year, on their phones, and put it on our social media channels as well as their own. Influencers. Couple of sports stars. Our owners, even. The flight that went down was the one I'd assigned my father to film on. He was so nervous, you know? About the technology, about getting everything just right for me—"

"Desmond, you couldn't have known—"

Desmond gestured upward. There was a look of such desperate hopelessness on his face.

"He's gone," he said, as if relaying something that had happened last week and not almost a decade ago. A cry escaped Val's throat, and before she knew what she was doing, she threw her arms round him and held him as tightly as she could.

"I miss him so damned *much*," Desmond said, his voice rough and thick. "I couldn't live with myself. I *can't* live with myself. It consumes me, Val, every single damned day I have to wake up on this earth. Sometimes I sleep, and I wake up and I'm happy for a moment, and then I remember. My uncles, they blamed me, too. They put up a front for a while, but the bickering was too much, and they all left. I haven't talked to them since, but to hell with them. I've got this. I've managed without them for years."

"They left you," she whispered, and even she could feel the constriction deep inside his chest. "You were mourning, and they left you!"

"They were right to do so," he said bitterly. "I concocted the stunt. He wouldn't have been on that flight if it wasn't that stupid campaign I designed—"

Val tightened her arms around him and squeezed. She buried her face into the place where his shoulder met his neck. He didn't respond but neither did he push her away. When she finally pulled away, his face was as calm as if he'd never told the story; then, he cradled her face roughly with his palm.

"Don't you see, Valentina? Don't you get it? Fine, I'll say it. I can't love you the way I…the way I might have. Not when—Not when I'm like this."

I can't love you the way I might have.

Was he saying what she thought he was? She couldn't fathom it, couldn't breathe even, because he was looking at her with so much longing in his face that it twisted deep inside her chest.

"I hope you know how badly I want you," he said, his voice hoarse. "But I can't. Valentina, do you understand? It simply isn't fair to you."

She found her breath. "Who says you get to decide that for me?" she demanded. 'This is exactly why I can't say yes. You'll never give us a chance for anything more.'

"Valentina—!"

And yet— she wanted him. And in this close proximity, she couldn't pull back. She stood on her toes and wrapped her arms around his neck. And then, yes, oh, yes, he was pulling her against him and kissing her with slow, hot lips. He was murmuring things she could only half understand, and holding her trembling frame the way she'd been longing for. She was helpless beneath him. Well, maybe not so helpless. After all, it was she who stumbled back into her room, pulling him with her. It was she who tipped her head backward so he would have access to that soft, sensitive place on her neck that they both loved. And it was she who yanked down the neck of her camisole, freeing her aching breasts. She who whimpered "please" against his mouth. She who placed his hands on her burning skin.

Val didn't know how to comfort him, or what would help him accept it from her. All she knew was that the aftermath of making love to Desmond Tesfay always felt intimate, safe, familiar.

She wanted to grant him that intimacy now, and she knew instinctively that if he left the room now that wall would go up—and go up forever. She couldn't offer him more than this, but she could at least offer him this.

She likely would come to regret the impulsive, heated decision, but that was tomorrow's problem.

When her silken sleeping shorts and camisole had been removed and he was finally, finally inside her, she rocked her hips back and forth, trying to drive him deeper. Harder. Faster. She was so slick that it was hard for either of them to maintain control. He was groaning and growling in her ear, making sounds that might have been sobs were his eyes not bone-dry. And after, when he slipped from her and lay panting beside her, staring at the ceiling, she turned into him, looped her arms round his neck and did the weeping for him.

CHAPTER FOURTEEN

THE NIGHT OF Desmond and Val's marriage celebration party—spearheaded mostly by Hind—drove Val into unprecedented waves of anxiety. She was going to have to lie to potentially thousands on a public stage.

Seeing their faces definitely made it all the more real. And now, when she was supposed to be getting ready for the lavish party Hind and Sheikh Rashid were hosting for her and Desmond, she was sitting on the bed in her room in the staff quarters of the sheikh's estate, lost in a doom-scrolling session from hell. It'd been easy enough to find the story; one article led to another, which led to another, which led to yet another. Dreadful articles, with titles that grew all the more accusatory as the story moved from the investigation phase, to blame, to backlash. Desmond wasn't actually named in more than one or two, but the story and the airline's subsequent collapse were heartbreaking.

She hadn't seen Desmond since that night, at her own request. She needed time to nurse that bruised tender thing that had emerged from that night's conversation, and he said gently that he understood.

And she'd gotten her period, too, much to her relief. *That* was a complication that might have had her lose her grip on reality, at this point.

More than once she slid the solitaire off her finger, looking at it as if it were some foreign object. The thing *would* sparkle, despite all her doubts, even in the dark.

She'd never owned something so beautiful in her life. Desmond, it seemed, had a talent for making things beautiful, whether it was rings, or planes, or kisses, or—

You miss him.

Having seen this part of himself that he'd revealed only made her feelings all the more tender.

He couldn't love her the way he may have wanted to.

But that was practically a *declaration*, wasn't it? And Val had no idea what to do with it, only knew that her cheeks burned whenever she thought of it or of his face when he'd said it.

In love with *her*?

The thought was not nearly as terrifying as it might have been. If he cared for her in that way, couldn't she…? Didn't she…?

She countered this by trying to convince herself that he was right.

He was right, and she was practical to the core, even if her common sense had occasionally failed her. She would be sensible. She would ignore the throb between her legs. She would ignore the fact that she wanted nothing more than to follow him back upstairs, to wrap her arms around him, to let him hurt within the comfort of her embrace, to ask him to make love to her. She would ignore how much she wanted to sleep curled around him and wake in his arms. Part of her wanted to cry out that it could work, that she could make herself part of that life…

Are you delirious?

She'd finally been handed freedom, and here she was, doing her best to enter into another kind of bondage. The bondage of being wanted, but not being loved.

How could she settle, again?

And anyway, weren't all men disappointing, in the end? Even if they didn't mean to be?

Val was jolted from her reverie when the doorbell rang. Her hand flew to her throat as she hurried to answer it, then groaned inwardly when she looked through the peephole. Hind was on the doorstep with two attendants holding large metal boxes and a rolling case. Even through the peephole she could see that the girl was vibrating with excitement.

She sighed and pulled the door open, then yelped as the younger girl practically leaped on her.

"Aren't you excited? This is Gifty, to do your makeup and give you a facial—she worked for the Ugandan first lady," she stage-whispered. "Joyce will help you with your nails and hair, and we'll both help you get dressed. Ladies, come on," she ordered, kicking off a much-abused pair of designer mules at the door.

"Hind, this is absolutely not necessary."

Hind snorted. "Of course it's necessary. I've seen what you wear to Baba's parties."

"Hind!"

"Sorry," the girl said conciliatorily. "You're very pretty, though."

Val could only roll her eyes.

Taking this as assent, Hind commandeered every square inch of Val's modest sitting room, throwing open the black-out curtains to let natural light pool on all surfaces, lighting a Diptyque candle, setting up makeup lights and an enormous mirror, pulling out a tiny JBL speaker that flooded the space with a mix of American hip-hop, Khaleeji music and, bizarrely, Robbie Williams.

"I just love this song!" Hind declared, spinning about till

the ends of her *shayla* fanned out like the wings of a bird, setting everyone in the room laughing.

Val was touched by the girl's display of affection. It was something a cousin or a younger sibling might have done for her with just as much excitement at one point in her life, before she'd cut off her entire family for a man who'd done nothing but take advantage of her from the beginning. Afterward, she'd shut other people out as a result of the shame that had characterized her life. She had no close friends. She socialized occasionally with fellow staff members or members of the many expat WhatsApp groups she was in, but there was certainly no one who would go as far as to do this.

Val's bathroom was quickly transformed into a mini spa. Her hair was washed and oiled with products that smelled of lavender and the sea. Tingling preparations were smoothed onto her skin, left to sit and wiped off with soft cotton pads that left her feeling cooled and soothed as air penetrated her skin. Her hair was sectioned and then styled into soft twists and pinned into an elegant updo that framed her face with shining black curls. Hind's chatter required little response; murmurs were enough, and most were lost beneath the relentlessly cheerful pop music, anyway.

Dear Hind. In an odd way, her sweetness made up for every moment of exasperation Val had endured during the girl's teenage years.

She couldn't remember the last time she'd been so indulged.

Oh, wait, maybe she could. It was before her wedding, holed up in a midrange hotel overlooking the French Quarter. Then, she'd been surrounded by family and friends, none of whom she'd seen in years. Family and friends that had no idea that she was celebrating a pretend marriage today to a man they'd never met.

It was just…

How had she let this happen? How had she gotten to a place where she'd become so isolated? Malik hadn't only stolen her money; he'd stolen her agency, her self-confidence. She'd allowed him to finish the job her parents had started. She hadn't even tried to stand her ground with them.

Val picked up her mobile and toyed with it absent-mindedly. She could call her mother—she could call her right now. But how the hell would she even begin to explain what had happened to her over the past several years?

As if the mobile could hear her innermost thoughts, it rang so suddenly that she jumped, sending a jar of berry-colored powder clattering to the floor. She slid out of the room amidst Gifty and Hind's exclamations and scrambled for a broom and damp rag and went out onto the balcony, which was the only place in her apartment that wasn't currently jumbled with beauty products. She answered the mobile on the third ring.

"Val." Desmond's voice was rich and low.

She said nothing.

"You all right?"

She took a breath of perfumed air. "Hind has been here for two hours. She brought *stylists*. She won't stop playing Robbie Williams."

"Robbie *Williams*?"

"She said she wanted to play something from my generation."

His laugh reverberated through her body. She closed her eyes. "You ready?"

"Absolutely not. I feel sick to my stomach."

"Keep your focus on what's important." He paused, and in that moment Val wanted to ask him how preparations were going for his pitch, and how he was doing, and if he was dreading tonight as much as she was and whether he missed her at all. She wanted to say that she'd read all the articles, all the stories, and her heart ached for him. But she didn't.

She'd asked for distance, and she would do well to remember why.

The Majestic Gold Palace was situated in a desert oasis a little way from the city; Val had made the trip many times before for one event or another. It was part royal residence, part hotel, part events center, part resort, and tonight, it gleamed for her in the soft purple-orange twilight, framed by shadowy desert sand. Desmond had sent a car to collect her about an hour before the event, and as the Jaguar crawled sedately up the road to the palace, Val pressed a hand over her chest, willing her heart to beat just a little slower.

Ground-level floodlights illuminated the sand-colored buildings and they gleamed in the twilight. Motifs of beaten gold representing the early days of Bahr-al-Dahab flashed and twinkled, and the main dome, the centerpiece of the estate and a marvel of architecture that had been studied for years, stood proudly atop the main building. It was decorated with soft mosaics that seemed to blend and change as seamlessly as the stirring of the sea. From where she was, it looked as if the colors were dancing across the fading sky. Val rolled down the window, partly for fresh air and partly to take in the heady smell of jasmine, balmy and sweet, wafting from the low bushes that lined the road.

Hind, thank goodness, had elected to travel with her parents, so Val was alone, which gave her time to collect her thoughts and do her best not to have a panic attack. The sheikh loved any excuse to throw a party, and the union of his daughter's companion with one of the United Kingdom's rising stars of business and enterprise was something to be celebrated.

The pathway leading to the entrance was lined with polished onyx and ebony tiles, reflecting more light from ornate jewel-studded lanterns that flanked the path. The metalwork cast dancing shadows on the stones. Lush plants in vibrant green also lined the entryway, including the jasmine trees for which the palace was famous. The driver passed through a stone arch with an intricate frieze racing round it, and she could see Desmond, hands folded, looking tiny against the massive double doors of gleaming wood.

There was no one else outside, except for a traffic warden in a white *candoura* with a reflective jacket over it. He was directing the cars to a side entrance. Only Val's car was directed so close to the front stairs that she could have touched them from the back seat if she'd wanted to. Desmond opened her door with a smile, the gesture taking over his handsome face.

"You made it," he said simply, and Val's body flushed with mingled shyness and heat. He drew her out of the car and his eyes skimmed her body—possessively, she thought—and that little flutter went up her spine again.

This, she thought, was not helping at all.

Her gown, chosen by Hind, was of the palest blue sprinkled delicately with a handful of midnight blue crystals. It fit so tightly to her hips and legs that she was only able to take tiny steps forward, tottering slightly in heels of the same shade of midnight blue. A translucent overskirt in the same color cinched in her waist and flowed out, giving the illusion that she was rising from a bed of mist.

She'd never worn something so lovely before. And now that she was close enough, she could see that Desmond's close-fitting tux was of the same midnight blue. Above it, his skin glowed brown and gold and she ached to touch it. And as if in response to what she felt inside, he laughed a bit shakily.

“Good evening.”

Had she ever seen him so awkward, so unsure of himself? She was disarmed enough to let him draw her close, and she marveled at how very natural it felt.

“You look lovely,” he said, reaching up and running the back of his hand down the curve of her cheek, well below where Gifty had accentuated the curve of her cheeks with blush, highlighter and tiny crystals that she assured her wouldn’t fall off.

“It’s all thanks to Hind.”

“And you smell…” He dipped his nose into the hollow of her throat, even as his hands closed round her waist, made tiny by the best corsetry that money could buy. It was distressing, how easily her body softened against his. This wasn’t for show because they were the only ones in sight. They were alone, and he seemed as eager to touch her as she was to allow him.

“Just practicing for inside, yes?” he said in such self-mockery that she had to laugh. It sounded unnatural, even to her. What a disaster they were!

But maybe for tonight, and tonight only…?

How many times, her inner voice jeered at her, was she going to use that excuse to justify falling into bed with him?

“Desmond,” she began, then stopped. The gentle knuckles on her cheek were traveling down, down to her chest, where her dress dipped dangerously low.

“Hind called and warned me you’d have a neckline that needed good jewelry,” he said, and there was a smile in his voice.

"I've an enormous ring. I don't need anything else."

"You're my wife, and every business magnate, socialite and princess will be in attendance this evening." He paused. "This isn't just for us—this is about the deal. His Excellency accepted my proposal yesterday."

"He did?"

"Yes, he did."

"Congratulations."

"Thank you." His voice was quiet and warm, and that hand of his was still exploring. The quiet hum of insects, the smell of jasmine, the gleaming door, the shadows, the dancing lights…it lent this night a fairy-tale quality that made her a little dizzy. Her breasts tingled and her awareness of him grew all the more intense. She flinched when she felt something cold and hard slide over her skin, but relaxed when she realized that he was fastening something round her neck.

"Sapphires," he said. "Turn your head—there are earrings, too."

She did so, dutifully, standing quietly as he took off her simple, classic studs and holding still as he put them in her ears. He dropped the earrings he'd removed into her hand. "You'd better put these in your handbag, if you've got one."

She did, numb fingers fighting with the clasps on her clutch. She glanced at her reflection in a dark window and what she saw was a woman so sophisticated she barely recognized herself. As if in a dream or a sequence from a surreal film, she saw Desmond reach out, turn her around, and lower his lips to hers. Softly. Assuredly. And feeling, she thought with a twinge of panic, not one bit like pulling away.

CHAPTER FIFTEEN

WAS THIS WHAT it was like, being so absolutely consumed by a woman that it drove out all other thoughts?

It was as if Desmond was floating above the realities of both their lives, elevated by the magic of the evening. His self-imposed seclusion from the world didn't come into play. The fact that this whole thing was built on a lie. Her marriage, for goodness' sake. He'd meant to stay away from her as much as he could, but he couldn't keep his hands—his lips—from devouring her skin and mouth any more than he could keep from breathing. He smelled vanilla and sun-warmed flowers and the distinct sweet musk of her skin—a sweetness that had clung to him in memory since their first encounter.

He didn't know how long they kissed in the darkness outside that palace of gold; all he knew was that it was something he'd longed for. When the doors creaked open and they sprang apart just in time to make themselves decent, and both laughter and applause spilled out onto the entryway, he glanced at her face, her lovely, starry-eyed face, and for the first time in almost a decade he wondered. He wondered if this wasn't something he might want after all, although he knew in his heart that he didn't deserve it.

Sheikh Rashid's round benevolent face beamed out at them; Hind was at his elbow, resplendent in rainbow-colored silk that drifted round her in bright waves. At her elbow was a gaggle of young women that Desmond recognized vaguely from local social media; the curly-haired girl, he knew, was from Egypt and married to a Jamaican real estate mogul, and a tall, thin Emirati woman in a lavender pearl-studded abaya had her own skincare line…

"Some pictures, please, maybe?" Hind suggested, and they were lost in a haze of flashbulbs. Hind told them breathlessly that she was lighting up her stories with clips of the party.

"Don't tag me in anything!" Val yelled, to Desmond's amusement, but she might as well have been calling to the wind. Her charge was off in a cloud of Tom Ford and yet another bevvy of rich housewives were there to kiss her cheeks, to look critically at her dress and to whisper behind jeweled hands to their friends about the nobody from nowhere who'd managed to entice this handsome, wealthy young entrepreneur into marriage. They'd googled him of course. Aside from some very well-curated photos, his profile was as scanty as hers.

"Just let the girl have her fun," he whispered in her ear after the last of the well-wishes had been shared and the ladies melted into the crowd.

"I can't." He could tell that Val's teeth were gritted, even under the layers of contour and highlighter she wore. Her fingers were tight on his arm. "I'm married, in case you forgot!"

"You're also in Asia," he said dryly. "And trust me, almost nothing that happens in this region is going to register over there."

"I'd thank you *not* to make any generalizations about my country. And you're wrong." Val looked about ready to faint. "There was the World Cup, don't forget, and I was just approached by a producer from *Dubai Bling*."

"So?"

"So? It's on Netflix!"

"I'll ensure any stories stay buried," he said.

"You can't. That's not how social media works." She looked resigned now, although she was still fingering the sapphires at her neck as if they were choking her. "I hate secrets," she said, her voice wavering as if she were near tears.

Desmond paused as his stomach constricted into a knot. He grabbed her wrist to get her attention, and she turned to face him.

"I hate parties," he said, and smiled down at her. The corners of her mouth flickered up in return.

"Ask Hind not to mention you by name or post anything with your face in full shot. People do it all the time. It'll be okay."

She didn't look convinced, but at least she nodded.

"Now, come on. The least you can do is enjoy your own party, honey."

"Don't call me that."

"Why not? You're warm. You're sweet. And, sometimes, yes, you're quite sticky—"

"Desmond!"

"I'm only a man, and you've left me with some absolutely delightful memories."

She let out a mortified snort, but her eyes had brightened. He sighed in relief.

Bullet dodged, at least for now. And the absurdity of this party would do much to remind him that this was all fake.

And that the fact that he was in love with Valentina—he couldn't think of her as Val again—could not matter. He mentally ran through the list of justifications he'd been turning over in his mind for days.

He was a mess.

Valentina was finally escaping one horrible relationship. It wouldn't be fair to ask her to get into another, especially when he had so little to offer.

Sheikh Rashid had spared no expense on this event; the older man loved to host, and every moment had been carefully curated to ensure that his guests had the best possible time. A string orchestra with harps, tinkling bells and traditional strings played in the palace's lush gardens. There was the main hall where dancers, jugglers and illusionists wandered through groups of people, entertaining as they went, and small hidden corners for guests that wanted more private conversation, and a women-only hall for some of the more conservative female guests to meet, gossip and adjust their scarves to show off the magnificent dresses they wore underneath.

Instead of a big sit-down dinner, tables set for eating were scattered throughout the ground floor so attendees could load their plates and cluster round their friends and family members. It felt, all in all, like a real wedding. The sheikh blustered through an overlong but good-natured, fatherly speech and released his guests to an evening of entertainment.

Desmond shook hands until his own felt quite numb. He kept an eye on Valentina the whole time. She was as serene as always, beautiful in her gown, and gracious toward everyone who greeted her. She did not protest when he tucked her hand in the crook of his arm, and instead leaned into him, her warm body relaxing against his body as it had done so many times before.

Mine.

It wasn't true though, was it? Not by a long shot. And yet, this, tonight, felt very real. He squeezed her waist—he loved the way her body curved, the valley of softness and warmth that was there—and felt the stirrings of arousal. He grasped for a line of conversation that would distract him.

"How does it feel to be the center of attention?" Desmond said.

"Awful," Val said, and he was surprised to see that she was very near tears. He put his arms around her, turning ever so slightly to shield her as much as he could. He began to sway gently to the music of the harp, and pressed his cheek close to hers.

"You look so beautiful," he said. It was honestly the first thing that came to his mind.

"Desmond!" her eyebrows came together.

He laughed, but the sound had no humor behind it. "Perhaps we should go somewhere quieter so we can talk?"

Val stared at him disbelievingly for a minute, then picked up her skirts and strode off as quickly as they would allow. It wasn't easy finding a place; it seemed that the party had grown fuller by the moment. Val finally shooed away a teenage couple who were canoodling in a palm tree–festooned corner and they scuttled away like rabbits. She turned on Desmond.

"Well?"

"You're free. Officially. Your debts have been paid."

Val's hand flew to cover her mouth; her eyes were wide and dark. "That's impossible."

"No, it's not. I facilitated it myself a few days ago."

"A few days—" Val's voice broke off. "But how—?"

"We had a bargain, sweetheart." The endearment rolled off his tongue so easily; he almost bit it at the slip.

Val hadn't noticed. She pressed her hands to her face then jumped a little when she was greeted by one of the daughters of the sultan of Brunei.

"Not here," she replied softly. She greeted people, posed elegantly for a couple of pictures, and made small talk. She went to Sheikh Rashid and kissed his wrinkled cheek, and hugged Hind.

"*Mabrook*, dear," Sheikh Rashid said warmly. "You know, Desmond, she's a very good girl. I've often wished she would settle down with someone like you who can take care of her."

Val's polite smile was fixed.

"You've hit almost half a million followers," Hind said excitedly, thumbs racing frantically over her mobile's screen.

"Oh, Hind." Val's face settled into the first genuine smile he'd seen since they'd spoken in the alcove. "Stop making reels for a minute and look at me, lovely."

Hind's eyes were bright above her pointed chin. "Thank you for making this night so beautiful," she said, and the girl beamed.

"Oh, Val, I know I'm a brat sometimes, but I hope I'll have what you have one day." She paused. "Well, not like him exactly, he's not my type at all."

Excuse me? Despite his discomfort, Desmond raised his brows.

"No offense."

"None taken."

"I mean, you're tall and all, but you're also very slim and I like men who are—"

Sheikh Rashid tactfully cut off Desmond's sputtering defense about green juice and CrossFit. "Desmond, I'll see you first thing tomorrow, so we can put this bride to bed. You can deal with the other bride tonight." And, chuckling at his own wit, he walked off with Hind, who made a gagging face over her left shoulder.

The party had reached that lazy, languid point where people are softened by food, drink and conversation. Even the music seemed quieter. It was a good time to leave, and Desmond placed his hand on her lower back and bent to speak in her ear.

"Now?"

She nodded, and they headed outside.

Unlike the rather sedate, elegant gathering inside, the outside held the more cheerful partygoers; Hind had done her work well. People were milling about on the lawn of the palace entryway, taking pictures in front of the lanterns, dancing and eating canapés circulated by waitstaff in white jackets. All he could focus on was her face, however, and the fact that she looked—

"Valentina…"

She smiled a little, and he knew. He shoved his hands deep into his pockets, a dull knot in his chest tightening.

"London?" was all he said, and quietly.

She shook her head, once, quickly, and the first of several tears broke loose from her eyes. "Desmond—I'm sorry."

"I understand." And truly, he did.

She could not commit to him, not without the assurance of his love. And it was the only thing, despite his fortune, that he was too broken to give.

"Malik responded to your team," she managed, wiping her eyes. "I'm going to go home, Desmond, and finish what you were kind enough to start. But Sheikh Rashid–"

Desmond shook his head. He was the least of their worries. "I'll figure something out." At this point, to his surprise, he barely cared one way or another whether they kept the deal. It all seemed so—juvenile now, so unimportant. "Do you plan to quit?"

She nodded. "He's expecting it, I think, and expects that

I'll be leaving to—your home. To be your wife. He's not going to ask any questions, Desmond. You're fine on that front."

So he'd be returning to London alone, after all. He felt his shoulders sag with the type of weariness he hadn't allowed himself to feel in a very long time.

He should have told her this. He should have said it out loud, but his tongue was stuck to the roof of his mouth and the words didn't come.

"You're right," she said. The anger had gone and now her face was drawn and sad. "I'm not ready. You're not ready. I should actually thank you. You've made me less of a fool than I could have been."

"Valentina—"

"I understand you think it's for my own good, Desmond. Perhaps you're right."

CHAPTER SIXTEEN

VALENTINA LEFT BAHR-AL-DAHAB as soon as a replacement could be trained to help with Hind, clearance letters from the bank in hand. She squeezed Desmond's hand in a sisterly fashion, the same fashion they'd adopted since the night of their party, living on opposite sides of their villa, meeting in the middle for a strained meal once or twice, trying to prove to themselves that they were both unaffected. Promised to be in touch.

Desmond dropped her off at the airport himself. He didn't ask what her destination was, he didn't use any of his resources to find out, and she didn't volunteer the information. Her beautiful face looked drawn and there were hollows beneath her eyes. She didn't kiss him. She barely *looked* at him.

"I'll come back for any events you deem necessary," she croaked.

He shook his head. "I've put you through enough, don't you think?"

At that, she laughed, but it was a raspy, painful sound. "Yeah." She reached out a hand for him to shake as if they were business partners wrapping up a deal. In some ways, he supposed they were. He took her small, soft hand in his, and felt something hard against his palm. When he looked at it he had to clear his throat.

It was the vintage solitaire she'd picked out on that flight from London, what seemed like an age ago.

"You could keep it, you know," he said.

She shook her head. "You've given me enough."

It was true, in some respects, but it hadn't been enough, had it? He shoved his hands in his pockets and watched her hips sway gently as she walked away, disappearing into the airport security line. She'd refused his offer to fly her wherever she wanted to go, no questions asked.

It was probably for the best.

So Desmond went home and he got to work. Now that his relationship with Val had been completely dissolved, he saw clearly that the only thing that had been fake was his conviction that he'd be able to leave unscathed. Whatever they'd had, it had been as real to him as the blood running through his body.

Worse than that, he missed her. Missed her enough to wonder for the first time in ten years if there was something that could occupy his mind more than the Flight 0718 disaster, or the deal that was already pumping hundreds of thousands into his accounts. Never had doing the right thing felt so wrong.

He used long nights in the office and back-to-back meetings to keep thoughts of her at bay. But then, inevitably, his body would succumb to tiredness and he'd wake up dreaming of her.

He lay there hard and aching, his longing for her pushing out the faces of the victims from his memory that he'd spent so many years obsessing over. They were gradually being replaced by memories of laughing with her in his office in London, of sipping champagne with her in a gilt opera house, of chasing Hind all over London. And most vividly, that last night, when he'd pinned her down in the cool darkness of her bedroom, where she'd gripped him as if—

Something had broken in him that night that had allowed her to seep through the cracks and take hold somewhere deep inside. Part of him wondered if his bruised mind had merely replaced one obsession with another. The other part of him wondered if—and he could barely even allow the thought to skim his mind—if he had grown to care for her, if he *could* deserve her…

He could not complete the thought. Instead, he dove into the Sheikh Rashid project with an energy that left his team looking on helplessly half of the time as he tore through deliverables and made Sheikh Rashid look pleased every time he submitted a report.

"I knew you were the man for the job," he said, patting Desmond's arm, his face florid with satisfaction. He did not ask about Valentina, who he assumed was in her new bridal home, preparing it for their new life together; he did not comment on Desmond's sunken face or wild eyes. Hind, however, who had resumed her internship, did look at him from under heavily mascaraed eyes that were dark with curiosity. The teenager had surprised him these past few weeks. She'd showed up on time, paid attention and actually contributed to her team's project. His social media marketing manager had approached him about giving her more responsibility and perhaps featuring her in some content—she was the daughter of the owner, after all!

He avoided her to the best of his ability, but she lingered after a team meeting.

"Val hasn't been answering my messages," she said, by way of an opening.

Desmond had prepared for this. "She hasn't seen her family in a few years. I told her to go and enjoy this time off, and I'll join her later after your father's project wraps up."

Hind compressed her lips; she did not look convinced at all.

"You must miss her."

"You have no idea," he said truthfully.

Hind was still standing there, twisting her rings round and round on her fingers. She looked very young and very apprehensive. He sighed, inwardly. What did she want from him? Praise? He'd give it if it got her out of there quicker.

"I'm pleased with your work," he said after a beat. "Very fresh and quick-witted."

"Oh." She looked surprised, as if she hadn't been thinking of that at all. "Thank you," she said almost shyly. "I like it."

"You're good at it."

Another beat, and she was still there. Desmond sighed inwardly; it was ridiculous that a sixteen-year-old was driving him out of his own office but he really didn't want to continue the conversation. "Well. If you'll excuse me…"

"Did I mess something up?"

Their words overlapped each other. Hind chewed the inside of her lip, then repeated herself. "Did I do something wrong?"

"What do you mean?" asked Desmond, trying very carefully to keep his face bland.

"I mean, the night after the party." Hind's voice was growing softer and softer. "I didn't mean— It was all that social media stuff, all the attention, all the pictures…"

"Hind."

"It was my fault. I knew Val wouldn't like the exposure and I did it anyway. People were just so into her. Into both of you." She waved a hand in his general direction.

"I mean, you're like, so old, but *mashallah*, you made for some good content—"

Old? He tried his best not to look as offended as he felt.

Surprisingly, Hind took the hint. "And now she's not here," she said, staring at the ground. "I know something's wrong. Val *always* answers."

"Hind..."

"Do you think she's mad at me?"

"I'll tell her to call you," he promised, and unceremoniously ushered the girl out. "Don't feel guilty, Hind. It's self-indulgent and won't get you anywhere. As long as your intentions are good, you can feel sorry about how something turned out. You can learn from it, but you shouldn't feel guilt."

"But that's impossible," she said after a pause.

"It *feels* impossible but it is not actually impossible. You should concentrate on the lessons learned, not the fallout from what happened." As the last words left his mouth, he paused. Hard.

You could be talking about yourself.

No! the little voice deep inside his chest hit back, licking up like a flame he'd been tending for years. *She didn't hurt people the way you did.*

But was it really so different? Would he have reacted differently to Flight 0718 if someone had advised him the way he'd just advised Hind? Or, if he'd sought out someone who could help him work through the pain of what he'd done?

He realized after a long moment that he'd been holding his breath. He released it, slowly, then rubbed his aching jaw.

He knew exactly what it would take to get help. Hell, this wasn't his parents' generation. He had access to the best care, the best therapy, that existed, both mentally and physically. What had held him back was the fact that he knew it would hurt like hell, working through this—and that abandoning his guilt felt like abandoning the victims of Flight 0718. They'd suffered, so why shouldn't he?

Then, a still, small voice somewhere inside, a voice that had been stoked to life by Val's gentleness, spoke as if in a whisper.

You've invested so much in their healing. Why not your own?

Why not, indeed? He was looking at himself clearly for the first time in years. The years ahead stretched before him like a yawning abyss. What would they look like? Would he continually push away what felt so perfect? Had Valentina Montgomery and that one mad night been a catalyst for freedom for him as well as for her?

He hoped, but he was afraid. Desmond lifted his hands and ran them over his head. He could go and see her. Find her. Explain why he'd pushed her away. The memory of the way Val had looked at him during those dark nights in London when there was no turmoil, when she unfolded in his arms like a bud to the sun…

What would it be like, to return fully the affection he'd seen written all over face? What would it be like to be free to love her? What would it be like to deserve her?

Could he do it? And if anyone was worth it, wasn't it Valentina Montgomery?

It had been so long since she'd been in the States that Valentina felt like a stranger. Sand and desert heat seemed more natural to her now than the lush greenery of North America. Everything here was Technicolor-bright, blurring her eyes with expanses of green. Even the air felt different. And here, in her family home in New Orleans, a feeling that she'd missed so much was combined with an odd sense that time had stood still. It was home, but it wasn't *her* home, not anymore.

She'd vacillated between surprising her mother and letting her know in advance that she was coming. In the end, the prospect of, at best, an incredibly awkward reunion and, at worst, giving her mother a heart attack, she had decided to call. When she announced that she was coming to visit, her mother was completely silent on the other end of the line.

"Mama?"

"I'm here." Her mother's dulcet, buttery-warm accent sounded a bit garbled through Valentina' s mobile. "I'm just trying to figure out one, how long it's been, and two, why you want to come *now*."

"Mama—"

"I don't think I'm out of order, wondering about these things, baby girl."

It was the old name from her childhood that brought the tears up, and she snuffled them back. She was so tired of crying. She'd cried more since she'd met Desmond Tesfay than she ever had over Malik, despite what he'd done to her. "I— It's hard to explain over the phone."

And where would she start? Her stubborn insistence on marrying Malik? Her husband's mistreatment of her, and subsequent abandonment? Her time in prison for debt that was not her own? Nearly a decade working as a glorified nanny? And now—and this was her most colossally foolish move so far—falling in love with a man who she would owe for the rest of her life but could never repay?

Nearly forty years of consistently bad decisions, nearly forty years with little to show for it except her terrible taste in men and no idea whatsoever what to do now.

"Mama, I'm so ashamed," she whispered. "I haven't done anything right since I left."

The long silence that followed lasted thirty-seven seconds. She knew because she counted.

"Come home, honey."

And so, she had. Tired, jet-lagged, haggard, with no more than a single suitcase of belongings. When her Uber dropped her off in the driveway of the two-bedroom house where she'd grown up on North Villere Street, she'd tried her key in the door and found it still worked. And the moment she entered, she smelled the rich creaminess of beans. Fried fish. Honey-and-butter-laced cornbread that was crisp at the edges. Greens, with smoked ham. And there was her mother—a little thinner and looking a little more tired, with a mouth that trembled when she finally laid eyes on her daughter.

"There's time for us to have it out after this," the older woman said, her voice low and rich. "But, honey, let me hold you for a minute."

And when Valentina was enveloped in the softness of her mother's arms and smelled talcum powder, White Diamonds and the cool cucumber melon scent of the body lotion she'd been using since the nineties, she closed her eyes and lost herself in being loved, although she surely didn't deserve it.

She'd abandoned her mother as readily as Malik had abandoned her—and for what? Why?

Foolish, foolish pride.

CHAPTER SEVENTEEN

"I NEVER LIKED that fool husband of yours," her mother said decidedly two days later, and Valentina smiled inwardly. There was a time when she was younger, and even more foolish than she was now, that she'd have flared up and taken offense.

"You likely were right, Mama."

"It wasn't him, per se," her mother replied. Her words were as slow and deliberate as they'd always been, with a dash of something outside of her Louisiana accent—a confidence and emphasis on what she said. "Although he was as slick as a greased sow. It was you. You…shrank around him. You were shy already, and he was so strong."

Valentina smiled. "I didn't want to be shy. I wanted to see the world."

Her mother harrumphed. "You did, that."

"It wasn't all bad." Especially in the early days, before her husband's single-minded ambition completely took over. But then again, wasn't it really? She remembered long, languid meals out at opulent restaurants, designer bags, him nagging her to dress "younger," whatever that meant. Sex where she counted backward in her head, willing it to be over faster. Him calling her a lazy lay, no matter what she did. The fact that she'd never had an orgasm with a man until—

"It wasn't about bad and good. It was about his character. Even bad men do good sometimes. I was worried because you hadn't seen enough of the world to be able to pick a good man yet."

"If I didn't, it was because I'd never met one." Valentina had to swallow hard against a prickling in her throat.

"I know. I think my trying to keep you safe backfired a bit, in that. But there's no sign of him now. Are you going to tell me what happened?"

"I want to," Valentina said. "I'm just afraid I'll break down."

"You've always been scared of crying." Her mother's lips lifted at the corners, not quite a smile. "It's okay, honey. Let's eat."

She might cry anyway, Valentina thought ruefully, watching as her mother took a large willowware plate down from the cabinet, the same set she'd been using as long as Val could remember. It'd been passed down from her grandmother to her on her wedding day and would one day be Valentina's. She decanted a hearty spoonful of jambalaya from the battered steel pot on the stove, then set it in front of her daughter.

"I'll probably be in the mood to serve you until next week," she joked, then saw to her own plate. Valentina waited, hands folded in her lap, until her mother was seated, before she picked up her heavy silver spoon.

Flavors exploded on her tongue the moment the first grains of rice touched it: thyme, oregano, pepper—plenty of pepper, just the way she liked it; tender pieces of chicken; rich, spicy sausage; the subtle sweetness of tomato and Vidalia onions. Things she couldn't even identify, it'd been so long. The Middle East had every cuisine in the world available—she'd eaten cheeseburgers in Dubai, Thai food in Qatar, Nigerian food in Abu Dhabi, and American chain restaurants in all those places. But she hadn't eaten Louisiana cooking in ten years. Her husband hadn't cared for it, and after he'd abandoned her, she'd lost heart and hadn't wanted reminders of the family she'd abandoned for him.

"I've got corn, too." Her mother spooned *maque choux* onto her plate as well. "Fresh cream, from one of those farmers' markets all the young people are going on about."

"I always thought *maque choux* was such a fancy name for such a simple dish."

Her mother chuckled. "Eat up."

Valentina combined the corn and peppers with her rice, the way she had when she was a kid. She liked the candy-sweetness of the corn alongside everything else. As she ate, something was loosening in her chest—a knot that had been there since she'd arrived in Louisiana with a headache from crying on a sixteen-hour flight.

It finally allowed her to speak.

"He left, Mama," she whispered. And then the whole story poured out, her spoon clattering down on the willowware because if she took another bite she'd stop talking and might never start again. When she'd finished, the food was cooling on both their plates and her mother was staring across the table at her as if she were a stranger.

"So… Malik left you in debt," her mother said slowly. "And you went to prison? In the Middle *East*?"

She swallowed hard. Her mother's face was losing color. "Yes."

"Are we really so bad, that you couldn't phone home for help?"

It was very hard not to cry. "You had—I didn't—I felt like I was taking up space, Mama, after you married Russell. It was time to make my own way. And I made such a fuss about marrying him that I… I couldn't."

Her mother looked faintly sick.

"And then you worked as a *maid*!"

"A nanny, Mama." Valentina tried not to regret opening up about what had happened. "A companion. To young ladies."

Her mother ignored this correction. "And then you met a man that paid off your debts?"

She knew how it sounded. Val looked down at the table. When her mother didn't speak, she looked back up to find her mother was staring at her, something indecipherable in her eyes.

"You *pretended* to be his…*wife*?"

"Yes, ma'am," she said softly. The various colors were congealing on her plate and she chose to focus on them.

"Can you show me— What does he look like?"

Valentina looked up a photo from the celebration event and showed her mother. His head was tilted and he was looking at her with an intensity in his eyes that leaped off the screen. And *her* face…

Her ears began to burn.

There was a silence through which all she could hear was the ticking of the kitchen clock and the humming of the air conditioner.

"He's handsome," her mother said.

"Yes."

"I thought you said he was younger than you."

"He is. He's just…tall." Well, that and his experiences had probably etched years onto his face. But she didn't want to get into that now.

"Were you—? Did you—?" her mother paused delicately so that her meaning was clear.

"We did," Val admitted.

Her mother pursed her lips. "And you came running back here."

"It's not like you think, Mama. He was…he's a good person. I just, I couldn't…"

Her mother watched her flounder for a long moment before putting her daughter out of her misery. "Do you love him?"

Heat rushed to Valentina's cheeks. "Mama. No!"

"Huh."

Valentina took in a breath that exhaled on a very shaky laugh. "He's *entirely* inappropriate, Mama. He's younger than me, for one thing. He's just signed a big deal that will keep him out there, and now that my debts are paid off, I have nothing to do there anymore. And he…well, he doesn't want me."

Even as the words came out, Val heard how unconvincing she sounded. Her mother's raised eyebrows seemed to agree. She forged on. "He took me to the airport, and I gave him the ring back. He didn't stop me."

"There was a *ring*?"

"It was part of the ruse, Mama. Trust me. We both knew it couldn't work."

"Did you give him *any* indication that it was a possibility? That you wanted it?"

"Why are you being so hard on me?" Val burst out, and then began to cry huge noisy sobs, all the emotions of the past weeks breaking through the self-imposed walls she'd put up.

"All I know," her mother said, "is that you come home after nearly a decade, tell me this fantastic story about a man who cared for you when you didn't have anyone else, and you looked as if I'd punched you in the gut when I asked if you loved him. It's not unreasonable to think that maybe you do."

"Mama," Valentina managed to say through her tears. "I think… I *think*…maybe I do love him."

* * *

The heat of the Louisiana summer came as it always did with the bitter, oily smell of exhaust from the road and the heavy damp smell of rain that always threatened to fall. Summer brought a hum of mosquitos at night, hopping frogs, fireflies illuminating the sky and the slow creep of warm, swampy air that left a sheen on the skin and encouraged the mouth to hang slightly open to aid in breathing.

Valentina wasn't ready for it at all. It was different from the heat of the dry Gulf, and it caught her off guard. She spent many mornings on the front porch, sipping iced peach sweet tea and applying listlessly for local teaching assistant jobs. It was too hot to sew, too hot to go to Armstrong Park and too hot to trail behind her mother where she worked painstakingly on her roses and magnolias in the little garden at the back of the house, the old jazz standards her father had recorded years ago playing out of the scratched boom box she'd had since the early nineties. They'd been alone all these weeks; her stepfather, Russell, was away, visiting family with his daughters, and for that, Valentina was grateful.

Valentina brooded and dabbed at the perspiration trickling between her breasts.

"You'll stay here," she said to herself, "until you decide what you want to do."

She still hadn't told Desmond. She would, of course, but processing it all and thinking about what this new stage in her life meant took priority.

Part of her was grateful for this new beginning—making up with her mother, being free of debt and of Malik. The freedom to start a new life, on her own terms. But a part of her also mourned the loss of the *beginning* of something with *him*; the beginning of something she felt like she'd abandoned, despite wanting it very much. It was nothing like how she'd felt when she fell under Malik's spell back in the early days. Then, she'd quickly been overwhelmed by the force of his personality, coupled with her desire to be swept away somewhere that wasn't NOLA.

She pushed aside her laptop and sat up straight, taking another slug of iced tea. It seemed to pool in her throat, tightened by a nervous tension she couldn't explain. She pushed away her tumbler and picked up her mobile. Aside from a couple of texts from Hind, one from Sheikh Rashid's office about her severance pay, notifications from a food delivery app she hadn't read and a couple of responses from job-hunting websites, there was nothing. It was unsettling, seeing such stark evidence of her isolation over the past several years.

Enough of that.

She scrolled to Desmond's number. Their last exchange was the morning she'd flown back to the US. There was no acknowledgement in the messages of what had happened between them only hours before.

As if she had summoned him by thought alone, a bubble suddenly appeared under his name.

I'm in Louisiana.

Valentina stared at the phone, stunned. She didn't drop it, but she was close. Before she could gather herself together enough to call, he was texting again. Then she did yelp, because the phone rang, startling her so badly her hand jerked out, spilling the tea precariously close to her laptop. She snatched the machine out of the way of the expanding puddle and answered. "Hello?" If she'd had any doubt about her feelings for him, it dissolved as her core heated and her heart pounded.

"Valentina." His voice was low and restrained. They were both silent for nearly a full minute before she spoke.

"You're in Louisiana."

"Yes." He paused. "Don't worry, I'm not going to show up on your front step. Not without your permission, anyway. It was impulsive flying over without saying anything to you, but I'm happy to go home unless…" He stopped. He sounded so unsure of himself. "Unless you'd be willing to see me."

She closed her eyes.

"Valentina?" He hesitated. "Sorry. Val. You're just always Valentina, to me."

Being back home, where she had always been known as Valentina, had shifted something inside her, and that included the use of the name she'd rejected for so long. Perhaps it was part of her admitting that she was still vulnerable to love.

"Valentina is fine. Yes, I'm here." The hand gripping the phone was now incredibly sweaty. "And… I'm willing."

"I'll be real with you," Desmond said, and his voice was now so quiet she had to strain to hear. "I'd like us to go out, maybe to dinner, and…talk, I—" His voice broke off. "Sorry. I'm doing a terrible job at this."

"Yes," she said. Her heart was thudding so hard in her chest she could barely hear her own voice. "Yes, I—I can meet."

He was *here*! He'd come.

And need was, once again, clawing at her insides, just in response to the sound of his voice.

CHAPTER EIGHTEEN

IT WASN'T EASY, or grand, or beautiful or dramatic—it was none of the things that'd had his imagination in a choke hold since he'd heard her voice. As he walked through the door into the dim coolness of the near-empty restaurant, Valentina stood. He tucked his hands deep inside his pockets and slowed his walk so he could better take her in.

She was a little thinner in the face. She wore a sundress the color of buttermilk that glowed against the rich brown of her skin, and she was wringing her hands. She didn't say a word. And when he reached her and peered down into her face, when he saw the expression there and the way her pulse hammered in her throat, not to mention her eyes, and how they—

She crossed her arms. She was wary. Watchful.

"What are you doing here, Desmond?" she asked.

He'd thought he was ready for this question; ready to articulate what was in his heart. He'd practiced on the plane, for goodness' sake. But when she looked at him, all he managed to get out was, "I wanted to see how you were."

Disbelief crossed her face. "I'm fine."

"Have you…found a place? Are you settled here? Are you—?"

"Desmond," she cut in tightly. "I'm touched that you

came all this way to check on me, but I don't think it's good for either of us to—"

Damn, he was handling this badly!

"Fine, I lied. I'm not here to check on you. I needed to explain why I did what I did. I didn't have the words then, but now—" He stopped and collected himself.

Valentina was staring at him. Her arms were still crossed protectively across her front, but at least the anger had left her face.

It was time. If he couldn't speak now then he never would. She was worth it. He began to speak quietly, so quietly and hesitantly that he barely recognized his own voice.

"I'm not good enough for you," he said.

Something in her face shifted, something subtle.

"I don't know if I can…be with you without hurting you," he continued. "There's just so much that's messed up about me, Valentina. I don't know if I have the strength to work past it, or be what anyone needs. I know I don't deserve you. And you—"

"You always do this." Valentina shook her head, her face sad. "My ex-husband criticized me because I was never good enough, and now you're abandoning me because you think *you're* not good enough? You don't get to *decide* that, Desmond. Just like you shouldn't have paid off my debt without telling me. You claim you're doing things for my benefit, but you're giving me no say. That's not *fair*, Desmond."

Her eyes had begun to glimmer.

"You're such a good man, Desmond," she said. "Malik wasn't. But you do actually have something in common."

He stiffened, and she smiled a little.

"You're incredibly proud people. It just manifests differently. And love, love works because it kills pride, every day. It means you're naked to each other, every single time. You have to be brave enough to be vulnerable, and you can't do that." She chewed her lip for a moment and then looked intently up into his face. "You denied us the possibilities we could have had."

Desmond clenched his jaw so hard it hurt. Those soft-spoken words pierced him more effectively than the slimmest needle; he could feel them burrowing beneath his skin, threatening to break it open. And it must have shown on his face because she reached out and placed a hand on his chest.

"You've told me everything about yourself except what's in here," she said, and his insides contracted so painfully he had to turn his head away for a long moment.

"Desmond?"

Run! his senses commanded. And he could have; it would have been so easy. He'd get back on his jet and run for his life—the life he'd carefully curated for himself. But instead, he set his jaw and stayed.

Things had to change at some point. It had to be now or he'd lose this magnificent woman for good. So he'd do this, even though he felt physically ill, and his chest was tightening painfully.

"I wanted to protect you," he said after a long moment.

"You wanted to protect yourself," she corrected, and dropped her hand. She looked wan suddenly, as if the direction the conversation had gone had taken every last bit of energy from her. "I wasted years of my life with a man who hid so much from me, Desmond. I can't repeat that—I *won't*—no matter how well-intentioned it is."

They stood in silence for a long moment, her words echoing in his head.

You've told me everything about yourself except what's in here.

She was right, wasn't she? He'd given her everything but what had mattered the most. And he'd hurt her in the process.

He raked a hand over his head, disturbing the curls that had gotten much longer in the days they'd been apart. "Will you sit with me for a while? Please, Valentina."

Valentina was sure he could hear her heart thudding in her chest because it was echoing so loudly in her own ears. Desmond sat across from her, looking wearier than she'd ever seen him, but there was something in his expression that was new.

He's softer.

He smiled at her a little. "Is this the place with the lobster pot pies?"

The corners of her mouth tugged upward. "You remembered."

"I remember everything you've ever told me." A waiter materialized out of the shadows, seeing a break in the intensity of the conversation, and Valentina ordered two of the pies. Desmond added a bottle of white wine.

When she frowned at the extravagance he smiled and said, "I've missed that look."

"I'm sure you have."

It was surely too late to pretend that she didn't want him, that her heart didn't ache for him, and he wouldn't have flown all the way over here unless he felt *something* for her, too. The way he looked at her, as if she were something to treasure… The near-reverent way he touched her, even on that first heated night when they were strangers…

Desmond's fingers crept across the table as if to brush hers, but stopped short.

"Everything you've said is true," he said.

She let out the breath she'd been holding.

"I am too proud," he added. "I didn't give you a say. I'm sorry, Valentina. The last thing I wanted to do was hurt you, or to remind you of Malik. I should have talked to you and given you a choice so you could decide what you wanted for yourself."

She closed her eyes briefly. She was tired of thinking about Malik. He was in the past, and she only wanted to think about Desmond now.

"Valentina, I love you."

He said it so simply and without fanfare that at first she wasn't sure she'd heard him right. Her eyes flew open. His face was sober, but the intensity in his dark eyes stole her breath away.

"Desmond…"

"Do you really think it's so impossible?" He shook his head. "We *fit*, Valentina. I don't know if you feel the same, but I know I love you. I'm also a messed-up man from a messed-up family situation and I never want you to regret me. But you're right. I don't get to decide that. And I'm sorry."

He loved her He loved her, and he'd *come* for her.

"Valentina?"

There was a lump in her throat so large it hurt. "I'm just…processing."

They were interrupted by the arrival of a fragrant basket of bread with parsley-studded honey butter, and wine so cold the condensation slid down the side of the glass. The server decanted for both of them, then left.

Desmond picked up one of the heavy ceramic plates and scooped out a large spoonful. It was just as Valentina remembered—golden-brown pastry, rich, creamy gravy, and tender bites of sweet lobster. Her stomach growled in anticipation, but she couldn't put a bite in her mouth. Not yet.

"Desmond?" she said, and her voice came out so quiet

she wasn't sure he'd hear, but she was powerless to do more in that moment.

"Yes?"

"I'm not sure what we can be," she admitted. "It's so strange, things being different now. But I do know that I'd like to try. With you. If that's…"

Brightness flashed across his face, transforming it completely although his expression changed little. "Valentina!"

"It was such a whirlwind, the first time," she said. "I barely had time to register what was happening before I was married and gone. But this time, I want to do it right. We'll date—" the term sounded laughably backward and she winced even as it came out of her mouth "—and spend time together. I'm trying to repair my relationship with my mum, and possibly my stepfather, and that'll take time. And you…"

"I'm working on things. Talking to someone." He looked so uncertain—more uncertain than she'd ever seen him before. "I…contacted one of my uncles, as well, and we've been talking."

"Desmond, that's wonderful."

"It's strange as hell." He lifted his brows. "I'll tell you more. But later."

She nodded and her next breath shuddered through her whole body; the tension was leaching out, a little at a time.

Desmond Tesfay was in love with her.

"I love you, too," she said. "Let's eat."

They ate magnificently. They talked. They laughed. They shared.

For the first time, without any reservations or awkwardness.

And for the first time in nearly ten years, Desmond Tesfay felt at peace.

When they emerged from the restaurant the sun was setting in a soft mosaic of purples and grays and oranges, and the air had cooled.

"We should get back, before the mosquitos eat us alive," Valentina murmured.

He nodded. "My hotel isn't far from here."

She hesitated, just for a moment. "You could…come home with me, Desmond. It isn't far, and I'd love you to meet my mother."

"I'd like that."

She stood on her toes and tipped her face back, offering herself freely. All thought ceased; he bent lower, hovered over her upturned face for just a moment, and kissed her.

It felt so different this time. He still wanted her just as much as he ever had, but it was without the desperation of trying to hold on to something that constantly slipped through his fingers like sand. He'd never felt so free to kiss her with such tenderness, to take his time, to show her his whole self without fear of judgment.

And when she put her arms round his neck and tucked her face into the nook where his neck met his shoulder, he knew that time no longer mattered, not for them.

* * * * *

MAID TO MARRY

DANI COLLINS

MILLS & BOON

For you, Dear Reader,
for your endless love of romance.

PROLOGUE

Five years ago

MAYBE HER FATHER was right, Stella Sutter thought as she hurried to prepare more drinks. Maybe lying did send you to hell, because that's where she had ended up.

It had only been a little fib!

Yes, I have worked in a bar before, she had told the chalet manager. Because she had. As an after-hours janitor.

She had also worked at other chalets. *Those* managers had only ever asked her to make up beds and scrub toilets or, at most, brew a cup of coffee. This was her first week working for this new resort, which seemed to target a younger crowd with ads showing après-ski parties and hot tubs big enough for groups.

Stella had been thrilled to get on with them. They provided accommodation as part of their compensation package, which was only a shared room with three other girls, but rent was outrageous in Zermatt. She was grateful for whatever she could get.

She wasn't supposed to be here tonight, though. One of her new roommates had wanted to keep skiing with someone she'd met on the piste this afternoon and asked Stella to cover her evening shift. At other chalets, that meant tidying up after dinner and turning down beds, so Stella had agreed.

When Louis, the chalet manager, asked if she could stay longer to help pour drinks, what else would she say but yes? Her roommate had already bragged about how great her tips were.

They had better be. These people were hooligans.

At least a few of them must be famous, though. A photographer had tried to get her to talk about them when she'd been on her way in. She had said with all honesty that she didn't know anything about any of them.

Louis had since told her the guests were a father and his two grown children from the UK. The brother and sister were models for the family clothing brand. The son had been out all day and the father had left for a dinner date. The daughter, whose name was Carmel, was the only one here, and she seemed eager for everyone to get wasted off their faces.

"Girl!" Carmel shouted from the terrace.

Louis had cranked up the pulsebeat of electronica and opened the doors to the terrace, letting in icy winter air and the giggles and whoops of the dozen drunks simmering in the bubbling hot tub.

"What's her name again?" Carmel asked. "Sheila! Where's our drinks?"

Carmel was English, so Stella replied in that language. "Coming."

"She's coming," someone repeated, and they all laughed hysterically.

Stella didn't get the joke, but suspected it was dirty. They were making a lot of remarks that were outside the bounds of good taste. She kept looking to Louis to settle them down, but he only seemed to encourage it.

"Sheila." Louis padded in, leaving yet another trail of puddles for her to mop up. He wore only a small red bathing suit and his ponytail. He was at least ten years older than the group of twentysomethings. She had a feeling he got a commission on the bottles they opened, because he was not shy about ordering her to do it.

"Stella," she reminded him.

"Whatever. You have to get the drinks out faster." He was consuming alcohol as quickly as everyone else. "I thought you said you'd done this?"

She pointed to a tray. "These ones are ready."

"Just bring those bottles and the corkscrew. They don't care about clean glasses."

They didn't care about anything. They were trashing the place. Stella's roommate was going to kill her when she arrived in the morning. That's why she was trying to tidy behind these louts. They were impossible to keep up with, though. They were tracking water everywhere, spilling drinks and dropping food. She had a feeling one couple had gone into an empty bedroom. That bed would need stripping and remaking before she left.

She hurried outside to where the rectangular tub was set into the terrace, putting everyone's chins and shoulders at the level of her ankles. All the women had lost their tops.

Carmel was standing in the waist-deep water so she could display her breasts for inspection. Stella averted her gaze only to crash it into a pair who appeared to be having sex in the corner of the tub.

"Nine-point-nine," a man judged Carmel's chest. "Want a ten? Put them here." He lifted his splayed fingers with invitation.

Carmel laughed and pointed at Stella. "What about her?"

"Her?" The man turned his head to give Stella a bleary-eyed once-over. "She's a two. Too tall. Too serious. Too many clothes."

Gales of laughter followed.

Not for the first time, Stella questioned her wisdom in running away last year. Not that she'd been underage. She'd turned eighteen a week later. Technically that made her an adult here in Switzerland, but in her father's eyes, eighteen had meant she was old enough to marry a man twice her age and start making babies.

Stella had already seen how much responsibility children were, and how they hemmed a woman's choices. After their mother died, Stella had been the primary caregiver to her younger brother and sister until their father remarried. Even after Grettina joined them, Stella hadn't had a life outside of school and helping at home, especially after Grettina had the twins.

Escaping in the dead of night hadn't been her plan, but her father had forced her hand and she didn't regret it. She was doing what she could to continue helping Grettina and her siblings, sending money home when she could, though. She needed this job.

So she kept an unbothered look on her face and served the drinks. In the last year of carving her own path, she'd had a lot of dodgy experiences. This might be the foulest behavior she'd had to tolerate, but it was only one night. A few hours more at most. She could stand it.

Or so she believed. Until it got worse.

"I bet she's an eight under those clothes." The man traced a curvy shape through the air while eyeing her chest in a way that made her deeply uncomfortable. "C'mon, love. Strip down and join us. Show us what you've got."

Stella looked to Louis, who ought to be putting a stop to this harassment. He was settling back into the tub and Carmel was straddling his lap. They were kissing passionately.

"Someone has to get the drinks." Stella forced a smile.

"Pour mine then." The perv stood to hold out his filmy pint glass.

She had really hoped to see a tip by now—which she might if that man stood any taller in the water. This was dreadful, but she definitely wouldn't be paid if she walked out.

She took the cap off a bottle of beer and leaned out to pour it into the man's glass.

He dropped his glass into the water and, as she was reacting with astonishment to that, grabbed her wrist and yanked her into the tub.

Between the fall and the plunge beneath the hot, bubbling surface, and a very real fear that came from not knowing how to swim, Stella floundered in panic.

Within seconds, she was pulled up into the man's arms amid gleeful shouts of laughter. He grabbed her backside to grind himself against her pelvis while he tried to get his mouth over hers.

"Stop it!" She was still sputtering for breath and blinking water out of her eyes. She thrust her hand over his mouth, turning her face away while trying to fight out of his hold.

It was all a big joke to everyone. They were cheering him on—

The music shut off abruptly and a man's furious voice demanded, "What the *hell* is going on?"

Everyone fell silent in shock. For a moment, the only sound was the gurgle of the tub jets and snap of the bubbles while they all stared at him.

Stella's first thought was that he was younger than she expected from someone with such a deep voice and forceful personality. He was only mid-twenties. He wore a cream-colored ski jacket with black piping and black ski pants. His hair was short on the sides, curly on top, but the curls were crushed from whatever hat he'd been wearing. His black brows sat in severe lines on his swarthy face. His long cheeks were hollowed, his mouth hard.

"It's just Atlas," Carmel said with disgust. "My brother. I thought you were out for the night?"

"It's midnight. Are you all right?" His gaze met Stella's, then swerved to the man who still had his arms locked around her. "Let her go."

Stella was finally able to find the bottom of the tub with more than her toes and wade toward the steps. Her clammy clothes adhered to her skin and the icy air struck through them, making her shudder. She hunched her arms into her chest, teeth starting to chatter as the cold penetrated.

Behind her, Carmel mocked, "It's *midnight*? Who are you? Cinderella?"

"Where's Oliver?" Atlas shook out one of the towels Stella had left in a stack on the covered shelf and handed it to Stella, continuing to glower at Carmel.

"He knew I was having friends over so he went out." She shrugged.

"All of you get out. *Now*," he ordered.

"Ignore him." Carmel flicked her hand before she re-straddled Louis.

Atlas cursed under his breath and noticed Stella huddled in the towel.

"Do you have anything to change into?"

She shook her head. Even if they did have spare uniforms here, nothing ever fit her. She was tall and busty and, despite the number of meals she'd been forced to skip in the last year, had a very round bottom.

"Come with me." He shut the doors to the terrace as they walked inside, waved off her concern for the drips she was leaving on the floor, and led her down a flight of stairs into a bedroom.

She faltered at the door, never comfortable around male anger, even when it wasn't directed at her.

Atlas dug into a drawer, pulling out a folded pair of dark green joggers and a matching hoodie. He dropped them on the bed.

"Have a shower. Warm up. I'll get rid of them." He brushed past her.

The shower at her rooming house was down the hall. It was always tepid, always in high demand and always looked moldy despite the fact that she had scrubbed it herself with bleach.

At the very least, she needed to quit dripping on these hardwood floors. She locked herself in the bathroom and stripped off clothes that had been a big purchase for her very thin wallet. She wrung them out as best she could and left them draped on the edge of the tub while she showered.

Until she'd hopped on a train and gotten herself a bed in a youth hostel here in Zermatt, then began taking any housekeeping work she could find, she had never seen anything like these shiny chrome fixtures or these roomy shower stalls with their elegant tile work and fragrant shampoos. She had certainly never used one.

It was such a pampering experience, she could have stayed there all night, but she made herself hurry through it, then dry off with one of the warm, fluffy towels from the heated rack.

The clothes Atlas had provided were very good quality, making her anxious about returning them. The drawstring pants were too long and the pullover hoodie was a size too big. The neckline drooped open across her collarbone and the cuffs fell to her knuckles.

They were soft against her skin, though. Cozy. The pullover held traces of a woodsy cologne filled with subtle notes of smoke and cedar and leather. Wearing his clothes was an intimate experience. It made her feel enveloped by him. Claimed.

She shook off a hot shiver and squeezed her hair with the towel. She didn't have a comb and wouldn't presume to use his to re-plait it. She wound the length into a bun that she secured with the pins she'd removed to wash it.

She would need a plastic bag to carry her damp clothes home. There should be one in the housekeeping closet.

She strode back into the bedroom with purpose and nearly ran straight into Atlas.

He had his back to her and wore only his briefs.

"Oh!" She blushed as though she'd never seen a man half-dressed in her life when she'd spent the evening confronted by bananas in hammocks.

Look away, she ordered herself. *Retreat!*

But she was frozen in shock. Awe, actually. He had broad shoulders and a long spine. All of him was long and lean and his skin held a natural olive tone that was much darker than his sister's creamy complexion.

"They splashed me." His voice was thick with fury. He shot his legs into jeans, pulling them up over his muscled buttocks. As he closed the fly with a terse zip, he turned to face her. "I told them to leave or I'll call the police. They're like crabs in a bucket, incapable of getting out. I'm calling them anyway, to report that man who was groping you." He patted his jeans and looked around as though trying to locate his phone.

"No," she squeaked with panic.

"No to the police? Why not?" He jerked his head toward

the door. "Listen to them. They're out of control. I saw him assault you. He needs to know he can't get away with it."

But the police would want her name. They might discover that her father had reported her for theft—which she was guilty of, even if it was a petty amount.

She looked past him toward the door, wanting to leave, but accosted by her strong work ethic. The place was a mess.

He misinterpreted her expression.

"Don't worry. I won't let him touch you again." As a fresh round of cheers rose outside, he sent another look of disgust toward the closed door. He picked up a green Henley and tugged it over his head. "I'll throw him out myself. I'm looking forward to it."

Her stomach tightened with unfamiliar swirling sensations as she glimpsed the thatch of his armpit hair, then watched his muscled chest with his brown nipples disappear as the shirt dropped to finish hiding the path of hair that bisected his flat, six-pack abs.

She had never understood the mesmerized giddiness that other girls—grown women like those outside—exhibited around men. In this second, however, she had an inkling. Tendrils of admiration unfurled inside her, making her want to touch him. She actually licked her lips, confused by the intensity of the compulsion because it was so new. So strong.

"What's your name?" The timbre of his voice changed. The simmering anger was gone, replaced by gruff curiosity and something else.

She lifted her gaze to find he had one thick brow quirked. His mouth held a curl of amusement.

Oh, no. He'd caught her ogling him. She hated when men did that to her. Now she was guilty of it.

"Um, Stella?" she replied in a voice that squeezed through her tight throat.

"Um, Atlas," he mocked drily, and held out his hand.

Boiling in embarrassment, she took a nervous step forward.

The second his warm palm connected with hers and his fingers closed in a firm grip around her hand, she felt as though a jolt hit her heart, stalling it in her chest. A fresh flood of heat suffused her, this one vastly different from shyness. It had roots in the pit of her belly and moved outward through her limbs, leaving a sting in her nipples and between her thighs.

Which was mortifying. Nothing like that had ever happened to her. She only hoped he didn't know, but the way his eyes narrowed made her fear that he did. Which caused her stomach to swirl and tighten and her body to swelter even more.

"How old are you?" He slowly released her hand. His gaze was traveling all over her face, leaving a sensation that felt as though he traced her features with his fingertips.

"N-nineteen. Next week." She couldn't fib with him, not when his dark gold irises were piercing into her soul.

"I'm twenty-six." There was finality in his voice. Rejection? But he continued to study her face as though looking for answers to something. She couldn't tell what he was thinking behind his inscrutable expression. That she was too young? Too *obvious*?

She got distracted by his eyes again. She'd never noticed a man's eyelashes before. His were long and thick with a hint of curl. They would have seemed feminine along with his full, sensual lips, but his sharp cheekbones and rugged jawline balanced them out. She had never really noticed a man's lips either, but she found herself wondering how his would feel pressed to hers.

A fresh tingle of awareness made her start to smile shyly even though she didn't know why.

His expression altered. He looked away briefly, as though undecided. When his attention came back to her, his features were stiff with conflict, his brows low with dismay.

"*Are* you all right?" he asked. "I can take you home after I get rid of them."

"I'm fine. I was more upset about having nothing to change into. Thank you for this." She plucked at the front of the hoodie. "I'll bring it back in the morning."

"Keep it. It suits you." Satisfaction lit his gaze as he centered the seams on her shoulders.

"I couldn't." She smoothed a hand down the front, loving the fleecy feel of it against her skin, but the movement revealed that her nipples were stiffly poking against the fabric.

She shot a look upward to see his nostrils flare. He swallowed and pressed his mouth flat while dragging his attention back to her face. His hands slid from her shoulders to clasp her upper arms, not pulling her in, but not holding her off either.

Stella was the least sophisticated woman she knew, but she'd spent a year watching people her age hook up. She understood the small signals, even if she had never participated.

Until now.

She moved forward, feeling as though she stepped into a bubble with him, one that floated in sunshine while the rest of the world turned to rainbows.

"Thank you for..." She wasn't sure what she was thanking him for. The clothes? The rescue? This feeling of lightness and possibility?

She tilted up her face. She was too new to the mating dance to make more of a move, but it was enough for him to tighten his hands on her arms and draw her closer.

"Are you sure?" His thumbs moved restlessly, making the cotton shift against her arms.

She nodded, even though she wasn't entirely sure what she was asking for, only that she wanted to know how it worked, this thing called sexual attraction. She wanted to know how to kiss.

He bent his head and touched his mouth to hers.

That's all it was for three long seconds—a feathery contact that barely grazed her softened lips before she felt him start to retreat, leaving her stinging with disappointment.

A small sob of yearning panged in her throat. Her hands closed into the knit of his shirt. She pushed into her toes, seeking *more.*

His breath hitched, then his mouth opened with more hunger over hers. More command.

It was a fresh plunge into suffocating heat and blurred light and wild sensations that were panic-like, but also exhilarating. She didn't know what to do, which was terrifying, but he did. With a sweep of his tongue, he encouraged her lips to part and the intimacy of it sent a spike of delight straight into her belly.

Moaning, she leaned into him, offering more of herself to be consumed. She didn't realize she had pressed right up against him until his hard chest was crushing her breasts. His hands roamed down her back, ironing her tighter into him. She loved the strength and confidence in the way his hands moved over her, unhurried but thorough. She had the discomfiting urge to have her backside fondled, but she didn't know how to tell him that without stopping the kiss and she never wanted to stop this kiss. It was a world unto itself, one that was velvety and dark and perfect.

She realized that waffle knit and denim were abrading her palms. She was cruising her hands over his back with discovery while her whole body undulated in an attempt to get closer to his. Her hand brushed the pocket of his jeans, intrigued by the abrasion of denim over flexed muscle.

A gruff noise resounded in his chest. The world tilted. The side of the bed hit the backs of her knees and the mattress arrived at her back. She gasped and opened her eyes to the sight of him on one elbow as he loomed over her.

"No?" His expression was stark, eyes hazed with the same sort of spell that had been cast over her.

"Yes," she whispered, because she already missed the feel of him against her. She slid her hand into his hair and urged him to kiss her again.

He pressed his weight across her and plundered. It was glorious. Intoxicating. She met the dab of his tongue with her own, reveling in the sensation of falling in slow motion down a long, dark tunnel. She loved the feel of his hair! She sifted her fingers through the springy thickness and found the indent at the back of his neck and died a little death when his hand skated over her breast, then splayed to take firm possession and massage it.

A sharp, raw need combusted between her thighs. A dampening heat that *ached*. It was so intense, she heard herself whimper.

He rasped something against her mouth in a language she didn't recognize and buried his mouth in her throat. The undeniable shape of his erection was against her thigh. Never had she thought she would find that enticing, but she wanted to touch it. To be under him. She wanted that *there*.

A caress arrived against the bare skin of her stomach and climbed to her naked breast. The cup of his palm made her breast swell and tingle.

He lifted his head to look into her eyes as he scraped his thumb across and around her nipple, sending more lightning strikes into her loins.

"Let me see. I want to suck it."

The grit in his voice sent shivery prickles across her skin. The sheer audacity of what he was asking made her turn her face into his biceps and close her eyes. But her hand found the edge of the pullover where it was bunched against his wrist. She started to draw it upward.

As swirls of cool air crept across her torso, the door swung inward, letting in the noise of the party.

Atlas abruptly moved his hand to her back, rolling her protectively into his chest and cradling her there while his voice turned to a rusty knife blade. *"Get out."*

"See?" Carmel said. "He's right here, getting off with the maid."

What? Stella twisted against the band of Atlas's arms, craning her neck to see Carmel was sagged into the room, clinging to the door latch. She was dripping wet and clutched a towel to her naked breasts.

"Just like Daddy," she pronounced with venom.

Atlas pushed into the mattress, springing away from her and off the bed, slashing Stella with a glare of blame.

Stella sat up, trying to get her bearings, only then noticing the man with iron-gray hair in the hall.

"Really, Atlas?" the man said.

Stella's heart lurched from fresh shock to something more appalled. For once in her life she felt small, but in the worst possible way. Belittled. Looked down on.

"I told them I was calling the police. I'm doing it now." Atlas yanked his ski jacket from beneath Stella's hip.

She scrambled off the bed and tugged at the clothes she wore, ensuring she was fully covered.

"They're on their way." The older man sideswiped Stella with a lip curl of disgust. "Get rid of her. Then help me get rid of the rest." He stalked away.

"Oh, no." Carmel pouted with exaggerated sympathy while her eyes stayed bright with malicious laughter. "Daddy's mad."

"Get dressed." Atlas caught his sister by the shoulder and steered her from the room, nudging her toward the end of the hall and pulling the door closed behind him without looking back at Stella.

She clutched her stomach, feeling sick and humiliated and scared. Had that man said the police were on their way?

She peered out the door and saw Atlas had his back to her as he stood in the doorway to another bedroom. "Sober up and *grow* up," he ordered.

From another part of the house, there was a confusion of drunken giggles and terse responses.

Stella seized her chance to slip down the stairs and into the staff closet, where she jammed her feet into her boots and yanked on her coat. As she stepped outside, she could already see the flicker of blue lights bouncing off the snow-capped roofs below.

The photographer had been joined by another. They were smoking and one perked up when he saw her. "What's going on in there, love? Big party?"

Thankfully, Stella's hat was in her pocket. She jammed it on her head as she veered down a back lane to avoid those men and the approaching authorities.

It was a frigid walk home, one filled with shuddering

cold, distress and disappointment and confusion. Would she have given herself up to Atlas if his sister hadn't interrupted them? She hadn't dreamed that kisses and sex could feel like that. She'd felt helpless, not against Atlas, but against herself.

This was how it happened. This was how women found themselves in the snare of child-rearing and dependence. She was lucky his father had put a stop to it, she supposed, but she still felt denied and humiliated.

As if that bitter walk home wasn't punishment enough, she received another blow at dawn. Her roommate shook her awake and waggled her phone in front of her.

"What the hell happened last night? We've all been fired. We have to be out by nine."

CHAPTER ONE

Present day

COMING TO ZERMATT hadn't been Atlas Voudouris's idea and he already regretted agreeing to it.

Iris, his soon-to-be fiancée, had set it up. After dating for several months, they had needed a holiday away from their families and social circles and the prying eyes of gossip rags to discuss their future.

Iris's friend owned a group of chalets here, and in return for extending them a complimentary stay, Atlas would owe the man a favor. It was exactly the give-and-take connection he was marrying Iris for. He had no objection to that, especially because the paparazzi hadn't figured out yet where they'd gone.

Staying in Zermatt also allowed him to reach out in a very casual way to a sticky business contact, one who happened to be staying in Cervinia, on the Italian side of the Alps. Atlas had been trying to partner with that man for two years, but had barely managed more than an introduction. If he could finally grease those wheels, it might be worth the discomfort of being here.

But being here was uncomfortable. He couldn't deny it. He'd been agitated since their arrival last night, unable to sleep because he kept bumping up on a memory he'd been trying to shake for five years, one where he had behaved *just like Daddy.*

He'd made a pass at a woman who was too young for him. Maybe she hadn't been as inexperienced as he had initially judged her. She had been passionate as hell, completely undermining his good sense, but she had been in trouble with the law and she'd been one of the staff at the rented chalet.

That was close enough to messing around with a taverna owner's daughter to make Atlas want to go back in time and kick himself.

Which was impossible, obviously. Instead, he walked around with a splinter he couldn't dig out from under his skin. She wasn't even here! Young people moved through ski resorts like migrating birds, landing for a season before moving on to greener fields.

He didn't *want* to see her. As of last night, he and Iris had agreed to become engaged, likely to marry within the year. They would announce it in London this Saturday.

Oliver would be smugly pleased. He had handpicked Iris for Atlas, which rankled more than it should. Iris was charming and intelligent and beautiful. It didn't matter that Atlas wasn't particularly attracted to her. Passion was not something either of them expected from marriage.

They each had their own reasons for agreeing to it, though. For Atlas, it would give him a clear line toward taking the helm at DVE, the global conglomerate his father currently headed. Oliver's family had started DVE as a publishing enterprise two hundred years ago. Through the twentieth century, it grew into a media and broadcasting powerhouse, but would have collapsed under the tech revolution if not for the clothing line Oliver's wife had started before she died. The Davenwear athletic and wearable tech brand had propped up the rest of the company, thanks to Atlas's fame and his sister's notoriety. Once Atlas began climbing the ladder within DVE, he'd diversified into green and renewable energy, among other forward-thinking interests.

Taking over at DVE was more than a claim of his birthright—which was what Atlas's mother had urged him to do when she had sent him to his father at fourteen. No, after nearly two decades of investing every part of himself into DVE's growth and success, Atlas had earned the top spot. He could wait until his father died, which was unlikely to happen soon, considering Oliver was a very healthy sixty-four, or he could marry the woman Oliver had picked in exchange for Oliver's agreement to retire.

They would make their announcement at Oliver's birthday party at the end of the week, putting the wheels in motion for a transfer of power.

I'm getting what I want, Atlas reminded himself.

Yet he remained on edge.

Maybe if they'd gone skiing today, he would have worked out this restlessness. It was snowing heavily, promising fresh powder, but Iris was a fair-weather skier. Besides, after coming to their agreement last night, they'd had some shopping to do.

Atlas could have had the jeweler come to them, but despite five floors and ten bedrooms, the chalet felt claustrophobic. He brought Iris to the shop in the village where she had spent the last hour sipping mimosas and discussing designs with the goldsmith while Atlas mostly stared out the window.

He wasn't looking for anyone in particular. It was generic people-watching because it would be rude to work off his phone while his new fiancée ordered up a twelve-carat square diamond flanked by a pair of two-carat trapezoid-cut diamonds in white gold.

He signed off on the eight-figure price tag, then told them to box up the pair of ruby earrings that had also caught her eye.

When they left, she looked across the street to a boutique so he walked his credit card into the shop and left her there to browse.

The shop owner invited him to sit in their lounge. He could have ordered any food or beverage of his choice, but he claimed a desire to look at watches and walked down the street to the coffee shop.

Dissatisfaction dogged him the whole way, amplified by the lift of a camera phone as he passed a woman on the street.

Celebrity was yet another price he'd paid to Oliver for the benefits of being his son. Yes, Atlas had gained recognition on his own. His gold medals as a swimmer had earned him a healthy following online and modest sponsorships had flowed in, but Oliver had parlayed Atlas's good looks and athletic success into elevating the Davenwear line. Between that, and Carmel's weekly scandals, and the attention that his socialite dates invariably attracted, Atlas remained a magnet for media attention.

He ignored it as he always did and opened the door to the coffee shop, stepping back because a woman was on her way out. She wore a fitted winter jacket and a sky-blue hat and checked her own step, flashing him a friendly smile that fell right off her face.

His entire world skipped from its groove. Had he conjured her?

He'd forgotten how blue her eyes were. There was a lake in Australia that held that same saturation of blue, but he'd never seen it anywhere else. Only there and here, in her astonished stare.

Something flared in those mesmerizing depths, but it was quickly eclipsed by horror. She tossed him a begrudging "Thanks" in the colloquial Swiss German and brushed past him. She was carrying a takeaway coffee and a paper bag that presumably held a pastry, judging by the aromas floating out from the shop's interior.

"Stella." He let the door close and remained outside with her.

She halted next to one of the empty bistro tables, staying under the awning where the sidewalk was still bare. Beneath her short jacket, she wore gray plaid trousers tucked into tall boots. The wool fabric clung lovingly to the valentine of her ass.

"I didn't think you recognized me." She turned and offered a stiff smile. "It's nice to see you again, Herr Davenport."

He'd heard enough lies in his life to recognize one. And *Herr Davenport*?

"Voudouris," he corrected. "Oliver Davenport was never married to my mother." Reporters continued to mislabel him because Oliver did. In fact, Oliver had made it clear that the quickest way for Atlas to take the reins at DVE would be to adopt his father's name, but he never would.

"You look well. I hope your family is well also." Another lie. One so great, she had to clear it from her throat. "Are they here with you?"

"No." He ignored the opportunity to say he was here with his fiancée. The weight of that knowledge scorched like acid in the pit of his stomach while the rest of him drank her up like an elixir.

She'd come a long way from a soaked, ill-fitting uniform. Her clothes were good quality, her jacket zipped halfway so it flared open to frame her ample breasts.

A fantasy of mapping her figure with his hands, with his *lips*, arrived so suddenly it was as though it had never left. As though the craving had sat as unfinished business in the depths of his most carnal urges.

No. He was the rational one in his family. The one who *wasn't* driven by emotion and ego and libido. He kept all of that on a tight leash.

He was not *just like Daddy.*

"You've lived here all this time?" That thought annoyed him for some reason.

"Yes." She looked over her shoulder. "I run the front desk at Die Größten Höhen. Greatest Heights."

"I'm at Chalet Ruhe—"

She nodded with familiarity so he didn't bother naming the resort, especially because someone entered the shop behind him, forcing him to take a step closer to her.

She stiffened.

Now he was close enough that she wasn't backlit by the brightness of the falling snow. He could see her features better.

She looked very much as he remembered her. Her hair was hidden beneath her hat and she wore no makeup. She wasn't pretty in the classic sense, but he wouldn't call her plain. Her nose was narrow and her eyes widely set. Her upper lip was thinner than her lower, the corners of her mouth sharp, but he remembered exactly how plump and erotic her lower lip had been against his tongue.

Then there was that combative chin.

Why he found the thrust of it so riveting, he couldn't say, but he was both distracted and intrigued. She had had this same outward politeness and meek air back then, but like today, it was at odds with a bone structure that proclaimed she had a stubborn personality. It made him want to mine for the real Stella.

Which was a disconcerting impulse, especially today of all days. The edginess that had been plaguing him returned a thousandfold.

"I should—" she began.

"Where did you go that night? I was going to take you home." He didn't mean to speak over her, but he had always wondered if she had arrived home safely.

She must have. She was here, alive, snorting with disbelief.

"You left to avoid the police." He'd always wondered about that, too. "Is that why you kissed me? To keep me from calling them?"

"What? *No.*" Stella's stomach had been rolling like a cement mixer from the second she'd started to thank a stranger for holding a door only to come face-to-face with her nemesis.

How did he even remember her? Most people forgot her in five minutes. She might be tall, but she wasn't memorable otherwise. She was ordinary and deliberately quiet and had a boring personality because she never did anything interesting. She kept her head down, worked hard, and stayed out of trouble.

Yet here she was, faced with a man who had only grown more handsome over the years. He wore tailored trousers over heavy-soled, laced boots and a quilted winter jacket with the Davenwear logo. His jaw was clean-shaven, his hair shorter than it had been five years ago. Snowflakes were melting on his black curls and his eyes still held that compelling light in their bronze depths. His mouth—

Don't look at his mouth!

Her brain was zigzagging, trying to undo this meeting while her composure was just as confused. Part of her wanted to run away screaming. An equally unnerving elation pinned her feet to the ground while something in her sang, *It's you!* Which didn't make sense. She wasn't happy to see him. She low-key hated him and his family. High-key, really, because of all the hardship they'd caused her. The *shame*.

"Why then?" he demanded.

Why had she kissed him? He could pull all her fingernails before she would admit she'd been overdue for her first kiss. And that she'd wanted it to come from *him*.

"I thought the police might look me up and call my father."

"What if they had? How old *were* you?" he demanded with an appalled glare.

"Nearly nineteen. I told you that." She looked to the lid of her coffee to be sure she wasn't spilling any. "I took some money from him when I left. He was angry. I've since paid him back." She wasn't sure why she told him that. It didn't really exonerate her and it wasn't a good memory. Repaying her father hadn't prompted any sort of forgiveness. He'd never loved her the way a father should and never would.

"Being assaulted by drunks was preferable to living at home?" It was a grimly perceptive summation of her childhood.

She jerked her shoulder in a half shrug, then looked into the falling snow.

"I should go. I'm on my lunch break and I don't want to lose my job. Again." It was as spiteful as she would allow herself to be. This town existed on tourists, especially the rich ones. She hadn't risen to the position she enjoyed by talking back to them.

"Again?" he repeated, stepping forward to catch at her

elbow before she could turn away. "What do you mean? My father had the chalet manager fired. Which he deserved." His unflinching stare dared her to contradict him. "You weren't fired, too?"

"Of course I was. *And* kicked out of my residence." She closed her hand tighter on the bag holding her croissant and disdainfully lifted her elbow from his loose grip.

He narrowed his eyes. "Why?"

"Why do you think?" she choked out. "I only went into your room because you invited me." She leaned in even though the weather had reduced the pedestrians to near zero. "I didn't mean for anything to happen."

Heat consumed her and her voice wavered as she stared at the angry slant of his mouth. Those stern lips had ravished hers. His clenched hand had cradled her naked breast. His erection had pressed against her thigh.

"I didn't think *you* were a victim of anything," she continued shakily. "But I was accused of taking advantage of a guest. 'Fraternizing for my own gain.' Because you lent me clothes that you get for free, I guess? They refused to pay me the wages they owed me as punishment."

She'd actually been slut-shamed with a blistering lecture in front of the office staff when she'd gone in to protest. She still writhed on the flames of that humiliation.

"And now you've ruined my appetite!" She set her coffee and croissant on the nearest table, turned up her collar and stepped into the falling snow.

"Stella." He caught her arm again.

Some wicked, sinful, foolish part of her was thrilled. She twisted to face him, held her breath, pulse fluttering in her throat as she waited for his apology. Waited for him to say something meaningful. Something that told her he'd thought about her as often as she'd thought about him.

"That shouldn't have happened. None of it." He was speaking under his breath, his words a cloud of breath that was heavy with dismay. "I shouldn't have kissed you."

"Well, you *did*." She yanked her arm free, crushed and mortified with herself for that moment of— Oh, she didn't want to dwell on how adolescent her rush of hope was, wishing impossible things. "Leave me alone." She offered one final glare of rancid fury, then hurried away.

Did she feel like a coward for her retreat? Not really. Some fights weren't worth having. Sometimes running away was all you had.

She had worked hard to become someone who could get through a confrontation gracefully, though. That altercation had not been her best moment.

Usually, she was dealing with a guest who didn't really affect her on a personal level, though. Atlas was the opposite. As aggrieved as she'd been all these years, he was also the man against whom she continued to measure all others.

Which made no sense. He wasn't *that* special. She met rich, handsome men every day. Some even flirted with her. Why did this particular man stick in her memory like a burr? Had she been so young when she met him that she had imprinted on him or something? Because she had grown up a lot since then. She'd dated and kissed and…

Okay, that was it, because all those later kisses and fondles had left her cold. No one had ever made her blood simmer the way standing in the snow, in the street, arguing with Atlas Voudouris did.

She didn't want him stirring her up again! She'd already spent too many hours looking him up and wondering and wishing and dreaming…

That way lay madness.

But against her will, pins and needles were jabbing all

over her, as though she was thawing from that long walk home without gloves or socks when her hair had been wet and her self-esteem thin as a tissue.

It was painful. Distressing.

Her father had always warned her against lust and boys and fooling around. Sure enough, when her hormones had awakened under Atlas's kiss five years ago, her attraction toward him had gotten her fired and she'd lost her home. She'd tried to seek him out the next day, but he'd been gone, leaving her floundering.

The entire experience had left her cautious about her body's natural reaction. She didn't really think it was a sin to feel passion, but she had been glad on some level that her interest in sex had grown muted, allowing her to believe she was safe from suffering lust-related disasters again.

Other times, though, she had wondered if Atlas had left her a little bit broken. Which was deeply unfair, because she didn't know how to mend that sort of damage.

Now she knew he was here in Zermatt and all her stupid longings were reawakening, ones that not only wanted him to rescue her from this rocky journey called life, but even more, she wanted him to touch her. Kiss her. Would it feel the same? She was dying to find out.

She cringed at herself, running through every single word that had passed between them, picking it apart, trying to be happy that she'd told him to leave her alone.

Which he would, because he had said he wished he had.

What a horrible thing to say! She never wanted to see him again in her life.

"Why don't we have an early dinner?" Iris said when Atlas joined her for a drink in the sitting room between their two bedrooms.

He'd just spent an hour swimming laps so he was hungry, but she was putting more than a meal on the table. With her engagement ring on order, he had a green light for lovemaking.

No, thanks.

He flinched inwardly at his distinct lack of interest, especially because he definitely wanted sex. He was frustrated as hell. That's why he'd swum himself into exhaustion, but his libido was fixated on plaid trousers and a belligerent chin and electric-blue eyes.

He poured himself a scotch, trying to work out how to tell Iris, *I can't. Not tonight. Maybe never.*

It was a sobering thought, one he needed to look at from all angles before he pushed the button that would detonate everything he'd spent months—years really—putting into place.

And for what? A woman who justifiably hated him?

I only went into your room because you invited me. I didn't mean for anything to happen.

Neither had he. He'd arrived into the chaos of the party in time to see her yanked into the tub. Her uniform had been soaked and clinging to her generous curves, but it had been a uniform. He had averted his eyes from the thrust of her nipples and the way the fabric had adhered to the notch in her thighs. He didn't prey on the help and he didn't let anyone else do it, either.

But fifteen minutes later, she had walked in on him changing. She'd been wearing his clothes and they'd looked damn cute on her. He remembered trying to exercise some restraint, but she'd stepped into his kiss and…

He closed his eyes against the memory. He'd relived it too many times for it not to spring forth in vivid detail, though. Heat. Softness. The fit of her breasts against his front. The smell of his body wash on her skin. The brush of her tongue against his own.

Somehow, they'd fallen onto the bed. Her passion had fed his and he suspected they would have gone all the way if they hadn't been interrupted. He'd never been carried away so quickly or completely. Not before or since.

He'd never been so tempted to kiss someone as he had been today, to see if their chemistry was still as potent. It had taken everything in him not to follow her into the falling snow, pull her around and *find out*.

He probably would have gotten himself a knee to the stomach. Or lower. She'd been trembling with bitterness and he couldn't blame her.

I didn't think you were a victim...

He wasn't.

It was no surprise that his father had turned her into one, though.

Ironically, Oliver saw himself as the primary victim anytime something went wrong. When that happened, someone had to pay. Never himself. It was never his fault. It wasn't Carmel's fault, either, for accepting an invitation to stay in a resort that specialized in wild parties, then hosting a dozen hard-drinking strangers. It wasn't Oliver's fault for going on a date knowing full well Carmel would let things get out of hand. It wasn't even Atlas's fault for failing to return in time to put a lid on it.

It was the fault of the staff for indulging a woman who lacked stopping sense—even if that staff included a teenage runaway living on the thin edge of survival.

Atlas tipped his head back. He should have tried to find Stella that night. Or the next morning before they left. He shouldn't have allowed Carmel's "just like Daddy" comment to get under his skin.

But he had. Chasing down a maid would have injected truth into his sister's accusation, not just in their father's eyes, but his own.

"Atlas?" Iris yanked him back to the chalet and the engagement he deeply regretted.

He turned, expecting her to be miffed at his inattention, but she wore an appalled expression and was staring at her phone.

"What's wrong?"

"Carmel just sent me a link."

He'd been ignoring his own phone. It was one of the reasons he loved to swim when he needed to think. Nothing external could intrude, especially whatever nonsense his sister was up to.

"Did you tell her we ordered the ring?" He wearily went back to his room to take his phone off its charger on the night table. "I told you she would try to interfere." Carmel felt threatened by his takeover from their father. She had made a career of blocking all his efforts.

"No, this is…" Iris followed him to the double glass doors that separated his bedroom from the sitting room. Her glare was accusatory.

He touched the link under the string of Carmel's *Ha-ha-ha-ha!* Photos appeared. Images of him. With Stella. From today.

He swore.

"It's not AI," Iris said shakily. "Is it?"

"No." They were authentic photographs taken through the window by someone inside the coffee shop, the glare from the glass only causing minimal reflection to diffuse the clarity. They hadn't raised their voices, but he couldn't help wondering if the photographer had overheard them somehow. Had there been music playing inside the shop? He couldn't remember.

The post was already going viral.

The ongoing speculation over whether he would propose to Iris had primed the pump, ensuring a photo of him with a different woman would be high-traffic gold. That's why some enterprising tourist had begun clicking the moment they recognized him.

DVE's team of legal, PR and image specialists were already reaching out to him. He'd missed two calls, but they had a draft statement prepared. They were paid to protect Atlas, the rest of the family and the DVE brand so their response leaned heavily on Stella being a crackpot opportunist setting him up for her own gain.

He swore again, this time more wearily.

"Who is she?" Iris demanded.

He ought to say, *No one*, but he couldn't make his lips form the words. But who was Stella to him? Really?

On the other hand, "no one" was a tough sell when the panel of images ran the gamut from her forced smile of politeness, then her leaning in with a look of scorned anger. There was one of him holding her elbow, then another with his hand hanging uselessly in the air after she had shrugged him off.

The worst interpretation was that he had accosted a stranger in the street. Looked at with a shred more accuracy, it was a lover's spat.

"We met briefly years ago."

"Meaning you slept with her and ghosted her." Iris sniffed with indignation.

"I've never slept with her." It was the truth, but Iris wasn't having it.

"It looks like you did!"

"I can see that." He wasn't going to repeat the false accusations that Stella had fraternized with him for her own gain. What a mess. "But it's in the past—"

"No, it's not! It's happening right now." Iris jabbed her phone, quoting, "'With an engagement announcement between Davenport and Makepeace-Reid expected any day, another woman has appeared with a vengeance.' Why *vengeance*, Atlas? I said last night I would tolerate discreet affairs. This is not discreet!" She shook her phone. "And I didn't expect they'd start before we announced our engagement."

"It's not an affair." He bit back an urge to say she was overreacting.

"You left me in the boutique to *meet* her."

"We bumped into each other."

"Do you really expect me to believe that?"

Hell, he barely believed it. Iris was entitled to her outrage, but it was bringing down his carefully assembled house of cards.

As she started back to her bedroom, he asked, "What are you going to do?"

"Go back to London. What are *you* going to do?"

This was his chance to save their engagement. His only chance.

Go with you.

The iciest logic in his brain urged him to say it. To do it. He should go straight back to London, issue a statement that pushed Stella firmly under a bus, patch things up with Iris and take over DVE. That's what he wanted, wasn't it?

"I'm scheduled to heli-ski with Zamos tomorrow," he reminded her.

Iris's laugh was a high-pitched wobble before she delivered a stone-cold, "I'm keeping the earrings."

CHAPTER TWO

STELLA WAS PROUD of herself for not stalking Atlas online, not even when she returned to her small flat in the top of the four-story walk-up.

Looking him up was a bad habit she had largely conquered because the humbling truth was, she didn't need to. She had memorized his backstory long ago.

Atlas was usually described as Oliver Davenport's son from "a brief relationship with Rhea Voudouris," daughter of a Greek restaurant owner. At the time of his birth in Greece, Atlas's father had been married to an heiress who started a line of athletic wear as a lark, under the DVE umbrella. When she passed from an unspecified illness, Oliver took it over.

In his teens, Atlas moved to live with his father in England. He'd been excelling in junior games as a competitive swimmer, which explained his powerful shoulders and lean hips. Within a few years, he'd won three golds and a silver at the Olympics.

His good looks and status as an elite athlete made him a natural for becoming the face of the athletic wear line. Through his late teens and early twenties, he was often posed with Carmel, Oliver's legitimate child, next to pools and on rocky outcroppings atop mountains. Carmel was waif-thin and sulky next to Atlas's broody strength. They made a striking pair and Carmel's frequent scandals sent their images viral on a regular basis.

Over time, Atlas quit modeling in favor of working directly at DVE. Oliver was the majority shareholder and CEO, but Atlas was seen as his successor, which kept eyes on him as an industry titan worth watching.

Then there were the women.

That was the real reason Stella refused to look him up anymore. Every time she did, she was accosted by a photo of him with a beautiful, wealthy starlet or heiress. It shouldn't bother her, but it did, probably because it reinforced exactly how different they were.

Honestly, with the world as his playground and an army of foot soldiers to fetch and carry for him, she had to wonder what he'd been doing walking into a shop in Zermatt today, but she refused to seek answers online.

Because it didn't matter. He was dead to her.

Even if she did keep replaying their conversation, alternately wishing she had said more, or less, while also rehearsing what she would say if she ever got the chance to speak her mind again.

I shouldn't have kissed you.

If only *she* had said that to *him*, rather than letting him say it first. Why did it sting so much to hear it?

She was staring into her refrigerator, trying to decide what to make for dinner, when her phone began to ping and ping and ping.

Concerned, she picked up her phone. Not her family, but it seemed to be a work emergency. Her coworkers, including the evening desk clerk and the manager of the hotel, were all sending texts. Every message was some variation of, *Is this you?*

The links and screen grabs showed her outside the patisserie, arguing with Atlas.

"Nooo..." she groaned, flicking to scan the articles.

She'd been identified by name along with where she worked. Staff at the patisserie could have provided that information, she supposed. She was there several times a week.

But "a source close to the couple" was quoted as saying, "Atlas planned to propose to Iris while they were on holiday." An accompanying photo showed him in a tuxedo with a stunning woman in a gorgeous dinner gown. She was delicate and elegant and she was the daughter of a viscount.

Stella's stomach plummeted with inadequacy, then dropped again as she saw she was being framed as a home-wrecker, interfering in what was otherwise a fairy-tale courtship.

"Seriously?!" she gasped.

He could have said something about her when she asked about his family. Instead, he had jumped right into asking where she had gone that night—as if it was any of his business—and accused her of kissing him as a distraction tactic.

Now the whole thing was being twisted.

How could this be happening? No one at the patisserie would have suggested she was anyone's Other Woman. People who knew her knew she barely dated, let alone got involved with men who were committed elsewhere.

The evening clerk texted.

People are calling to ask about you. Someone just asked me where you live. I didn't tell them.

She was already swimming in outrage. Now she plunged into an icy pool of horror at the idea of being swarmed by paparazzi. She'd seen celebrities get mobbed while visiting here. It was horrible.

Hurrying to the door to her balcony, she twitched the drapes enough to see down to the street, but it was dark and the lanes were narrow and deep between the closely set buildings. It was difficult to tell whether those were locals and tourists going about their evening or someone more nefarious lingering in the shadows, hoping to catch her through the glass.

Ew…

She dropped the curtain into place and texted her supervisor.

I don't think I should come in tomorrow.

Agreed.

That was the swift reply. Then:

I notified Head Office. They're unhappy the hotel name has been brought into it.

"That's not my fault, is it?" she hissed, then quickly texted back.

Is my job on the line?

I'm not sure.

That was the heart-stopping reply.

That man. What an absolute life-imploding toad!

She didn't have Atlas's number, but she quickly found the landline for Chalet Ruhe. Before she could dial, a call from an unknown number came up. Then a text from her downstairs neighbor.

She ignored the call and read the text.

Are you expecting company? Someone tried to get in as I was leaving for dinner. They said they knew you.

Don't let them in, she replied, and began to panic.

The building was mostly used for short-term rentals. That last text had come from the ski instructor who had told her about this apartment two years ago, but tourists who were only staying a week would think nothing of letting someone in to knock on her door.

Her brain slipped into the self-preservation mode that had gotten her onto a train to Zermatt the first time. She threw her laptop and a few overnight things into her shoulder bag, then dressed for the cold. A hat with earflaps wasn't out of place. Neither was the wide scarf she layered up to her chin. At the last second, she thought to put on a different coat from the photos. This one was long and quilted, built for the coldest temperatures winter could throw at her, which she loved when she needed it, but it turned her into a shapeless lump of beige, something she hoped would disguise her on her way to the train station.

She would go to her stepmother's until this blew over.

Please let this blow over.

The twins' birthday was coming up and they both needed shoes. Beate's application fee for the music academy was due soon, too. Stella helped with all of those costs.

She needed her job.

As she trotted down the stairs, she heard voices in the foyer.

She had reached the floor where the ski instructor lived so she slipped down the hall to their door and punched random codes into their keypad, pretending to be entering while she listened for the footsteps to climb the stairs behind her.

Whoever it was took them two at a time then halted, making her scalp prickle.

"Stella."

She snapped around to see Atlas with his hand on the newel, one foot on the first step of the next flight. His gray wool topcoat hung open over black trousers and a pale gray turtleneck. He wore five-o'clock shadow and a scowl.

"I thought you lived on the top floor?" he said.

"How do you know that?"

"Unimportant. Come. I have a limo waiting." He sounded crisp and remote as he stepped back to wave her toward the stairs.

She didn't move. "You need to fix this. I might lose my job."

His mouth flattened. "Let's talk in the car. If my people can find where you live, so can the paps." He waved again.

She hesitated, wanting to talk this out but, "Is your fiancée there?"

"I don't have one. Go," he insisted with a point down the stairs.

She tsked. "I didn't even want to speak to you," she reminded him as she hurried down the stairs in front of him. "You're the one who turned it into a scene. Now—"

"Wait until we have privacy." He caught her arm to halt her as they arrived in the foyer. He glanced both directions through the glass of the exit door, then, with a curt nod, opened the door and ushered her straight into the open back door of a waiting limo.

He slid in so fast behind her, he sat on her coat.

The door slammed, and in a powerful move, he gathered

her and scooched her along, settling her just as quickly while shoving his hip against hers.

She was no delicate flower like the fiancée he claimed he didn't have. It was both thrilling and disconcerting to be enveloped by his long arms and powerful chest and the faint cloud of a fading cologne. He could easily overpower her and she was letting it happen.

She wiggled to settle into her spot, putting space between them, but feeling cold as she did. Wary and frightened.

The driver slid behind the wheel and was away before she'd found her seat belt, let alone her composure.

"Are you taking me to the train station? That's where I was headed," she said as she clipped.

"To go where?"

"My stepmother's."

"Where's that? Doesn't matter," he dismissed with a brush of his hand. "They'll figure it out and look for you there. Text her. Tell her no matter who asks, she should say, 'No comment.'"

"They're going to badger my family?" She had a flash of her father's reaction and cringed, then quickly texted Grettina. She said she would call to explain as soon as she could. "That's the train station," she pointed out as the limo shot right past it.

"That's where the photographers think I'm headed. We're going to Cervinia."

"That's four hours!" It was on the Italian side of the Alps, absolutely the wrong direction for her.

"We'll go over the top."

"The cable cars don't run at night."

"Stella." His tone was insulted, but he didn't say anything more because the limo was pulling into the heliport.

"Oh." That answered that. "But I don't want to go to Cervinia," she pointed out.

"You'd rather be eaten by wolves? Because I had to jump from an e-taxi to a limo to lose the photographers who were staking out the chalet. We have about five minutes before they realize this is where I was really headed. They'll see you're with me and everything will grow exponentially worse. Let's talk on the other side."

"This feels like a kidnapping," she told him crossly. One she facilitated by jogging up the stairs to the helipad that mostly serviced heli-skiing and sightseeing tours of the Alps.

Minutes later they lifted off. She was alone in the back seat while he was next to the pilot looking as though he knew what he was doing up there.

She took a few breaths, trying to calm her pounding heart. This was all happening too fast. Was he really saving her? Or managing her?

She shouldn't have come with him. It had taken a lot for her to become as independent as she was. A *lot*. But she had a good life in Zermatt. One that sustained her and allowed her to help Grettina. One that made her feel valued and secure and confident.

Now, as the moonlit Matterhorn slid behind her, she felt as though her connection to her safe place and the life that she'd built stretched and snapped like a rubber band.

She could get it back, she reassured herself. She had her ski pass in her wallet. That would get her onto the cable cars. A taxi around the base of the mountain cost the earth, but she had a credit card if she had to resort to taking the ground route. There were trains, too. One way or another, she could find her way home.

They didn't descend into Cervinia, though. Not the

proper part of the town. They landed on a private helipad next to a chalet built on the edge of a small lake on the outskirts. It was a mountain retreat that didn't seem to have a plowed road into it. Four people on snowmobiles were riding away from it.

How would she get anywhere from here? Snowshoe?

A flutter of panic went through her. This was exactly the kind of situation she had run away from—being under the thumb of a man who held all the cards while she had none.

Atlas hopped out and opened the door beside her.

"Come," he shouted, reaching to unbuckle her. "The pilot wants to get back to his dinner."

He helped her down from the helicopter and used the flap of his coat to shelter her as they ran from the cloud of snow that was stirred up by the churning blades. As soon as they were at the door to the house, the chopper lifted off again.

"The house is fully stocked, but I told them to release the staff," Atlas said as they entered to shake off the snow in the ski room. "My people will arrive tomorrow. In situations like this, I don't want anyone around me who isn't on my payroll."

"Like me?" she suggested, stomach tilting with the knowledge they were alone here.

She hung her jacket and sensed him stilling as he looked at her.

"That was a joke," she said.

"I know." A muscle pulsed in his jaw. He turned away to remove his own things.

She glanced down, wondering if she had something on her shirt.

She'd worn this cashmere sweater over black trousers to work today. Her wardrobe was a careful curation of high-quality consignment shop items. In Zermatt, designer labels often wound up in the secondhand shops. The trick was finding things in her size that flattered her figure, but she was a decent hand with sewing so she was usually able to alter something to make it work.

This pearl-pink pullover was simple and classy beneath the blazer she wore at work and she loved the feel of it, but she suddenly realized how closely it hugged her torso and breasts.

She glanced up again, but Atlas was stowing his boots on the shelf, profile stiff.

"This feels like we've pulled a bank heist," she muttered. "What the *hell*, Atlas?"

"Fun fact, that's not the first time I've heard that this evening. We need to discuss how we're going to respond." He held open an interior door, inviting her to walk down a hall past a glass-enclosed fitness room.

At the end was a flight of stairs next to a wall of glass that looked onto the indoor pool. Windows on the far side of the water offered a view to the snowy outdoors. A lounge on the end was surrounded by lush tropical plants, and sun-lamps were installed on the ceiling. Moody blue lighting reflected off the veined marble on the walls, making the whole place look magical.

An elevator pinged. She hadn't even seen it, but Atlas had touched the call button and the doors slid open next to the stairs.

"What's to talk about?" She stepped inside the elevator and immediately regretted it. It was too small. She could smell the winter air still clinging to his hair and skin. "Can't you make a statement that the photos were taken out of context and make it go away?"

"Those sorts of statements look really stupid if the other party makes their own statement that contradicts it. Have you talked to anyone?"

"*No.* Like who? Why would I?"

"For money? What?" His brow went up as she swung an affronted look on him. "You were unjustly fired five years ago. You might have seen this as an opportunity to receive compensation for that."

"I don't want compensation. I want to keep a low profile so I can keep my job. My *life.*" The doors opened, allowing her to stomp off the elevator in a dramatic exit, but she paused to get her bearings.

He came up behind her, not touching her, but making her prickle with awareness as he halted just as abruptly.

They took in the rooms that flowed one into another beneath exposed wooden beams. The decor was mostly white and earthy browns. Glittering chandeliers were turned off above a massive sectional, but Tiffany-style table lamps glowed in mosaics of violet and scarlet and amber. Cozy reading chairs were tucked into nooks beside the massive stone fireplace that separated the main living room from the dining room. The marble dining table had sixteen empty chairs and a floral inlay that was an absolute work of art. In front of her were huge windows and double doors that led onto an upper terrace and what was likely a beautiful view of the lake and the hilly dales surrounded by sharp peaks looming above.

The kitchen was an open space with an island and eating bar. Places like this usually had a professional kitchen on one of the lower floors where the bulk of food preparation happened. Breakfast would be served here and the chef would prepare meals here if asked, but it was mostly a place for guests to make cocoa and find snacks after midnight.

She moved to the refrigerator to take inventory. "Have you eaten?"

"No. I should have asked the staff to leave something.

Do you want a drink?" He moved to where the bar was in shadow and clicked on the track lighting above it.

"White wine, thanks." She pulled out milk, flour and eggs. Crepes were her standby when she didn't know what else to cook. "What would I even say?" she asked. "If I talked to reporters?"

"Exactly." There was a faint pop as he removed a cork from a bottle of wine. "That my sister held a wild party five years ago? There's front-page news." His voice was deeply sarcastic. "That I kissed you? I did." He shrugged it off as nothing, not looking at her as he poured her glass. "That my father fired you without cause? It's all true and does very little harm to any of us."

"Except me. They're already making out like I broke your engagement. My employer doesn't want to be associated with that. I've worked really hard for that job, Atlas. Can you *please* make a statement that your lack of a fiancée has nothing to do with me?"

"I would if it were true, but it's not." His mouth formed a humorless twist as he brought both drinks to the island.

"What do you mean?" She paused in reaching for the glass, heart swerving in her chest. "I didn't do anything! I didn't even know she existed."

"You're still the reason Iris went home without me."

"How?" Stella cried. The pink in her cheeks had started to fade, but rushed back in. That chin of hers was looking for a fight, but the tension around her eyes and mouth deepened with distress. "Is that really what you're going to say?"

"No. Probably not. I'm still deciding. Do you want me to cook?" He was even hungrier than he'd been when Iris had suggested an early dinner four hours ago.

"As if." She turned to set the crepe pan on a burner and pulled more ingredients from the refrigerator.

"I can cook." He was a grown man who had learned to take care of himself long before his father's staff had begun doing it. "My grandfather owned a taverna. I started working there as soon as I was tall enough to carry an empty plate to the sink."

"I'll let you clean up, then."

He leaned on the wall where he was out of the way, still skeptical she wouldn't want revenge for losing her job five years ago.

He was distracted by noticing her hair was longer than he'd suspected. It hung in an intricate golden braid that resembled a herringbone pattern. As she moved, it swished across her back, drawing him into a fantasy of catching it and wrapping it around his fist while he ran his free hand all over the cashmere that hugged her full breasts.

Damn it, what was it about her? Each time he saw her, he reacted as though he'd never seen a female figure before. Yes, hers was exceptional, but he'd seen many exceptional beauties in his lifetime. They'd been throwing themselves at him from the moment his first whisker had appeared. He was careful about how and with whom he had sex, but he had enough of it that he wasn't in a state of parched need for it.

That's how Stella made him feel, though. As though he would die if he didn't touch her. Like he needed to *have* her. The urge to stand behind her and bury his lips in the side of her neck pulled like a magnet.

"Why is it my fault that your engagement is off?" she asked stiffly.

Because he couldn't keep himself from looking for knicker lines beneath her trousers.

He made himself stare into his glass, doubtful she'd appreciate hearing his compliments on that front. Or rear, as it were.

"Our engagement was not official." He'd already had his assistant cancel the order for the ring. "It was more of a business agreement anyway."

"Really?" She glanced over, nose wrinkled with skepticism. Disapproval maybe?

He shrugged.

"Our fathers are friends." Iris's family was the quintessential broke aristocracy, desperate for an influx of cash. Oliver was eleventh in line for an earldom, so he considered himself a peer of the realm. He had this common, bastard son, however. One he wanted to elevate with a marriage into a titled family. "Iris is well connected socially, but I had concerns about how successful we'd be. She wants a man of leisure, whereas I've crafted my life around taking over DVE. I just bought a home in Greece, but she prefers London. In many ways we weren't compatible. Hence the separate bedrooms."

Stella paused before throwing the mushrooms into a pan of melted butter.

Yes, he had told her that deliberately. He wanted her to know.

The mushrooms began to sizzle.

The irony was, he loathed himself anytime he showed the least similarity to his father, yet he had been about to repeat Oliver's mistake. Oliver had married the woman his parents had put in front of him, then cheated on her with Atlas's mother. With countless women, in fact, but Oliver had learned his lesson after the first pregnancy. He took precautions after that.

Atlas wanted to believe *he* would never break his vows, but this hum of desire for Stella had lingered like a ringing in his ears. Now it was a cacophony crashing around his chest.

She glanced over again. “I still don’t understand—”

“My PR team wanted to issue a statement that would make all of this go away. For *me*. I refused to leave you to take the brunt of it.” That was something his father would do. “Iris read my reluctance as more significant than it is.”

“What were they going to say?” she asked with alarm.

“That you’re an opportunist who orchestrated the photos for profit.”

“Why are rich people so *awful*?” She flipped a crepe.

“I didn’t let them do it, did I?” No, he had made a few blistering phone calls, warning his staff that Stella was not a scapegoat. Then he’d told them to find her so he wasn’t leaving her to fend for herself against the inevitable deluge of photographers and trolls.

Iris had left for the heliport in a justifiable snit, reading plenty into what she had overheard. How could he deny his interest in Stella, though? He didn’t understand why he felt so protective of her, but he was.

While Stella seemed the furthest thing from grateful for his consideration or rescue. Her profile was stiff as she went into full production with the crepes: pouring, flipping, filling, rolling… All while stirring a pan of sauce and pulling roasted asparagus from the oven.

When she began plating everything, he topped up their drinks.

“This looks really good,” he said as they took side-by-side seats at the bar. She’d drizzled a creamy herb sauce across the mushroom-filled crepes, topped them with the asparagus spears and added halved cherry tomatoes on sprigs of basil. “Are you a chef?”

“I’ve taken sous-chef courses.”

"Is that the direction you want to go?"

"No." She took a bite, considered it, then picked up the saltshaker. "Before I left home, I thought I would go into accounting. I was shy and decent at math and I wanted to know how to handle money because we never had any while I was growing up. I had a crash course in finances when I got to Zermatt," she said wryly, handing him the salt. "But I realized a lot of little things could add up to better pay and opportunities. Bartending, first aid, cooking…" She waved at her plate. "I also realized I like hospitality so I took my degree in it, online so I could keep working."

"What do you like about it?" All he remembered about his time working at the taverna was late nights and a layer of sweat that felt like a crust while his mother complained about how sore her feet were.

"It makes me feel good to solve problems. Appreciated." She used the side of her fork to separate a bite from the rolled crepe. "And people interest me. I've realized that it doesn't matter if I'm shy or private. They'd rather talk about themselves anyway, so I just ask them about where they're from or what they do for a living." She shrugged.

"You're not shy."

"Because I've worked hard to overcome it." She closed her mouth over a bite of food.

"No." He rejected that. She was too confident, easily meeting his gaze—which many didn't have the nerve to do.

She lifted her brows in challenge.

"You dress tastefully, but in a way that allows yourself to be noticed and admired. You speak plainly and clearly. My lie detector says you're not being honest."

She gave a sniff of indignation and took another bite of food.

"Oh," he said with realization. "You're not being honest

with *yourself*." That was interesting enough to swivel him away from the very tasty meal to study her profile as her chin set at a militant angle.

"I think I know myself better than you do."

He bit back a laugh. He might not know details of her upbringing or her life in Zermatt, but he could read her like a book.

"You were born stubborn and assertive." It went bone deep. That was as clear to him as the modest gold hoops in her ears and the dismayed twitch at the corner of her mouth. "You were told to be something else, though. That's why you never felt comfortable in your own skin. That's why you ran away. Isn't it?"

"Is that Interpol on the phone?" She thumbed toward the desk in the corner, where a cordless landline sat. "Asking you to profile a serial killer for them?"

"Is that what you are under this good-girl act? A serial killer?" He waved at her. "*Prove me wrong.* Why did you run away from home?"

"I'll direct your attention back to the word 'private.' Which I definitely am."

"She said. Stubbornly and assertively," he mocked.

"Yes. I am stubbornly, assertively private. And you have destroyed my privacy with your fame. Or is it infamy? Either way, tell me how you intend to fix it."

He swiveled back to his own meal, polishing off several bites as he considered his options. Denying there was a relationship between them felt like a lie. The spark was there, still glowing hotly after five years of neglect. Power like that was dangerous. He was already too possessive and protective of her. He could tell that an affair with her wouldn't be as lighthearted as his liaisons usually were.

He shouldn't be contemplating an affair with her at all.

He wasn't a snob about dating a woman of means that were considerably more limited than his own, but he was highly conscious of the hypocrisy of it. His father had taken advantage of his mother, bowling her over with his wealth and status. Stella might possess self-assurance and ambition, but he knew which one of them had the upper hand here. The one with the house and the helicopter.

Besides, starting up an affair with her would push off his plans at DVE indefinitely. So no. He definitely should not have an affair with her.

But he really wanted one.

"Are you married?" he belatedly thought to ask. "Involved with someone?" The thought caused a cold wind to invade his chest, the kind that whistled through the cracks of a chasm.

"No. Why?" She gave him a side-eye of suspicion.

"Just making sure this isn't worse than it already looks," he prevaricated.

She carefully stabbed a cherry tomato with her fork.

"What if I do tell my side of it?" She fixed her gaze on the back wall of the kitchen while she chewed and swallowed. "I don't need to get paid for it. Your PR people could release it however they want, but it's true that your father got me fired and that's why I was angry with you. Doesn't that defuse the whole thing?"

"It might." Damn. Now that he knew she didn't have anyone else in her life, he couldn't keep himself from saying it. "Unless we have an affair. Then it looks like a poor attempt at hiding what they knew all along."

CHAPTER THREE

STELLA CHOKED ON her bite of tomato. She reached for her wine and sipped to wash down the acidic taste, then gave a little cough.

"What…um…?" She had to clear her throat again. "What gave you the impression I want to have an affair with you?" She tried to look condescending.

"You don't?" He angled to face her again, swinging his crooked knee outward so he subtly caged her. "Be careful, Stella. I have a very highly developed gauge for lies."

She tried to hold his unblinking stare, but challenging him put tension in her stomach and a quiver in her chest. Her face went so hot, she was probably as red as one of the tomato halves left on her plate.

"You want the truth?" She picked up her mostly empty plate and walked it around to the sink. "I wish I didn't hear offers like that as often as I do. I have friends who enjoy the perks of being someone's holiday fling, but I'm not one of them. If that's what you're after, try one of the apps." She held out her hand to take his plate.

Something was flashing in his gaze that she couldn't interpret. Not anger, but something very male and aggressive.

He slowly handed across his plate, but hung on to it until she locked eyes with him.

"I also recognize when deflection is being used to avoid

an outright lie. Speak clearly, Stella. You don't have to say yes to an affair, but if it's a no, *a hard no*, then say that. I'll drop it from this discussion and never bring it up again."

A million ants invaded her chest, scrambling around. She believed him. He was holding her gaze too steadily to be bluffing. He wasn't touching her, but he was gripping her in a way that demanded she be honest to the point of nakedness.

They were both still holding the plate and it seemed to conduct energy from him into her. The current traveled up her arm and into her lungs. Her throat became too tight to release the tiny word he had demanded. Her lips refused to form it.

Because it would be a lie.

Yearning had haunted her for years. What-ifs. She had buried them under anger and scorn, but they'd always been there in wayward dreams and hidden moments of reliving the most exciting kiss of her life.

That painful truth rose to make her skin feel too small for her body. Heat suffused her. Culpable heat. A distressing desire that only seemed oriented to him. It pulled dampness into her eyes.

"All right, then," he said quietly, and released the plate.

She set it in the sink with her own, clumsily, so the dishes clattered and jangled discordantly. Then she stood there, shaken.

"It's going to be okay, Stella."

"No, it won't," she choked. "This is going to ruin my life, isn't it?"

That was hitting her along with the harder truth that she couldn't pretend she wasn't attracted to him. He had all the advantage and it frightened her.

"*You* can go back to your life," she accused. "You're rich

and untouchable. If people ask you uncomfortable questions, you can get in a helicopter and go somewhere else. I'm never going to have that luxury. I'm always going to be the woman in the photos, the one who broke up your relationship. That is unfair, Atlas. I shouldn't be paying for one stupid kiss this many years later!"

She wasn't just talking about a kiss and a photo, though. She was talking about this other thing. This connection. Was it an obsession? She didn't know and she didn't want to examine it for fear of giving it even more life.

"It's deeply unfair," he agreed, coming around to her side of the island. "That's why I brought you with me. I'm going to protect you, Stella."

"For the low, low cost of an affair?" Her voice hit a strident note.

"No. I want that. Don't doubt it. But it's not a condition for my helping you."

"And how will you—" Her phone began to jingle in her bag. "That's likely someone in my family, worried sick over the headlines."

She leaped on the excuse to move away from him and catch her breath.

"Hoi, Beate." She switched to German as she accepted the call. "I'm fine, but I had to leave Zermatt—"

"Pappa's here," Beate hissed.

"At the house? Why? Grettina let him in?"

"He wanted to have dinner with us. He says he lost his job and his apartment. He says he has to stay here."

"*No.* Tell him I'll cover his rent."

"He owed so much he was evicted."

"He hasn't been paying? Why didn't he tell me?" She knew why. Because he hated that she wasn't beholden to him. He hated that she had defied him and forged an independent life and that she couldn't be manipulated the way the rest of the family could.

"He can't stay, Beate. You know how that will go." She started for the stairs, then turned back to collect her glass of wine, avoiding Atlas's frown. "Have you called Elijah?"

"He came when I texted that Pappa was here. He's trying to talk him into going to a hotel, but you know what Grettina's like." Their stepmother wouldn't put him out. He was the father of her twins.

"Is he really evicted? Or just playing on her sympathy?" Stella closed herself into one of the bedrooms, barely taking in the faux rustic decor of iron bed frame and refinished washstand as a night table. She sat down on the fluffy white duvet.

"They locked up his tools until he pays his back rent, but told him not to come back. He has nowhere to go. Oh, here's Elijah."

Elijah was the next eldest and lived at the dorm of the university.

"What is going on with you?" Elijah demanded quietly as he came on the line. "Beate said there are photos of you with a man?"

"Don't worry about me. What about Pappa?"

"I'm getting him a hotel, but I can only afford a few nights." Elijah had a little more influence over their father because he was a son and that earned him a shred more respect than the women in the family, but Elijah only worked part-time because he was in an accelerated engineering program at the university. "I can't keep him from coming back tomorrow when I'm in class."

"I'll book the hotel and put it on my card." Stella got a discount because of her job. It only worked if the affiliated hotel had a vacancy, but it made it more affordable. "I'll cover his rent if we can find a place for him. You and Beate search, too." She didn't bother mentioning it should be far enough away that Pappa would need to take a train or bus to get to Grettina. They all knew what was best.

"He's talking like he did last time. Adamant he should stay with his wife and children. Sanctity of marriage and all that," Elijah said grimly.

Grettina was too kindhearted to argue that "for better or worse" didn't mean she had to put up with his worst.

"I'd come to help but… That's the other thing. Paparazzi might turn up asking about me. If Pappa talks to them…"

"He won't. I'll get him to the hotel tonight," Elijah promised. "Is there anything I can do for you?"

"No. I'll book the hotel right now and send you the details. Give everyone my love." She ended the call and hissed out her breath. Then she took a big gulp of wine and tapped to book the room.

She had her own rent to worry about, but she didn't let those worries creep in. She sent the confirmation to her brother and told him to let her know when their father was at the hotel.

With heavy steps, she carried her phone and empty wineglass back to the kitchen. It was spotless. Maybe Atlas *had* washed a dish or two in his life.

He stood in the corner, hips leaned on the heavy desk. He set aside his phone when she appeared.

"What happened? That sounded like a family emergency."

"A small one," she downplayed. "I've dealt with it, but I should warn you. My father isn't online so he won't know anything about this…" She set her wineglass on the island and waved at the ceiling. "I doubt any reporters could find him since he's going to a hotel, but if they did approach him…" She shook her head. "He has strong opinions."

"How do I manage him?"

"The minute I figure that out, I will let you know," she grumbled, and hugged herself, already hearing her father's berating tone. *Tramp. Sinner.*

Aside from one moment of poor judgment, she had lived like a nun most of her life, yet her father took every chance to look down on her. A brazen, selfish girl. A disobedient runaway. A thief.

She was starting to think she might as well live the life he accused her of living, since he would never believe how chaste she really was.

Maybe that was a rationalization for something she longed for, though. She swallowed, but the sting of culpability remained in her throat.

"He's the reason you ran away," Atlas surmised.

"I don't want to talk about that. Tell me how you think you can protect me. Because I need my job." If he brought up an affair again…

His cheeks hollowed as he regarded her, then he reached for the drink he'd refilled and left on the desk.

"The most obvious way would be to find you an apartment with better security. It only took me two tries to walk into your building. You would need a detail of bodyguards, too."

She released a humorless laugh. "You're prepared to pay for that? And this bodyguard sits in the lobby while I go about my workday? The hotel will love that. *I* will." She gestured at herself facetiously. "That sounds very normal. Sign me up."

"I can find you a better place to work and live. What's your end game?"

"Career-wise? To earn my way up to managing my own hotel, not achieve it through nepotism."

"It's only nepotism if you're bad at it."

"It doesn't matter whether I'm good or bad! Having you support me does not convey to people that we only kissed once. I'm really angry with you, Atlas." There. Her conflict resolution classes were good for more than bolstering her CV. "You have put me in the impossible position of having to rely on you when my independence is very important to me. *Very*."

"Understood. I'm angry with you, too."

"For what?" she cried.

"For sticking in my head as unfinished business." He set aside his drink and let his hands rest on the edge of the desk beside his hips. "And you, Miss My Independence Is Very Important to Me, wouldn't have come here with me if it wasn't the same for you. We both feel this need to see where things could go. Let's acknowledge that and talk about a more realistic approach." His voice was a steady rumble in his chest that she felt like a vibration through her skin and into her bones. "One where I can protect you very easily because you're with me."

"You're serious. You want to have an affair." Her insides swooped and swirled as though she was strapped into a roller coaster. "We don't even know each other. We don't *like* each other." What if she was bad at it?

"The animosity between us is sexual tension. Aren't you curious to see what happens when we release it?" He uncrossed his ankles, but stayed leaning on the desk.

She stiffened, bracing herself for whatever move he might make.

"I'm not going to chase you," he chided softly. "Consent and all that. But let's at least talk about it."

Her nostrils burned as she sucked in a breath, ready to deny it, but she held her breath until her lungs were filled with fire. She couldn't make herself lie to him. How infuriating.

"Fine. I'm attracted to you," she gusted out. "Obviously." Now she was going to combust with sheer embarrassment.

She looked toward the windows, hoping he couldn't see how extravagant her dreams about him had been over the years because she didn't need her degree in hospitality to know he was only in the market for temporary entertainment, most likely because he was stuck with her right now.

Thus, the real question became: Did she want a fling with him? One that lasted only long enough for this publicity storm to die down?

"What's going on behind those beautiful blue eyes?" He still hadn't moved, but he somehow loomed larger. More impactful as he leaned on the desk, relaxed and watchful.

Her gaze slid down to his throat where his top button was open, then to the wide shoulders straining his shirt. His hands rested on the edge of the desk, but she remembered how they'd felt roaming her back and the sensual glide of his touch under her shirt.

Her nipples stung in reaction. With anticipation.

For all these years, she had longed to know what might have happened if they hadn't been interrupted.

"I am curious." It hurt to make that admission. She cleared her throat, writhing inside with self-consciousness. She wondered why she only reacted to him and she wondered what sex would be like. With him. "That doesn't mean I want to have sex, though. There's a big difference between thinking about it and doing it." She had thought about it many times. She'd never had the nerve to *do* it.

Because she'd never wanted sex in the same way that Atlas made her want it.

"A kiss then. I've wondered all this time whether it would be the same." He lifted his hand, inviting her to come to him.

It was a few steps and a journey across a desert and an ocean and a continent. A galaxy.

Then his strong hand was closing over hers, drawing her to stand between his feet. She thought she might be shaking. Dreaming.

Perhaps he noticed because he cupped the side of her neck and just looked at her, expression very somber. His narrowed gaze left pinpricks of sensation each place it touched—cheek and brow and lips. Shoulders. Throat. Breasts.

Time stretched out with excruciating tension. She couldn't have felt more exposed if she'd been naked. She closed her eyes, but that only made her more aware of the way her body was flooding with heat. Of the way his hand shifted to cradle her jaw. His body heat was like a physical aura that radiated across her skin. Her heart began to stumble and race.

Then his mouth brushed hers, tickling and sharp. A tease. A test? She didn't know if she passed. She only knew that her hands were closing into his turtleneck. She kept her eyes closed, but leaned in, seeking the smoothness of his lips. The firmness she recalled so vividly—

With a gruff noise, he slid his arms around her and pulled her deep into the vee of his legs, lashing her to his chest as he claimed her with a powerful kiss.

She was instantly overwhelmed, yet greed rose like a monster from within her. Without conscious awareness, she found herself responding urgently, pressing into the kiss and seeking his tongue with her own.

This was the kiss she'd been chasing since their first one, the kind that swallowed her whole. The kind that seemed to lift her from the floor and pull her into a maelstrom of sensations—firm hands shaping her back and hips, the hard plane of his chest crushing her breasts, the *heat.* Her arms curled themselves around his waist and her fingers found the bumps of his bowed spine. His thighs were such a hard cage against the outsides of hers, they hurt to press against, but she did it anyway, liking that sensation of his indomitable strength.

The plunge into this wildness should have terrified her, but beneath her overwhelmedness was familiarity. This was *exactly* how it had been before. They were picking up from where they'd left off. Everything felt good and right and necessary.

He grasped her plait and dragged it down her back, forcing her to lift her chin and expose her throat to his hot breath and the scrape of his teeth and a lick against her carotid artery. Heat flooded into her loins and some primal instinct made her seek relief by pushing her mound against the thick column behind his fly.

With a growled noise, he straightened and twisted. In a powerful move he sat her on the edge of the desk.

Now he was between her legs. Her knees lifted of their own accord, tilting her pelvis into a more welcoming angle. Her calves found the firm shape of his buttocks and pulled him in, urging him to settle the ridge of his erection against the ache in her core. *There.* She moaned into his mouth.

He muttered something in Greek and pulled her hips closer to the edge, then swept an arm behind her. There was a tumble of something heavy and the smash of broken glass. She thought she smelled the pungent scent of alcohol, but she only hugged his hips with her knees, rising into the slow, rolling grind of his sex against hers.

His hand burrowed beneath her top, pushing aside the cup of her bra so he could capture the naked swell of her breast in his hot palm.

She arched, startled by how sensitive her skin was to his touch, as though she felt the whorls of his fingerprints. Then she did what he'd asked her to do five long years ago. What she had wanted to do that night. She dragged the hem of her sweater up, exposing her bra-covered breast.

His nostrils flared. The lust in his eyes scorched her swollen breast. He dragged the cup further away and exposed her distended nipple, then dropped his head to capture it with the hot pull of his mouth.

Such a knifing slash of pleasure shot through her, she cried out, toes curling in delight.

He lifted his head. "Good?" he rasped.

"Yes," she moaned, letting her eyes blink open long enough to be confused by the beams in the ceiling. She'd forgotten where she was.

Then he was licking and teasing her nipple again, plunging her back into ecstasy while pulsing the tip of his erection in exactly the right place to coil the tension within her. She was aroused more than she knew how to bear and writhed, needing to escape that excruciatingly intimate pressure between her thighs because she was arriving on a ledge that couldn't hold her. It was too narrow, but each wriggle of agony pushed her closer to toppling off it.

"Atlas," she gasped.

He sucked her nipple again, hard, and she *shattered.* Ragged noises came out of her, noises she'd never made in her life. She shuddered in release, clinging to him, ankles locked behind his back, keeping him pinned in place while the contractions racked her.

As she sobbed helplessly, still in the throes of her orgasm, he brought his mouth to hers. His body was tense and his hips were heavy where they pinned hers to the desk. His kiss was passionate, and hungry, but sweet. Almost tender.

"You've wanted this as badly as I have," he said with a gritty laugh against her trembling mouth. He ran his restless lips along the edge of her jaw. "I've never been so hard in my life. I have a condom on me if you want to change your mind about having sex."

"Wh-what?" Her body was molasses, her brain incapable of thought.

"I always carry them." His thumb caressed beneath her ear. "It's not premeditated." He looked at her through weighted eyelids, cheeks flushed, but he clearly had all his wits about him while she was still trying to gather hers after completely abandoning herself.

The hand she slid to his shoulder was pure reflex. She needed air. Space to think. It was hitting her how quickly she had lost herself. Why did he always make her behave like this?

"Wise." He straightened, drawing her to sit up and helping her straighten her clothing. The tension in his expression changed to something more contained. "We should discuss the ground rules before we go any further."

Ground rules? She didn't know how to talk about sex. She didn't know how to do it! Everything about them was unequal, especially this. Look at him. He was completely in control and she had none. The embarrassment creeping over her was so profound, so visceral, her throat burned. Her eyes stung, making her blink to stave off tears.

“Stella.” He dipped his head, brows crashing together. “Did I hurt you? Why are you crying?”

How utterly humiliating. She was acting like the virgin she was—as though that had been her first orgasm ever.

When it was actually the first one that someone else had delivered, but that was no excuse for acting so callow.

She wanted to run away again. Far away. She let herself imagine quitting her job and catching a train and starting over where no one knew her—which was a ridiculously melodramatic reaction to something that had only gone a little further than the encounter they’d had five years ago. What must he think of her?

“Stella.” He touched her chin, trying to make her look at him.

She brushed his hand away and ducked her head.

“I—” She gulped back her rush of emotion. “I didn’t mean for this to happen.” She meant the tears. This was awful. “Can you—” She pushed at his chest until she was able to slide off the desk, but her knees still felt soft.

He caught her elbow and she pulled away, fearful she’d fall straight back into his arms. Straight back onto her back.

“You’re perfectly safe, Stella.”

No, she wasn’t! She was going to have an affair with him and he would break her heart and destroy her life even worse than he already had.

But not yet. Not yet.

“It’s been a long day.” She stumbled down the stairs and locked herself into the bedroom again.

CHAPTER FOUR

ATLAS BARELY SLEPT.

After leaving Stella's bag outside her door, and knocking briefly to tell her it was there, he worked himself into exhaustion in the fitness room, then went to bed in the primary bedroom on the top floor.

He felt her two floors beneath him, though. He felt every roll of her body between the sheets, heard every sigh. He held the scent of her skin in his nostrils and imagined the brush of her hair against his cheek.

Had he pushed her too far, too fast? She'd had her legs around his waist and had bucked beneath him. She had pulled her shirt up herself and said "yes."

Her climax had been so sweet, her aftermath so buttery soft, he'd wanted to eat her up.

Then he'd said something that made her freeze up. Was it the condoms? He was always careful to protect himself and his partner. He was diligent about consent and always conscious of the power dynamics between himself and his lovers.

Taking advantage of the help was too much like his father, but this entire scandal was too much like one of Oliver's sordid affairs. No matter what happened between him and Stella, it would have repercussions around Atlas taking over DVE. He really should pick the option of sending her back to Zermatt with whatever protection she needed and get on with his life.

He might have seriously considered it if he hadn't been so immersed in their kiss that he'd nearly joined her when she climaxed.

With a frustrated curse, he threw off the covers and decided to swim off his frustration, remembering as he pulled on a robe that he didn't have a swimsuit, which was par for the course right now.

To hell with it. He'd swim naked. It wouldn't be the first time. Maybe he'd get lucky and Stella would join him.

He half expected she had snowshoed out of here in the dead of night, but he glanced into the ski room on his way to the pool and saw her boots and jacket were still there.

An hour later, he showered off the salt water and took the elevator to the main floor, where he entered an aroma of coffee and pastries.

Stella was in a robe, sitting at the island eating fruit with yogurt and muesli.

"Good morning," he said, testing the waters.

"Good morning." She sounded subdued, but her eyes were bruised with sleeplessness. "I can make eggs if you want a bigger breakfast."

"My staff should be here soon." He moved to the espresso maker, set his cup and selected cappuccino.

As he waited for it to whir and pour, he felt his phone vibrate in his robe pocket.

Zamos. Atlas had remembered to text him last night to cancel the heli-ski and let him know he was staying here in Cervinia. He had invited Zamos and his wife to lunch. It was a long shot, since the other couple would have seen the headlines by now, but he was loath to pass up a chance to connect with the man.

Atlas wouldn't have been surprised if Zamos ghosted him, but the reply had been:

Our son is teething. We're staying in today. You're welcome to join us here for lunch.

Huh. Zamos and his wife were an extraordinarily popular power couple. His wife was known especially for her shrewd recon skills gleaned through gossip and other social connections. Was she trying to get an early scoop on Atlas's personal life?

Atlas replied, then pushed his phone back into his pocket and picked up the filled coffee cup. When he turned, Stella was watching him with a somber expression.

He started to say, "About last night—"

"I need to tell you something." She spoke over him, looking and sounding so grave, he tensed.

"About your father?"

"What? No." Her brows came together in confusion. Then she tilted her head. "Because I said he might become a problem, publicity-wise? No. Um. No, I don't think he knows yet. We'll circle back to that. No, this is about, um, last night. I'm really embarrassed."

"Don't be." It was an erotic memory he would cherish for the rest of his life.

"Not just about..." She blushed and looked into her bowl.

"You don't owe me any explanations. No means no. I'm fine with it." He reached out to set his cup on the place mat next to hers and picked up a plate, helping himself to a croissant she must have warmed in the oven.

"No, that's not—I didn't mean to cry. It was a very weird day and you're...*you*. You're a lot, Atlas."

"That sounds like an accusation," he said drily. "I'm not sure what my crime is."

"I don't *do* this." She closed her eyes, face bright red. "I didn't know what to say. How to tell you that I'm new to this."

"Because I mentioned ground rules? I'm not into anything kinky." Although he definitely could be, if she had something in mind. "I only meant we should be clear about our expectations. Don't you usually talk things out beforehand?"

"No. I mean, yes. I've definitely had *that* conversation." She kept stirring her yogurt without taking any. "It's always been a very quick no. Which usually puts an end to the conversation. Kind of like last night."

He paused with his croissant halfway to his mouth, plate at the ready to catch the crumbs, thinking he understood, but also thinking he couldn't possibly be hearing her correctly.

"Always?" he clarified.

"Every single time," she said with a firm nod, gaze fixed on her spoon.

He set the pastry back on the plate and rubbed his fingertips against his thumb. The whisper of noise was the only sound until he cleared his throat.

"You're…"

"Don't call me that," she warned. "Talk about a crime. People virgin-shame as much as they slut-shame."

"You're twenty-three," he finished. "And very sensual."

"You don't know that," she muttered.

"You smelled everything as you were cooking last night. It looked and tasted delicious. You wear cashmere and keep petting your robe. You blush every time I look at you as though you feel it."

"I'm blushing because I was raised to believe that wanting sex is a sin!" she cried. "Especially outside marriage. Which doesn't mean I'm holding out for that. That's not what I'm saying." She put out a stalling hand. "I'm saying that, until recently, I hadn't met anyone who seemed, you know, worth risking going to hell for."

He supposed that was a joke, but had to ask, "Recently? Or five years ago?"

"Both," she threw at him with annoyance. "Getting fired for something that wasn't my fault was awful, but what you did was worse. You set the bar up here." She marked a spot in the air above her head. "Everyone who came after you was bland in comparison. I was waiting to feel something again and of course it had to be *you*."

Atlas set aside his plate, equally frustrated. "Why the hell do you think I never slept with Iris?"

"You have not gone five years without sex."

"No." He felt inexplicably chagrined as he made that admission. "But I thought the way I felt with you that night must have been a secondhand high from those lunatics in the tub. I've looked for chemistry like it ever since and never found it. Not until I saw you again."

"Don't say things like that," she said crossly. "I'm gullible enough to buy it. If you want to talk ground rules, I insist on honesty. Don't play on my lack of experience."

"Honesty is rule number one for me, too," he shot back. "Tied with monogamy."

"I think I've established that other men are not a problem," she grumbled.

"Good." Was he smug? Hell, yes. "I had this week booked as vacation. We can go anywhere you like, but seeing as I have a party in London on the weekend, I suggest Paris or Milan, to find you something to wear. You'll need cocktail dresses, too. You'll have a little time for shopping when we're in Athens, but we can order them now for Australia."

"What? No. I can't." Her eyes flared with shock.

"Why the hell not?" If she had yanked a leash tied around his neck, he couldn't have been more irritated or thwarted.

"Because I have to be back at work next week and gadding about with you would only make things worse." Stella's body was aching from a restless night. Her eyes were dry and her mind still in turmoil. "I put in a request for personal time this week." To deal with her father, but she kept that to herself. "Hopefully, things will die down again by Monday, but I help my stepmother with expenses so I can't risk losing my job."

"Screw your job. I'll cover whatever you need as long as we're together."

"I'm not taking money for sex! That's not the kind of relationship I want with you." She had friends who went into Sugar Daddy situations and good for them. She didn't care how other adults conducted themselves, but relying financially on a man was *not* for her. "I thought about this a lot last night and I've realized..." She drew a breath and let it out with the decision she'd made in the predawn hours. "Sex needs to happen or I'll never get over you."

Stella wasn't sure how she had expected Atlas to react. Invite her to his bedroom, perhaps? He seemed like a man of action, but he only stared at her, expression inscrutable.

As the potent silence grew, the rat-a-tat of an approaching helicopter intensified.

"That's my staff." He looked toward a window that faced the helipad.

She slid off the stool and moved to where she could see it.

"That's huge!" A helicopter three times the size of the

one they'd arrived in descended onto the pad. It had a row of four windows and she saw silhouettes in every one of them. "How many people is that? I'll get dressed."

"Don't bother. They brought fresh clothes for you."

She wasn't about to meet a dozen strangers in a bathrobe.

She went to shower and emerged to find bags of Davenwear on her bed: yoga pants and velour joggers and smart hiking trousers. There were sports bras with more cross straps than a spider's web, fitted T-shirts and snuggle-soft pullovers.

She tried on the black yoga pants with the flared pant leg. The V-neck T-shirt plunged to make the most of her cleavage and the pink chenille jacket was like pulling on a hug. She instantly felt relaxed yet able to run a marathon.

When she came upstairs, she found a half dozen strangers busily working off laptops and scribbling on pads, preparing snacks and wiping down tables. They all treated her the way she treated guests at the hotel, pausing to acknowledge her with cheerful eagerness to please.

Atlas was in a meeting in the den, she was told. She accepted a coffee and retreated to her room to browse for an apartment for her father. He had gone to the hotel under duress, mostly because Elijah had told him Grettina would use the room if he didn't.

After an hour or so, heavy footsteps approached her open door. Atlas appeared. He had shaved and wore jeans with a collared shirt beneath a dark blue pullover. His expression was still remote enough to make her stomach sink. Why did he seem so angry with her? She had told him she would have sex with him. Wasn't that what he wanted?

"We have a lunch date. We need to leave in fifteen minutes," he informed her.

"Where are we going?" She looked down at her clothes

and touched the plain braid she was wearing down the front of her shoulder.

"Rafael and Alexandra Zamos have invited us to their chalet. You don't need to change. I want to keep it casual. I've been trying to connect with him for years and he's finally giving me an opening, but this is a social visit. Were you given ski pants? We're taking the snowmobile. They might be in the ski room." He vanished from the doorway like smoke.

She quickly looked up the couple they were meeting. They were very rich, which was no surprise since they were contemporaries of Atlas. Rafael seemed self-made after getting his start in shipping. His wife was an American heiress who had attended boarding school in Europe.

"Do you think they're expecting you to bring Iris?" she asked when she met Atlas in the ski room.

"When I canceled the heli-skiing, I told Rafael that Iris had gone back to London. His wife stays on top of gossip and instructed him to ask me if it would be four for lunch so I'm confident they know who I'm bringing. If you're uncomfortable at any time, tell me. We'll leave."

And quash a relationship he'd been chasing for years?

"I'm surprised you haven't run into them in Athens. They live there," she said as she pulled on periwinkle-blue ski pants over her yoga pants, then adjusted the suspenders.

"After my mother died, I sold the taverna and didn't go back to Greece for years. I only bought my home in Athens recently with a plan to be there more often. I haven't had much chance to use it yet. I travel a lot."

"I'm so sorry. When did you lose her?"

"About a year before I met you. Breast cancer." He zipped his jacket.

"Is that when you went to live with your father?" The timing didn't seem right.

"No." He handed her a helmet so she could fit the straps.

He didn't offer any context on his childhood, firmly keeping walls in place between them.

"Do you want your own machine?" he asked.

"Not unless you want me to have my own. I can get from A to B if the terrain isn't too challenging, but I'm not very good."

"Ride with me, then." They finished bundling up.

Outside, he let her settle onto the seat first. It was fitted with a passenger seat behind his that was positioned a little higher and had a small backrest.

When she nodded, he straddled the seat in front of her. They checked that the headsets were connected and he started the engine, then told her, "Hold on."

She snugged herself into his lower back and leaned forward to fold her gloves on the front of his chest.

He took it slowly across the unbroken snow, but the blanket was so powdery, it kicked up around them like bubbles of champagne, making her grin.

A moment later, he arrived on the packed track and opened the throttle.

It was a sunny day, turning up the contrast of white snow against blue sky. Their speed rippled her clothes and she had an excuse to hang on a little tighter. It felt glorious, even if there were thick, insulated layers between them.

He slowed a few times and stood to take them through some crests and dips, but within the half hour they were in the more populated outskirts of Cervinia. He followed a track upward toward a beautiful older chalet that backed onto a forest and had a view of the valley. It had the charm of a well-loved private home and the staff exuded an air of ownership as they took their helmets and outerwear.

A gorgeous couple stood as they were shown into a

sumptuous living room. Rafael was tall and dark like Atlas and almost as handsome. Alexandra was the epitome of American beauty with a slender, elegant figure, shiny ash-blond hair and confidence that radiated like sunshine. She wore leggings with a tunic-style top and minimal makeup, which immediately put Stella at ease that she wasn't underdressed.

Alexandra's curious gaze skimmed her, seeming to note Atlas's hand in her lower back.

The inspection made Stella brace for a judgy remark, but Alexandra only said, "We were so relieved when Rafael saw your text that you weren't skiing. Atticus is teething and had us up half the night. I really didn't want to leave him when he's not feeling well so it was nice to have an excuse for a lazy day. Shall we have a drink in the sunroom before we eat?"

"This is a beautiful chalet," Stella murmured as they walked through to the closed-in terrace. Overstuffed furniture was draped with colorful knit throws and tasseled cushions. A small gas fireplace kept it cozy while the windows overlooked snow-covered trees, village rooftops and the rugged mountainside.

"The decor is unique, isn't it?" Rafael sent an amused glance to the chandelier made of deer antlers. "It belongs to our friend's grandfather. He bought it when he married sixty-odd years ago. They only allow family to use it, so I guess that makes us family?" He directed the last to his wife with a tone of discovery.

Alexandra gave him a look that was filled with the sort of private joke amusement that only a couple perfectly attuned to each other's thoughts could share.

Stella immediately felt a stab of envy, wondering if she would ever have that with anyone. Not with Atlas. She cut him a glance, unable to read him at all and feeling rebuffed. She'd told him she wanted him to be her first and he had been cool ever since. Was that the issue? Was he turned off by her lack of experience?

He caught her looking at him and a spearing sensation went into her chest, one that emanated painful heat through the rest of her body.

His expression altered, not softening exactly, but asking a question. She gave him a small smile. She was fine. They didn't have to leave.

"I won't ask why you decided to come to this side," Alexandra said drily while looking between them as though she'd seen their byplay. "It sounds like you live in Zermatt, Stella?"

"I do. I grew up near Bern, but I moved to Zermatt when I was eighteen."

"You're lucky. This is a beautiful part of the world." Alexandra leaned forward to pick up her Aperol spritz, adding in a self-deprecating tone, "I say that like I want it for myself. The truth is, our son is an excuse. I was already complaining it was too cold to ski. I always think snow sports are a fun idea until I arrive on the mountain and remember that snow does not fall in temperatures anywhere near seventy degrees."

"Sasha is a delicate hothouse orchid," Rafael teased, picking up her free hand and kissing her knuckles. "I'll take everyone skiing when they arrive," he promised her. "You can stay with Atticus if you want to."

"That's probably the only way I'll get to hold my own baby," she said ruefully.

Stella tried not to stare, but they epitomized what she wanted in a relationship—someone who knew her well and offered casual affection and had a nickname for her. Someone whose small shows of support demonstrated deep understanding and indulgence. Someone who loved her the way Rafael clearly loved his wife.

She caught Atlas studying her again and replaced whatever yearning was on her face with a helpful smile. "Please let me know if you decide to ski our side. I can connect you with anything you might need—passes, guides…"

It was something she did regularly as part of her job, but she thought she felt Atlas stiffen as she said it. Why couldn't she do anything right around him?

"Good to know. Thank you." Rafael nodded with appreciation.

The conversation meandered from ski conditions to the book on the table—a romance that Stella had been meaning to pick up for herself—to whether this or that person was reputed to be in town.

Stella didn't feel too excluded by the name-dropping. She was familiar with the lofty families and celebrities who owned homes or made regular visits to the area. She even contributed snippets of intel on who was likely to make an appearance at which time of year.

Alexandra was an absolute queen as a hostess, guiding them to the dining room and keeping the conversation moving without being intrusive. They were finishing dessert when she abruptly rose.

"That's Atticus." She nodded to the maid, who had come in with a baby monitor. "We gave the nanny the day off so I'll get him. He's liable to give you a cold shoulder since he's not feeling well, but would you like to meet him?" she asked Stella.

"I'd love to," Stella said sincerely, even though she suspected an ulterior motive in being asked to come upstairs.

Alexandra asked the maid to prepare a bottle and led

Stella to the nursery, where she gathered up the infant who was fussing in the crib. He wore fuzzy blue pants with a matching shirt and had lost a slipper during his nap. He rubbed his face into his mama's shoulder as she cradled him there.

"Your bottle is coming, little man," Alexandra soothed, petting his sweaty curls and straightening his clothes.

"He's gorgeous." Stella tilted her head to glimpse his flushed cheek and dark eyes and the pudgy fist he was gnawing. "How old is he?"

"Six months. He was premature, so more like four. His teeth are on the early side, if we count from his due date." Alexandra patted his diaper to ensure it didn't need changing. "The truth is, I'd always rather be home with him," she confided. "Whether he's happy or grumpy. He's our little miracle. I only agreed to ski today because the men were doing the heli thing and Iris would have— Never mind. I'm speaking out of turn."

Stella doubted Alexandra ever made a social misstep. She was providing an opening for Stella to spill some tea on Iris or Atlas or herself.

"Not at all." Even before she had worked with the public, Stella had learned how to walk the thorny spaces around telling the truth without implicating herself or blaming anyone else. "I can't speak for Iris or her reasons for leaving, but the photos completely skewed a very tame story. Atlas and I met when he came to Zermatt five years ago. We hadn't seen each other until yesterday. The only reason I'm here with him today is wingman. I think he was hoping for exactly this—that I would chat with you and give him a chance to talk privately with your husband."

"Yes, I know," Alexandra said with a good-natured smirk. "That's why I invited you up here. Ah. Thank you."

She gratefully took the bottle from the tray as it was delivered, then offered it to the baby, sinking into the rocking chair as he took it. "I'm not prying, Stella. People think I'm a gossip because I listen to it, but I don't repeat it. Not to anyone but Rafael. He and I are a team. We protect each other by sharing what we learn about the players on the other teams."

"That's an overstatement of my relationship with Atlas," Stella assured her. She absently plucked the rumpled blanket from the crib and folded it, leaving it across the rail. "I don't actually know him very well at all. I don't think that's something he allows and I'm just as guilty of keeping to myself. Maybe we're all like that." She perched on the edge of the daybed and tucked her hands between her knees.

"Guarded? Life knocks us around and makes us that way, doesn't it?" Alexandra was looking tenderly to her baby. Her smile held a poignant quality. "Sometimes letting your guard down pays off, though. It does with this little one. And Rafael, of course."

"How did you know you'd be safe to do that with Rafael?" Stella asked curiously.

"I didn't," Alexandra said with a rueful shake of her head. "Not at first. Honestly, I don't think you can know until you take that leap of faith and find out. It's a gamble."

Stella shook her head, already knowing she didn't have the courage for high-risk stakes like that. She steered the conversation back to Atticus and his teeth.

As the women left, Rafael invited Atlas into the den.

He was reluctant to be out of earshot for Stella. Rafael's wife seemed unfazed by his bringing her, but that didn't mean she wasn't a cat behind closed doors. His own sister could turn from syrup to strychnine in a heartbeat.

Despite her inner strength and determination, Stella was also sensitive and inexperienced. He was still processing that she'd never had sex. It made no difference to him beyond the fact that she needed a slower pace than she might have if she'd had other lovers.

No, he was far more disturbed that she wanted to end their affair within the week. His brain had nearly exploded at that. Hell no. There was no way a week would be long enough to burn out this chemistry between them.

She wouldn't let him support her, either.

That's not the kind of relationship I want with you.

She'd made his offer sound tawdry when he was only trying to facilitate her spending as much time as possible with him. He was in demand around the world. He wanted her with him and, if she had worries like a stepmother who struggled to make ends meet, he wanted to alleviate that for her.

"You went to considerable trouble to get this meeting. Let's get to it." Rafael closed the door, but didn't sit or invite him to. He leaned his hips on the desk, comfortable, but no longer the amiable host. Now he was pure CEO.

"You've avoided me for years," Atlas pointed out. "Are you now seeing there are several fronts where DVE could partner with Zamos International and benefit both?"

"I've always seen opportunities between our two companies," Rafael said blithely. "I approached your father eight years ago with a proposal and he slammed the door in my face. It wasn't a business decision. It was personal. He saw me as an upstart, which I was, but he wanted to keep me down. He wasn't the only one who treated me that way. I don't forget a single person that did." Or forgive, was the heavier implication.

Typical Oliver. He believed himself better than everyone else and therefore entitled to the success he enjoyed.

He didn't even work for it. He succeeded in spite of his bloated sense of self-worth, not because of it. The reality was, Atlas had been responsible for most of the gains at DVE in the last five years. The board knew it, even if Oliver refused to admit it.

"I'm not my father," Atlas said simply.

"No?" Rafael didn't look to the ceiling where the murmur of the women's voices could be heard, but Atlas recognized the comparison to Oliver's serial philandering.

"No," he asserted, but it felt less than true when he was jockeying for an affair with an innocent whose advantages were considerably fewer than his own. "I'd love to say yours is the only bridge Oliver has burned over the years. It's not. I'm doing my best to rebuild them. We have very different approaches. Give me a chance to prove that and I will."

"Is there any truth to the rumor you're taking over DVE?" Rafael asked bluntly.

"Oliver's retirement plans are confidential." Judging by Oliver's scathing email reacting to the photos of Atlas with Stella, those plans were postponed indefinitely.

"You're aware that Zamos closed with Casella Corporation last year? We're on the brink of a huge expansion."

Atlas gave a curt nod. It was the reason he had pushed so hard to meet with Rafael. Zamos International would be looking for funds to support and sustain the growth he was projecting. "That's why I wanted to meet with you."

"Now is the time to hammer out a letter of understanding, so our companies can expand together," Rafael said. "The most obvious is the volume of DVE products that Zamos can transport, but there are other areas where we can dovetail."

"Agreed." Triumph flared in Atlas. Closing a lucrative deal like this with Rafael would give him the leverage he needed with the board to support his takeover at DVE

"But I won't negotiate anything with DVE as long as Oliver is at the top," Rafael said flatly. "I don't trust him."

That punched the breath out of him.

If Atlas had been engaged to Iris rather than coming off this scandal with Stella, he might have had a shot at persuading the board to support him in replacing Oliver against his will, but right now he looked as impulsive and supercilious as Oliver.

There was a creak of floorboards above them.

"That's the women coming down. If things on your end change within the next few months, you and I will have a lot to talk about. After that, I'll be looking in other directions." Rafael moved to the door. "You have my number."

Atlas had come so far on his quest to claim his birthright. It was infuriating to have it set out of his reach *again*.

His frustration was blistering his insides as they walked out to the living room where Stella cradled a blanket-wrapped infant.

Atlas hadn't consciously recognized the itch of absence that had invaded his chest until it dissipated when he saw her. She was fine. Glowing even.

"Where's Sasha?" Rafael frowned with concern toward the stairs.

"Changing. He spit up on her." Stella's voice lilted with humor. "I offered to bring him down to you, but honestly, I want to keep him." Her arms firmed in a gentle hug around the baby before she gave him up to his father. "He's absolutely precious."

Her expression of longing caused a near-audible click in Atlas's head, one that was like the wheels of a combination lock aligning to open a vault. Inside, the solution sat as though it had been there all along, waiting for discovery.

The seeds of this idea had actually been sown when she

had said she was raised to believe she should wait for marriage, then told him she would only give him the rest of the week. He'd balked, instinctually knowing that wasn't enough time, but what would be? A month? A year?

And while he was indulging himself with her, he would only put off his search for the wife he was being pressured to take, to earn the board's support of his leadership at DVE.

What if *she* was his wife, though?

His mind began to race so quickly, he barely heard them continue speaking.

"He's on his best behavior now," Rafael scoffed good-naturedly. He protectively cupped his son's head as he dropped a kiss on his cheek, then tucked him against his shoulder. "You should have heard the names he was calling me last night."

"Slander. He's been a perfect gentleman as long as I've known him. But I gave Alexandra the name of a teething gel I always recommend to guests. If you have trouble finding it here, let me know. I know where to get it in Zermatt and can have it sent over."

"We'd appreciate that."

Alexandra returned and offered coffee.

"It sounds like you have busy days ahead, once your family arrives," Atlas said. "We won't take up any more of your time." Besides, he had his own plans to leap on. "We'll see you again soon, though. Athens, likely." He used *we* deliberately. And *soon.*

Rafael's eyes narrowed shrewdly as they shook hands and departed.

"How did your meeting with Rafael go?" Stella asked as she set her helmet on the shelf in the ski room back at their own chalet.

"Good." Atlas set aside his boots and gave her a look she couldn't interpret.

"I thought it must have gone very well." He'd had a gleam of purpose in his eye when he and Rafael had joined her in the living room. A determined sort of energy had been coming off him as he'd sped them back here to the chalet. It was still there, practically shooting out in rays that wrapped around her to draw her in. "When you told Rafael that *we* would see them in Athens, I wondered if that meant you were getting lawyers or some other team together. It sounded promising."

"I was referring to you."

"Me?" She hung her jacket and slipped her suspenders off her shoulders, stripping down to the light jacket and yoga pants she wore beneath. "I can't go to Athens. When? For how long? I only have a few days off and I may have to visit my family."

"We're going to deal with your family together, Stella, because I have a new proposal for you. A real one. *Marriage.*"

CHAPTER FIVE

STELLA GAVE HER head a shake. "I'm sorry. I didn't hear you properly."

"Yes, you did."

"No. That's not…possible." Her heart was beating really fast, filling her ears with a drumming sound. She wanted to run.

Run.

"Let's go somewhere private to discuss this."

They took the elevator to the top floor. It let them out in a sitting room with a wall of windows that gave access to a private balcony overlooking the lake. Through a pair of double doors, she glimpsed the wide bed he'd slept in last night. His room was tidy as a pin, so she assumed the staff had come in while they'd been out.

He closed the glass doors to the landing, giving them more privacy before he offered, "Drink?"

"I feel like you might have had one too many over lunch." She sank down on the moss-green love seat.

"Snowmobiles are as dangerous as motorcycles. I drank water." He poured scotch. Two of them. "A week is not enough, Stella. We need more time."

"For what?!"

His one brow went up in a silent *Shall I spell it out?* He offered the glass.

She blushed as she accepted it. "I told you I'm not holding out for marriage."

"I know, but marriage has become something I want. Today, Rafael confirmed my suspicion that Oliver is the biggest detriment to DVE's progress. Now I know how urgently we need a regime change. The board is aware of his shortcomings, but they want him to step down gracefully, which Oliver promised to do if I married Iris. They don't want to put another skirt-chaser in charge. This…" He waved between them. "If we have an affair, it makes me look just like him, but if you and I marry, I become a faithful, domesticated husband."

"Ha!" As if.

"Oliver cheated on his wife with my mother, Stella," he said gravely. "I would never do that to you."

She would love to believe that, but it was all too far-fetched. Rather than push back on that, however, she asked something she had always wondered.

"Why do you always call him Oliver?"

"Spite." His tone was pleasantly lethal. "It's my petty way of reminding him that he behaved like a bastard first. That he made me what I am."

"Does he call you that?" she asked, appalled.

"I don't care what he calls me," he said, but she suspected there was real pain behind the scoff in his voice. "The truth is, I've been known to live down to his labels."

"Is 'reckless' one of them? Because this sounds very impulsive, Atlas. Outrageous, even."

"It's not." He looked up from his drink. "In the past, I only had affairs with women who weren't interested in marriage because I knew it was something I would have to do for practical reasons. This is the most expedient reason of all—dethroning Oliver."

Wow. Some tiny part of her had wondered if he had begun developing real feelings for her in the short time they'd known each other, something that went beyond passion and a sense of obligation. How pathetic of her to imagine such a thing.

"I will also need an heir and a spare," he continued. "Until I saw you with the baby today, I've never pictured myself having kids with anyone, but—"

"Stop." She covered her face, appalled by how hurt she was and not wanting him to see it.

"It's the perfect solution, Stella."

"For who?" she cried. "What if I don't want to have your babies, Atlas? What if I want to have a career? Did you think of that?"

"You don't want a family? Ever?" He cocked his head with curiosity. "You seemed really taken with that baby."

"Holding a baby for two minutes is not the same as raising one. Looking after children is *hard*."

"That's the voice of experience?" He narrowed his eyes.

"Yes. After my mother died I had to look after my brother and sister." She didn't want to get into that bleak time, though, and rose to pace off her agitation. "I told you I'm still helping my stepmother. My sister is still at home, along with the twins Grettina had with my father. One of them has special needs, so she can only work part-time. My brother pitches in where he can, but he's at uni. Once he gets his engineering degree and gets a job, he'll be able to help out more, but for now it's on me to close the gaps in the finances and help with homework over the tablet or find a specialist if one is needed. That's enough responsibility, thank you. I don't need a baby on my hip while I do all of that."

"Your father doesn't help?"

"No," she said starkly. "In fact, half the time, I support him, too."

"Men who don't look after their children is my Achilles' heel. How much does your stepmother need to take the pressure off? I can hire people to ensure she's not stretched so thin."

"Don't try to obligate me! I know how those sorts of manipulations work, Atlas. I've lived them."

"With your father?"

"Yes. I told you he's a challenging person. But we manage." She brushed aside how painful that was sometimes. "As long as I have my job. I *like* my job. I have goals and opportunities there. I'm working my way up to manager. As soon as Beate is on her own, and Grettina isn't so strained, I'll transfer to different locations and see the world. I have a plan." It was a good one. A fulfilling one. It was one she had made *for herself.*

"You want to manage a hotel? I'll buy you one. You want to see the world, I'll take you."

"I can't believe you had the nerve to call *me* stubborn. Let it go, Atlas. The role of wife isn't some cookie-shaped hole you fill with the next one from the box. It's insulting that you think you can just shove me into it."

"I think I've made it clear that I want *you*, Stella. If you need a fresh demonstration of my interest, come here. I'm happy to provide it." He shot the contents of his glass and set it aside.

Her heart swerved and her veins stung with fight-or-flight reaction.

"Marriage is about more than sex." She looked to the doors to the foyer, ensuring no one was overhearing them. "If that's all we have, it's doomed to a very quick death."

"Oh, Stella. Is that what you're really holding out for? Love?"

"No," she insisted, while wondering, maybe? "I deserve

to be loved, Atlas." Anxiety pressed hotly behind her eyes as she declared that because she was loved, but she was also vilified by someone who was supposed to love her.

He sighed, expression turning condescending. "Love doesn't solve real-world problems. I loved my mother, but it didn't keep her alive. She loved me, but it didn't make raising me alone any easier for her. I don't think you'd be working so hard to help your family if you didn't love them, but it doesn't make that easy, does it? *I* can make your life easier."

He leaned forward to claim the drink she hadn't touched, then negligently dropped into an armchair.

"Let go of your romantic view of marriage, Stella. It should be a strategic alliance that improves your life. Marrying me gives you the means to help your family. It spins our scandal into something viewed as respectable. If it doesn't work out and we divorce in a year or two, you'll possess the resources to protect yourself from any fallout."

"I believe that sort of arrangement is called fortune-hunting. I'm not interested in being that kind of person."

"Your desire to be independent borders on a fault. This arrangement gets both of us what we want."

"Like Rafael? Do you seriously want to marry me to cut a business deal?"

"You say it like that's the only one I'll secure once I'm at the helm of DVE. But yes. I do."

"*They* love each other, you know. You must have seen it."

"Rafael and Alexandra?" He gave a snort of harsh cynicism. "Their marriage was notoriously tactical. Alexandra had a grudge against her parents so she married a man who came from humbler roots than mine. Rafael married *way* up. He wouldn't be anywhere near where he is if Alexandra hadn't used her position to make introductions for him."

"Well, I can't get you those sorts of things, so why would you even consider me?"

"I don't need that the same way Rafael did," he said blithely. "Having a physical connection with my wife has become my highest priority."

"I never imagined I would say this, but I would rather have casual sex with you."

"And I would rather wait until we're married." He tilted his glass against his complacent smile.

"What are you going to do?" she mocked. "Hold out until I ask you for a ring?" This was the most ludicrous conversation she'd ever had.

"I'm confident you'll break first. Based on last night."

She called him something she'd never called anyone to their face before. She said it in German, but the way his expression frosted told her he got the gist of it.

He moved fast, catching her at the door to the foyer, stopping her from opening it by setting his hand over hers on the latch.

"Sex is a big deal for me," she hissed as she yanked her hand from beneath his and turned on him. "Not because I've never done it, but because my father's voice is in my head, calling me every name you can think of. The *one* time I let things go too far, I got fired for it. Now you're mocking me for how I acted last night? I'm already ashamed of it. You don't have to make it worse."

"Don't be ashamed. Don't you dare."

He tried to turn her face to look at him and she knocked his hand away, stubbornly keeping her blurred gaze on the fading afternoon beyond the window.

"Damn it, Stella. I don't like losing. It makes me fight dirty, but there is nothing wrong with how you reacted last night. It was incredible. I want that for as long as it lasts.

If you want a divorce when it burns out, fine. But it's already lasted five years. It will last at least that again, I promise you."

"As if I want to tie my life to someone who makes me feel small the minute he's angry with me! Been there, done that, and I took a train to Zermatt to get away from it. Now let me out before I start screaming."

With a muttered curse, he opened the door.

That couldn't have gone any worse, Atlas thought, as Stella's footsteps retreated down the stairs.

Then he heard her shriek from the lower floor.

He leaped toward the stairwell and peered down at her. "What happened?"

"They fired me, didn't they?" She shook her phone at him. "Three months' pay as per my contract since they don't have cause, but they believe they do have cause in terms of damage to the company reputation so I'd better leave without a fight. Also, they're putting out a statement that I don't work there so the buzzards will get out of their lobby. Thanks a *lot*!"

She stomped down another flight of stairs and the slam of her bedroom door resounded through the house.

Fantastic.

He went down to the main floor and his PR manager picked up her head from studying the screen on her laptop.

"I'm guessing we're not any closer to our own statement?"

"No." Damn it.

He walked into the den where a pair of lawyers were working, closed the door and issued fresh instructions that he hoped would be a good use of their time since he wasn't giving up on marrying Stella.

He went to her door, prepared to hear crying or glass breaking or even the sound of the helicopter while she flew herself out of here.

Instead, he heard her speaking German.

"It's not a waste of time. Or money. You're not quitting, Beate. No. Don't listen to him. You're *good.* We'll find the money." A lengthy pause, then, "That won't happen. I'll move in before I let him do it. I may have to. Don't tell Grettina, but I've lost my job. They didn't even give the scandal a chance to die down. No, it's not like that. He's someone I met a long time ago, but that's not why I'm calling. Are you able to go visit the apartment today? The one from the link I sent you? If not, I'll come tomorrow—"

Atlas rapped his knuckles on the door.

Stella opened it and held up a finger at him, continuing to speak into her phone.

"There are? How many? Hmph. But they only spoke to Grettina? Not the little ones? Good. And Pappa doesn't know? That's good. Let Elijah know they've been there. Hopefully, he can keep Pappa at the hotel. If he comes to the house…" She touched her brow. "Look, I have to go, but I'll text you my plans in a little while. Give everyone my love."

"Your sister?" he guessed as she ended the call.

She nodded and sank onto the edge of the bed. "You were right about them finding my family. Three different reporters were at the house today, asking Grettina about me. I thought I could go there, but…" There was no anger or blame in her voice, just worry and weariness. She dropped her elbows onto her knees and buried her face in her hands.

"Tell me what's going on with your father," he insisted as he closed the door.

She winced as she lifted her head, as though he was physically twisting her arm.

"Upstairs, you said he made you feel small and that's why you ran away." He angled the only chair in the room to face her and sat down in it, putting their feet toe to toe.

She flickered her gaze to the closed door.

"I'm not going to judge you," he assured her. "My father refused to acknowledge me until he saw a use for me. I have so little respect for him, I'm plotting to take his job. You can't shock me."

She stopped clicking her thumbnails together and frowned at him. "Do you really hate him for making you? Because people can't help who they're attracted to."

"They can control how they act on that attraction," he shot back. "They don't have to take advantage of a naive girl who's never been off the island where she grew up. They don't have to hide the fact that they're married and leave without saying goodbye. They especially don't have to call her a liar when her father calls to say she's pregnant. Maybe they could send her some money to help raise their son, instead of refusing outright to have anything to do with either of them."

"Did he really?"

"Yes." It still filled him with rage and disgust and guilt for existing. For stalling his mother's life when she might have had thousands of other opportunities if she hadn't been a young single mother.

"Did she have any help at all? Family?" she asked with concern.

"My grandfather. He owned the taverna where she worked. He looked after us as well as he could. Things were lean, but we never went hungry."

"You miss him," she noted.

"I do," he admitted with an old pang that came of wishing he'd made that old man's life easier, too, instead of harder.

"How did Oliver come back into your life?"

This wasn't what he wanted to talk about, but maybe if she understood what drove him, she'd be more inclined to take his side. To agree to the marriage.

"My mother wrote to him after my grandfather died. I was winning at local competitions and showing promise for national competitions, getting attention online, but the cost of training and travel was beyond what the taverna could fund. She wanted to send me to Athens where I could attend a school with an elite athletics program. I was willing to give up swimming altogether, but she saw that it was a step toward greater things, so she insisted on asking Oliver for help. His wife had recently passed and he was realizing that Carmel was ill-suited to taking over DVE. He didn't want to lock himself into another marriage and start over with a new baby. I was fourteen, smart and ambitious. He could have paid my mother off with a modest settlement and continued to keep my existence quiet, but he offered to acknowledge me as his heir so long as I went to live with him and attended the schools he chose."

"That must have been hard on her." Her brow pleated.

"It was." It had been hard on both of them. He'd been homesick as hell. "But she wanted me to claim what she viewed as rightfully mine. At first, that was an education and a standard of living she couldn't give me. The training alone was worth my weight in gold medals. You don't get to the Olympics by taking lessons at the community pool. I hated leaving her, but my allowance was generous enough I could cover her living expenses and still have plenty left over for myself. She kept the taverna open and worked there on and off, but she didn't *have* to. For that, it was worth making a deal with the devil."

"You really see him that way?"

"He forced me to model swimsuits. What do you think?"

A small giggle escaped her. She covered her mouth, contrite. "I'm sorry."

He shrugged it off. "Now tell me about your father."

She winced with dismay. Sighed. Then tucked her hands under her thighs and spoke to the floor.

"He's very strict. Religious, but only in the way that suits him. He acts like he's holding us to a proper standard and warns us we'll be punished for our sins. Spare the rod, spoil the child. That kind of thing."

"He hit you?" Cold fury wrapped like a cold fist around his heart.

"Mostly me, after my mother died. I didn't know how to cook or keep Beate quiet."

"How old were you?"

"Ten."

He bit back a string of curses, not wanting to interrupt her when she was finally talking, but he could hardly hear her through the rage rushing in his ears.

"She'd been ill for a while and didn't see a doctor. I don't know if that was Pappa claiming prayer should fix it or if she believed it. He's very difficult to stand up to. Last night he told Beate to give up her music. She's very talented, but he said she's not good and it got into her head. He told her it costs too much and it's indecent for a woman to sing and play piano and she ought to be ashamed that it takes her from helping Grettina with the little ones."

"Did *she* let him hit you?"

"Grettina? No. I mean, she couldn't always stop him, but she's always had a knack for calming his temper. She's as devoted to the church as he is. That's how they met, but she walks the walk on how she thinks people ought to behave. Kind and generous and forgiving. I sometimes think she married him for us. Me. I was thirteen and he didn't know what to do with me." She gestured wryly at her chest, but there was a flash of deep pain behind her eyes. "*I* didn't know what to do with me."

He closed his fists on his knees, thinking about her father telling her sex was a sin, blaming her for the maturation she couldn't stop. That must have been so confusing as she developed into her voluptuous figure.

"Grettina feels strongly about her marriage vows. He's the father of her twins so I understand why she felt so compelled to try to make it work, but he takes advantage of her." Her brow crinkled with distress. "I don't think she would have even considered leaving him if I hadn't run away. And sent her money to give her the means."

Her chin set at a remorseless angle.

Such a fierce warrior of a woman. So young to be so strong and determined. Brave. He was awed and deeply proud of her for fighting so hard to get where she was. To get away.

"Why did you run away? What happened?" he asked softly.

"Pappa found someone he wanted me to marry. Not someone with a billion-dollar company." She sent him a pithy look. "Just a man with a farm, but he has strong feelings about a woman's place. About mine." Her gaze dropped again, pensive. "I was looking forward to university so I could finally live by my own rules. One day he said he would take me to see a school in Bern. I was so excited." Her mouth curled with cynicism. "It was an hour to Bern, but he told me to pack for the weekend. Even Grettina found that strange, but we knew better than to question him. He took me to Visp, where he introduced me to a man who was twice my age and said we were getting married in the morning."

Atlas's heart lurched. "That's medieval."

"I was terrified. But talking back to him was..." She shook her head. "I sat there and listened to them negotiate a price like I was a dairy cow. I realized I wasn't going home no matter what happened. We were given rooms because my father was staying to sign the permission papers—I was still a few days shy of my birthday so he had to. I got up in the middle of the night, took my birth certificate from his wallet along with all the money he had, and caught the first train leaving the station. It took me to Zermatt."

"And he reported you for that? I thought Oliver was a piece of dirt."

"Not a contest I want to win, but yes. He did. Once I turned eighteen and knew he couldn't force me to come home, I called Grettina to let her know I was safe. She told me he'd been to the police. I don't think it was a high priority for them. It was a petty amount and I was old enough to be on my own, but I was scared enough I didn't want to talk to them that night we met, in case they told him where I was. I did pay him back, though. Around six months after I met you, actually." She brightened. "I found a lost dog and claimed the reward. I owed my father two hundred euros and that man he wanted me to marry offered him twenty-five hundred for my hand. That woman paid me *five thousand*. For a *dog*. Whenever I see a poster for lost pets, I look for them like they're Easter eggs."

The humor in her voice invited him to laugh at her, but he was the furthest thing from amused. He was sick and incensed and more determined than ever to bring her under his protection.

She sobered.

"So now you know why I don't want to marry anyone. Not for money. Not to become a baby machine," she said.

"He's trying to worm his way back into your stepmother's home? That's what these calls are about?" He pointed toward her phone. "Can you involve the police?"

"Grettina doesn't want to. They can't do much anyway. She and Pappa are separated, not divorced. He's not physically abusive, not to her, and he knows hitting is a redline where the twins are concerned. At the same time, Grettina can't bring herself to put him on the street. He's the father of her children. Not a good one, but their father and mine. So I'll find him a job and a place to live. He's a carpenter, but he's slowing down with age and blows up with temper over the littlest things, which gets him fired. Usually, I pay his rent until he finds something else, but this time he didn't tell me he had stopped paying. They've kicked him out for good. It's so frustrating."

"Whether you marry me or not, I will help you, Stella. But let me paint a picture of the solutions available to you as my wife. You will have the means to buy each of them a home as far apart as you deem sensible. Those will be yours to keep forever. Don't make that face. It's the sort of thing that was in my agreement with Iris. *Listen to what I'm offering.* Your father will never be homeless again, not unless you put him on the street yourself. He won't have to work. You'll have a very generous allowance, one that will make it possible for you to support all of them while maintaining the lifestyle expected of my wife. Your stepmother will never have to feel guilty that she's not taking him in because *you* will be taking care of him."

"That's so mercenary."

"It's a strategic move that betters your life and that of your family."

"By locking me into life with a stranger."

"Did your stepmother know who she was marrying? I imagine she thought she was in love with him, but what did she get out of the union? Three children who weren't hers and two more she's raising alone. Make a smarter choice, Stella. Make the choice that betters your life and everyone you care about."

"But what happens if we don't work? If—"

"It will all be spelled out in the prenup. I've already promised you two houses, an allowance, and a hotel to manage. What else do you want?"

She blinked, then her chin came up. "Full custody of any children we have, in the event of divorce."

"Ha!" She was trying to scare him off with a deal-breaker, but it told him that he had her. That allowed him to smile even as he said, "Never. We will share custody *if* it becomes necessary. And their home will be Greece."

"I'm not having children for at least two years," she warned with a staying finger. "If we're still married after that, we can *discuss* trying to start a family."

"Deal." He rose to extend his hand to shake.

After a long moment of consideration, she set her jaw at its most militant angle and stood to accept it.

He held on to her hand when her grip relaxed and brought it to his mouth. "I have one more condition," he said against her knuckles.

"What's that?" Her fingers fluttered like a snared bird in his.

"We marry tomorrow."

CHAPTER SIX

"I DON'T ACT that fast," Stella blurted, snatching back her hand.

What had she just done?

"The hell you don't," he scoffed. "You make careful plans for yourself, then seize opportunities when they present. That's how you wound up in Zermatt."

Was this an opportunity? Or a trap? And if she had realized the struggles she would face, she might not have done it.

That wasn't true. She was grateful to her teenage self for making that bold decision.

What would Future Stella think of this choice, though?

Her mind kept falling back on her conversation with Alexandra, when she had said she and Rafael were a team, and Atlas saying that marriage had started out as a tactic for each to get what they wanted.

It gave her the courage to make the leap and offer a jerky nod of agreement.

"I'll have a draft of the prenup for you shortly." He moved to the door, then paused. "If you want your family at the ceremony, I can arrange it, but I can't tolerate your father being there."

"I don't want him there, either." Other brides might want their father to give them away, but Pappa had tried to do that once already. She wouldn't let it happen again. "Will your family be there?"

"No," he said decisively. "I'll tell them when we get to London. Can you trust your family to keep it under wraps for a day or two?"

She thought of the twins, who were eight, and Pappa asking questions about why they'd been away.

"It's probably best if it's just you and me." She was used to keeping secrets from all of them. It wasn't the best dynamic with her family, but it had always felt safer. The less they knew of what she did, the less they had to confess to Pappa and be berated for it.

"I'll release the hounds," he said with a smirk, and left.

She lowered onto the bed again, trying to assimilate what she'd just done, but she wasn't given much time to react. Within a few minutes people began asking for her time, drawing her into meetings on everything from the correct spelling of her middle name to her mobile number, blood type and shoe size.

When the draft for their prenuptial agreement came through, she nearly fainted at the amounts Atlas was putting at her disposal. She tried to protest and Atlas said it was in line with his agreement with Iris. He told her they would marry in Denmark, since it had no residency requirement and was closer than Gibraltar. They would leave first thing in the morning.

Stella ran the agreement by a lawyer friend in Zermatt. Her friend charged a premium for dropping everything to read it within the hour and suggested an addendum to cover fertility treatments should that arise, but otherwise didn't spot any red flags.

With that, Stella ran out of reasons to turn back, but she was still trying to wrap her head around having a future with Atlas. She would be his wife and, eventually, the mother of his children. That would bind her to him for life the same way Grettina was bound to Pappa. It was daunting, but after tossing and turning all night, agonizing over whether she was making the right decision, she woke to a text from Beate.

Pappa had turned up wanting breakfast. Somehow, he'd caught wind of the photos.

Beate didn't tell her what he was saying, but Stella could imagine. He already thought Stella was a show-off for "wasting good money" on a hotel. He never missed a chance to criticize her. From the time she'd begun showing early signs of womanhood, he'd blamed her for it. He'd wanted her to shoulder the role of an adult woman where their household was concerned, but had resented that she had grown into one.

As she thought back to all his hypocrisies, something fierce rose in her, something that wanted to show him he'd been wrong when he'd tried to choose a husband for her. If she was going to buckle to the institution of marriage, it would be on her terms. It would be a marriage that allowed her to get the upper hand with her father once and for all.

"You're still here," Atlas said when they met for breakfast. He looped his arm around her and set a brief, minty-fresh kiss on her lips.

"You had doubts?" She touched her mouth, which was buzzing from that light contact.

"You have a history as a flight risk." He was teasing her, running his hand down the tail of her braid in the lightest of playful tugs.

It was a bright day of broken clouds when they lifted off, affording her a good view as they flew into Geneva. There, they boarded his private jet and reviewed the final prenuptial agreement. By the time they landed in Copenhagen, her e-signature was being requested.

Nerves accosted her then. The reality of what she was doing loomed larger as they were driven to a beautiful hotel in the town center and shown into a luxurious suite with a sun-drenched parlor, a balcony with a view of the harbor and a claw-foot tub in the bedroom.

A stylist was waiting with the dress she'd picked out.

She grew teary at that point, wishing she had asked Beate to be here. She suddenly felt very alone. This was how she'd felt on arrival in Zermatt. It was a new world to her, one where she didn't know anyone. Where she didn't know how she would make her way.

Was she throwing away her independence on a gamble that wouldn't pay off?

Atlas came in and the woman left.

"Wow." He halted to take in her satin A-line dress in winter white. It was tea-length with an off-shoulder neckline, simple and elegant. At least, that's what she had thought, but she brushed self-consciously at the fall of the skirt.

"It's not too simple? Or too sexy?" She had long ago learned there was no hiding her curves, so she might as well make the most of them.

"You are exactly the right amount of sexy. You look beautiful." His gaze touched the baby's breath the stylist had woven into the braided crown she'd arranged atop Stella's head. "I meant to ask you to keep your hair down, but I look forward to watching you take that apart later."

When they consummated their marriage. The air in her lungs evaporated.

"You look very nice, too," she said shyly. He was in pinstriped trousers and a dark gray morning coat. "Would you mind helping me with this? I forgot to ask her to help me put it on." She showed him the thin chain and offered her wrist. Her fingers were twitching with nerves, making it impossible to close the tiny catch. "It's my 'something old.' Beate gave it to me years ago. She won it at a fair and saved it for my birthday. It was in my laptop bag from when I had to have the catch fixed."

She braced herself for him to say something dismissive as he took it. It wasn't even real gold.

"Had I known, I would have bought a charm for it." He fastened it and the brush of his fingers against her skin made her pulse trip. "Instead, I bought this." He reached for an embossed bag he'd set on the table and withdrew a wide velvet case. Inside was a necklace with matching earrings.

She gasped, not insulting him by asking if they were real stones, but she did say with shaken hope, "A loan?"

"No, they're yours. A wedding gift."

"Atlas." She couldn't imagine what he'd paid for the intricate setting of marquise and pear-shaped diamonds set into a vine-like design. "I don't know what to say."

"You know what I want you to say. 'I do.'" He drew a circle with his finger, urging her to turn so he could fasten the necklace.

After he did, his touch traced the vee in the back of her dress, tickling against her skin until he reached where the buttons formed a line down her spine.

"These look designed to slow down an eager groom."

Trembling, she moved to the mirror to admire the necklace, which was so stunning it blinded her. She shakily removed her small gold studs—which had been an act of defiance since her father said only harlots pierced their ears.

She inserted the diamonds and the sway of their drops made her more aware of herself and how feminine she felt. The necklace was a weighty reminder of the magnitude of the step she was taking, but there was no going back. Atlas was holding the door, watching her with such a look of possessiveness, the air crackled.

It only took a few minutes to reach the courthouse. Inside, a young man greeted them. He held a small bouquet and had a satchel over his shoulder. He wore a dark suit and an excited expression.

"Stella, this is Yana, from our London office. He works closely with my assistant, Derik. He has agreed to help us until Derik is back from vacation, but if you find you're compatible, you may want to keep him as your own assistant."

"I don't think I'll need one, will I?"

"You will," Atlas assured her. "Think of all those phone calls and incidentals you pick up for guests at the hotel. Yana will do that for you so you can spend your time on more important things."

"Like you?" she teased.

"Exactly." His mouth tilted with dark satisfaction.

"It's an honor to meet you, Miss Sutter," Yana said in accented English as he offered the bouquet. "The wedding planner is upstairs, finalizing the paperwork. Shall we go?"

The chamber was surprisingly romantic with a vaulted ceiling and ornate murals on the walls. The ceremony itself was only a few minutes, but unhurried and filled with wishes that they embark on a life of caring and friendship.

As they exchanged rings, pincers of uncertainty took hold of her heart, but if she had harbored any girlish dreams around marriage or her wedding day, they had featured this man.

She had never imagined it would truly happen, though!

Even so, his hand was settling against the side of her

neck. He sealed their marriage with a too-brief brush of his lips against hers.

At the last second, as he was about to draw away, he pressed back to crush her mouth with his own. It didn't hurt, but it sent a deep sting through her—excitement and a sort of appeasement, but also stoked the fear she had barely acknowledged. That she wasn't enough. That the things he made her feel were too big. Too much.

When he drew back, she discovered her hand was clenched around his lapel. Her mouth burned and her heart thudded. She felt ravaged.

But wanted. Needed, even.

She blinked back emotive tears and signed the papers with a pen the stylist had lent her as her "something borrowed."

Yana took their photo on the stairs a moment later, offering congratulations as he lowered the camera.

They were married.

Chilled champagne waited in the room along with fresh strawberries, a selection of chocolates, an extravagant arrangement of flowers, and a blend of essential oils for the bath labeled Relax and Romance.

"Yana thinks of everything," Stella remarked, taking off the cap to inhale the aroma of rose, jasmine and sandalwood. It did nothing to ease her nerves.

"I requested this." Atlas popped the champagne.

As he poured, her phone gave a few pings where it sat on the dresser. She had deliberately left it here while they went to the courthouse so she wouldn't be distracted by it. Now she set aside the bottle of oil and picked up her phone.

"I'm used to keeping it on for work, but I'll mute it—" She cut herself off as she saw she'd received several emails from Atlas's staff: a copy of their signed agreement, a confirmation of a bank account opened in her name, a listing from a property agent she'd spoken to yesterday, and access to a joint calendar, among other things.

She liked to think she could roll with whatever life threw at her, but this was *so much.*

Atlas offered her a tall flute crackling with bubbles. "You look nervous. Would you like to fill the tub and see where it takes us?" The quiet rumble of his voice made her skin feel tight.

She turned off her phone and left it on the dresser.

"I'm afraid that I won't live up to your expectations and you'll regret all of this," she admitted, then sipped to wet her dry throat.

"What about your expectations?"

"I don't have any."

"The hell you don't." He sounded amused. "You've waited to have sex because you wanted it to feel a certain way. Do you think I'm not wondering if I can live up to *that*?"

He looked the furthest thing from worried or insecure, though. He looked hungry.

She swallowed.

"That means you'll have to be very clear about what you want," he said in a voice that settled even lower, becoming almost velvety in its timbre. "You'll have to say *yes* and *more* and *harder*. I won't make you say *please*."

She choked on her champagne.

He took the glass with an admonishing look. "This is my best suit."

He set both glasses near her phone.

"I don't know what I want," she confessed in a strained voice, then had to ask, "What do you want?"

He made a rumbling noise of consideration as he shrugged out of his jacket and loosened his tie, gaze traveling from her hair to her cheek to her shoulders and onto her throat.

"I want to watch you take your hair down and undress. I want to see you in only that necklace while you ride me and I feel your hair all over my chest."

She gasped. Her hand went to the necklace, but only because her pulse pounded so hard, she thought she might dislodge it.

"Am I coming on too strong?" He sounded amused, but his voice held a rasp that suggested he was keeping himself in firm check. "This is what sex is, Stella. If you want it to be good—and I know you do—then we have to say what we want and trust the other one will set the limits if it's too much. I have very few."

"Limits?" She suspected she didn't have any, not where he was concerned. She was standing here fully dressed, but already felt naked. Vulnerable and raw. But excited.

His eyes narrowed. "If you're not ready for that, keep your hair up. We can go for an early dinner."

"No, I—" She reached for her hair and began searching for pins. Which felt like the most blatant action in the world. It felt like saying, *Yes. More. Please* and *harder*. It felt like begging.

She half expected him to laugh at her, but when she dared a glance toward him, he was watching her intently as she let the sprigs of baby's breath fall and unwound the tail of her plait, then began to unravel it. His hands flexed as though he was resisting the urge to touch her. To hurry her. That gave her an unexpected thrill. A sense of power as she realized how much control he was exerting over himself.

When she had combed her fingers through her hair, fan-ning the long, rippling tresses around her shoulders, she asked, "Do you want me to keep undressing?"

"Yes." The gritty word dropped like a hard stone in the quiet of the room. His urging was like a tangible force. Command rolled off him in aggressive waves.

Which should have had her hurrying to comply, but the strangest urge to defy him struck her. Not defy. *Provoke.* She didn't know what possessed her, but she bent to pick up the hem of her dress and hooked her fingers into her underpants, sliding them down and off while letting the skirt fall back into place.

She kicked away the white cheekies and straightened to see an incandescent mix of astonishment and lust consume his expression.

"Is that how we're playing?" He came toward her and cupped her head and smothered her mouth before she could finish saying, "Yes."

His tongue swept between her parted lips, plunging her into a passionate kiss while she was still absorbing the erotic sensation of the silk lining caressing her bare bottom and thighs.

I'm not wearing underwear. He knows it.

She wore a strapless bra and wished she didn't have that, either.

This was a very immodest way to behave, but she reveled in it. His hands roamed in circles on her backside, stimulating her with the heat of his palms and slippery glide of satin against her skin.

The press of his erection nudged where it had the other night. It was even more enticing now that she knew what he could do for her. She pushed into him, urging him to do what he had done then.

He spun her to the bed and came down on the mattress

with her. His weight crushed her and his mouth plundered her lips and her only complaint was that she'd lost that delicious pressure between her thighs.

"Atlas," she gasped, turning her head away to catch her breath.

"Tell me what you want," he said as he levered himself up and off the bed. "This?"

Before she could respond, he adjusted her angle on the bed. Her skirt rode up as he dragged her closer, leaving her exposed to him.

She tried to pinch her thighs together, but he dropped to his knees and hugged her leg, then pressed a damp, open-mouthed kiss to the inside of her knee.

"Do you not want my mouth here, *asteri mou*? Or here?" He set his mouth higher on the tender skin inside her thigh, eyes bronzed with iniquity. "Tell me."

In that moment, she knew she would never have the upper hand with him. Never.

Her heart lurched even as her pulse tripped with sexual excitement. Provoking him had unleashed a ferocity in him that she had no hope of outgunning, but as he gently sucked a love bite into her skin, she groaned in capitulation.

"Yes." She squeezed her eyes shut. "Please. More."

He teased her, making her wait for the trail of kisses to work in pinprick sensations toward the ache in her center.

"Please," she heard herself pant again, right before his touch delicately parted her folds and the heat of his mouth captured her most sensitive flesh.

It was distressingly intimate and deeply pleasurable. Sinful, probably, but she couldn't bring herself to stop him. She was seduced. Melted into liquid iron, heavy and glowing and molten.

"There. More. *More*," she moaned.

His long finger entered her slippery channel, moving in delicious cadence with the sweep of his tongue in such a perfect dance she thought she must be levitating off the bed. She was nothing but sensation, trying to capture the most intense waves with the knowledge there was something even greater beyond the break.

Then the crash happened, cracking her in half with the force of it, suffusing her in more pleasure than she could stand. Her cries of inhibition filled the room and he kept up his caress through the crisis and into the aftermath, only slowing when her contractions were fading to twitches.

She was boneless and buttery then, still trying to recover as he closed her legs.

"Do you know how long I've wanted to do that?" He rolled her onto her side and settled behind her so he could open the buttons down the back of her dress. "Five *years*."

Soft kisses peppered her shoulders and spine as he opened the dress, making her twitch in the liminal space between satisfaction and returning arousal.

"I liked making you come apart like that," he whispered hotly against her ear. His lips nibbled along the rim. Her scalp tightened and her strapless bra relaxed. A shiver chased down her naked spine while his restless hand brushed bra and dress away so he could cup her breast. "I'm going to be deep inside you when it happens again," he promised.

His diabolical lips trailed to her nape, but as he shifted his mouth to the side of her throat, there was a pull on her scalp.

"You're on my hair."

"I need a condom anyway." He lifted off the bed and stripped his clothes. "It's in our contract."

He was joking, but she checked in pushing off the last of

her clothes. Part of her wanted to say *You don't have to*. She wanted to feel him. At the same time, she was disconcerted to realize he still had the capacity to think of something coldly practical when really, he could have done anything to her at this point and she would have thanked him for it.

He drew a condom from the box in the night table. "Do you need lube?"

She shook her head.

"I don't want to hurt you, Stella." He leaned down to kiss her and slid a very proprietary hand between her legs as he did, caressing with a light, sweeping touch against her damp folds.

She tensed, shy, but he was in no hurry and, between kiss and caress, she was easily seduced into lying back on the bed. He gently invaded with one finger, then two. It was so flagrant, and fluttered such intense sensations through her, she bit her lip.

"Hurt?" He stilled.

"No."

"You're tearing up." He carefully withdrew.

"Because it's so…" She stopped herself from saying "big." "I really want this. You."

I feel like you're taking all of me. I'll have nothing left.

This marriage was a disaster of the best and worst kind.

He kissed her again, tenderly, then applied the condom. He piled the pillows against the headboard and brought her with him as he settled back against them, guiding her to straddle his hips, but he only had her settle her damp core against the rigid line of his erection.

"Do you have any idea how beautiful you look right now? Rosy and aroused…" He brushed the fall of hair away from her breast and over her shoulder, then cupped the swell, lifting it. "Let me suck your nipple."

She had to catch at the headboard as she leaned forward, then jolted at the sensation of his hot mouth closing around the tip, pulling with light suction. Her legs were open; he was fondling her backside, reaching to touch her again, making her writhe while gently torturing her with the flick of his tongue against her sensitive nipple.

"And the other," he demanded when he released her.

She bit her lip, wanting this, but wanting the other. Wanting to belong to him. She arched, trembling with arousal.

He dropped his head back and looked at her through hooded eyes.

"Now you're starting to look like I feel."

As though he was being torn apart? As though the heat billowing through blood and flesh and lungs was burning him alive?

"I can't wait anymore," she said helplessly and yes, there were tears in her eyes. "It's been a long five years."

"It has," he said in a voice like gravel. "Take me." He held himself steady and set his hand on her hip, guiding her.

The sensation of impaling herself on him was imposing and stark and deeply intimate. She was nervous, but too shaken and weak with arousal to fight gravity. Too ready and curious and trembling with need.

"There's no hurry," he admonished in a murmur, keeping his fist wrapped around his shaft so she could only feel the breadth of his tip filling her.

"I don't want to wait anymore." The ache of longing rang in her voice.

His breath hissed in and he removed his hand to clasp her waist.

She sank fully upon him, shuddering at the pinch as his length filled her. It was carnal and real, so very blatant, but good. It felt right. Like a culmination. Like she was meant to be right here in this moment in time, looking into his golden eyes.

As she panted and tried to adjust to this new experience, his touch pressed lightly into her tailbone, inviting her to move.

She did and her entire body felt stroked. Sensuality fluttered through her as she began to rock her hips in a rhythm set by instinct and the clasp of his hands on her hips. Her breasts swayed and she leaned down to kiss him, moaning with pleasure into his mouth.

It was perfection. Joyous, beautiful perfection that was building with each grind of her hips, with the way his tongue flicked into her mouth and his hands moved across her skin.

She didn't care that all of Denmark could probably hear her. She rolled her hips, wanting more, wanting him deeper. He wrapped his arm around her to keep her hips secured to his and slid down on the bed, then began to rise up to meet her, fingertips digging into her hips. The coil within her tightened, the urgency gathered.

"Atlas, Atlas…" Within moments, it was happening again. She was splintering into a million pieces.

She held herself very still as climax washed over her, hands splayed on his hard chest, thighs gripping the hips that were pinned high beneath her.

But there was no easing her into the afterglow this time. When the tension began to leave her body and she dragged her eyes open, she found his were alight with a feral gleam. In a move that reminded her he'd been an Olympian, he rolled her beneath him, and thrust once, deep, to secure their connection.

She cried out as fresh nerve endings were seared by steel and friction.

"Too hard?"

"No." She brought her knees to his waist and locked her ankles in his lower back. "More. *Harder.*"

He was no delicate novice at this. He wasn't brutal, but he unleashed his strength, making love to her in a way that did nothing less than claim her. While his kiss stole her breath and his arms caged her, he built one powerful thrust on another until sensations were twisting through her like forked lightning, making her writhe at the intensity of it. The pleasure was too much to bear.

She was trapped, though. Trapped in a world that had shrunk to him. Only him. The damp heat of his chest rubbing her breasts, the tension of his shoulders, the crash of his pelvis into hers. His smothering mouth and the scrape of his teeth at her jaw and the incredible tension that gripped them both.

When they were both sweating and making animalistic noises, when the ferocious pleasure was threatening to kill her, Atlas rasped, "Come now, Stella. *Now.*"

She did.

Atlas managed to get them both between the sheets and should have passed out the way Stella did.

Hellfire, she was beautiful, looking like Aphrodite with her hair spilling around her generous curves and her skin still flushed with orgasm. Her face was serene, innocent if not for the lips that were swollen and pink from their kisses.

He pushed the sheet down to his waist, still hot. Still recovering. Not just physically, but mentally.

He had known sex with her would be spectacular. He hadn't expected it to be *that.* She was completely uninhibited, bringing out a primal side of him he'd taken pains to bury deep in the back of the cave.

An undeniable possessiveness had been expanding in him since the photos had come out. Sooner than that, probably, but the moment he realized she was under threat, he had felt compelled to protect her. There was a disconcerting other side to that coin, however, one that recognized the threat she posed to him. In the last hour, she had taken him to his breaking point and would continue to do so. He was vulnerable to her now and, because she was his wife and he was obsessed with her, she made him vulnerable to anyone who might attack her.

His practical mind had seen this marriage as a single path to several benefits: a wife he genuinely wanted, sex with a woman who had quietly obsessed him for years, and proof that he wasn't his father. He hadn't seduced a virgin while married to someone else. He married the virgin he wanted. He intended to treat her like a goddess.

Marrying Stella had been the right thing to do. He couldn't regret it, but he recognized that things had changed for *him*. He wouldn't remain faithful out of an arrogant desire to prove he was better than his father. It went far deeper than that. He tried to imagine wanting someone besides Stella, anyone, and it didn't compute.

She was the one he wanted. The only one. He had her and that should be enough to satisfy the beast within him, but there was an itch to hunt still pacing within him. He wanted more from her. He wasn't sure what it could be, but it bothered him that this craving sat in his gut even as his blood was still slowing from being inside her.

He wasn't aware of falling asleep, only knew the waterfall he heard didn't make sense. He was in a hotel in Denmark. Married. Wasn't he?

He snapped his eyes open and found her side of the bed empty. Her jewelry sat on the nightstand.

"Stella!" He came up on an elbow and there she was in a hotel robe, hair piled atop her head in a messy bun.

She finished pouring oil into the running tub and closed the bottle. "Do you mind?"

"No." He sat up, letting the covers fall to his waist. "How do you feel?" Sore enough she needed the bath?

"Embarrassed," she admitted in a voice he barely heard over the rush of water.

"Why?" He threw off the covers and stood. "There's no shame in what we did. Even if we weren't already married."

"No, but…" She bit her lip, rueful. Her lashes flickered, suggesting her gaze had gone to the twitching flesh between his thighs.

"What?" he prompted, stalking toward her, growing smug.

She lifted a defensive shoulder, so damned cute with her blush and pert smile, he wanted to kiss her before she could reply.

"I woke up and thought, 'Why isn't he awake? I want to do it again,'" she confessed.

Oh. Conceit poured in a line of heat from his throat to his torso to his loins, pulling him into arousal as he drew her into his arms. "You can always wake me for that. I'll never be mad."

"You look angry right now." She sent a teasing look to the aggressive thrust of his erection. "Can I, um…?" Her hand hesitated to take hold.

"That's part of our shared property now, *asteri mou*. Help yourself."

She hummed a noise of amusement and gently gripped him. Her hand was soft, her touch hesitant, but deeply seductive all the same.

He cupped her jaw and kissed her while she explored, learning the shape of him. His own fingers found the opening in her robe and discovered that she had, indeed, been thinking about this. Her wet heat called to him. He wanted to taste her again and imagined her tongue where her thumb was riding the sweet spot on his tip.

Desire rose so sharply in him, he had to cover her hand to still it.

"Should I stop the water?" she asked in a voice soaked with arousal.

He glanced at how slowly it was rising.

"We have time. But why don't you watch it, just in case. Turn around and hold on to the edge of the tub."

Her eyes flared with shock, then glittered with libidinous interest before she did exactly as he'd commanded.

Oh, she was dangerous. If he wasn't careful, she would have him wrapped around her finger before he knew it.

He remembered to get a condom, barely, then returned to sweep the robe up to the middle of her back, before losing himself in her perfection.

CHAPTER SEVEN

ATLAS HAD HATED his father's boxy, institutional brick manor house from the moment he'd arrived here at fourteen.

The country estate was an hour from London and Atlas had felt every minute of that rainy drive today, exactly as he had seventeen years ago. On that first day, he had left his mother behind in Greece. Today, he left Stella in his penthouse in London, but the knowledge she was there, not next to him, pulled at him like a barbed hook in his skin.

She was busy choosing a gown for the party Saturday night, the one where he would steal focus from his father's celebration of his sixty-fifth birthday. As a courtesy, Atlas was warning him, face-to-face. Man-to-man.

"The prodigal son returns," Carmel said when he entered the parlor where she lounged in her silk pajamas, legs draped over the arm of the chair, hair spilling off the other side as she tilted her head back to look up at him with a smirk. "Shame about Iris."

"It all worked out in the end." He kept his left hand in his pocket. "Where's Oliver?"

"In his library, writing you out of his will if there's a god. What do you mean it worked out? How?" She gathered herself to sit up and tucked her legs under her.

"I'll tell you after I talk to him."

"Sounds ominous. Do I need to call my sponsor?"

"Perhaps." He had legitimate concerns about her reaction to his marriage.

Carmel had celebrated a year of sobriety last month and had begun taking her position with Davenwear more seriously. She was in a good place, but she was a mercurial person and she'd always felt threatened by him.

"Your life won't change, though," he assured her. "No matter what happens, I'll always look after you. I hope you believe that."

"Said the scorpion to the frog. 'It'll be fine. Just get me across the river,'" she mocked.

"I'm not the scorpion." He chinned toward the stairs.

"And I'm the frog? What are you? The river that drowns us both?" She dropped her gaze to his trousers. "Why are you acting like you're twelve and found a hole in your pocket?"

To hell with it. He showed her the band on his finger.

"Who?" she demanded, eyes brightening with alarm.

"Stella. The woman from the photos."

"That hotel maid?" She cackled. "Who made her wedding gown? *Mice?*" She rolled back into the cradle of the chair and picked up her phone. "Good luck with Daddy. I'd say it's been nice knowing you, but we both know it hasn't."

"Charming as always." He didn't bother pointing out that Stella had worked her way to managing the front desk and walked out. He found Oliver in his suite, having his final fitting for the tuxedo he would wear tomorrow night.

"You," he sneered when Atlas strode in after a brief knock.

"I need a moment with my father, Enzo. *Per favore*," Atlas said to the tailor.

The man who had had his hand on Atlas's inseam for

more than a decade helped Oliver remove his jacket and left with it, closing the door behind him.

Oliver stepped off the riser and moved into the sitting room, where he pulled the stopper off a decanter of brandy. "How the hell did you let yourself get caught?"

Not "Who is she?" or "What happened?" but "How dare you get caught?"

"You've put me in a terrible position with Makepeace," Oliver continued with crisp annoyance. "He's already putting the thumbscrews to me, demanding a placement for his nephew. The boy is an absolute disaster, but I don't have a choice now, do I?"

Oliver only understood the world in terms of power and manipulation, backstabbing and back-scratching, which was why Atlas had decided to play his game and win it.

"I met Stella the first time we went to Zermatt, for that winter shoot when Carmel was nearly arrested." That was an exaggeration, but Atlas enjoyed reminding his father that police had come to the chalet. "You met her, too. Briefly. Then you had her fired."

Atlas had debated whether to tell his father that. God knew Oliver wouldn't remember her and likely didn't remember the incident beyond a scandal he'd had to clean up. Atlas didn't want Stella's position as a chalet girl to come out later, though, when Oliver might think he could embarrass her with it.

"You've been poking her all this time?" Oliver made a face of distaste as he handed Atlas one of the glasses of brandy. "Tell me it's finally over. I don't care what it cost, but why haven't you made a statement yet? What the hell have you been doing for two days?"

"Getting married. The announcement will go out shortly."

"*Married.* Not to her? That had better be a joke. Good

God, she's pregnant?" His lip curled in distaste. "Not so high on your horse now, are you?"

"She's not pregnant," Atlas said with malicious cheer. "I married her because I wanted to."

"You're not that stupid, Atlas." Oliver hitched his trousers as he sat in his favorite throne-like armchair. "What could she possibly bring to a marriage? Is she secretly sitting on a fortune?"

"No, but neither was Iris."

"Iris was a valuable alliance. The Makepeace-Reids offer credibility and lineage. Esteem."

"You keep trying to polish me into legitimacy," Atlas noted with a humorless shake of his head. "I'm never going to be anything but your bastard son, Oliver. It's time to accept that."

"I will not," he said with great indignation. "Are you seriously asking me to condone your marriage to a chambermaid? Dragging my name down as you do?"

"I don't use your name, do I?" Atlas taunted.

"Quit being a child. I was already married." Oliver put on his testy voice, as though his marital status would have made a difference when they both knew he would never have married Oliver's mother. A taverna waitress? No. His contempt for Atlas's mother was as plain as his derision of Stella. "I refuse to accept this," Oliver declared. "Annul it or I'll strike you from my will."

He could try. After a paternity test and all these years of being recognized as his son, contributing to the wealth Oliver continued to enjoy, Atlas had a very good shot at contesting any changes and they both knew it. Atlas also had a fortune in his own right, built on early investments and his work at DVE. He could weather losing the assets Oliver had promised him.

"We can turn this into war if you want to." Atlas let him see he was completely unbothered by the prospect. "But let me remind you that the board has held off on voting for me to replace you because I was single. Now that I have a wife—"

"You have a pawn you're trying to turn into a queen. They will see through this mopping of a scandal. You're no better than me, Atlas. They know it as well as we both do."

"I cleaned up my scandal in the most honorable way possible." Yes, that was a dig against his father's countless conquests who'd been paid to disappear when they became inconvenient. "I've spent years demonstrating sound judgment and responsible leadership. One stumble doesn't erase any of that. Most importantly, if the board decides they can't support me, they can watch me move to greener pastures. I'm young enough to start over. Are you young enough to continue running DVE without me? To guide it into the future? Are you strong enough to fend off whoever they choose *instead* of me?"

Oliver lowered his drink, realizing with a choke of astonishment, "This is a coup."

"It is." Atlas saluted him with his own glass. "You can decide how bloody it will be."

In the fog of getting married and celebrating with nonstop sex, Stella had failed to fully process what marrying Atlas meant for her *life*.

Everything changed quite literally overnight. She had not only left her home and job behind, but lost the person she had always been. She was no longer the clerk behind the desk or the voice on the phone who assisted others. She was surrounded by people doing that for her, all respectful and cheerful and trying to anticipate her needs. They made her bed and carried her bag and ran her bath and poured her coffee. She was not one of them.

It was a startling shift that was even more apparent when she spoke with her family.

They were shocked and perplexed by her marriage, of course, not knowing how to react, especially since she had run away to avoid the marriage her father had tried to force on her. She didn't have boyfriends and didn't talk about wanting a husband so this was completely unexpected.

Elijah was particularly concerned about her. Stella was older and had left home to live on her own terms years ago. She always took lead on standing up to their father, but suddenly he had a lot of questions about how vulnerable she was. Who was this man she'd married? Would he treat her kindly? Had their father driven her to this with his latest selfish actions? Elijah's concern was sweet, if unnecessary.

Atlas met Elijah over a video call and reassured him that he was very invested in Stella's peace of mind where their family's welfare was concerned. He promised to bring her for a visit before they left for Australia, then asked Elijah how he thought their father would best be managed.

After a long discussion among the three of them, they arrived at a plan. The property agent found a house in a solid middle-class neighborhood that was badly in need of updates. Stella told her father the truth, that her husband had purchased it for her and she wanted her father to live in it while he renovated and modernized it.

Pappa grumbled that it would be expensive and a lot of work, but she had a budget for him that included hiring tradespeople as well as covering a meal delivery service so he wouldn't have to worry about groceries and cooking.

"I can hire a stranger to do it if you'd rather, but they

may not do the work as well as you." She knew how to play to his ego.

Her father's taste ran to minimalistic and ultrapractical, but he valued quality and his workmanship was always excellent. His perfectionist tendencies were part of his temperament problems, so Stella expected there would be delays around electricians not being considered up to snuff or plumbers balking at his telling them how to do their job. He was very single-minded when he had a goal, though. She hoped the house would consume him enough to take his attention off Grettina and the rest of the family.

Grettina insisted she didn't need anything, of course. Stella quietly took over the payments on her lease and asked the agent to find a property that would be suitable for Beate when she moved to Austria to continue her music studies.

As the pressure eased where her own family was concerned, the pressure with Atlas's began to rise.

Returning from his meeting with Oliver, Atlas had said ominously, "He's weighing up his options." Atlas then made calls to a number of the board members, advising them of his marriage.

The formal announcement came out overnight, creating a deluge over the next two days of nonstop gift deliveries and countless messages of congratulations with invitations to yachts, summer homes, galas and dinners. People couldn't wait to meet Atlas's mystery bride and reporters and paparazzi were clamoring for photos and statements, but his father and sister were noticeably absent in the sea of well-wishes.

Stella would meet them shortly. She and Atlas were arriving early for Oliver's birthday party at the family estate, planning to stay the night. They drove through a gauntlet of cameras at the gate, but thankfully had privacy once they were inside.

She was so nervous her fingers were pure ice when Atlas helped her from the car.

He frowned in concern. “Don’t worry. Short of challenging me to a duel that I would win, he knows I have the upper hand.”

She wasn’t sure how that was supposed to reassure her, but she found a smile as they climbed the steps and walked through the door that the butler held open for them. Atlas introduced the man as Chester.

Chester bowed his head with deference. “It’s an honor to meet you, Mrs. Voudouris. May I take your coat?”

“I’ll take it.” Atlas was very chivalrous that way, Stella was learning. He seemed to enjoy these small excuses to touch her, often adding a caress against her neck or a squeeze of her shoulder while he held her chair or helped her dress. Or undress.

Today, as she skimmed her arms free, there was no sign of affection, though. When he spoke, his voice had chilled. “What are you trying not to tell me?”

“I suggested calling you last night, sir,” Chester said in a somber, barely audible undertone. “Miss Carmel is unwell.”

Atlas swore sharply and looked toward the archway on their left. It seemed to lead into a drawing room of some sort where staff were busily polishing and decorating.

“Where’s Oliver?” Atlas snarled, handing off her coat and starting that direction, bellowing, “Oliver!”

“Upstairs, sir,” Chester said with a small clear of his throat.

As Atlas turned to start up them, a man appeared in a quilted robe on the gallery.

“*Must* you behave like the street mongrel you are?” Oliver Davenport looked exactly as Stella remembered him, right down to the scathing glower at his son that somehow ignored her and disapproved of her all at once.

"How long has she been drinking?" Atlas demanded.

"How long do you think? You left here at eleven ten on Thursday, so eleven eleven. Perhaps you should have anticipated collateral damage when you were plotting your revolution."

"You're saying it's my fault? Of course you are." Atlas took the stairs two at a time. "Why haven't you taken her to the clinic? She's likely dehydrated."

"The party was her idea. She'll only discharge herself and come back for it."

"I cannot believe you." Atlas brushed past him.

Stella stood frozen in place, shock turning to apprehension as Oliver finally took notice of her.

For a long moment, he stared down at her. Then he snorted in dismissal and walked away.

"Perhaps I could show you to your suite, ma'am?" Chester offered. "I believe the stylist is arriving soon. I'll have her sent up once you've had a chance to settle in."

"Thank you. Um…unless Atlas needs my assistance with his sister?"

"One of our maids is with her. Please." He guided her to the stairs.

As they reached the top, they found Atlas supporting Carmel as he walked her toward them along the gallery. She wore crumpled silk pajamas; her hair was lank, her skin sallow.

In a slurred voice, she complained, "I had a year. You ruined it. I hate you so much."

"I know," he said grimly. "You can tell the counselor all about my many offenses, but let's get you there."

"This is her?" She picked up her lolling head as they came even with Stella. "Daddy said you're not even pregnant. You must have done something really vile, in bed or out—"

"No, Carmel," Atlas said dangerously. "You hate *me*. Never go after Stella or I really will make your life miserable. I'll be back in time for the party," he told Stella before he walked his sister down the stairs.

The party would go on?

She blinked in surprise, but followed Chester as he showed her to an apartment-like suite where he left her with a maid and a promise that tea was on its way. The maid was unpacking her things into the bedroom closet and looked horrified when Stella offered to do it herself.

Stella paced back to the sitting room, trying to get her bearings in the place Atlas had spent his adolescence and young adult years. His personality wasn't stamped here much. The decor was masculine with a sturdy desk and heavy armchairs in the study, a long sofa and big-screen television in the sitting room, and a wide king-size bed in the bedroom. A selection of his clothes were in the closet and there was a shaver on the charger in the bathroom, but those things could have belonged to any man.

Above the bed was a beautiful triptych of an island she presumed was Atlas's birthplace, given the white buildings against a blue sky surrounded by turquoise waters. On the night table stood a framed snapshot of a young Atlas—perhaps five or six, judging by his missing teeth. He was hugging the waist of a pretty woman who had her hand on his shoulder. Her other arm was around a smiling heavyset man beside her. They stood on the stoop of what must have been the family's taverna.

Was this all he had of them? she wondered.

Love shone out of their faces in blunt contrast to the scene that had taken place when they'd arrived. How often had he had to take Carmel to a clinic? Many times, she suspected, considering the resigned tone he'd used when he'd said she could tell the therapist about his many shortcomings.

She heard the door to the sitting room and came back, hoping to see Atlas had returned, but braced for Oliver. She wouldn't be surprised if his father had decided to barge in and verbally attack her, blaming her for his daughter's condition.

It was another maid, rolling in a tray with a tea service and a tiered stand filled with crustless sandwiches, scones, jam, tartlets and cakes. She asked if she could set it up on the table by the window overlooking the rose garden.

"Please." Stella noted the staff seemed subdued, but not nearly as affected by Carmel's condition as Stella was. They'd obviously been through this before.

She thanked the young woman, then sat, not really hungry, but it would be a long evening. She used the time to browse her phone. She didn't know much about addiction beyond learning how to respond to overdose in first aid and reading HR policies on drug use, so she read up on recovery and support while she ate.

The stylist came in shortly after she finished and Stella was tied up with her for the next few hours. Her nails had been done yesterday, but it still took ages to have her makeup applied and her hair curled, combed out, then pinned back from her face to fall in ripples down her back.

Her gown had been a difficult choice, finding the balance between her debut as Atlas's wife and trying not to upstage whatever his sister might wear, for fear of getting off on the wrong foot. She'd chosen a beaded one-shoulder gown in mauve that clung to her figure and split over her left thigh, revealing her cute peep-toe shoes with their double ankle straps.

She was fully dressed, necklace and earrings on, mouth dry as she contemplated whether she would have to go downstairs alone when Atlas strode in.

"You're ready. Good. Guests are arriving." He scraped his hand against his five-o'clock shadow. "Give me a minute to shave and change." He began peeling off his shirt as he walked through the bedroom toward the bathroom.

"Is Carmel all right?" she asked, trailing him.

"No. But I've seen worse. They're giving her fluids and will keep her while she dries out. I'll check on her tomorrow before we go back to London." He clicked on his shaver and began running it over his face.

She hovered, feeling useless until he turned off the shaver and walked around her toward the closet.

"It's good they had a bed available," she said, trying to find a bright side.

"We founded the place. She's got her own room with her name on the door." He dropped his trousers and kicked them away. "That is a very dark, tasteless joke. I shouldn't have said it." He pulled on his tuxedo pants and left them open while he shrugged on his shirt.

"Do you want to talk about it?" she invited.

"No." He buttoned and tucked, zipped his fly, then tied his bow tie perfectly, first try, without a mirror. He shot his arms into his jacket, shrugged it into place and shot his cuffs.

He looked insanely handsome and so remote it hurt her heart.

As he closed the buttons on his jacket, he finally looked

at her again, scraping her appearance from top to toe with his critical gaze. “Did you get the ring?”

“What ring?” She glanced toward the study. “Chester left something on the desk.”

“It’s for you.” He strode through and picked up the glossy black bag with satin ribbons for handles. Inside was a box upholstered in red and tan leather tied with a gold ribbon. “Bloody packaging,” he muttered, pulling it apart to reveal a smaller box, this one black velvet. “Granted, the average thief would have given up by now…”

He offered her a huge blue sapphire surrounded by diamonds. When he slid it onto her finger, it fit as though made to sit against her wedding band—which she suspected it had.

“It’s beautiful. Thank you.” She had begun to lose her shyness when it came to touching him, but she felt awkward as she stepped closer and kissed the corner of his mouth.

“Lipstick?” he asked, wiping at the spot as she drew back.

“No, it’s fine.”

“Good. We should go.”

He was so aloof. Was it the stress of his sister’s condition or did he blame her for it?

She made herself find a smile as she tucked her hand in the crook of his elbow and accompanied him to the stairs.

CHAPTER EIGHT

HE SHOULD HAVE expected it, Atlas berated himself as he was forced to say, yet again, “She’s not feeling well.”

All the guests were longtime family friends and business associates. They knew “unwell” was code for “relapse.” Their reactions ranged from murmurs of compassion to less sincere, more judgmental brow lifts before they turned their attention to Stella.

His wife was weathering her own spectrum of reactions from polite welcome to undisguised curiosity to a few greetings that were more askance.

If she found it uncomfortable, she didn’t show it. She smiled warmly and asked appropriate questions and complimented gowns all while giving away very little about herself despite being grilled relentlessly.

“I grew up near Bern, but moved to Zermatt at eighteen. That’s where I met Atlas five years ago,” she said for the thousandth time, touching his arm and smiling up at him. “I didn’t expect we would rekindle things, but here we are, stealing the limelight from the guest of honor. Have you known Oliver long?”

She was actually an artist at deflection. If he wasn’t in such a foul mood, he would have appreciated that sooner. He would have noticed the stress around her eyes.

He was winning all the prizes for selfishness today, wasn’t he? God, he wanted this night over with.

Catching Chester's eye, he signaled that champagne should be served, then cut off the man droning on about his recent trip to the Amalfi Coast.

"Would you excuse us? It's time for the toast." Bringing Stella with him, he wove through the crowd to the ballroom where a chamber orchestra was assembled on one end.

The conductor nodded when Atlas appeared next to him and gracefully closed out their piece, stepping down so Atlas could bring Stella onto the dais in his place.

With the music silenced and staff circulating with trays of filled glasses, people gathered into the room and quieted, offering their attention to him and Stella. Atlas handed her one of the tall flutes that Chester brought and kept one for himself.

"First, if you haven't had a chance to meet my beautiful wife, Stella..."

She really was beautiful. The color of her gown made her eyes look purple. Each time he looked at her, he wanted to kiss her. To be alone with her and hold her. To lose himself completely in her so he could escape himself. Until there was no part of himself left.

"...then that is your loss," he continued. "Because we're leaving right after our first dance. We're still newlyweds, after all."

That earned a knowing chuckle.

"Where is Oliver?" Atlas scanned to where his father had come in from the terrace to glare at him.

Oliver hadn't said a word to Stella yet. He'd been avoiding them, not that Atlas had bothered making a point of introducing them. They were in a firm standoff of clashing wills.

"At sixty-five, my father continues to astound me," Atlas said with more sincerity than anyone could know. How could he be so neglectful? How? "Our relationship hasn't always been smooth sailing—" He paused for the laughter that understatement provoked. "But I anticipate he'll have more time for sailing and other relaxing pastimes very soon."

There. The gloves were off and on the floor between them.

A speculative murmur went through the crowd, hardening his father's expression.

Atlas grimly lifted his glass. "Please join me in wishing Oliver the health and happiness he deserves."

Rot in hell was what he really meant.

Glasses went up along with cheers of "Hear, hear."

They stepped down and the conductor led a chorus of "Happy Birthday" before switching to a waltz.

"I'm not much of a dancer," Stella warned Atlas as he guided her onto the floor.

He didn't care if she stood on his shoes and let him shuffle her around. They needed to start the dance portion of the evening so they could get the hell out of here.

She was actually a lovely dancer, easily matching his lead, much the way they were in bed. His father danced by with one of the women from the board—a widow he slept with on occasion and was likely trying to seduce onto his side against Atlas.

Atlas didn't take the chance that his father would ask them to switch partners. He cut the dance short and swept Stella out the front door to his waiting car.

"Oh! I thought—" She looked over her shoulder.

"There's a spa hotel up the road. I had Chester arrange it. We have bags in the back. I can't make you stay here."

He couldn't stay here. He was liable to smother Oliver in his sleep.

Stella's shoulders went down a notch, letting him know how much tension she'd been carrying while she'd been here, but she gave him a wary look as they slid into the car.

Thankfully, she didn't say anything until they'd arrived at the vine-covered estate house that had been converted into a luxury hotel. It offered fitness facilities and spa treatments along with a farm-to-fork restaurant and other exclusive amenities. Carmel spent as much time here as she did at rehab so he knew it was a top-notch place.

Their room was actually a stand-alone two-story cottage in a converted granary. Upstairs was a four-poster bed beneath a skylight. A small balcony overlooked a private garden lit with fairy lights. Downstairs, in the sitting room, wine sat on ice next to a basket of fruit, cheese, chocolate and crackers.

"Are you hungry?" Stella asked.

"No." Not for that. Maybe this confined space had been a bad idea.

She sent him a considering look before she came across and slid her arms around his waist.

He stiffened.

"Do you want to talk?" she asked.

"No."

"Get drunk?"

"Hell, no." He was always careful how he used alcohol, having seen the dark side of abusing it.

"Do you want to make love?"

"Stella—" He took hold of her upper arms, which were bare and warm and smooth. Inviting. "I'm not in a very romantic mood."

"Have sex, then? Or—" The next word she used lifted his brows into his hairline. "Did you think I don't know that word?" she chided. "I've stubbed my toe."

He choked on a laugh. Then shook his head. "I can tell when I'm being managed. You don't have to pacify me."

"It's not pacifying. It's..." She frowned. "You're upset

and you've put up a wall because of it. I understand why, but it's a mental stubbing of a toe. All that energy needs to go somewhere. Why not me? You'll make it good for me. I know you will. And when we're naked, I feel close to you."

He shook his head. "You're still new to this." He was reminding himself because he was in a mood that would push boundaries if he wasn't careful.

"I am." Her lips tilted into an enigmatic smile. "And I've been thinking I want to try something I haven't done yet." She started to lower to her knees.

"Wait." He tightened his hold on her arms.

"You don't want me to?" She blinked in surprise.

"I do. Desperately," he said through his teeth.

"Then let me."

He held her for a few pulsebeats of indecision, then, "Put a cushion down so you don't hurt your knees."

Atlas heard a creak on the stair and jerked his head up, realizing Stella was gone from beside him.

"Where are you going?"

"I need my bag."

"I'll get it." He came up on his elbow, but she was already down the stairs.

He fell onto his back again, listening until she crept back up and took her bag into the toilet.

He had a thought to check his phone, to see if there was news about Carmel, but his brain was still dull with sleep and his body still lethargic from an excess of sex.

Stella had destroyed him, utterly destroyed him. First, she'd taken him in her mouth and generously caressed every which way he guided her to do. She had been right about the energy within him needing an outlet, though. As much as he'd wanted to let her take him over the edge, he'd also wanted to punish himself on some level. To hurt. And he'd needed some semblance of power to combat the helplessness that stalked him.

Before he lost control, he had picked Stella up and tipped her onto the couch to ravish her in the same way. Claiming her with his mouth and his touch and every part of him, again and again, on every piece of furniture he could abuse—the coffee table, the stairs, the bench at the end of this bed. He'd had her cling to the bedpost while he knelt behind her and covered her hands and buried his mouth in her neck while burying himself in her body.

Each time he made her cry out and spasm with joy, he'd exulted in his ability to do so. He'd tested the limits of their eroticism until, at some point, the urgency within him had reached its breaking point. He'd exploded within her. Finally, their raw, frenzied connection had turned slow and sensual and become a tender sprawl across the soft mattress.

They had passed out, naked and sweaty and spent. Now the predawn glow at the edges of the curtains was coating the room in a liminal gray light.

She came back to bed on tiptoe, still in the hotel robe, fingers working to braid her hair.

"I'm awake," he told her, and pulled back the covers on her side.

"I think I'm getting my period. My back hurts." She sat on the bed, legs curled to the side while she continued binding her hair. "I wanted to put something on."

"Are you sure I'm not the reason your back hurts? I think I might have broken my own." His whole body was aching as though he'd trained for hours.

"I'm sure." She was reaching the end of her tail and held it while she searched in the pocket of the robe. His bow tie came out, and she used it to tie off the braid.

"Sacrilege." He reached for the braid and lightly rolled the length around and around his fist, pulling her in slow motion to lean down and kiss him.

She did, becoming pliant as she splayed her hands on his chest, but she lifted her head to say, "I'm not broken, but I think I'd rather wait and see."

"I was just saying hello." Maybe avoiding what he knew she deserved. "And thank you." He released her hair and found her knee beneath the slit in the robe, appreciating the feel of her soft, cool skin.

"Can I ask something before we go back to sleep?" She braced her arm on the far side of his waist so she was bridged over him, hip leaned into his side. "Was Carmel's drinking really our fault? She's upset that you married me?"

"Her drinking has nothing to do with you, Stella. Don't ever let either of them get into your head that way. Unless you pour a drink and hand it to her, there is no way it could be your fault. She began drinking herself to blackout in her teens. If we want to point fingers, we can look to the genes on her mother's side where there's a history of addiction and alcohol abuse, but that's not her fault, let alone yours."

"Yet I get the sense you're blaming yourself."

He drew a deep breath against the weight of Carmel's struggles.

"I carry a lot of guilt where she's concerned," he admitted. "She lost her mother about a year before I came to live with them. That's when her drinking started, at boarding school. She was already struggling academically. She has some learning challenges and grief didn't help. She began acting out, getting suspended."

"She probably wanted to come home."

"Perhaps." He nodded. "But when she did, I was there. She wasn't aware I existed until I arrived. Suddenly, she learned her father had not only had an affair while her mother was pregnant with her, she had a brother who was entitled to half the estate. I remember overhearing her crying, trying to understand, and Oliver said to her, 'Someone has to take over. You're not up to it.'"

"That's horrible."

"It was. She felt rejected. Usurped. It's not that she's not capable of working alongside me, but she's never applied herself because her anger and drinking were always in the way. I've often questioned whether it's worth being Oliver Davenport's son, but I stuck it out because my mother wanted me to claim what she saw as my birthright. I've invested years of my life into DVE. I'm definitely a better leader than Oliver, but Carmel thinks I have a master plan to steal it from both of them. Oliver plays us against each other. I'm dead sure he fed her some line about my marrying you so I could cut her out. That's why she has always sabotaged my relationships. She feels threatened. Our photos? Iris would have seen them, but Carmel made *sure* she saw them. She knew I'd have leverage with the board the minute I had a wife."

"Aren't you trying to stick it to Oliver, though? A little? You were needling him with your toast."

"I was." He winced with remorse and fury. "But what kind of man uses his daughter's illness as a weapon? Do you know why he didn't take her to the clinic? He wanted me to see her like that." Sick and weak and soured by vodka. "He wanted me to feel responsible."

"But you're not, Atlas." She brought his fist to the spot where her warm breastbone was exposed by the lapels of the robe, cradling it there. "You care about her. I can see that."

"I do." Agony sliced through his chest as he thought about how much damage had been done to Carmel through the years. "But I swear he would rather she died so he wouldn't have to deal with her any longer."

She released a small noise of sympathy and pain and brought his knuckles to her lips, kissing it better, but only making the ache inside him throb deeper.

"That's what I come from," he said, swallowing the thickness from his throat. "That's what I cause by existing. By claiming what's mine."

"Oliver had the affair, Atlas. Does Carmel never see his role in it?"

"Where do you think she gets her victim mentality? None of this is Oliver's fault." He threw his free arm over his head. "In his opinion, my mother was a slut waitress who trapped him by having his son. His bastard was getting attention on the sports channels so he had to acknowledge me before my paternity came out. His daughter failed to live up to his expectations so he had to bring in his second string. I keep telling Carmel that she should trust me, not him, but she desperately wants Daddy's love. He can never be the villain in her eyes. Only me."

"And it hurts." She rubbed her soft cheek against the backs of his fingers.

"I don't expect her to love me or accept me, but my taking over isn't just about besting Oliver. It's what's best for all of us," he asserted, believing it. "I should have seen our marriage would cause her a setback, though. I was being like him. Going after what *I* wanted." Going after Stella. He could see how he had roped her in with his selfish logic, binding her to him no matter the cost, so he could have everything he wanted in one ruthless move.

A chill of self-contempt invaded his chest, but Stella was shifting to blanket herself across his chest as a weight of plush velour and warm curves and that unique scent of almonds and honey.

The rope of her hair slid across his neck. He picked it up and pressed the cool, bound silk to his lips, deeply aware of the way she captivated him, making him disregard the consequences of his actions.

He wanted to replace Oliver, not be like him, but the more enthralled he became with her, the more he felt the ruthless, self-serving blood that ran in his veins.

Stella was still thinking about all that Atlas had confided when they drove to Carmel's clinic after breakfast.

His frankness and genuine torment over his sister had allowed her to glimpse who he was deep inside—a man with a strong conscience and a desire to protect the vulnerable. A man worth loving.

As she had curled up against him, she had felt her heart cracking open in a way that scared her. She had learned to protect herself with calm smiles and carefully chosen words and behind-the-scenes maneuvering, but he was sliding past all those defense mechanisms.

It had been concerning enough when she'd realized how much physical power he had over her. Not brute force. He would never wield his strength against her—not in a way she objected to, anyway. He preferred to assault her senses so she bent willingly. When his hands trapped hers or his thighs held hers open, she was always weak with passion and was thrilled by the rough exertion of his strength. He never hurt her when they were like that and that had already begun building her trust in him.

Now her thoughts and feelings felt impossible to disguise from him. It was a terrifyingly unguarded sensation. She wasn't sure how to deal with it. She wanted to withdraw the way he seemed to do without effort, but all he had to do was give her hand a small squeeze and she was smiling with shy joy, unable to hide how much she was won over by his tiniest show of affection.

They arrived at a stone building at the end of a shady drive and walked inside, past a brass plaque that read Aster Lane Retreat. The building wasn't big, possibly holding ten or twelve rooms. There was a dining room, which was empty, and the sound of a piano from a parlor she couldn't see.

They were shown to a small, well-tended garden surrounded by a tall stone wall where Carmel reclined on a lounger. She wore pink Davenwear joggers, a matching jacket and sunglasses.

"Yech," Carmel sneered when she saw them. "Here to gloat?"

"I wanted you to meet Stella. Properly." Atlas turned a nearby chair and caught Stella's ponytail, drawing it up and away so she wouldn't trap it behind her back as she sat. "How are you feeling?"

"Hungover. Obviously." Carmel turned her head to study Stella from behind her lenses. "Daddy said he got you fired when we were in Zermatt that time, and you two have been doing it ever since. I don't remember you," she added with deliberate dismissal.

"You might not remember me saying yesterday that Stella is off-limits," Atlas said in a tone of quiet warning. "Now you will. And no. We haven't."

"No?" She looked to him.

"I wasn't expecting this marriage, either," Stella said evenly. "I know how it makes me look. I feel like I should apologize to you for it, but I can't. I don't regret it." Even when Atlas seemed to be dismantling her hard-won self-reliance with only the brush of his touch on her shoulder.

Carmel's mouth tilted into a sugary smile, as though she wanted to make some disparaging comment, but she must have thought better of it because she asked, "How was the party? Was I missed?"

"Always," Atlas replied. "Everyone asked about you."

"Did *Daddy*?"

Silence. There was only a latent buzz of a bee moving from rose to rose nearby.

Carmel made a choking noise and looked away from both of them.

"I don't think he was speaking to Atlas because of me," Stella murmured. "We didn't stay long. We spent the night at a spa Atlas said you like. I had them put together a basket of things you've bought in the past. The front desk said they'll leave it in your room." After they inspected it.

Carmel rolled her head to look up at Atlas.

"What can I say?" he drawled. "She's *nice*."

"Then what the hell is she doing with *you*?"

"A fair question." He extended his hand toward Stella. "We'll go. Text me if you need anything."

"What could I possibly need, Atlas? My life is perfect."

"Good. Mine, too." He wove his fingers with Stella's, but she had the sense he was being ironic, which sent a pang into her heart.

Their marriage might not be perfect, but she wanted to know she made his life better on some level. That he didn't *regret* marrying her.

But maybe he did?

CHAPTER NINE

THEY WENT TO GREECE, spending a few nights in Athens, then Atlas flew them to the island of his birth as a mini honeymoon. Stella was curious about it and he discovered a surprising nostalgia in him as he drove her around, pointing out landmarks and the taverna and sharing memories from his childhood. The April weather was warm enough to swim in a cove and Stella seemed to enjoy poking around the shops in the village afterward.

"Life here seems idyllic," she said as they ambled across a field toward some ruins the next afternoon. "Would you want to raise your family here?"

"Ours." He caught the disconcerted look on her face at how quickly he'd made the assertion.

"Presumably," she said, and rolled her lips together.

"I would like to raise our children here," he decided as he scanned the horizon. The paparazzi had hardly bothered them while they'd been here and the pace of life was slower. "But I'm glad we're waiting to start making them."

"Oh?" Her expression sobered. "Why?"

"I wonder what sort of father I'll make." So did she. She had started birth control, allowing more spontaneity in their lovemaking, which he loved, but he understood it was her way of protecting herself against being locked into a life with him.

"Because of Oliver?" She frowned.

"Yes." He felt a tic in his cheek and motioned her to keep walking.

"You're not like him."

"I married you with malice aforethought."

"Not toward me." They arrived at piles of rocks set in rectangular lines. They could have been the walls of an ancient temple or a bath, a stable or a home. It was impossible to tell. "The way you talk about him, it doesn't sound like he engages in much forethought ever."

"True," he snorted. But he was still using their marriage as leverage with the board.

"You don't have to model yourself on him, you know. What about your grandfather? It sounds like you were fond of him."

"He was a good man," he recollected, heart squeezing with grief and affection. "If you couldn't afford coffee or a meal, he made sure you had one anyway. He encouraged my swimming."

"He must have been very proud of you."

"I guess." He hesitated, then admitted, "Growing up, I felt like a burden on him as much as my mother. If I hadn't held her back, my grandfather could have retired. Instead, they were chained to the taverna. That's why I sold it when I could. It felt like something I had trapped them into keeping."

"Did they really feel that way, though? Or are you projecting?"

"I don't know. We didn't talk about it much. The few times my mother brought up contacting Oliver to help out, my grandfather shut her down. It was a matter of pride, I think. My mother told me that when my grandfather told him she was pregnant, Oliver threatened him with a lawsuit that would have ruined him if they pursued a paternity claim. The taverna was all he had. I hate myself for taking all that Oliver has given me and turning on him with it, but I never want to be helpless against the Olivers in the world as my grandfather was." He rubbed his jaw with agitation, then dropped his hand.

He could feel her studying his profile and tried to distract her.

"It's too bad the road is so busy here." He nodded at the abandoned building below. It had been scorched by wildfire, leaving the walls blackened and the surrounding olive grove charred but recovering. "Otherwise, this would be a good location for a villa."

"Do you know what it was? It looks like it had a pool."

"It was an inn. Most tourists want to be on the beach, but cyclists and backpackers liked it." It had a stellar view and access to these ruins and other good hiking trails.

"Do you think it's for sale? You promised me a hotel," she reminded him, shading her eyes. "I was so angry at being fired, I was going to ask for something in Zermatt and compete against my old employer, but why be spiteful? The best revenge is to be happy, right?"

"Is that how you think I'm behaving with Oliver? Spiteful?"

"No." She lowered her hand, brow crinkled. "Do you?"

"That's what Kendall called me yesterday." He was one of Oliver's cronies on the board. "I told him I can strike a deal with Zamos if they put me in charge. He told me to quit being vindictive."

"What did you say?"

"Nothing that's fit to repeat." But there was a ruthlessness in him. He knew what he wanted and had come too far to give up. "Do you really want this place?" He jerked his chin at the eyesore that was the damaged building. "It's a lot of work."

"I know." She wrinkled her nose, grinning. "But I think I do."

"I'll see what I can do."

They left for Australia a few days later, stopping by her stepmother's home on the way. Grettina insisted on putting out a huge wedding lunch to welcome Atlas to the family, but everyone was on pins and needles with Pappa there.

At one point, Atlas encouraged Beate to visit them in Athens after she finished school.

"Stay the summer with us," he coaxed. "Stella would enjoy that, wouldn't you?" He looked at her. "We could take you on a cruise around the islands."

"Beate is needed here," Pappa insisted. "To help Grettina with the twins."

"I understood Stella was organizing a housekeeper for you?" Atlas said to Grettina.

"Oh, I can manage," Grettina demurred. "The children are older now—"

"Who the hell do you think you are?" Pappa snarled at Atlas. "This is my family. I know what's best for them. Keep your nose out of it."

The ice that descended over the room froze everyone in place.

"Pappa," Stella began, dying of embarrassment.

Atlas squeezed her hand. "I'm Stella's husband. Her family is now my family. And let me make my position crystal clear, Herr Sutter. I will never prevent Stella from seeing any of the people she loves. In fact, I'll create as many opportunities for that as possible. I will take every measure to ensure her loved ones are safe and well, up to and including calling the police if one of them is threatened in any way. Do you understand me?"

Pappa's eyes widened with outrage before he turned on Stella. "Are you going to let him speak to me that way?"

"Atlas is his own person, Pappa. He's not asking Grettina to control *you*, is he?" She managed to keep her voice steady even though her heart shook in her chest.

As her father looked fit to blow, Elijah stood. "I should get back to studying. I have an exam tomorrow. Let me take you home, Pappa."

After a potent silence, Pappa threw his napkin over his plate. "In your *new* car?" He sent another scathing glance at Stella, who had purchased it for her brother so he could get to Grettina at a moment's notice, if necessary.

Stella kept a look of equanimity on her face and rose to embrace her brother, thanking him for coming and, in a quiet look of understanding, for taking so much of the burden of their father on himself.

After Pappa was gone, the crackle of tension noticeably dissipated. They visited a little longer with Grettina. When they were preparing to leave, one of the twins shyly asked Atlas, "Can we visit you, too?"

"Of course. Do you like to swim? We have a pool," Atlas said.

"Oh, dear," Grettina chided. "I'll never hear the end of it until we see it." As she hugged Stella, she whispered, "I like him. I'm happy for you."

"Thank you. And you don't have to bring the twins," she urged Grettina. "We could take them for a week and you could take time for you."

"I wouldn't know what to do with it," Grettina dismissed.

Stella let it go, but would press her again when things calmed down.

"Thank you," she said to Atlas when they were in the air, on the way to Australia. "I know that wasn't pleasant, dealing with my father." She was still mortified.

"My father hasn't even spoken to you yet," he reminded her, mouth thin with disgust.

"I worry that marrying you wasn't enough to hold up my side of our bargain, though. You're doing all these things for me, making it possible for me to look after my family. You're ready to protect them yourself, but you don't have what you were trying to get."

"DVE? That'll come." He spoke with offhand confidence, but now he was looking at her in the way that made her skin feel too tight. "I definitely have what I wanted, though." He leaned over and set a lazy, inciting kiss on her mouth. "Shall we go into the stateroom?"

They did, and undressed without ceremony, pulling back the covers to sprawl across the bed.

She released a sigh of pleasure at the simple act of lying naked with him, lazily kissing and caressing. She had thought their first few times were powerful and wonderful—often intense and mind-blowing—but it kept getting better. She was more confident now, sliding her thigh against the outside of his, arching and licking into his mouth, enjoying how he hardened against the thatch between her legs.

He knew how hard he could suck her nipple and that he could dominate her with the hot iron of his body pressed over hers. He knew how to caress her and when she was ready for him to push her legs open and thrust deep.

She gasped, eyelids fluttering at the electrified sensations.

"Too hard?"

"Perfect." She danced her fingers along his ear and the

back of his neck, tilting her hips so he was seated as deeply as she could take him. Then she opened her eyes, finding him watching her with a glittering look that was carnal and possessive.

"You could have had this without the ring," she murmured. "It's what I wanted, too."

"I like the commitment." The weight of his hips pinned hers while he trapped her hand to the mattress by weaving his fingers between her own, flexing his grip so they both felt the hard gold of her wedding band against her tender skin. "I like knowing you're mine." His mouth twisted. "That's a primitive a thing to say, I know."

"I think I was yours the moment I saw you," she admitted, feeling defenseless as she admitted it, but it was true. She wasn't just falling in love with him. She was deeply in love with him. Irrevocably. "It scares me how much I want to be with you. To be yours."

He drew in a breath that swelled his chest, eyes glittering with satisfaction, but flashing, too. "Why does it scare you?"

"Because I fought really hard to support myself and feel secure and confident on my own. Now…" Now she was dependent on him in so many ways.

"You don't trust me to look after you?" His expression grew taut with dismay.

"I do," she said, but even she heard the hesitation in her voice.

His eyes narrowed.

"I believe I can trust you," she amended. "Sometimes I think I'm losing myself, though. In you. Us. I don't think it's the same for you. That feels unequal. A lot of this feels unequal." He possessed her heart, but he wasn't offering his own.

He murmured something and let his head drop so he could feather his lips against the edge of her jaw, almost an apology.

"Being soft hasn't served me, *omorfiá mou*. Any weakness I've shown has been exploited. You're already a vulnerability on my part. I have to be careful how great a weakness I let you become."

She couldn't help her small sob of hurt.

His gaze filled with consternation. "Look at the way I coerced you into marrying me, so I could have this." He slid his big body against her, domineering and thrilling as he withdrew and returned, every bit as overwhelming as always. "I want you exactly where you are, Stella. I'll give you anything you want to keep you right here. That's not the behavior of an honorable man."

"I don't want things, though. I only want you."

She couldn't have him, though. Not in the way he had her. She could see it in the way his expression remained impervious as he moved again, watching her, ensuring her pleasure with each thrust. Inflicting pleasure on her, tender but merciless, until she was digging her nails into his shoulder, cresting the hill, sobbing in joy.

Then he cradled her and murmured Greek endearments into her hair and did it again.

Atlas kept reminding himself that if he had engaged himself to Iris, Oliver still would have dragged out his retirement plans. The only difference would have been the amount of leverage Atlas would have had to make it happen.

By taking Stella as his wife, and making that declaration at Oliver's party, Atlas had thrown down a gauntlet, putting pressure on everyone to pick a side. He didn't have the luxury of patience, not if he wanted to strike that deal with Zamos.

Oliver, in typical fashion, didn't see the wisdom of jumping on an opportunity. He was fighting Atlas's efforts, gathering his forces and leaning on allies, trying to convince the board that Atlas had lost his judgment and that Stella had trapped him with her feminine wiles.

Atlas was on his own charm tour, proving that his leadership continued to be rock-solid, but he couldn't help wondering if there was a grain of truth in Oliver's snide accusations. He had married Stella for carnal reasons. He wanted her *all the time.*

He wanted to believe this frustrated urgency, this sensation that something remained beyond his reach, was caused by the tenuousness of his future with DVE. That once the board backed him, and he had what he'd sought for nearly two decades, he would finally feel settled.

But he had this feeling that Stella wasn't his, even though she was at his side unfailingly. They spent two weeks in Australia where he shored up his position there and in the Asian sectors, then visited America on their way back to Europe.

Stella did everything she could to assist him. She dressed the part, played gracious hostess, learned who was who, and was always so sincerely curious about people they fell straight under her spell.

Her support felt strange to Atlas. He had never had a partner. He'd had a grandfather and mother who had sacrificed too much on his behalf. He had had coaches and teammates who encouraged him, but he alone had done the work in the water. His sister had always undermined him out of fear and his father had held him back out of a similar sense of vanity and threat. Even his allies on the board were more concerned with their own interests than his.

Stella wanted him to succeed. Not for her sake, but for his.

It was a disconcerting dynamic, especially because Atlas saw himself as her protector. He remembered what it had been like to come into the world of high society, of boys' clubs and catty cliques. She might not be chronically shy, but she was sensitive and private and, because of his celebrity status, much of her life was already on display and up for judgment.

She faced all of it head-on with warmth and grace.

And, as of tonight, was helping him achieve a small win he doubted he would have had otherwise.

"Stella," Alexandra Zamos greeted them as they entered the ballroom of an Athens hotel. "We're so glad you two were able to make it. Hello, Atlas. It's good to see you again. Congratulations on your recent marriage. How lovely."

"Thank you for inviting us." He kissed the cheeks she offered while Rafael did the same to Stella. He heard Stella ask after their son and Rafael assured her he was well.

"This is not my first fundraising event, sir," Alexandra admonished cheekily. "New husbands are notoriously generous. I'll leave you to peruse the jewelry in the silent auction while I introduce your bride to people she absolutely must meet."

Alexandra pulled Stella into the crowd. The itch of her absence immediately got under Atlas's skin.

"This invitation really was about raising money, then?" Atlas asked Rafael. He had made it clear he wouldn't work with DVE so long as Oliver was in charge, but things might have changed on his end.

"Sasha is very passionate about helping teens and young women who've been preyed on by powerful men. She's been wanting to check in with Stella." Rafael brought his flinty gaze to Atlas, telling him those two statements were not unrelated. "Your marriage was very sudden."

Atlas held his gaze, not flinching at the insult even though it felt like a spit in the face. "I just let her walk into the jungle with your wife. Should I be worried?"

"No." Rafael's gaze flashed with affront. "Sasha likes her."

"So do I," Atlas drawled. "We had our reasons for moving quickly." One of which was definitely Rafael's business, but he wouldn't show all his cards.

"There are rumors your father is on his way out."

"We'll see." Eighty percent of executive conversation was poker, but this was too important to bluff. "We're heading to London next week for quarterlies. Announcements will be made then."

Ah, there she was. His scanning gaze had finally spotted Stella conversing with a handful of people. She was smiling, looking relaxed and engaged. Some of his tension eased.

"I see some people I need to speak with, but there's a tennis bracelet of blue and white sapphires I expect you'll want for Stella. They'll go nicely with her ring. Be warned. I plan to run up your bids. I like to see my wife smile, too."

Atlas prickled, feeling caught revealing his crush on his own wife, but Rafael was already walking away.

The other man wasn't wrong, though. It cost him a pretty penny, but the bracelet was perfect for Stella. He made sure that he won it for her.

CHAPTER TEN

THEY'D BEEN MARRIED two months by the time they returned to London. Atlas said they needed to be in town ahead of the quarterly board meeting, but Stella suspected his real purpose was collecting Carmel from her stay at the clinic.

Atlas had spoken to his sister at least twice a week while she'd been there. Stella had noticed it was always under the guise of asking something about work, but it allowed him to check on her and let her know he was there if she needed him, not that she seemed to want anything to do with him.

Carmel faltered when she saw them waiting in the lobby for her.

"Did Daddy demote you to chauffeur?" She searched in her handbag for something.

"I haven't spoken to him since the party, but I told Chester to expect us for lunch. Unless you'd rather stay in the city?"

"God no. I'm not ready for the brunch circuit." She set aside a romance novel and found her sunglasses, putting them on her nose. Then she picked up the romance novel and waved it at Stella. "Thank you for these. I haven't finished this one, but I got through everything else and left them in the library. It's a nice change from all the *Positive Thinking Solves Everything* dreck that's in there."

"I'm glad you enjoyed them." Stella had ordered boxes of books for Carmel three times, mostly to let her know she was thinking of her. "I started reading romance to improve my English, but they always make me feel better if I'm having a rough day."

"Did you read the one where the hero is a minotaur?" She dipped her sunglasses down her nose to peer over them.

"Oh, I know!" Stella couldn't help laughing. "It's good, right? But also, what?" The premise involved milking bulls.

"Group therapy turned into book club over that one. Does *he* know you're reading books like that?" She thumbed toward Atlas.

"What book? What minotaur?" Atlas frowned between them.

"Shh," Stella admonished. "What he doesn't know is not hurting him. At all."

"Are you saying my brother is reaping the benefits from you reading sexy books? Ew… No. Too much information." Carmel pushed the bridge of her sunglasses up her nose and tossed her hair, but she wore a reluctant smile of amusement as she sailed out the door.

"Do I?" Atlas asked in an undertone as he held the door for Stella to follow Carmel.

"Are you complaining?"

"Not at all. But I draw a line at putting on animal costumes."

"Your loss," she teased, making him smirk.

They continued to banter and talk books as Atlas drove them to the estate, but Carmel grew subdued as they arrived. Chester let them into the cavernous foyer and directed them to "the afternoon parlor" where Oliver waited. He stood at the fireplace holding a glass of something amber.

"Brandy?" Atlas said with angry astonishment. "On the day your daughter comes home from sixty days in rehab?"

That's when Stella realized why Atlas had been so intent on bringing Carmel home himself. She really was married to the most protective, lovable man in the world.

"Not to worry, Daddy. I'm completely cured. Just like last time," Carmel said with deep irony as she walked across to offer her cheek.

"Good to have you home, love. I've missed you," Oliver said indulgently, then lifted his malevolent gaze to Atlas. "What makes you think *you're* welcome here after causing this?" He jerked his head disparagingly at Carmel.

"I thought we could lunch together like adults and discuss the transition. Or define our battle lines," Atlas said, tone cool and even. "Your choice."

"Lines," Oliver scoffed. "As though you don't cross them when it suits you. You love to pretend superiority over me, then walk in here using women as your shield."

So he had noticed Stella was here. He hadn't spared her a single glance so she had presumed she was invisible.

"*I* use women?" Atlas snorted.

"You put your sister in a sanitarium like a Victorian husband with his hysterical wife, to embarrass me at the party and divide the two of us." He waved between himself and Carmel.

"I put myself there, Daddy. I've had to accept that." Carmel clutched her elbows, looking as though she wanted to say more, but Oliver ignored her as he continued attacking Atlas.

"You kept a chambermaid as your mistress for years then married her when you got caught, purely to stick a knife in my back!"

"That's not what I did." Atlas sent a sharp glance to

Stella. They hadn't had a lengthy affair, but the rest was not inaccurate. She knew it as well as he did.

She rolled her lips inward, pinning them closed, deeply uncomfortable.

"Why did you marry her, then?" Oliver demanded. "It wasn't her fortune or her connections. She doesn't bring anything to your marriage except a great pair of—"

"Careful," Atlas said through gritted teeth.

"Too close to the truth?" Oliver mocked. "You're not fit to run DVE if you can't recognize a gold digger when you see one. Well done, girlie." Oliver finally acknowledged her. "I've seen some slick operators in my time, but you really found your mark with this one, didn't you?"

"Don't speak to her if that's how you're going to talk," Atlas cut in sharply. "And you don't have to listen to this," Atlas said to her gruffly. "You can wait in the car if you want to."

"I'm here to support Carmel." Did they all forget she was fragile as a newborn right now? Did they forget she was *here*, hugging herself and looking wan? "Would you like to come to London with us?" Oliver looked to be in a vile mood. Stella would never leave one of her siblings to handle her father alone if he looked like this.

"No." Carmel shook her head, body tense and expression stiff.

"Oh, she's good," Oliver said with sarcastic admiration. "I bet she told you she loves you to get her hands on all of this. Didn't you?"

"No." Stella reminded herself this man meant nothing to her, but she still felt stripped raw under his contemptuous regard. It was too familiar, compelling her to push back and assert her truth. "But I do."

"Love him? I'm sure." Oliver choked on a withering

laugh. "I've never understood why they call them working girls when they never want to *work*."

That was deeply unfair yet hit a tender spot in Stella. She had worked *so* hard for everything she had and had resisted becoming reliant on Atlas, but here she was, looking like the opportunist Oliver judged her to be. It stung to her very core.

Her throat closed, making it impossible to defend herself while Atlas visibly swelled with anger. He seemed to expand while his face darkened and his mouth tightened. So did his fist.

"I married her so *I* could get my hands on it," he said with icy fury. "Does it feel good to see the monster you created in your own image? One who uses innocent people to get what he wants?"

"It always comes back to your mother, doesn't it?" Oliver said tiredly. "She was no victim, Atlas. She wanted it. She threw herself at me and made out fine, exactly as planned. Exactly as this one will." He waved pithily at Stella. "Exactly as *you* will."

Atlas swore. "No. You have dangled DVE like a carrot for seventeen years. Tomorrow, I'm taking what's mine. You can step down or I will leave DVE and take a third of its capital and assets with me. Yes," he added grimly as Oliver's face reddened with outrage. "I'd rather destroy it than let you keep what *I've* kept alive. You have met your match, Oliver, because I *am* you."

He waved Stella toward the door.

"Will Carmel be all right?" Stella asked once they were in the car.

"Chester knows to get her help if she needs it." Atlas had made that clear after last time. God knew Oliver wouldn't do anything. "I'm sorry you had to go through that."

"I don't care about him or his opinion of me." She sounded like she was being honest, but it was the ugliest blowup he'd ever had with his father. His attacks on Stella had infuriated Atlas, but far worse was his own behavior.

He had taunted Oliver by saying he was his mirror image, but it was hitting him that the words were too true. Appallingly true. He had ruthlessly used Stella in an attempt to get what he wanted. Even Rafael Zamos had seen it. Atlas could pretty it up with sparkling baubles and generous gifts and attentive lovemaking, but the truth was, he had used Stella's worries over her family to achieve his own ends.

I bet she told you she loves you.

No. But I do.

His heart had nearly come out of his throat when she had said that. It made his behavior that much worse. That much more like Oliver, who had encouraged a woman to fall for him purely to appease his own desires.

Atlas couldn't stand how far he'd sunk to his father's level. It drenched him in disgust and self-loathing.

They didn't speak again until they were in the penthouse in London. The housekeeper had finished for the day and, since they hadn't been sure of their plans, hadn't left any meals.

"Should I make something for lunch?" Stella asked. "Or would you rather order in?"

"Did you mean it?" he asked, unable to hold the question in.

"What?"

"When Oliver asked if you loved me."

She stiffened. Shadows of indecision swirled in her eyes before her expression softened, becoming so naked and defenseless, it dropped his heart even further, until it was churning with his gut.

"I would never lie about something like that. I wouldn't lie to *you*," she said.

He flinched. "How could you?"

"That's not a real question, is it?" she chided as she came to set her hand on his arm.

He stepped back, withdrawing from the contact because it created thorny sensations that pierced more than his arm. They went into his chest and his throat and his belly. The magnitude of her confession, of her tender feelings, was too big inside him. Too heavy.

"It's okay if you're not there yet," she said in a voice that wavered. "We're still new."

Yet. The expectation in that word was so loaded, it only made him feel worse about what he'd done.

"I don't deserve your love, Stella." He doubted he ever would.

"Of course you do. You're a good man, Atlas."

"Ha!" He ran his hand down his face.

"Please don't question my judgment," she said with quiet dignity.

"Were you in that room?"

You love to pretend superiority, then use women as a shield. You married her to stick a knife in my back.

"It's *my* judgment you should question," he said tightly. "I've been behaving exactly the way he does. Think about your future, Stella. If I'm capable of this today, I could be worse tomorrow. Do you want me leaving you pregnant to fend for yourself and our child? Encouraging you to drink yourself to death?"

"You wouldn't do that."

"You don't know that. His poisoned blood is in me. I've turned into him to fight him and now that's what I am. Run while you have the chance."

"I'm not leaving you, Atlas," she admonished with a flex of injury across her face. "I love you. I want to be with you."

"And I refuse to use your feelings to keep you here. I'm liable to use your feelings to destroy you."

"You're not making sense." She tried to approach him again and he stepped back again. Her shoulders fell. "If you care about me enough that you want to protect me, then you're not a bad person. You're not like him," she insisted.

"You don't know the thoughts in my head." The rage. The desire for revenge that wanted to stop at nothing to vanquish Oliver once and for all.

"No," she agreed. "But you do care about me, don't you?" Her faltering smile fell away as she searched his eyes. Anxious lines etched in around her eyes and mouth. "A little?"

The pang in her voice matched the ache in his chest. Yes, he cared about her. So much he couldn't look at her because she would see it and he refused to manipulate her. He refused to keep using her.

He clenched his teeth so hard he thought his molars would crack.

Stella knew how to hide her emotions, but it took all her effort to breathe through the pain of this rejection.

When Atlas had told Oliver he was using her to get the better of him, she had heard a certain truth in it, but she'd believed their connection went deeper than that.

As the silence dragged on, ringing with his refusal to say he returned any scrap of her feelings, she had to accept that he did not.

She swallowed, trying to assimilate the agony of being in love with a man who was letting her down. She had overturned her life for him, allowing herself to become dependent on him emotionally as well as financially. She had sworn she would never let this happen, but she had. What a foolish, horrific, devastating mistake.

"I..." Her voice didn't want to work. She blinked, trying to clear the hot sheen from her eyes. "I'll go see my family." Run away. That's what she would do. *Again.*

She pulled out her phone and began tapping.

"I'll arrange the jet," he said in a graveled voice.

Oh, he couldn't wait to get rid of her, could he?

"There's a train in two hours that connects in Paris. It will get me there by morning."

"You're not taking the train overnight."

"Excuse me, Atlas, but you just told me to look after myself because I can't trust you to do it." Her voice was ragged but hard as she snapped her focus back to him.

She heard his breath hiss in as though he'd been punched.

"I'm perfectly capable of looking after myself and I will." She booked the sleeper, already anticipating crying her way across the continent. "I have to pack."

CHAPTER ELEVEN

He had to let her go. It destroyed him to do it, but he had to.

If you care enough about me to want to protect me, then you're not a bad person.

It was a paradox, though. How could he protect her if she wasn't where he could see her? Touch her? Feel her asleep beside him and know she was safe and warm and happy?

How could he be a good person when he was hurting her by pushing her away?

"Text me when you arrive," he said as she shouldered a small bag on her way to the door.

She only released a choked noise, barely acknowledging him as she left with her chin high and her mouth trembling.

She did text, though, while he was staring at his breakfast, incapable of swallowing a bite.

Here.

If she had been able to think of a shorter word, he was sure she would have used it.

He drew a breath that held more acid than relief.

Sleep had eluded him. He'd kept pushing himself to go over the points he would make to the board this morning, but his heart wasn't in it. What was he trying to prove? Yes, he believed he was better equipped to lead DVE into the future, but did he expect to feel validated by being awarded that role? Legitimate? Accepted? Was he still trying to get what he thought his mother had deserved from her very brief affair with Oliver?

He was making a case that he was better than Oliver, but if he was using his father's underhanded tactics to achieve his ends, did he deserve to run the company?

He arrived at the DVE building still unsettled and had a brief meeting with his assistant, Derik, and other key personnel. When they made their way to the boardroom, he bumped into Carmel in the hallway.

"I didn't expect you," he said. She usually voted by proxy, typically giving her support to Oliver, so there was no reason for her to be here unless she was hoping to gloat after Atlas lost.

"It's only my future that's being decided." She touched the diamond stud in her ear, still looking wan and brittle from her stay in rehab, but her eyes were clear, her color good, and her appearance impeccable. "I was going to stay home and watch reality television, but I finished that book Stella gave me and thought she'd like to read it. Is she here?" She looked past him toward the office they'd just left.

"No. She's in Switzerland."

"Oh. Is everything okay?" She almost sounded sincere in her concern.

Don't tell her.

He knew she would use it against him in the meeting, but he seemed to be on a full bender of self-destruction because he snapped, "No, it's not okay, Carmel. Yesterday she had a taste of what she married and rightfully spat it out."

"She *left* you?" she asked in a shocked hush. "But what about this meeting?" She motioned toward the boardroom where everyone was taking seats. "You married her for this."

"I know that." He pinched the bridge of his nose, feeling as though he was being drawn and quartered. Pulled in too many directions.

Because he hadn't married her for this. This takeover had been the justification he'd used to make sense of his desire for her. After one brief meeting, she had stayed in his memory for *five years*. She hadn't been gone twenty-four hours and he felt as though he'd had a limb amputated.

He never should have let her go.

His phone vibrated and he reached to silence it, but saw Stella's face on the screen.

"Stella." Words piled up in his mouth. He didn't know where to start.

"It's Beate. We're in the hospital," her sister said with an unsteady hiccup. "Pappa pushed Stella down the stairs."

"What?!" His shout was so loud, everyone inside the boardroom stopped to look. He snapped his fingers at Derik and started toward the elevator.

"Don't say that!" He could hear Stella saying in the background. "Give that to me. Atlas, I'm fine." Her voice came on the line, adamant but shaken. "It was more of a stumble."

"Are you hurt?" he demanded, heart stumbling.

"I put out my arm to stop my fall and it needs an X-ray. I told Beate you're going into a meeting and that I'd call you later. You should have let it go to voicemail."

"I don't care about a stupid meeting, Stella. I'm leaving now. Get the jet readied for Bern," he ordered Derik, who was hurrying alongside him with the rest of his entourage. "Where's your father? Did he hurt anyone else?"

"The police took him for questioning. One of the neighbors saw it and called them. At least this time it's not his word against mine."

"*This* time?" He nearly lost his mind.

They all crowded into the elevator, but he stopped one of the suits and pointed him back the way they'd come. "Tell them my wife is in the hospital. They can have their meeting without me."

"I'm telling you I'm fine," Stella insisted. "Oh. They're here to take me to X-ray. Go into your meeting. Call me after. I—I'd like to know how it goes."

They would talk in two hours or less, he resolved as he ended the call and ran his hand down his face, shaken to his core. What had he expected would happen if he let her go back there alone? What an *idiot*. What a blind, callous idiot he was. Even if she forgave him, he never would.

As he climbed into the back of the SUV, Carmel slid into the seat on the other side, taking the spot his assistant would normally use.

"What are you doing?"

"Coming with you." She made a show of straightening her pleated skirt.

"No." He held up his hand to keep the driver from shutting the door, even though some tourists were aiming their phones to catch a snap of both of them inside the car. "I know you enjoy it when I suffer, but this amount of schadenfreude is in poor taste, even for you." He flicked his hand, ordering her to leave.

Her mouth pursed. "You would go with me if the situation was reversed." She leaned to see Derik, who was hovering with confusion. "Get a message upstairs. Tell them if Daddy is left in charge, and Atlas takes all his money out of DVE, then I'm taking Davenwear and all of my share of the assets, too. I refuse to stay on a sinking ship."

Atlas was floored. "Is that really why you came in today?"

"I'm not as blind to Daddy's shortcomings as you think I am," she said haughtily. "I'm learning how to look after myself, same as you. Now let's go." She waved with annoyance at the men on the curb. "We have a flight to catch."

The door slammed and the driver got behind the wheel while Derik took the passenger seat, already relaying Carmel's message to someone over his phone.

"Will she be okay?" Carmel asked with quiet concern as they pulled into traffic.

"I don't know."

Physically, it didn't sound too serious, but emotionally, Stella had to be traumatized. He wasn't even there and he was filled with anguish.

He should have been there.

"I hope so."

The greater question was, would *they* be okay?

On that, he didn't have much hope at all.

Stella was making her police report from her hospital room, waiting for the fracture in her forearm to be cast, when Atlas strode in.

"My husband," she blurted as the startled police officer held up a stern hand.

Her heart nearly burst with shock and joy at the sight of him. She had cried most of the journey from London, berating herself for falling in love with a man who had seemed to feel nothing for her at all.

She had been so hurt, so angry with him and herself, she hadn't wanted to call him after her tumble. Beate had thrust her phone in front of her face to unlock it and placed the call herself.

The truth was, Stella hadn't believed he would come if

she asked. He'd made it clear that he didn't love her and she'd thought that was the end of it.

"How bad is it?" Atlas stopped next to her bed, hands coming out and pausing in midair before he gripped the rail. His gaze swept over her from the collar of her hospital gown to her legs beneath the blanket, then came back to the arm that was elevated on a pillow and wearing an ice pack.

"A hairline fracture in my wrist. As I was just explaining to..." She motioned with her good hand to the officer. "I called Pappa to say I was visiting Grettina, in case he wanted me to look at anything at the house."

She explained about the house she'd purchased for him and why.

"He came over an hour later, angry that I was staying with Grettina when he wasn't allowed to. He said I should stay in my own house and let him resume living with his wife. Grettina came to the door so I stepped out to stand beside him. She told him she wanted to stick to their arrangement where he comes for dinner once a week to see the twins. I offered to order a car so he didn't have to wait for the bus and he lost his temper and elbowed me. I lost my footing and fell down the stairs." Eight of them.

She had to take a moment to push back the horror as she had realized there was nothing but air beneath her foot.

Atlas's grip on the bed rail looked strong enough to bend it like a paper clip.

"Has this happened before?" the officer asked.

"I made a complaint a few years ago." She rushed to get out the rest so she never had to speak of it again. "It turned into a he said, she said, but that's why Grettina left him. She was worried he would continue to lash out physically, especially with the little ones. Pappa was advised to go through an anger management program, but he never did."

"Where is he now?" Atlas asked sharply.

"He's in custody," the officer said. "He'll likely be held overnight. We have the neighbor's statement. I expect he'll face criminal proceedings." The officer gave her contact details for a social worker who could provide mental health and other supports.

"I saw Beate in the hall," Atlas said once the officer was gone. "Where is Grettina? Is she safe?"

"Elijah is with her at the house." He had arrived when the police did. "He's going to drive her and the twins to visit her cousin in Berlin. Her cousin's husband is a divorce lawyer. Beate will stay with Elijah until school finishes."

"And you'll come home with me."

"I—" As she had sat here in the numbness of shock, certain her marriage was over before it had properly started, she had wanted nothing more than to be where she had always felt safe. Where she felt empowered and independent and sure of who she was. "I was planning to go to Zermatt."

His expression shuttered. "To close your apartment?"

Her neighbor had cleaned out her refrigerator the day after Stella left with Atlas, but—

"I'm not sure." She searched his gaze, trying not to feel a lilt of hope at his presence here. "What happened at your meeting? Do you even need a wife anymore?"

His expression spasmed. He looked to the door as it opened.

The nurse came in with a wheelchair to take her to have her arm cast.

The wheelchair wasn't necessary. Stella was able to walk and not the least bit dizzy or lightheaded, but Atlas helped her off the bed and into the chair, then followed her into the hall, where Beate sat with Carmel.

"Hello," Stella said with surprise, putting up her good

hand so the nurse would pause next to the pair of women. "I didn't know you were here," she said to Carmel.

"Atlas nearly fainted when he got your call. I thought I'd better keep an eye on him. I hear your father makes ours look like Santa Claus. Oliver's been told to clean out his desk, by the way," she informed Atlas offhandedly. "You're in. The announcement said it more nicely, but it's effective immediately. How long are you here?" She looked back at Stella.

"I'll be discharged as soon as I get my cast." It was done then. Atlas had what he wanted from their marriage. He *didn't* need her.

"Pity." Carmel pouted with disappointment. "Beate and I were putting together an order for some really spicy books for you. Have you read this one?" She pointed at her phone and looked to Beate. "I nearly got pregnant just reading about this guy."

Beate snickered.

It was a pity, Stella thought. She and Carmel might have become friends if they'd had the chance.

She looked at Atlas, aware that his sister liked to exaggerate for comedic effect. He might have rushed to her side out of a sense of duty, but he hadn't been *that* upset. Had he?

"I'll be here when you get back," he said, giving nothing away.

While Atlas waited for Stella to be discharged, Beate left to meet a friend. She had arranged to stay with her while Elijah was taking Grettina to her cousin's and the other girl was off work, so Beate was meeting her downstairs.

"Atlas." Carmel crossed her legs and clasped her knee, leaning toward him. "This is how my therapist talks to me. Atlas, what brings you here today? Use your 'I' statements."

She had been surprisingly decent this whole time so he didn't tell her where to go. Even so, "Pass."

She sighed and sat back. "It wasn't your fault, you know. My stumble."

"You asked me if I should call your sponsor. I should have." He pushed his hands into his pockets, looking down the hall, willing Stella to come back even though she'd only just left.

"No. *I* should have. I wasn't even that upset when you told me you were married. Not until Daddy came downstairs and started saying things to get me worked up. The worst part is, I knew what he was doing. He was drinking in front of me, wanting me to fall off the wagon so he could make it your fault. I let it happen because..." She shrugged, mouth twisting into deep remorse. "Because I want him to love me."

"I know." Atlas watched her eyes fill with tears. "I don't blame you for that."

"He doesn't, though." She wiped under one eye, expression tightening. "In therapy, we're always talking about making sure the people around us will support our sobriety and he doesn't. He never has. You do, though. I don't know why, since you can't stand me."

"I can stand you a little. When you're not being horrible." It wasn't entirely a joke, but he added more sincerely, "I don't blame you for resenting me. I would, in your shoes."

"I shouldn't, though! You're the one who gets me into rehab and calls while I'm there. You're the one who says 'good job' at work. And now you have this wife who is not a vapid witch like Iris. She's *nice*. Please tell me you haven't really ruined it with her? Why would you do that?"

He drew a breath and held it, shaking his head. "I don't know. Why do you hurt yourself when you're mad at him?"

"Oh, Atlas. You don't care enough about him to let him affect you like that."

"After yesterday, I saw too much of him in me. I want better than that for her."

"Then *be* better. Gawd. It's not that hard." She waited a beat before adding facetiously, "For you."

He looked again for Stella. What was taking so long?

"You love her, don't you?" she asked gently.

His heart was beating outside his chest, calling to Stella, but he'd spent too many years hiding his closest feelings from this woman. She had used them too many times to hurt him.

"I thought you were going to cry, Atlas. When you got that call. I've never been so scared in my life because I really didn't know what I could do to help you if you'd lost her." She rose and squeezed his arm, smiling and nodding past him. "Here she comes."

His entire being settled as he saw Stella being wheeled toward him.

He hadn't known what he would do, either, if something more serious had happened to her.

"You're here, Atlas. Not in London. You have your priorities in order. You're not like him."

That moment of danger had put everything into perspective for him, though. When it counted, he had no problem walking away from the nonsense of life toward the meaning of it.

That's what she was, he realized. All these weeks since meeting her again, he had suffered an indefinable sensation of Stella being beyond his reach. He realized now he'd been holding her off. He had known that she would become his world and that meant letting go of all those other things that had consumed him.

They were inconsequential now, though. None of it mattered so long as he had her.

As she rolled to a stop before him, she seemed to come to rest inside his heart.

She was his everything. He didn't know how he would make up for the hurt he'd caused her, but he was damned well going to try.

CHAPTER TWELVE

STELLA DIDN'T KNOW what to make of the fierce light in Atlas's expression so she held up her arm, speaking to both of them.

"They said the fracture was small enough a splint would be enough support while it heals."

"That's good," Carmel said. "Your sister has gone with her friend and I'm off to Milan for some research and development. That's what I call shopping." Carmel wrinkled her nose. "Now I'll go talk to the press so you two don't have to. Don't worry. I'll make it all about me," she added toward Atlas.

It must have worked because only a few photographers lingered when Stella had dressed and was finally discharged.

By then, she was utterly done in, even though it was only late afternoon.

"Where are we going?" she asked with confusion as his driver took them to a private airfield.

"You said you wanted to go to Zermatt."

"Oh." She had thought he would insist on Athens or London. She had hoped he would insist she come home with him.

"No?" he prodded.

"Yes," she decided, even though it took all her effort to

hold on to her composure. She needed to know that when her world fell apart and she was left to fend for herself, she *could*. But she was going to struggle to say goodbye to him again.

He came aboard the helicopter with her.

"You're coming with me?"

"Yes." He frowned, but didn't hesitate to take the seat next to hers.

She nearly wept with relief. She was so tired from her sleepless night on the train and distressful morning, she didn't fight the drop of her head onto his shoulder as they lifted off.

She snapped awake when she felt something soft touch her brow.

He lifted his mouth away from the kiss against her forehead. "We're here."

"Oh." She was completely disoriented.

This had been the longest day of her life, but the sun was only sinking against the mountain peaks, not yet fully down. It had only been two months since they'd left, but the snow was gone from the valley bottom and the meadows were bright green.

"This is my favorite time of year," she told him as they left the helicopter and walked toward a waiting e-taxi. "Do you mind if we walk?"

Neither of them had luggage and he was still in the suit he'd put on for his board meeting. She wore the yoga pants and the loose top she'd been wearing when her father had arrived. When she crossed her arms against the breeze, Atlas took off his jacket and draped it over her shoulders.

"This is where I walked when I arrived the first time," she said as she led him to the bridge that crossed the river. "I didn't know the city so I came all this way from the train station before I realized I should have gone the other way. I was so frightened and angry. I didn't have any sort of plan. I only knew I was going to *show* him." She laughed at her vague, juvenile goal.

Atlas didn't, but he was watching her, listening intently.

"It was autumn and so pretty, all golden. I fell in love with the mountains and the freedom to make a mistake and go the wrong way. Everything was hard—finding a place to live…cleaning up after drunks… But lots of young people were here, making it all seem doable." Seasonaires arrived every winter to work and finance their ski habit. She'd felt like one of them. "At first, I thought everyone knew what they were doing except me. I felt like an ugly duckling among swans."

He made a noise of disagreement.

"I did. I was tall and didn't know what was trendy and wore awful clothes. But after a while I realized no one had anything figured out. That's when I began to find my place here. To know who I was. People liked me. They valued me at work. I had friends who were in my same boat, broke and eating noodles in a cup and were behind on whatever classes they were taking."

She waved at an acquaintance across the river who motioned *Call me* and *Drinks*. She nodded, but already knew she wouldn't be staying long enough to do it.

She had outgrown her life here. Zermatt had been her chrysalis. It was time to break free and become something bigger. But what? A backpacking explorer? An innkeeper in Greece? A CEO in a global chain of hotels?

A divorcée?

"That's good news about DVE," she said, testing the waters. "Congratulations."

"I don't care about that." His voice was hard. His expression altered into something softer as he met her surprised gaze. "I care about *you*, Stella." He swore and ran his hand over his face. "Do you have any idea how sick I felt that I let you go home alone? Even before this happened?" He motioned at her arm.

"You 'let' me?" She paused on the bridge to watch the water travel under her feet. "I came here the first time because I was tired of asking permission to live my own life."

"I let you *go*," he stressed. "I pushed you away and let you think I didn't care. I hated myself the minute you were out of my sight, but I thought I was doing the right thing." His tone turned contrite. "How could you love me if I hated myself? I was saving you."

"I don't need saving, Atlas. I know how to save myself."

"I know." He leaned his hip next to her and covered her hand, stroking her cool knuckles where they were exposed by the plaster of her splint. "It's something I admire so deeply in you. I hope you know that?"

She swallowed, so moved she teared up.

"What I really wanted to say was no, you can't go. Stay in London while I'm in that meeting because I need you. You, Stella. Not a wife. *You*. I thought if I told you I love you, it would be coercion. Emotional blackmail. I didn't feel I deserved your love. I still don't." He scowled to the other side of the bridge. "Not when I'm hoping that telling you I love you will bring you back to me."

"It's not coercion if it's *true*. Is it?" she asked with a streak of hope jolting her heart.

"It's as real inside me as air and blood and bone," he said with quiet heat. "It's so all-encompassing, saying the words isn't enough. But if loving you means giving you your independence..." He swallowed. His gaze filled with agony. "I'll find a way to do that."

As she looked into eyes that wanted to hand her the world even when it would cost his soul, she saw the bigger sky and the broader universe she could fly into. The love in his eyes filled her with a sense of expansion, one that made her turn and set her good hand on his jaw.

"What if knowing you love me makes me feel free to be exactly who I am? What if I believe you'll support me no matter what, and that makes me feel so big and powerful, I can do anything?"

His features relaxed into tenderness. Admiration. Intense joy. He cupped her face.

"What if holding you up makes me feel stronger? What if all that light inside you chases my shadows away?"

"What if we're better together?"

"More than we would be on our own." He nodded. "I believe we could be. Do you?"

"I do." She said it with as much solemn conviction as the first time she'd said those words to him.

She didn't know what their future looked like, but she already knew it would be wide and wonderful.

They kissed softly, keeping it chaste because they were in public, but it still had the impact of a thousand volts of wildly pulsing electricity. It still made her eyes sting and her heart feel too big for her chest.

"Do you want to go to my flat?" she asked.

"I'll go anywhere with you. I thought I just made that clear."

She'd never seen such a lighthearted gleam in his eye. They both smiled all the way to her building and held hands up the stairs.

"I like to claim I live in the penthouse," she said of her studio apartment, since it was tucked into the rafters at the peak of the block, with only one neighbor across the landing.

"Should we keep it as a love nest?" He moved around the tiny space, taking in the childish art that the twins had made at different times, the photo of her and Beate, the framed diploma that proved she had a degree and— He frowned. "Why is there a man's bicycle on your balcony?"

"Because I'm too tall for the ones that are marketed to women. Elijah thinks it sends a message that I don't live alone."

"You don't." Atlas closed the drapes. "Not anymore."

She tried to pull her shirt over her head and quickly ran into a struggle thanks to the splint.

Atlas stilled her hands. "I want to hold you, but wc don't have to make love if you're not up to it."

"I want to," she insisted with a pang. "I want to feel close to you."

He kissed her, first with tender reassurance, then with the passion they had kept bottled while they'd stood on the bridge. Within moments, he was helping her undress and throwing off his own clothes.

Then he sat on the bed and drew her to straddle his lap, guiding her legs behind him once they were joined.

"I didn't know I could love anyone this much," she confessed as she folded her arms behind his neck and set damp kisses in his throat. "I don't know how to make you feel it."

"I do, though. It hurts. In a good way." He pulled her hips tighter to his. "Like I'm using muscles I didn't know I had."

"Maybe you are," she teased, smiling against his mouth, then arching to brush her breasts against his chest while clinging to his neck.

With a low groan, he gathered her and rolled so she was on her back. Now he had all the leverage, but she didn't mind that he was taking charge. She trusted him to give her what she needed. He always did.

Afterward, they lay tangled under the covers, nude and replete, not speaking, only caressing and enjoying the closeness.

"I have to be in London tomorrow," he said eventually. "Will you come with me?"

"Of course."

"I'm going to tell them I'll work out of Athens."

She nodded. "I'd like that."

He rolled onto his elbow and set his hand on her stomach. His lips parted, then he seemed to think better of what he wanted to say.

"What?" she prompted.

His gaze was rueful. "I was looking for you when I came here with Iris. Not actively. I genuinely believed you would have moved on by now, but I couldn't help keeping an eye out. Then I nearly walked right into you and I knew I couldn't marry her. I didn't want to admit it, not in the moment, but I knew. You're laughing at me."

"No," she said, but she was smiling. "I'm laughing at us."

She rose and walked naked to the wardrobe where she pulled a boot box from the shelf. She set it on the bed so he could open it.

"I thought so many times about sending this to you with a note. It felt too desperate."

When he shook off the lid and found his own clothes, he chuckled.

"This is convenient. I thought I was going to have to wear one of your dresses when I run out to collect dinner." He rose and pulled on the pants. "They still look better on you. Although…" He drew her into his arms. "Naked will always be my favorite color on you."

She looped her arms behind his neck, liking the brush of his chest hair against her breasts.

"You were a dream for me. A fantasy. One I didn't think could come true." She hugged him and looked around at the home she'd made for herself. "I'll miss this place, but I'm looking forward to dreaming new dreams with you and seeing them come true."

"Me, too. But if one of your fantasies includes dinner tonight, I suggest you put on some clothes or I'm taking mine off and we won't leave that bed until morning."

"I have cans of soup."

"Decision made." He tumbled her onto the bed.

EPILOGUE

Two years later

THE TWINS WERE firmly in their tweens and filled with opinions about what was cool and what was boring and whether the other one had correctly relayed a story or not. Their visits were always a busy week of laughter and beach-combing, playing in the pool and staying up past bedtime to finish a movie.

Which made sending them back to Grettina a relief, but a poignant one. Grettina had taken up painting so she always went on a retreat when the twins were in Athens. She would send snapshots of still lifes and landscapes and always looked rested and pleased if eager to reunite with her children. They lived near Geneva these days. Beate was in Austria and Elijah was the only one who had contact with their father and only intermittently.

As they reentered the quiet penthouse, melancholy descended over Stella.

"I love them, but I love having you to myself again," Atlas said as he brought her a glass of white wine.

"Oh." Her heart took a small dip.

"What? You weren't going to work, were you?"

They had both taken the week off so she definitely had a thousand emails waiting for her, but that wasn't it.

"I was going to say something, but now..." She looked into the wine. "Maybe not."

"What?" he prompted.

"I was going to say they're growing up so fast. They both asked me if we were going to have a baby and I thought maybe that's something we should talk about?"

"I was waiting until our anniversary next month," Atlas said. "As per our contract."

"Oh." She started to bring her glass to her smiling lips, paused. "What if I went off the pill and we just see what happens?"

"Let's definitely see what happens." He took their drinks and set them aside.

"I took one this morning," she reminded him. "There's no point starting *now*."

"Rehearsals improve the odds of success." He backed her toward the bedroom. "Or so I've heard."

It didn't take much work at all. The timing didn't work the first month and she had a horrible cold the second month, interrupting their best intentions. Three months later, however, she was checking with her staff at the inn when she realized her period was late.

She did a test, then hurried to Athens, rushing into Atlas's office at the top of the DVE building.

"Stella." He stood up as she burst in. "What's wrong?"

"I'm late!" She ran around his desk and threw herself into his arms. "I did a test. I'm pregnant!"

"What?" He caught her, laughing, arms tight and heart hammering against her own. "Really?"

From the speakerphone, she heard Carmel's voice. "Ugh. Now I have to learn how to be nice to *children*? The things I do for you people."

"Carmel's on the phone," Atlas said with irony as he let

Stella's feet touch the floor. "We'll pick this up tomorrow," he told his sister, reaching for the button.

"Fine. Congratulations, I guess," Carmel said, but she sounded more indulgent than sarcastic. "I hope you're very happy."

"Thank you." He hung up and scooped his arms around Stella again. "You're sure?"

"That I'm pregnant? Or that I'm happy? *Both*."

"Both" turned out to be a prophetic word. They welcomed twins the following spring. They were all very happy.

* * * * *

Did you fall in love with Maid to Marry*?*
Then don't miss out on these other dramatic stories from Dani Collins!

The Secret of Their Billion-Dollar Baby
Her Billion-Dollar Bump
Marrying the Enemy
Husband for the Holidays
His Highness's Hidden Heir

Available now!

ROYAL BRIDE DEMAND
LaQuette

'Reigna.' He called her name with quiet strength that let her know he was in control of this conversation. 'I am Jasiri Issa Nguvu of the royal house of Adébísí, son of King Omari Jasiri Sahel of the royal house of Adébísí, crown prince and heir apparent to the throne of Nyeusi.'

Her jaw dropped as her eyes searched for any hint that he was joking. Unfortunately, the straight set of his jaw and his level gaze didn't say, 'Girl, you know I'm just playing with you.' Nope, that was a 'No lies detected' face staring back at her.

'You're…you're a…prince?'

'Not a prince, *the* prince. As the heir to the throne, I stand above all other princes in the royal line.'

She peeled her hand away from the armrest and pointed to herself. 'And that makes me…?'

He continued smoothly as if they were having a normal everyday conversation and not one that was literally life-changing. 'As my wife, you are now Princess Reigna of the royal house of Adébísí, consort to the heir and future queen of Nyeusi.'

COMING SOON!

We really hope you enjoyed reading this book.
If you're looking for more romance
be sure to head to the shops when
new books are available on

Thursday 24th April

To see which titles are coming soon, please visit

millsandboon.co.uk/nextmonth

MILLS & BOON

afterglow
BOOKS

SCAN ME